SHIFT

Also by Dale Peck

Sprout

Body Surfing

The Lost Cities: A Drift House Voyage

Drift House: The First Voyage

What We Lost

Hatchet Jobs

Now It's Time to Say Goodbye

The Law of Enclosures

Martin and John

SHIFT

A NOVEL

Tim Kring and Dale Peck

Crown Publishers · New York

Copyright © 2010 by Tim Kring

All rights reserved.
Published in the United States by Crown Publishers, an imprint of the Crown Publishing Group, a division of Random House, Inc., New York.
www.crownpublishing.com

CROWN and the Crown colophon are registered trademarks of Random House, Inc.

Library of Congress Cataloging-in-Publication Data

Kring, Tim, 1957–
  Shift / Tim Kring and Dale Peck.—1st ed.
    p. cm.—(Gate of Orpheus trilogy ; part 1)
  I. Peck, Dale. II. Title. III. Series.

  PS3611.R547S55 2010
  813'.6—dc22   2010005470

ISBN 978-0-307-45345-7

Printed in the United States of America

Book design by Lauren Dong

10 9 8 7 6 5 4 3 2 1

First Edition

To Lisa, Amelia, and Ethan
                    —T. K.

To my husband, Lou Peralta,
for his unwavering love and support
during the writing of this book
                    —D. P.

Contents

yet the gods sent Orpheus away from
Hades empty-handed . . .

—Plato, _Symposium_

The apparition appeared at 11:22 a.m. over I-35, in the two-
hundred-foot gap between the north- and southbound lanes where the inter-
state passed over Commerce Street. Traffic was heavy at that hour, but
moving well: twelve lanes on 35, average speed sixty-six miles per hour,
another six on Commerce traveling only slightly less fast. When the flaming
figure appeared in the sky, the results were predictably disastrous.

According to the Texas State Highway Patrol, thirty-five vehicles col-
lided with one another, resulting in seventy-seven injuries: cuts and bruises,
whiplash, broken bones, concussions, at least three seizures. A pregnant
woman went into labor, but both she and the baby—and, remarkably, ev-
eryone else involved in the pileup—survived the trauma. In addition to the
injured, another 1,886 people claimed to have seen the apparition, making a
grand total of 1,963, a figure later confirmed by both the Dallas Police De-
partment and the Dallas Morning News. *It was this last number that sent*
the story, already ricocheting around the airwaves and the Internet, into the
stratosphere.

12/30.

11:22.

1963.

The time, date, and year that the thirty-fifth president of the United
States had been assassinated, less than a quarter mile due east of the
sighting.

It was possible—possible, though infinitesimally improbable—that this
sequence was just a coincidence. Why hadn't the figure appeared at 12:30 p.m.
on November 22, skeptics were soon enough arguing on chat shows and blogs,
the actual date and time of the assassination? What was harder for them to
dismiss was the fact that every single witness, all 1,963 of them, reported
seeing exactly *the same thing. This wasn't a fuzzy image of a crucified Jesus*
on a piece of toast or the shadowy outline of the Virgin Mary in an MRI. In
fact, none of the twenty-six traffic and surveillance cameras with a view of

the area recorded anything besides the accident itself. Nevertheless, each and every witness reported seeing—

"A boy," Michael Campbell, twenty-nine, told one reporter.

"A flaming boy," Antonio Gonzales, fifty-six, told the paramedic bandaging the gouge over his left eye.

"A boy made of fire," Lisa Wallace, thirty-four, told the person who answered the 800 number of her insurance carrier.

"He looked right at me."

"It was like he was looking for someone."

"But it wasn't me."

There was a palpable sense of disappointment as witness after witness made this last admission, as if they'd somehow failed a test. But then their spirits perked up when they reported that they'd felt the boy coming, as if the privilege of witnessing his appearance was a blessing on the order of those bestowed on the sainted receivers of visions at Guadalupe, Lourdes, Fátima. One after another, witnesses reported the sensation of a tremor in the roadway that came up through their cars and was absorbed by fingers and toes and bottoms—the kind of vibration Mindy Pysanky, a California native, described as "like the start of an earthquake." Hands tightened their grips on steering wheels or door handles, eyes scanned mirrors and windshields for the cause of the disturbance, which appeared—no matter where people were, whether they approached the area from north or south or east or west—directly in their line of vision, facing them. Looking them straight in the eye, and then looking away.

"I saw him as clearly as I see your face," said Yu Wen, fourteen.

"His eyes were wide open," said Jenny McDonald, twenty-eight.

"His mouth was open too," said Billy Ray Baxter, seventy-nine.

"A perfect O," said Charlotte Wolfe, thirty-six, adding: "It was the saddest face I ever saw in my life."

"Not just sad," Halle Wolfe, Charlotte's daughter, eleven, clarified. "Lonely."

The boy blazed in the air "for three or four seconds," a figure that caused almost as much furor as the previous numbers, as lone gunman supporters lined up against conspiracy theorists over whether the apparition was some kind of otherworldly endorsement of the Warren Commission's findings or those of the House Select Committee on Assassinations. No matter which side you were on, however, it was hard to say what the flaming boy could have had to do with a crime whose forty-ninth anniversary had gone largely un-remarked-upon a month earlier. Not one of the witnesses said he reminded them of the dead president or his (presumed) assassin. In fact, almost every-one expressed disinterest in the unnerving string of numbers when it was relayed to them, let alone the proximity of the sighting to Dealey Plaza, the Texas School Book Depository, the grassy knoll.

One thousand, nine hundred sixty-three witnesses. All of them seeing the same thing: a seraphic figure ten feet tall, arms and legs trailing off in ropes of fire, a corona of flame rising from his head. The empty shadows of his eyes scanned the crowd while a silent cry leaked with the smoke from his open mouth. Sixty-two percent of witnesses used the word "angel" to describe the appearance, 27 percent used the word "demon," the remaining 11 percent used both. But only one man said that he looked like Orpheus.

"From the myth," Lemuel Haynes, a businessman "from the East Coast," told Shana Wright, on-air correspondent for the Dallas-Fort Worth NBC affiliate. "You know, turning around, looking for Eurydice, only to see her dragged back down to hell?"

Wright, who later described Haynes as "elderly, but still fit, with a large build, dark hair, and mixed complexion," said that the witness told her he'd just landed at Love Field and was on his way to a meeting.

"What a lucky coincidence," Wright recalled telling him, "that it should show up at the same time you did," to which Haynes replied:

"Luck had nothing to do with it."

According to Wright, she then asked Haynes if he thought the apparition had anything to do with the Kennedy assassination. Haynes looked over Wright's shoulder for a long time—at the Texas School Book Depository, she later realized, which was just visible through the famous Triple Underpass—before turning back to her.

"It has everything to do with it," he said, "and nothing at all," and then his driver, "a middle-aged Asian man with a wiry build," knocked her cameraman unconscious and took the memory chip from his camera.

By the time Homeland Security arrived at the scene, they were gone.

PART 1

THE MONROE DOCTRINE

We owe it, therefore, to candor, and to the amicable
relations existing between the United States and
those powers, to declare, that we should consider any
attempt on their part to extend their system to
any portion of this hemisphere, as dangerous to our
peace and safety. With the existing colonies or
dependencies of any European power we have not
interfered, and shall not interfere. But with the
governments who have declared their independence,
and maintained it, and whose independence we have,
on great consideration, and on just principles,
acknowledged, we could not view any interposition for
the purpose of oppressing them, or controlling, in
any other manner, their destiny, by any European
power in any other light than as the manifestation of
an unfriendly disposition towards the United States.

. . . It is impossible that the allied powers should extend their political system to any portion of either continent, without endangering our peace and happiness: nor can any one believe that our Southern Brethren, if left to themselves, would adopt it of their own accord. It is equally impossible, therefore, that we should behold such interposition, in any form, with indifference. If we look to the comparative strength and resources of Spain and those new governments, and their distance from each other, it must be obvious that she can never subdue them. It is still the true policy of the United States to leave the parties to themselves, in the hope that other powers will pursue the same course.

—James Monroe, 1823

The big man with the cigar pinched between thumb and fore-finger towered over the bound, quivering form of Eddie Bayo, one foot on the fallen man's throat like a gladiator stamping victory on a vanquished foe. The foot was shod in a woven leather sandal—less gladiator than plain old huarache—and the sock had a hole in the big toe, but even so, it was pretty clear who was in charge.

The six-inch-long pencil-thin panatela had a name—it was a Gloria Cubana Medaille d'Or No. 4—but the big man's name had disappeared along with his mother when he was a little boy, and for two decades he'd thought of himself only by the cipher bestowed on him when the Wiz plucked him out of the orphanage in New Orleans: Melchior. One of the three Wise Men. The black one, to be specific, which told you something about the way he was perceived in Langley, as well as about the Wiz's less-than-genteel Mississippi brand of humor.

Just looking at him, you couldn't say for sure. His skin had been described by various adjectives ranging from "olive" to "swarthy" to "high yellow." One of the maids in the orphanage had told him to embrace his "redbone" heritage, and his favorite whore in Havana's *Central* bordellos called him *"café con leche,"* which amused him no end—especially when she said he was "good to the last drop." But none of this changed the fact that after twenty years in American intelligence—and despite the fact that he stood six feet two inches tall, with shoulders like cantaloupes and thighs reminiscent of wooden barrels—he was still referred to as the Wiz's pickaninny.

So: Melchior.

He raised the cigar to his mouth to bring up the cherry. The glowing tip illuminated full lips, aquiline nose, dark eyes that gleamed with singularity of intent. A copious amount of brilliantine wasn't quite able to eliminate the curl in his thick, dark locks. He could have been Greek, Sephardic, a horseman from the steppes of the Caucasus—although, in his brass-buttoned, double-breasted navy linen suit, he looked like nothing so much as a sugar *hacendado* from before the *revolución*. The suit had in fact belonged to a former plantation owner, until he'd been executed for crimes against the proletariat.

Not that any of this mattered to Eddie Bayo.

"I don't wanna have to ask you again, Eddie," his captor said in Spanish not just perfect, but perfectly Cuban, albeit in a guttural kind of way.

"Fuck your mother," Bayo gasped against the foot on his throat. His snarl didn't really come off, given that his upper lip looked like a slug that'd been ground beneath someone's heel—which, in fact, it had.

Melchior brought the glowing tip of his cigar to Bayo's right nipple. "My mother, being long dead, has a snatch that's too dried up for my taste." Flesh sizzled; smoke tickled his nostrils; Bayo's throat convulsed beneath the foot on his Adam's apple but all that came out was a strangled gurgle. When Melchior took the cigar away, Bayo's nipple looked like a volcanic crater. A dozen more black and red coronas were scattered across his chest, although it would have taken a particularly rarefied eye to notice that they occupied the same relative positions as the major Hawaiian volcanoes. Geography had been one of the Wiz's first lessons to his protégé, along with the importance of keeping yourself amused.

A hole flashed behind the notch of his lapel as Melchior reached into his breast pocket for his Zippo, and he rubbed it lightly between his fingers; he could just feel the dried blood that kept it from fraying.

"You're running out of skin, Eddie," he said, relighting. "I'm gonna have to go for the eyes soon. Believe me when I tell you, few things hurt more than a cigar in the eye."

Bayo said something unintelligible. Behind his back his bound hands audibly scratched against the splintered floorboards, as though he hoped he could still dig himself out of this one.

"What was that, Eddie, I couldn't make it out. Your mouth must be dry from all the screaming. Here, let me help." Melchior grabbed a long-necked bottle of rum, poured the shot on Bayo's chest rather than in his mouth. Bayo moaned as the alcohol burned his wounds but didn't actually start screaming until Melchior sparked his lighter against the spilled rum. Six-inch tongues of flame danced on Bayo's skin for almost a full minute. A boxer once told Melchior that you didn't know how long a minute was until you stepped in the ring with Cassius Clay, but Melchior was pretty sure Bayo would take exception to that statement.

When the flames finally went out, Bayo's skin was bubbling like a pancake that needed turning over. Melchior puffed on his cigar. "Well?"

"Why should I . . . tell you . . . anything?" Bayo panted. "You're just gonna . . . kill me . . . when you get . . . what you want."

Melchior's lips curled around his cigar in a private smile. In the past two decades he'd heard people beg for their lives in more languages than the Hay-Adams had flags flying from its facade. But truth be told (and like most people who worked in intelligence, he'd long since forgotten what the word meant) he'd never actually killed someone in cold blood. Oh, he'd commissioned half a dozen hits in his day, shot his fair share of men in combat, but always under orders. Never once had he taken the law into his own hands, let alone gone Double-O on someone. But he was tired of Cuba—tired of this and every other banana republic and oil emirate and strategically significant sand spit he'd been deployed to over the past twenty years, and, now that the Wiz had been retired, he knew he was only one suicide mission away from being *under* the field rather than *in* it. He needed Bayo's confession. Not just to learn the location of his rendezvous with a group of rogue Red Army officers, but to earn the security of an office in Langley. The field nigger was finally moving into the big house, and wasn't *no one* gonna get in his way. Least of all Eddie Bayo.

"I like the No. 4," he said now, holding out the panatela as though evaluating it for purchase. "A simple cigar, but solid. Complements just about anything without overpowering it. You can smoke one with your morning coffee or wait till your after-dinner cognac. Hell, it even makes this disgusting Cuban rum taste okay. And of course the thinness"—Melchior jammed the cigar into the hollow of Bayo's left nostril—"allows for precision targeting."

Bayo's scream was like two plates of steel sliding against each other. The Cuban rolled and thrashed on the floor until once again Melchior put his sandaled foot on the man's throat.

"Roasted meat," he said, wrinkling his nose. "Lookit that. I finally found something the No. 4 don't go with."

"You don't get it," Bayo spat when he could talk again. "This is bigger than a two-bit thug like you. Russians won't back down. They got nothing to lose."

Melchior pulled his knife from its sheath.

"I don't got any safety pins on me, so I'm gonna have to slice your eyelid off so you can't blink. I imagine that'll hurt a fair bit, but it's gonna feel like heaven compared to the sensation of having your eyeball melted down like tallow. That's candle wax made from animal fat for an ignoramus like you. Like the kind the Nazis made from the Jews. You want your sister to see you looking like that, Eddie?" He dropped to one knee. "You want Maria to see her big brother looking like a burned-out kike blubber candle?" Melchior sucked at the cigar, getting it brighter and brighter. "How old is she now? Maria. Eleven? Twelve?"

"Not even you—"

"Yes, Eddie, I would. If it would get me off this shit-fuck island, I would gladly lay Fidel Castro on the altar of the Catedral de San Cristóbal de la Habana in front of a full congregation and stick a communion wafer on the head of my dick and shove it between what I assume, based on his beard, are a couple of incredibly hairy ass cheeks. And I wouldn't even *enjoy* that. Especially the hairy part. But Maria? She's a pretty girl. No one's ever stubbed a cigar out on *her* face. And no one ever will. Not if you talk to me."

He brought the cigar an inch away from Bayo's left eye.

"Talk to me, Eddie. Save us both the trouble."

Bayo had cojones, you had to give him that. Melchior was pretty sure it was the threat to his sister that broke him, not the pain. He whispered the name of a village about seven clicks away, close to the border of Las Villas.

"The big plantation south of town got burned out during the fighting in '58. Meeting's in the old mill."

Melchior jammed the cigar in his mouth and jerked Bayo to his knees. The seared skin of Bayo's chest split like wet paper when Melchior pulled him up, and a mixture of blood and pus spilled from the seam and ran down his stomach. But all Bayo did was bite his lip and close his eyes.

"You're a good man, Eddie. You can rest easy with the knowledge that your sister will never know what you did for her. Unless of course I go to the meet and no one shows."

Bayo didn't say anything, and Melchior exchanged his knife for his pistol, brought the gun to the back of Bayo's head. A shot to the back of the head sent a message. If you were going to execute someone, you might as well make it count. Still, the gun in his hand felt ponderously large and heavy, and Bayo's head seemed suddenly very small, as if, if Melchior's hand didn't stop shaking, he might miss. He brought the gun so close to Bayo's head that it tapped against his hair like a type-writer key worried by a twitching finger.

"They'll kill you, too," Bayo said, a desperate whine in his voice.

Melchior laid his thumb on the hammer to still it. "I'll take my chances."

"Not the Russians. The Comp—"

Bayo jerked to the left—even managed to get a foot on the floor before Melchior squeezed the trigger. Clumps of brain splattered across the room, along with his right ear and half his face. He remained up-right for a second or two, wobbling like a metronome, then fell forward. His cracked skull shattered when it hit the floor, and his head flattened out like a half-inflated basketball.

As the reverberations of the shot faded from the room, it occurred to Melchior that he should have cut Bayo's throat with his knife. He only had five bullets left in his gun. Four now. If Bayo hadn't lunged, he would've remembered that before he pulled the trigger.

"Damn it, Eddie. You went and ruined it."

Well, that was Cuba for you. It could take the fun out of just about anything.

Fifteen hundred miles north as the crow flies (no airplane had made the journey since the embargo had started in February) Nazanin Haverman walked into a dingy bar in East Cambridge, Massachusetts. Morganthau had selected the King's Head because it was far enough from Harvard Yard that the usual rabble didn't frequent the place, yet still well known among "a certain set," as he called it. Naz hadn't asked who the members of that set were, but somehow she suspected they were responsible for the smug graffito scribbled on a months-old mimeograph advertising Martin Luther King's March on Washington:

> W. E. B. DuBois went back to Africa.
> Maybe you should join him!

There was a mirror in the vestibule, and Naz looked in the glass with the disinterested gaze of a woman who's long since learned to inspect her war paint without reckoning the face beneath. She took her gloves off, easing the right one over the big ruby on her third finger, which she rubbed, less for good luck than to remind herself that she still had it—that she could still sell it if things got really bad. Then, keeping her gait as steady as she could—she'd primed herself with one or two gin and tonics before she left home—she headed down the narrow corridor toward the bar.

It hit her as she paused in the jaundiced light over the inner door. The cigarette smoke and the stale odor of spilled drinks and the urgent murmur of voices, the sidelong glances and equally circumspect feelings that accompanied them. A miasma of frustrated, sexually charged emotions swirled around her as palpably as the bolts of smoke, and against its press all she could do was fasten her eyes on the bar and forge ahead. Fifteen steps, she told herself, that's all she had to take. Then she could center herself around a tall, cold glass of gin.

Her form-fitting pearl gray suit directed the men's eyes to her hips, her waist, her breasts, the single open button of décolletage in her white silk blouse. But it was her face that held them. Her mouth, its fullness made even more striking by deep red lipstick that picked up the color of the ruby on her right hand, her eyes, as dark and shiny as polished stone, but slightly blurred, too—anthracite rather than obsidian. And of course her hair, a mass of inky black waves that sucked up what little light there was and radiated it back in oil-slick rainbows. A hundred times she'd had it straightened with the fumy chemicals Boston's blanched housewives used to relax their hair, a hundred times it had sprung back to curl, and so, in lieu of the elaborately sculpted coifs that helmeted the rangy blondes and brunettes in the room, Naz's hair was piled against her skull in a thick mass that framed her face in a dark rippling halo. There was too much of it for her to wear one of the pill-box hats that Mrs. Kennedy had made all the rage, so she wore a bandeau instead, perched precariously forward on her head and held in place with a half dozen pins that pricked at her skull.

The girls noticed her too, of course. Their stares were as hard as the men's, if significantly less sympathetic. It was a Sunday, after all. Business was slow.

"Beefeater and tonic, easy on the tonic," Naz said to the bartender, who was already setting a chilled Collins glass on the bar. "A splash of Rose's lime, please. I haven't eaten anything all day."

She tried not to gulp her drink as she perched herself on the bar stool, not quite facing the room—that would read as too obvious, too desperate—but not quite facing the bar either. The perfect angle to be looked at, yet not seem to look back. There was the mirror over the bar for that.

She brought her glass to her lips, was surprised to find it empty. That was quick, even for her.

That's when she noticed him. He'd stationed himself at the darkest corner of the bar, faced his drink like a defendant before a judge. Both hands were wrapped around the stem of his martini and his gaze was aimed directly at the olive at the bottom of the shallow pool. There was a sober expression on his face—*ha!*—as if he regarded what the drink was telling him very, very seriously.

Naz shifted her gaze to the mirror to study him more openly, tried to sort his vibe from the general miasma in the room. A new word, vibe. Part of the hipsters' jargon, which was creeping into the language like uncracked peppercorns that popped between your teeth. But you didn't need a special vocabulary to see that something was bothering this guy. A bitter olive that only a river of gin could keep below the surface. The sharpness of his eyes, the broad plain of his forehead below his dark hair, the delicate movement of his fingers all said that he was an intelligent man, but this wasn't a problem he could solve with his mind. His shoulders were broad, his waist narrow, and, though he hunched over his martini like a dog guarding a bone, his spine was supple, not bowed. So he was athletic, too. But there were some things you couldn't run away from. Some things only alcohol could keep at bay.

With a start, Naz realized the man was watching her as intently as she was watching him, his amused smile bracketed by a pair of C-shaped dimples. Caught out, she shifted her gaze from the mirror to his eyes.

"The last time a pretty girl stared at me this hard, my house brothers had written D-I-M-E on my forehead."

Naz reached for her glass, then remembered it was empty. The jig was up. She abandoned her empty glass and walked down to the end of the bar. If nothing else, she was pretty sure he was good for a drink.

Up close he was easier to read. His vibe. His energy. He was troubled, sure, but he was also horny. He was here for a drink, but he'd take something more if it came his way. It just had to be someone he could pretend was as complicated as himself. As—what was the word the beatniks liked?—deep, that was it.

She smiled as politely as her mother had taught her all those years ago. "Dime? Or perhaps *di me*. Spanish for—"

"'Tell me.'" An embarrassed chuckle. "It's rather more jejune than that."

"Jejune," Naz said mockingly. "In that case, *dit moi* indeed."

She'd fixed the accent—local, refined but also relaxed—and the shirt, which, though a little worn around the cuffs (French, fastened with tarnished silver knots), was bespoke. The knowledge that he was of the patrician classes emboldened her. She knew these people. Had been raised by them, manipulated by them on three different continents, and learned how to manipulate in turn.

The man shook his head. "I'm sorry, the story isn't repeatable in polite company."

"Well, why don't you tell me what you're drinking, and we'll start there."

He held up his martini glass. "I believe we are both drinking gin. Although I prefer mine without all that tonic, which only dilutes the alcohol."

"Oh, but the carbonation speeds its absorption, and the quinine is good for treating malaria, should you travel to exotic climes."

"I'm afraid summers in Newport is as far south as I've gone." The man waved a finger between their glasses as though it were a magic wand that could refill them—a task the bartender accomplished almost as quickly. "My grandmother swore that quinine kept her gout in check. She took an eyedropper full every evening, although I think the decanter of vermouth in which she took it had something to do with any salacious effects she realized. Salubrious, I mean." The man's blush was visible even in the dim light. "Salubrious effects."

Naz touched her G&T to his martini. They each sipped longly, then sipped again. Once again Naz prompted:

"D-I-M-E."

"Okay." The man chuckled. "You asked for it. As part of the initiation ritual into my finals club, pledges were required to submit themselves, if you take my meaning, to a female volunteer known as 'the coin mistress,' who translated inches to cents, which were then recorded on the pledge's forehead in indelible ink. Anyone below a nickel was refused membership. I was one of only three dimes, which, frankly, surprised me, since I'm pretty sure I'm one or two pennies short of the mark."

He fell silent for a moment. Then:

"I cannot *believe* I just told you that story. Actually, I don't know what's worse. The fact that I told the story, or the fact that I said I was one or two pennies short of the mark."

Naz laughed. "I feel as though I should say something about how much candy eight cents will buy, or nine—" She broke off, blushing even more than her companion, and the man waved his hands like a drowning swimmer.

"Bartender! It is very clear we are not drunk enough for this conversation!"

"So tell me," Naz said while they waited for their refills, "what has your brow so furrowed this evening?"

"I, uh—" The man's forehead wrinkled even more as he tried to figure out what she meant. "I have to get the first chapter of my thesis to my advisor by tomorrow afternoon."

"You seem a little old to be an undergraduate."

"My doctorate."

"A professional student. How many pages do you have to turn in?"

"Fifty."

"And how many more do you have to write?"

"Fifty."

"Aha." Naz laughed. "I can understand why you're so, um, furrowed in the brow area. What's your dissertation on?"

"Oh please," the man swatted her question away. "Can't we just start with names?"

"Oh, pardon me. Naz, I mean—" She broke off. So much for an alias. "Naz Haverman," she said, offering him her hand. "Nazanin."

The man's fingers were cool from his glass. "Nazanin," he repeated. "Is that . . . Persian?"

"Very good. People usually think I'm Latin. On my mother's side," she added in a quiet voice.

"Sounds like there's a story there."

Naz smiled wanly, sipped at her empty glass. "You haven't told me—"

"Chandler." His hand pressed hers so firmly that she could feel a pulse bouncing off his fingertips, though she wasn't sure if it was hers or his. "Chandler Forrestal."

"Chandler." The name made her conscious of her mouth. The lips had to purse to pronounce the *ch* and her tongue popped off her soft palate to voice the *d-l* combo, making her feel as if she'd just blown him a kiss. But it was the last name she commented on.

"Forrestal. I feel like I know that name."

Chandler offered her a pained smile. "My uncle perhaps. He was secretary—"

"Of defense!" Naz exclaimed, but inside she was less excited than suspicious. This seemed a bit . . . fortuitous, given the circumstances. "Under Roosevelt, right?"

"Navy under Roosevelt. Defense under Truman."

"Well. I had no idea I was chatting with a member of the political elite."

But Chandler was shaking his head. "I keep as far away from politics as I can. As you said, I'm a professional student, and if all goes well I will be till I die."

They both suddenly realized they were still holding hands and released each other simultaneously. A true gentleman, Chandler had eased off his bar stool to introduce himself. He slipped back on it now, but even so, Naz felt a closeness between them that hadn't been there a moment ago. She relaxed then. She'd been at this long enough to know when the deal was closed.

"Would you excuse me a moment? I have to powder my nose."

Camagüey Province, Cuba
October 26–27, 1963

The road to the village Bayo had named cut through a swath of jungle that had been cleared and grown back so many times it was all one height, like a thirty-foot-tall golf green. The dense weave of trunk, vine, and leaf was as intricately layered as chain mail. This, Melchior thought, was the real difference between forest and jungle: not some measure of latitude or climate, but the willingness of lesser plants to yield to greater. In the temperate zones, oak and maple and conifers choked out all the other life with their spreading canopies and root networks, whereas in the tropics lattices of vine strangled the trees— eucalyptus and palm mostly, the mahogany and lemonwood and acacia having long since been harvested. Strange succulents took root in the trees' bark and branches, leeching the life from them until they were left whitened skeletons. If he were prone to generalizations, Melchior might've seen something symbolic in this: the top-down stability of northern democracy versus the bottom-up anarchy of southern revolution. But a lifetime in intelligence had made him a practical man, one who dealt in facts, not abstractions, targets rather than causes. Eddie Bayo; his Red Army contacts; and whatever it was the latter hoped to sell to the former.

He cursed himself again for shooting Bayo. It was the kind of mistake he couldn't afford to make. Not tonight. Not after two years spent crisscrossing this godforsaken island. The only thing that gave him any hope was the fact that no one seemed to know anything about the deal. Cuba had more intelligence agents per capita than any place this side of East Berlin—KGB, CIA, the native DGI, plus God only knows how many paramilitaries hopping from one sponsor to another like the local tree frogs, fat, warty fuckers whose skin exuded a poisonous mucus (the frogs, not the paramilitaries, although the latter were if anything even more toxic). At any rate, the blackout suggested the operation was small. Melchior himself would have never gotten wind of it if he hadn't been keeping tabs on Bayo for more than a year. Two would be perfect, he thought now. Two Russians, two buyers, four bullets. All he had to do was make sure he didn't miss, or else he'd end up with a lot more holes in his suit than the one over his heart.

He reached the rendezvous without surprising anything more than one of the island's ubiquitous feral dogs. Melchior's relationship with them stretched back to the beginning of his time in Cuba: early on in his eight months in Boniato, he would toss dead rats through the bars of his window after lacing their corpses with strychnine. The guards used the poison as a rodenticide, but the inmates gathered up as much of it as they could, partly to use to kill one another (or commit suicide when they could no longer take their captivity), but mostly because the rats were the steadiest source of food in the prison. Later on Melchior, too, learned to keep the rats for himself, but for a while it was fun to watch two or three wretched mutts fight over a poisoned corpse, only to have the winner collapse in a pool of its own vomit. One thing you could say about the dogs, though: they knew the value of keeping a low profile. The bitch bared her teeth when Melchior's flashlight passed over her, but she didn't snarl or bark.

In fact, Melchior'd been hoping one of them might show up. He'd brought a sack of meat from Bayo's house, and he used morsels of it to keep the bitch trotting behind him all the way to the burned-out sugar plantation and the single structure still standing, though barely: the mill. Its main edifice, a large barnlike structure, was a dark shadow against the moonlit sky. The windows had been boarded up, but flickering light came from a thousand chinks in the siding.

Melchior made one man at the entrance. A perimeter check turned up no other guards or trip wires or jury-rigged warning devices. KGB would've never been this careless, he thought. He might pull this off after all.

He took the dripping burlap sack with the meat from Eddie Bayo's body—Eddie Bayo's house, that is, heh heh—and tied it over a tree branch about five feet off the ground. The bitch watched him curiously. Her tongue lolled out of her mouth and she smacked her chops greedily.

"Shh." Melchior jerked a thumb at the guard, who was so close Melchior could smell the smoke of his cigarette.

When the sack was secure, he moved out in a wide arc to the guard's left. Before he'd gone halfway, he heard the branch rustle as the bitch went for the meat. More important, so did the guard. His flashlight jerked in that direction. There was a louder rustle as the dog jumped again. The sound was loud and repeated enough that no one—not even a guard stupid enough to stand around in the dark with a cigarette clamped between his lips like a target—would've taken it for a person. But it was still enough to hold his attention, and while the guard peered to his left, Melchior drew himself about thirty feet off the man's right flank. He pulled his knife out and waited.

After the crashing had gone on for more than a minute, the guard finally went to investigate. Melchior moved in. There was no cover between the edge of the jungle and the barn. If the guard turned around, Melchior was dead. But he also had to wait to strike until the guard was far enough from the mill that no one inside would hear him if he managed to cry out.

He was twenty feet behind the guard. Fifteen. Ten.

The guard was almost at the bush. He'd seen the dog but not the sack of meat. He leveled his gun. Melchior was afraid he was going to shoot her. He was five feet behind the guard.

He felt the branch beneath the thin sole of his sandal even as it snapped. The guard whirled, which actually made Melchior's task easier. He aimed his blade for the throat, felt the cartilage of the man's larynx resist a moment, then the steel pushed through soft tissue until it lodged against the cervical vertebrae.

The guard opened his mouth but only blood came out, along with a last wet puff of smoke. Melchior separated the man's spasming fingers from the stock of his weapon with his right hand even as his left wrapped around the man's shoulders and, gently, as if he were saving a drunken buddy from a bad fall, eased the guard to the ground. He was still alive when Melchior leaned his head forward to ease the rifle strap around his neck, but he was dead when Melchior set his head back on the ground. As he stood up, he noticed that the bitch was staring at him intently.

"He's all yours."

Carbine fire marked the walls of the mill like the jumpy lines of an EEG, and the whole of the east side was scorched black. Melchior peered through the bullet holes, made out six men and a flatbed truck.

Two were clearly Russian: the dishwater crew cuts and holstered Makarovs gave them away. One of them stood slightly apart from the group, AK at the ready.

The other three wore gaudy suits and had their own guard posted with his own machine gun—an M-16, which was intriguing to say the least, since Melchior had now made one of the four as none other than Louie Garza, an up-and-comer in Sam Giancana's Chicago Outfit. Lucky, that's what he called himself. Lucky Louie Garza. How in the hell had he gotten his hands on a U.S. Army weapon, unless—oh, it was a beautiful unless!—the Company'd brokered a deal with the devil.

But that was something he could find out later. Right now he was more interested in what was hiding behind the slatted sides of the flat-bed truck. The second Russian had a large piece of paper in his hands with some kind of drawing or diagram on it. Melchior squinted, but the lines on the page were as indistinct as the threads of an old spiderweb. The tailgate was open, however, and he made his way around the corner of the mill and found another hole to look through.

"Ho-ly *fuck*."

Melchior took his eye away from the bullet hole, rubbed it, leaned forward again. He wasn't sure if he was delighted or terrified to see that it was still there: a metal box whose crudely welded seams were in direct opposition to the delicacy of the mechanism inside it. The word "Двина" was stenciled on the side in yellow letters. Melchior sounded it out. *Dvina*. He had to bite his lip to keep from swearing again.

Suddenly one of the men jumped to the ground, and Melchior snapped into focus. What was in the truck didn't matter until the six men surrounding it were eliminated. The two machine guns were the real problem. He positioned himself as best he could, having to work with the available chinks in the siding. He started with his pistol since he could re-aim it faster than the guard's bolt-action Carcano. He drew a bead on the Soviet guard just below the hairline of his scrubbrush–thick crew cut, fingered the crusty hole over his heart, whispered:

"*Timor mortis exultat me.*"

Just as he squeezed the trigger, he wondered what would happen if someone shot the bomb.

As Naz walked past the powder room to the pay phone, a tall figure stepped out of the shadows, his eyes lost under the low brim of a fedora.

"Jesus, Mary, and Joseph. You're some kind of genius at what you do, you know that?"

There was as much jealousy in the man's words as disgust, and Naz felt a chill run down her spine.

"Agent Morganthau. I didn't realize you were here." She jerked her head in the direction of the bar. "I was just coming to call you. I think he's ready to go."

"Looks to me like he came and went a long time ago." Morganthau was shaking his head. "I feel as though I'm witnessing the secrets of the harem."

There was something wrong, Naz thought. Morganthau was *too* disgusted. Too jealous. Remembering her suspicions when Chandler mentioned his family connections, she said, "Do you know him?"

Beneath the brim of his hat, Morganthau's thin lips curled into something that she thought was supposed to be a sheepish grin, but came off as a sneer.

"Chandler Forrestal. He was in my older brother's class at Andover. Captain of the lacrosse team and the debating club. Uncle was secretary of defense, Daddy ran one of the biggest pharmaceutical companies this side of the Atlantic until he gambled everything on a government contract that his brother personally blocked. He hung himself when Chandler was thirteen, and a year later Uncle Jimmy jumped out a window of the Bethesda Naval Hospital. Chandler went off to Harvard like he was supposed to, but instead of going prelaw he studied philosophy, then went for his doctorate in, what was it, comparative religion? Something ridiculous like that. I heard he even talked about becoming a man of the cloth. But I see he's become a man of the bottle instead."

Naz listened as Morganthau rattled off this capsule history, less interested in the facts than the vehemence with which Morganthau recounted them. Although she had no idea what had prompted his anger, it was clear he didn't just know Chandler: he'd set this up. This was more than a prank, or research for that matter. This was revenge.

"You make it sound like he's a murderer. Why should you care if he wants to study religion, or preach it for that matter?"

"Because he turned his back on his duty. His family. His *country*."

"Maybe he had something he had to do for himself. Before he could help 'his country.'"

But Morganthau was shaking his head. "Men like us don't have the luxury of ironic quotation marks, now less than ever. There's a war on, and the stakes, in case you missed the little brouhaha in Cuba last year, are bigger than ever."

All of a sudden Naz realized she was drunk. Drunk and tired. Terribly, terribly tired.

"Why are you making me do this?"

Morganthau's lips quivered. Smile or smirk, Naz couldn't tell.

"Because I knew he wouldn't be able to say no to you."

"Not *him*," Naz said. "*This*. You've said there are other girls. Girls who want to do it. Who find it exciting. So why make me do it against my will?"

Morganthau's head turned toward the main room, then back to Naz. He put his hand on her shoulder—not heavily, but not altogether lightly either.

"No one's making you do anything, Naz. Just say the word and you won't ever have to ask someone to buy you a drink again."

Morganthau's hand squeezed Naz's shoulder, not tightly, but not loosely either. His lips were visible beneath the shadow of his hat, moist, parted slightly, his breath hot in her face and laced with Irish whiskey. For a moment the two of them just stood like that, but then, when Morganthau leaned in for a kiss, she stepped back and shrugged his hand off her shoulder. Morganthau inhaled sharply. His head tipped back and for a moment his whole face was visible, the boyish charm disfigured by lust and contempt. Then he hunched forward and it disappeared again, although the feelings still radiated out of him like heat from an open oven.

He shoved a hand into his pocket. "Here. Give him this instead of the usual stuff."

Naz slipped the glassine into her purse, less wary than weary. "A new formula?"

"In a manner of speaking." Another mirthless smirk flickered over Morganthau's thin lips. "Give me ten minutes before you head out. I definitely want to set the camera up for this one."

Melchior was so focused on his target that he was almost surprised when a neat hole appeared in the Russian's forehead. A moment later the sound of his pistol going off slammed into his ears. The mob guard with the M-16 was already turning, and Melchior's second shot caught him rather more messily in the side of the head.

God bless Lucky Louie. Suspecting a double-cross, he immediately unloaded his gun into the remaining Russian. He fired wildly, and Melchior thought he heard the ricochet of a bullet bouncing off metal. Nothing exploded, though, so he kept shooting.

With a military target, Melchior's plan would have had much less chance of success. Soldiers would have kicked their way out of the mill at three different places, and even if they hadn't managed to take Melchior out, at least one would have gotten away, and with him any hope of that corner office in Langley. But these were mafia men. Thugs. Used to digging in against police officers who'd just as soon take kickbacks as tough out a gunfight. And certainly none of them was willing to be a sacrificial lamb: anytime Louie tried to give an order, one of the other two—Sal and Vinnie seemed to be their names—invariably screamed, "Shut the fuck up, Louie!"

Even so, it took twenty minutes for Melchior to pick off the first two, at which point Louie ran. Melchior took him down with a shot to the pelvis. Louie's left leg spun limply away from his body, and Melchior imagined the mill hadn't heard screams like that since the old *hacendado* whipped his workers for not processing the sugar fast enough.

Louie's gun lay inches from his body, but he was so blinded by pain that he didn't think of reaching for it until Melchior was virtually on top of him, at which point Melchior just stepped on his spasming fingers. The soles of his sandals were so thin that he could feel Louie's fingers clawing at the soft, fertile soil. Melchior kicked the gun out of reach and knelt down. Louie's mouth was clamped shut now, but he was still moaning like a dog run over by a truck.

"Who sent you here?"

Louie stared right at Melchior, but Melchior wasn't sure if he saw him or not. "*¿Qué?*"

"I'll tell your wife where you're buried," Melchior said in a soft voice. "Just tell me who sent you here."

Louie chewed air, but he seemed to be coming back to himself. The plates of his broken pelvis pushed visibly against his skin, but he tried to put on a brave face.

"I don't got a wife, tell my mother." He managed a wet chuckle, then said, "Same folks sent me as sent you, I'm willing to bet."

"I been in this pissant country two years. Whoever sent me here don't even know I'm alive anymore. So drop the macho act and tell me who you're working for. Is it just Momo, or is he representing outside interests?"

For the first time Louie seemed to realize that his captor knew who he was. He peered at Melchior curiously.

"Officially? Paychecks come via a sausage factory in New Orleans, but everyone knows it's a Company front. Banister's the cutout, but according to him the authority comes from higher up."

"Banister's a prick who'd say just about anything. But just for kicks: did he say it was Bobby or Jack or both?"

"Little brother."

"And did he say *why* Bobby Kennedy'd risk his and his brother's careers to hire the Chicago Organization to kill Fidel Castro, when he's got the whole CIA to do it?"

Louie coughed out another weak, wincing laugh. "Cuz Castro's still alive, you dipshit."

Melchior had to give that one to Louie. "What plan did they come up with for you?"

Louie rolled his eyes. "Poison pills. We was supposed to get them in his food somehow." He turned his head and spat blood. "You?"

"Exploding cigars." Melchior laughed, then jerked a thumb at the mill. "This is a little far from the Plaza de la Revolución."

Louie's eyes glazed over, and Melchior wasn't sure if he was dying, or thinking what his life might've been like if he'd managed to complete his deal. He could feel Louie's blood warming his knees as it soaked into the ground and was just about to kick the gangster when his eyes snapped back into focus.

"You got any rum?"

"Does a Cuban dog have fleas?"

"No more than a Cuban whore. Gimme a taste, and I'll tell you what you want to know. I'd just as soon go out of this world like I came into it: drunk."

Melchior pulled Eddie Bayo's bottle from his jacket and held it to Louie's mouth. Louie wrapped his lips around the neck and drank the smoky liquid like lemonade.

"Jesus," Melchior said when Louie finally came up for air. "That would hurt me more than getting shot in the hip."

"Yeah? Gimme your gun and let's find out."

Melchior laughed. He'd always been partial to a wiseass.

"So: Bobby sent you here to kill Castro. You didn't kill Castro but you're still here. What gives?"

Louie burped and spat more blood. "Bastard pulled the plug. Left us high and dry just like Jack did the Brigade." The disgust was audible in Louie's voice. "That's the problem with those smug Paddies. They don't follow through."

"Yeah, yeah, save it for the campaign trail. Do they know about tonight's meet? Does anyone?"

Now it was pride that filled Louie's voice. "Sam said there's always a way to make money in Cuba. Sugar, gambling, girls. But not even Sam knows about this."

"What about the Russians?"

"Vassily—that was the guy I was nice enough to shoot for you—Vassily says Russia's barely getting by. The people don't trust the government and the government don't trust itself. There's Khrushchev and his guys on one side, the hard-liners on the other. KGB's got their own agenda, Red Army's got theirs. If you worked *them* for once, put one against the other instead-a messing around in no-account places like Cuba, you might actually manage to *win* the Cold War."

"Yeah, but then guys like me would be out of a job."

Louie's eyes narrowed. "I thought you said the Company didn't know you was here. So who're you working for? Castro pay you off? The Reds?"

Melchior couldn't keep from smirking. "Let's just say one little brother's gonna have to buy me back from another."

"*Segundo?*" Louie pursed his lips, but all that came out was a wet stream of air. "I heard that when the fighting was over in '59 it was him who lined up what was left of Batista's men and shot them all. I'd take Bobby over that cold-blooded motherfucker any day—and I fucking *hate* those Paddy bastards."

"You do realize your boss gave Kennedy Chicago, which gave him Illinois, which gave him the election? What in hell have you got against him, besides the fact that he's Irish?"

"Ain't that enough?" Louie's laugh turned into a cough, and he spat up what seemed like a mouthful of blood. "Garza," he said when he could talk again. "Luis."

It took Melchior a moment to get it. "You're . . . *Cuban?*"

"Can't keep fucking with someone's country and not expect consequences. And Cubans is like Italians. They ain't ashamed to play dirty if that's the only way to win."

Louie broke off, panting heavily, but otherwise holding it together. Not crying and carrying on like Eddie Bayo, begging for mercy like a bully with a bloody nose. Melchior thought he would've liked the guy, if the circumstances had been different.

"I'm getting tired," Louis said now, "and my hip hurts like you can't imagine. Are we done with the twenty questions?"

"Just one more thing." Melchior jerked his thumb at the mill. "Are the keys in the truck?"

He had a bottle in his car. Vodka rather than gin. "Doesn't need a mixer," he said by way of explanation. She told him her landlady didn't allow coed guests ("Neither does mine") but if he was surprised that she insisted on this particular motel, so far out in East Boston that it was practically at Logan Airport, he managed to hide it. When he excused himself to go to the bathroom, she poured a pair of drinks and pulled the glassine Morganthau had given her from her purse.

Sometimes the stamps were blank, sometimes they had pictures on them. A rising sun, a cartoon character, one of the Founding Fathers. These depicted a bearded man. She thought it was Castro at first—it was the kind of joke she'd come to expect from the Company—then realized it was actually a William Blake engraving. One of his gods. What was this one called? Orison? No, that was some kind of prayer. Origen? She couldn't remember.

She was about to drop the stamps into Chandler's drink when she heard a door in the next room. She looked up and there was the mirror. It hung over the dresser, screwed tightly to the plaster. Naz had been in this room enough times to know that if you got right next to it you could see that it was recessed an inch into the wall. A design flaw, she'd thought—how many five-dollar motels went to that kind of trouble?— but Morganthau told her it minimized the dark corners out of camera range.

She stared at the mirror for a long moment. Then, making sure her actions were fully visible, pulled both stamps from the glassine, dropped one in Chandler's glass, the other in hers. She swished with her fingers, and in a second they were gone.

"Cheers," she said to the mirror.

"I suppose if I looked as good as you, I'd toast myself too."

She whipped around. Chandler stood in the bathroom doorway, his face wet, his hair freshly combed. He'd taken off his jacket and his white shirt hugged his slim torso. Her heart fluttered beneath her blouse. What am I *doing?* she said to herself, but before she could answer her question, she brought her glass to her lips. Warm vodka rasped down her throat like sandpaper, and she had to fight to keep the grimace off her face.

Chandler just looked at her a moment. She could feel his uneasiness, knew he was picking it up from her. If she wasn't careful, she was going to scare him away. But beneath that she could also feel his curiosity. Not lust—or not just lust—but a genuine desire to know this girl wrapped in clothes that, like his, were expensive but worn. For the first time in the nine months since Morganthau had recruited her, in the three years since she'd started doing what she did, she felt a mutual current between her and the man in the room.

"Naz?"

She looked up, startled. Somehow Chandler was beside her. His right hand cupped her left elbow softly, the way her father had always held her mother.

"I-I'm sorry," she stuttered, lifting her glass to her lips. "It's just that I—"

"Whoa there," he said, catching her hand. "That's mine, remember?"

"Oh, uh." Naz grinned sheepishly, handed him his glass. "I'm sorry," she said again. "I don't normally do this."

Chandler looked around the little room, as if her lie was somehow evident in the dingy walls, the scuffed furniture, the dusty TV with one bent antenna. The unerring way she'd guided him here. He touched his glass to hers.

"I'm here too," he said, and pounded his drink just as she had. The fingers of his right hand shivered and squeezed as the warm vodka went down, and she felt a tingle through her entire body.

"*Ice,*" he said when he could speak again.

Urizen, Naz suddenly remembered as Chandler grabbed a bucket and ducked into the hallway. That was the name of Blake's god. Blake claimed to have seen him in a vision, as she recalled.

She rubbed her arm and contemplated her face in the mirror—and what lay on the other side of it—and wondered what she would see.

o o o

In the nine months since Morganthau had recruited her, she'd slipped the drug to almost four dozen men. She wasn't exactly sure what he was hoping it would do. She only knew what she'd seen. One minute the men would be pawing at her, the next they'd jump back from something she couldn't see. Occasionally it seemed pleasurable. One time a man sighed, "Cerberus? Is that you, boy?" in a way that made her think it must be a long-lost childhood dog. But nine times out of ten the visions seemed terrifying, and half the men ended up huddling in a corner, swatting at imaginary tormentors. Morganthau suggested that the things the men saw—hallucination seemed an inadequate term, at least from her perspective; they were more like demonic visitations—were influenced by context. Since this was Boston, where Puritan roots ran deep, her johns had a tendency to manifest whatever pillar of judgment they most feared: the police, their wives, their mothers. Urizen himself.

Yet none of them felt as guilty as Naz. She was the whore, after all. The one who'd lived when her parents died. The one who traded her body for a few dollars and the numbing bottles of alcohol they bought. It was only after she'd ingested the drug that she allowed herself to admit that perhaps she hadn't taken it to defy Morganthau, or to find out what it was she'd been giving unwary men for the past nine months, but to punish herself even more than she normally did. To keep herself from getting close to the man who was even now staring into her eyes with a look of wonder on his face, a feeling of positive amazement radiating from his pores, as though he was asking himself what he'd done to deserve her.

She blinked, wondering when—how—he'd come back into the room. The ice bucket was on the table, fresh drinks had been poured. He'd even kicked his shoes off. One sat on the bed like a kitten with its legs folded beneath it.

"Are you cold?" he said.

She looked down and saw that she was still rubbing her arm where he'd held her.

"Want me to warm you up?"

He crossed the room in a black-and-white blur, and before she knew it his hands were on her arms again, rubbing gently. There was nothing fake in the gesture, or domineering, or sexual. He didn't knead her like a lump of human dough. He was just rubbing her arms to warm them up, and, helplessly, she pressed herself against him, turned her face up to look at his.

"My God," he said in a hoarse voice that was neither whisper nor groan. "You are so *beautiful*."

He gazed into her eyes and she stared back, looking for the thing that made him different from all the others. For the first time she saw that they were hazel. The kind of eyes that change color depending on how the light strikes them. Brown, amber, green. A little of each all at the same time. Flecks of purple, too. Blue. Pink. Amazing eyes, really. The irises were kaleidoscopes surrounding the tunnels of his pupils, and all the way at the back of that inky darkness was yet another spark of color. Gold, this time. Pure, immutable, like an electrical charge.

She knew what that spark was. It was his essence. The thing that made him different from every other person she'd met since she came to this country a decade ago. It was right there, flickering at her. Inviting her in.

Even after he closed his eyes and kissed her she could still see it.

She reached for it with her hand, but it was too far inside his head. She would have to go in after it. She had to push at the edges of his pupil to squeeze through, but once she was inside, it was roomier than she'd've expected: when she reached out her hands she couldn't touch the sides. Couldn't feel anything beneath her feet, either, and it was so dark that all she could see was the spark in the distance. For a moment she felt her own spark of panic, but even before she recognized the feeling she heard Chandler's voice.

It's okay.

She giggled like a teenager at a monster movie. The light seemed to have grown limbs, as if it were not simply a spark, a flame, but a person. A person on fire. She thought that should have scared her, but it didn't. There was no sense of torture from the figure leading her deeper inside Chandler, of agony or fear, but rather a sense of protection. Righteousness even. Shadrach, Meshach, and Abednego cavorting in the fiery furnace.

The spark was larger now. Had lost its limbs and taken on a more solid shape, taller than it was wide, flat on the bottom and sides but curved slightly on top. A tombstone, she thought at first, but when she got closer she realized that it was in fact an arched, open doorway.

It was only when she poked her head through that she saw the books. Thousands of them, stacked atop one another in spindly columns that sprang from the floor of Chandler's brain and receded into impenetrable heights. She'd thought the spark had been his essence, his secret, but now she realized it had only led her here. The real secret was hidden in one of these thousands upon thousands of moldering tomes. A slip of paper folded between the covers of some favorite childhood story long since migrated to the bottom of one of these hundreds—thousands—of stacks.

An embarrassed chuckle sounded off to the side.

"I thought it would look more like a cave. Dark, slimy, water dripping somewhere out of sight."

Chandler stood behind a stack of books just high enough to conceal his nakedness. She glanced down at herself, saw that she was naked too, and similarly shielded.

"Apparently you're a scholar." Even as she said it, she remembered what Morganthau had told her. He *was* a scholar, or at any rate a student. Harvard. The Divinity School. "So, uh, why books?"

Chandler shrugged. "Safer than the real world, I guess."

"'Politics,' you mean?" Naz made air quotes, although it seemed a fairly ridiculous gesture, given the context.

"In my family we didn't call it politics. We called it service. But from where I stood it just looked like servitude."

Naz laughed. "So, uh, what do we do now?"

"I'm not sure, but I think we're already doing it." Before Naz could ask him what he meant, he opened the topmost book on the stack in front of him. "Look."

Naz squinted. Not because the image was hard to see, but because it was hard to believe. It showed the motel room—the motel bed, to be precise, on which lay the apparently naked bodies of Chandler and Naz, although most of their flesh was covered by the blanket. But that wasn't the part Naz had trouble accepting. The vantage point of the scene was the mirror over the dresser. It was as though she was looking at herself and Chandler through the eyes of Agent Morganthau, whose husky breathing came in time with the rhythmic squeak of springs beneath his body. . . .

And all at once it was over. Naz was back in the room. On the bed. Under the covers. In Chandler's arms. Naked.

Wow, she thought. That was some trip. But then she looked in Chandler's eyes.

"Urizen?"

It took Naz a moment to remember the bearded man on the stamp.

"Oh no," she said, and turned fearfully toward the mirror.

The coo of a mourning dove eased Chandler from sleep. He let the percussive gurgle tickle his eardrums while the last images from his dreams faded from his mind. He'd been back in his grandmother's house, trapped at the table while the old battle-axe presided over one of her endless, tasteless meals. The really strange thing, though, was that the sooty portrait of his grandfather over the fireplace had been replaced by a one-way mirror behind which sat Eddie Logan, the annoying little brother of his best friend from boarding school. What was even stranger, Eddie was holding a movie camera with one hand and himself with the other. Chandler hadn't thought of Percy's pipsqueak brother in a decade. And what the hell was he doing with a movie camera?

Yet this was nothing compared to the other dream.

The girl.

He couldn't bring himself to voice her name, lest, like Eurydice, she should disappear at the first sign of attention. Instead he savored the residue of her voice, her eyes, her lips. Her kiss. Her body. God, he hadn't had a dream like that since he lived in his grandmother's house. Hadn't been that naively optimistic since his father had been alive.

And all of a sudden there was the other image, one that was never far from his thoughts, waking or sleeping. His father. Dressed in his three-piece suit, creases pressed, collar starched, every hair in place—a perfect imitation of Uncle Jimmy, as if sartorial splendor could mask the failure of his life. But in this memory one detail was out of place; namely, the noose that had jerked the tie from his father's waistcoat, so that it hung in front of his chest in grotesque echo of the tongue that bulged from his mouth. And the crowning glory: the piece of paper pinned to his jacket like a teacher's note on a toddler's shirt:

PUTO DEUS FIO.

The line was Emperor Vespasian's, uttered just before he died: *I am becoming a god.* His father had missed the first word of the quotation, however: *vae*, which could be translated as "alas" or "woe" or just plain "damn." Leave it to his dad to get it wrong right up till the end.

Chandler's eyes snapped open. Light filled the room, outlining everything in sharp relief, from the stacks of books piled three deep against the walls to the stack of dishes nearly as high in the kitchenette. He pressed his finger to the bridge of his nose to see if he'd fallen asleep wearing his glasses, but even as he did so, he saw them folded up on the bedside table. But still. The single room of his apartment, from the crumbs on the carpet to the cracks on the ceiling, was crystalline as a photograph. Weird.

He sprang from bed, his limbs snapping with energy. That was when he saw the bird. The mourning dove that had awakened him. It sat on the sill of the open window over the sink, pecking at crumbs of food on the topmost plate.

"Hey, little fellow. I didn't know your kind liked Chinese food."

The bird cocked one dark eye at him. Claws as thin and sharp as freshly sharpened pencil lead clicked and clacked over the sill, and its head and throat were a pearly gray that reminded him of something. The color of the girl's dress, that was it. He still didn't say her name. Didn't even think it.

He walked toward the bird slowly, worried that it might fly into the room. He talked to it softly, but the bird seemed completely unbothered by his approach. He was five feet from it, three, he was standing at the counter's edge. He reached toward the animal with his right hand.

"Don't be scared, little guy. I just want to make sure—"

Just before his hand touched it, the bird looked up. Cocked that one eye at him again. Except this time when Chandler looked into the eye he seemed to fall down it as though the dove's eye was an impossibly deep well. All the way down at the bottom a round, pale face stared up at him out of the inky water, only to disappear when he splashed through.

Naz.

He heard glass breaking, felt a sharp pain in his hand. The next thing he knew, he was standing over the kitchen sink. The window was closed, the glass in the bottom left pane broken. A thin trickle of blood ran down his hand and there was no sign of a bird. The dishes were still there, though, reeking faintly of mildew.

For a moment he stared at the blood trickling down his hand as though it might turn out to be another hallucination. He could feel the tiny pressure as the warm red stream pressed on each hair of his wrist, felt the weight of it pressing on the very vein that was pumping more blood to the wound. He stared at it until he was sure it was real, because if the blood was real, if the cut was real, then that meant she was real too. Only when he was absolutely sure did he say her name out loud.

"Naz."

The word rippled into the world like a sonic cry. Out and out it went, but nothing bounced back. But that didn't mean she wasn't real. It just meant she was lost, and he would have to find her. Like Eurydice, he told himself again, and did his best to forget how that story ended. Then, catching himself, he chuckled sheepishly.

"I have *got* to stop drinking on an empty stomach."

His protest rang hollow. He had no headache, no sign of a hangover. He wasn't even hungry, even though he usually woke up starving after a bender. He remembered drinking the day before—remembered drinking *a lot*—but it seemed to have had no effect. He looked at his body for some sign that he'd had sex but found no incriminating marks. Not that he usually found marks after sex, but still. After an encounter like that, you'd think there'd be some trace. But that made him think of his eyes. Of his oddly clear vision. He'd worn glasses for nearly two years now, and his deteriorating eyesight was the kind of thing that was supposed to get worse, not better. So why was he seeing with 20/20 vision this morning—20/15, 20/10—and why did he feel like it had something to do with what happened last night?

What happened last night?

"Nothing happened last night," he said out loud, but this protest was even more unconvincing than the last.

He filled the percolator and set it on one ring of his hot plate, opened the fridge, put a pan on the other ring of the hot plate, dropped in half a stick of butter and, while it melted, cracked a couple of eggs into a bowl. When the butter was sizzling, he poured the eggs in and scrambled them quickly, dumped some salt and pepper on top, ate them out of the pan. The coffee was done by then, and he poured himself a cup, added three teaspoons of sugar, and, more or less on instinct, sat down in front of his typewriter. He reached for his glasses by reflex, but they only blurred his vision—for a moment, anyway, and then it cleared again. He took his glasses off and the same thing happened: his sight blurred, then cleared, the sentence at the top of the page springing out in bold relief:

```
Toward the end of the Achaemenid era, the fire
principle, atar, representing fire in both its burning
and unburning aspect, became embodied in a demigod
Adar, a divine elemental akin to the four winds of
ancient Greece: Boreas, Zephyrus, Eurus, and Notus.
```

It was the thousandth incarnation of a sentence he'd been writing for the past three months. His goal was to trace the history of fire through the world's religions, from Akhenaten's replacement of Amun with the sun god Ra in ancient Egypt to Prometheus's theft of fire from the gods in Greece to the Persian incarnation of Adar and onward. His intention was to show how the sun, the giver of all life, is first deified (Ra), then demystified (Prometheus), then resignified (Adar) as human beings realize that fire, like a stallion, can be only partially tamed—which is why most religions contain an apocalyptic vision of the earth consumed by flames in a final judgment against mankind's hubris. It was this quasi-animist belief that Chandler believed was fueling the nuclear arms race: from primitive fire arrows to medieval trebuchets to nuclear bombs, humanity was doing the bidding of the fire god, building the tools that would enable it to realize its ultimate goal: the purification of the world through its annihilation.

He knew the arguments backward and forward, had scoured the dusty corners of every library between Cambridge and Princeton for supporting evidence. But every time he sat down at the typewriter, something stopped him. There was always one more fact he needed to look up, a distracting errand he had to get done. Chandler knew the truth, of course. The truth was that if he ever finished his dissertation he'd have to leave school. Go out into the world and make something of himself, and he knew how that story ended. Knew how it had ended for his father at any rate, and Uncle Jimmy, and Percy Logan, his best friend at Andover: a slab of white marble forty-two inches tall, thirteen inches wide, and four inches thick. For now he'd settle for the less frightening prospect of a blank sheet of paper.

And besides, this time there was no getting around it. He had to write *something*. His advisor had given him a deadline of 5 p.m. to turn in a draft of this chaper or she was going to cancel his monthly stipend.

He glanced at his watch—7:18. Just under ten hours to write fifty pages. Chandler didn't think he could fill that many pages even if, like the proverbial monkey, all he did was hit random keys for the next ten hours, let alone attempt to lay out a cogent argument spanning five continents and as many millennia.

He set his fingers on the keyboard, let his mind fill with the image of Adar. Like all fire, Adar was always moving from one place to another. To Chandler, he was like Hanuman, Rama's devoted servant, not as powerful as his king, but made invincible by unwavering fealty. Hanuman's chin was scarred by a lightning bolt when he was a child. Adar was the lightning itself: a limbed comet, a warrior made of pure flame—

The clacking of keys pulled him from his thoughts. He looked down, was surprised to see that he'd typed everything that had just run through his mind. He'd substituted the word "Urizen" for "Adar" (one of Blake's deities? he wasn't quite sure, although he could see the god clearly enough, beard and hair streaming in a cosmic breeze). Emboldened, his fingers flew over the keys. Words, sentences, paragraphs poured onto the page. One page, two, a third. In the middle of the fourth he needed to check a quotation but was afraid to get up. He knew the quote, could almost see it in front of him, written out on one of the thousands of index cards that filled a dozen drawers in his carrel in the library. And then, suddenly, he *could* see it:

```
There will be a mighty conflagration, and all men will
have to wade through a stream of molten metal that
will seem like warm milk to the just and a torrent of
igneous lava to the wicked.
```

He didn't ask himself how this was happening or if it could possibly have something to do with last night. When he finally looked up, it was just after four. A stack of pages sat next to the typewriter. He was about to count them when the number came to him: seventy-two. He had no idea how he knew this number, but he knew it was accurate. He threw the pages into his briefcase and ran out the front door. The campus was half a mile away. He was going to have to sprint if he wanted to get this in on time. He set off down Brattle Street at a run, but before he'd gone half a block he pulled up short. Something had caught his eye. A stack of newspapers at the corner kiosk. The *Worker,* of all papers. He glanced at the headline—FPCC AND DRE FACE OFF ON NEW ORLEANS RADIO— then realized it the words above the headline that had caught his eye. I.e., Friday, November 1, 1963.

Friday?

Friday?!

Never mind that he was able to see letters a quarter-inch high from ten feet away (and at a run to boot): if the paper was right, he'd some-how lost *five days.* He stood there dumbfounded, wracking his mind for some memory of the last 120 hours. Had he slept it all away? Wandered through it in some kind of alcohol blackout? An image of Urizen flashed in his mind again, stamped on a little square of translucent paper that floated in a glass of clear liquid for a second before dissolving. The taste of warm vodka was so palpable that his eyes watered.

Confused and frightened, he turned and walked back home. His key was in the door when he heard a throat clear. Even before he turned, he felt her. Her sense of barely controlled panic as she waded through the pyroclastic emotions streaming by with the other people on the side-walk. She was hunched inside a dark jacket, her face shielded by sun-glasses with lenses as big as the saucers on which espresso is served in cafes in the Latin Quarter of Paris. The most real thing about her seemed to be the ruby ring on her right hand, which she twisted ner-vously with the fingers of her left.

"Naz." Chandler's voice was as dry as the crust of food on the plates in his sink upstairs. "I—I thought I dreamed you up."

Naz didn't say anything for so long that Chandler thought she was just another hallucination. Then:

"I think you did," she said, and fell into his arms.

In the wake of his Caribbean sojourn, the Halls of Justice seemed bland and expensive. Terrazzo floors speckled black and brown like a wren's egg, buffed walnut wainscoting giving way to Listerine-colored walls. Sure, the slate roofs of Cuba's government buildings were leaking and the rococo wallpaper had been repatterned by gunfire. But the Cubans made all this seem intentional. Not decrepit or disheveled, but *déshabillé,* as the French would have it, which made the whole setup somehow alluring. Sexy even. Give the Communists a few more years and they would no doubt erect buildings like this one: fish belly–white on the outside, every bit as soulless within. But they'd never be able to afford the telling details: the all-pervasive hum of thousands of coffee-makers, Dictaphones, and air conditioners, and of course the immeasurable wattage of infinite fluorescence. Melchior pulled his hat down lower on his forehead. The Wiz always said a spy had only three natural enemies: cheap liquor, cheap girls, and bright lights.

On the beaded glass of the nearest doorway, three letters were stenciled in gold and outlined in black, like the office of a private dick in a forties noir:

D.D.P.

No name was painted on the door, but if he squinted Melchior could make out the ghostly outline of the words FRANK WISDOM just above the title. Whoever'd scraped the paint off had scratched the glass in the process, indelibly etching the Wiz's name into the door and rendering him more of a presence than he'd ever been during his tenure as chief of covert ops. This seemed a fitting tribute, since the Wiz had spent even less time in this office than Melchior had in the Adams Morgan apartment he'd owned for the past eight years.

The door opened. A gray suit appeared. The suit had a head. The head had a face. The face had a mouth. The mouth said:

"You can come in now."

The soles of Melchior's sandals squeaked on epoxied marble when he stood up. He twisted his left shoe a little, which made the sound louder, longer. To an observer it might've looked as though he was just being obnoxious, a high schooler sliding his sneakers on a freshly waxed basketball court. Indeed, his whole demeanor exuded contempt for protocol and propriety, from his too-long and slightly oily hair to his ill-fitting linen suit to the utterly ridiculous woven leather sandals on his feet. But in fact all he was doing was adjusting the inner liner of his shoe, which had bunched up because of the piece of paper folded between it and the sole. A piece of paper worth more than this whole building, although Melchior would settle for an office in it, as long as it came with a pretty secretary.

The man who'd opened the door showed him into the inner office, then, instead of leaving, closed the door, walked around Melchior, and took a seat at the desk. The nameplate in front of him read RICHARD HELMS. Melchior'd never met Helms in person, but he'd seen his picture in the paper often enough. This wasn't Helms.

Melchior was intrigued.

As soon as he sat down, the man seemed to forget about Melchior. He began flipping through the pages of a file on the desk. Melchior's presumably. Melchior noted with pride the thinness of the sheaf of pages. Agents whose tenure with the Company was half his had files two, three, four feet thick, but there were only twenty or thirty pages on the desk. Even so, he didn't like this self-important functionary looking at it. Where in the hell was Dick Helms? Given the fact that Melchior had worked side by side with the former occupant of this office for nearly two decades—not to mention the importance of the intelligence he'd gathered in Cuba—surely he rated a meeting with the current DDP?

Helms's surrogate continued to ignore him, so Melchior plopped into one of the green leather chairs in front of the desk. The surrogate sighed but didn't look up.

"I didn't ask you to sit down."

Melchior lifted both feet off the floor and held his battered sandals in the air. After fifteen months on his feet—and who knows how long on their previous owner—the soles were so worn that when he curled his toes the brown leather wrinkled like skin. So thin that you could see the outline of the piece of paper just under the leather of the left shoe, if you knew what you were looking at.

Finally the man behind the desk raised his eyes.

"I'm sorry Deputy Director Helms wasn't able to meet with you today. I'm Drew Everton. Acting assistant deputy director for the Western Hemisphere Division."

"How in the hell do they fit all that on your card?"

Everton rolled his eyes. "Would you put your feet down, please?"

Melchior smiled. "I just wanted the Company to see what I've had to endure for the sake of my country. I been walking around in a pair of huaraches for more than a year. My feet," he said, letting them plop one at a time to the floor, "are fucking *tired.*"

Once upstairs, Chandler didn't know what to do: sit Naz down and ask her a thousand and one questions or throw her on the bed and ravish her.

"I slept for five days. *Five days.*"

Naz shrugged. "I know."

Chandler pulled up short. "How do you know?"

He was behind her at that point. Her hair was looser than it had been a day and a half ago, fell down her back in lush ringlets. She wore a dark sweater, threadbare but cashmere. It clung to her back, which seemed as tiny and delicate as the thorax of a wasp. A skirt of pale gray wool rode softly over her hips; silk stockings added gloss to the curve of her calves. When Naz said, "You know how I know," Chandler started, because he'd been so caught up in her body that he'd almost forgotten she was in the room.

"Don't start in with that stuff about mind-reading and mental telepathy and extrasensory perception."

"All those terms mean the same thing. And I never mentioned any of them."

"ESP can refer to all sorts of phenomena. Remote viewing, precognition—"

"Would you be more comfortable if you predicted the results of next year's election?"

"I do not believe—"

"Chandler."

"—in ESP or secret CIA drug programs or two-way mirrors in seedy motels or—"

"Chandler."

"—the existence of a part of the brain called the Gate of Orpheus—"

"Chandler!"

Chandler, pressed against the wall, looked at Naz as if she were a rising flood and he was trapped on the roof of his house.

"Your father's name was John Forrestal."

"Anyone could have found that out. My family is well known."

"He hung himself from the chandelier in his office," Naz said over him. "'*Puto deus fio.* I am becoming a god.' What was *my* father's name?"

"How should I—"

"What was his name, Chandler?"

"Anthony," Chandler said helplessly.

"And my mother?"

"Saba," he whispered.

"Your mother disappeared after your father hung himself," she continued. "You always suspected your grandmother chased her away. What's Saba mean?"

"What's—"

"Answer the question, Chandler."

"A breeze. A gentle breeze." He looked at Naz abjectly. "How do I—how do we know these things?"

"Answer the question, Chandler. You know how."

"The . . . drug?"

Naz nodded.

"You gave me a drug. Someone—Morganthau?—made you give me a drug."

Again Naz nodded.

"And it opened the Gate. The Gate of Orpheus."

For the first time a look of doubt—fear—crossed Naz's face.

"That's the part I don't understand. Morganthau never mentioned anything about a Gate of Orpheus. I thought I was in your mind, or that we were in each other's. But now I think it was just you. Your"— her hands reached for a word—"consciousness somehow expanded into my mind. Into Morganthau's."

Chandler didn't say anything for a moment. Then: "He was really behind the mirror?"

Naz looked away. "He said he'd have me arrested if I didn't cooperate. Solicitation," she said, using the polite word. "He—"

"—photographs you," Chandler finished for her. "How many—? Forty-one," he answered himself. He answered himself because it was all there. Everything Naz had ever done. Her first sex, her first drink, her first time trading sex for drink. Somehow it was all in his mind. And he knew he was in her mind in the same way. All of him, residing forever behind those beautiful dark eyes.

He cleared his throat. "Morganthau's real name. It's—"

"Logan. Eddie Logan. I know. Now I know." She shook her head in wonder. "Do you remember what you said in the hotel room? You said, 'I'm here too.'" She took his hand, squeezed it as hard as she could. "I'm here, Chandler. *I'm here too.*"

Her touch sent an electric tingle through his body, and Chandler felt a dopey but wondrous smile spreading across his face. But at the same time there was fear: not of the connection, of how it came to be or what it meant for the future, but the idea that it might be lost somehow, someday. Because if he lost the piece of himself that was her, he would never be whole again.

Another quotation sprang to his mind. Not one he'd learned for his dissertation, just something he'd read somewhere, sometime. *The gods sent Orpheus away from Hades empty-handed, and doomed him to meet his death at the hands of women.* Plato, he remembered then. The *Symposium.* Unlike most classical thinkers, Plato hadn't revered Orpheus, but considered him a coward because he was unwilling to die for love. But that's stupid, he told himself. I'm not—

"Chandler?" Naz's voice cut into his thoughts. Her mouth was still open, but before she could say something else a knock sounded at the door.

CIA Headquarters, McLean, VA
November 1, 1963

"So." Everton took a cigarette from a gold case monogrammed
RH and lit it with a crystal lighter the size of an inkwell. "What's with the hat? Afraid I'll get a good look at your face, Melchior?"

Since it looked like he was going to have to deal with this fool, Melchior took a moment to scrutinize him. Or, rather, his clothes. Everton was clearly less man than mannequin, a prop wrapped in the uniform of his class. His gray wool suit, though perfectly tailored and brand-new, was ten years out of style (the lapels were practically as wide as a beauty queen's sash, for one thing, the serge so stiff it looked like it would stand up on its own). But that was hardly surprising: fashion trends would be beneath the notice of the acting assistant deputy director for the Western Hemisphere Division, and no doubt his tailor had been cutting his suits the same way since prep school. From the crisply symmetrical half-Windsor knot to the double peaks of his white pocket square to the gold Longines with its plain leather strap peeking out from his French cuffs, Melchior couldn't find a single aspect of the man that didn't reek of Wasp prudery. Even his gold wedding band, narrow as solder wire and (tastefully) unpolished, seemed to hide inside the hairs on his knuckle. Really, he was the type of man who could just disappear, and it would be months before even his wife noticed.

Melchior took his hat off and set it on Richard Helms's desk.

"I'm not the one who should be afraid," he said, pulling a Medaille d'Or from his breast pocket and lighting it with his Zippo. *"Drew."*

Everton's eyes followed the glowing tip of Melchior's cigar like a rabbit transfixed by a swaying snake.

"The elusive Melchior," he said, averting his gaze with difficulty. "I've always wanted to meet you, just to find out if you were real. That story with the slingshot still makes the rounds."

"You should see what I can do with a cigar."

Everton ashed so hard he broke his cigarette in half.

"I, ah, read about that in your report. Actually, I have a few questions about your account of your time in Cuba."

Melchior waved the cigar like a magic wand. "Ask away."

It took Everton another moment to tear his eyes from Melchior's cigar.

"Right. So. Twenty-three months ago you were dropped into the Zapata Swamp as part of Operation Mongoose. There were six people on your team: you, two American freelancers, and three Cuban defectors with contacts in the anti-Communist resistance movement. You yourself are reputed to have extensive and impressive field credentials from Eastern Europe, South America, and Southeast Asia, among other places, yet within a week of your arrival all three Cubans were dead, one of the freelancers had been deported, the other was MIA, and you were in Boniato Prison."

"That sounds about right." Melchior puffed contentedly. "Rip ever turn up? I owe that son of a bitch for ditching me."

A thick stream of smoke from the broken cigarette spiraled in the air between Everton and Melchior. Melchior could tell Everton wanted to put the cigarette out, but he just kept talking.

"After nine months behind bars, you claim that not only were you released, but were brought to the office of Raúl Castro and asked to keep an eye on Red Army activity in Cuba."

"He gave me this suit too." Melchior flipped open the left lapel, revealing the small hole over the heart. "Took it off a man he'd had executed. Was nice enough to have it cleaned first, but he left this *memento mori* to make sure I knew what the stakes were. Even threw in a pair-a shoes. Well, sandals, really." Melchior lifted his feet again, waggled them at Everton.

Everton threw up his hands, which caused the smoke from his broken cigarette to dance around like an impish genie.

"You *have* to realize the idea that Fidel Castro's *brother* hired a CIA agent to work for him defies credulity."

"With all due respect, Acting Assistant Deputy Director for the Western Hemisphere Division Everton"—Melchior sucked air dramatically—"the Company sent me to Cuba to try to get El Jefe to smoke an *exploding cigar,* so I'm not sure where you get off saying what's credulous or not."

"Desmond Fitz—ugh." Everton couldn't take it anymore. He grabbed a pencil and used the eraser to stamp out the broken cigarette. "Desmond FitzGerald read too many James Bond novels," Everton said when the smoke had finally dissipated, leaving behind the smell of burning *Hevea brasiliensis* sap, "and is a little too impressed by what Joe Scheider cooks up in his labs."

Melchior rolled his eyes. The exploding cigar had been a stupid idea, but it was hardly the point. "Why is it so far-fetched that a pair of totalitarian governments should be prone to the same factionalism that's in the process of ripping apart this country, not to mention this agency?"

"I don't—"

"Listen, Drew. I been back in the States three days. Just about the longest time I been here since I was thirteen. But it didn't take me more than three hours to see that there's been a shift. This country's splitting in half. Democrats on one side, Republicans on the other. Liberals and conservatives, reformers and old guard, beatniks and squares. What was the gap in the last election? A hundred thousand votes out of seventy million? High school elections have more swing than that."

"Kennedy won. That's all that matters." Everton didn't sound at all pleased by this fact.

"With a little help from Momo Giancana," Melchior said, "who, I gotta say, seems to be moving in very elite circles these days."

Everton's expression didn't exactly change at the mention of Giancana, but it stiffened with the effort of remaining impassive. "Fine," he said in a condescending tone. "Let's say you did meet with Raúl Castro. That still doesn't explain why he would task an American with the job of finding out what motives the Soviets might have for a Cuban alliance."

"With all due respect, Drew—which is to say, none—you got to stop thinking like a bureaucrat and start thinking like a spook. Segundo didn't trust his own men to get to the source of the problem. And even if they did, he didn't think they could fix it."

"By 'problem,' I assume you mean this fanciful notion that the Russians left nuclear weapons in Cuba? We have reconnaissance photographs showing the missiles being taken off the island."

"You have pictures of *boxes*. Those boxes could be filled with *matryoshka* dolls for all you know."

"Nikita Khrushchev isn't stupid enough to risk Armageddon for the sake of hiding one or two bombs on Cuban soil."

"Those are the dolls that sit one inside the other, by the way. Like Chinese boxes."

"I know what *matryoshka*—"

"Although I guess in China they just call them boxes."

Everton's ears were so red that Melchior was surprised they weren't oozing smoke like his broken cigarette. Melchior puffed on his cigar.

"Listen to me, Drew. Nikita Khrushchev might not be stupid enough to start World War III, but there are plenty of Russians who are. People whose objectives aren't the same as Khrushchev's, or the Kremlin's for that matter."

Everton snorted. "You're trying to tell me a rogue Soviet element was able to steal Russian warheads without anyone—KGB, CIA, or DGI—finding out about it?"

Don't forget the mafia, Melchior almost added.

"Actually, a lot of people knew," he said aloud. "Just not the who or the where. That's why Segundo hired me. He found it easier to stomach the idea of a small-scale CIA operation to remove one or two pirated devices than for his country to be blown off the map when word leaked that there were nukes on its territory."

"I repeat, we have no intelligence indicating—"

"Damn it, Drew, did you even *read* my report? *I'm* the intelligence. That's what you pay me for, remember?"

"We *paid* you to assassinate—" Everton cut himself off. Even in Langley, there were some things you didn't say out loud. "We paid you to deliver a box of cigars. Instead you drop off the radar for almost two years, and when you do show up it's smelling like rum and dressed like a plantation owner. Now, if you have any proof—"

"*Hacendado.*"

Everton folded his hands in front of him so tightly the knuckles turned white.

"What?"

"A plantation owner is called an *hacendado*, which you'd know if you paid any attention to the goddamn western hemisphere you're supposed to be in charge of."

Everton opened his mouth but Melchior spoke over him. "Twenty-three months I spent on that miserable little island, Drew, and I'm telling you there are Russian elements—call 'em rogue, call 'em crazy, call 'em whatever the hell you want, but they're using Cuba's proximity to the U.S. to move the Cold War in a whole new direction."

Everton's knuckles were so white they were practically green, and his pursed lips were equally pale, and the little crescents dancing in the hollows of his flared nostrils.

"Fine. If you have any proof of such a conspiracy, by all means, produce it now. And by proof I mean something more than a blazer with a hole and a stain that looks like it was made by an exploding cigar. Pen, I mean. An exploding pen."

For the first time all morning, Melchior's smile was genuine. This was his moment.

He reached for his shoe, but the look of disgust on Everton's face stopped him. He'd expected that look, even if he'd imagined it on Helms's face rather than some mid-level functionary's. Indeed, he'd planned the whole meeting around it. Had resurrected the ridiculous suit and sandals Segundo had given him and chosen an especially fragrant pair of socks so that the paper in his shoe would acquire a healthy tang of foot stink.

There was the look, just as he'd planned. The only problem was, it had nothing to do with Melchior's attire, Melchior's action, Melchior's words, and everything to do with Melchior himself. Melchior'd seen the same expression on the faces of countless anti–Civil Rights demonstrators in the newspapers he'd been reading since he got back. It was the face of a primly dressed white girl as she threw a tomato at a black boy walking into her school in Georgia. It was the face of a uniformed police officer siccing his German shepherd on a black man attempting to use the whites-only entrance of a cafe in Mississippi. It was the face of George Wallace taking the oath of office as governor of Alabama: "Segregation now, segregation tomorrow, segregation forever." Despite all the whispers referring to him as the Wiz's pickaninny—whispers that started, he knew, with the Wiz himself—Melchior had always done his duty to Company and country, and even if he'd often felt like a second-class citizen, he'd never felt *black*. But now he knew: as far as CIA was concerned, he was just as much a nigger as Medgar Evers.

His foot was still in the air, the sandal half off his heel. He let it hang there for one more moment, then reached down and slipped it back on, placed his foot firmly on the floor.

Everton's hands and face relaxed, and watery pink replaced greenish white as the blood flooded to his skin.

"I want to be completely candid with you. Deputy Director Helms didn't meet with you today because he was busy. He didn't meet with you because you are not worth his time. You are the product of a failed experiment on the part of the former occupant of this office. You and your fellow 'Wise Men.'"

"Caspar," Melchior said, his voice dangerously quiet. "Balthazar."

"I don't care if your names are Huey, Dewey, and Louie. Deputy Director Helms feels it's time the Company got out of science fiction and secret wars and returned to the business of gathering intelligence. The Wiz Kids were the first of the Company's ridiculous experiments, from which sprang Bluebird, Artichoke, Ultra, and now Orpheus. It's only fitting that the first should clean up the last."

Melchior's eyes narrowed.

"Orpheus?"

Everton was silent a moment. Then: "Did you ever meet Cord Meyer's ex-wife, Mary?"

"Are you kidding? I never even met Cord."

"Oh, that's right. The Wiz liked to keep you out of the spotlight. Or, who knows, maybe you kept yourself out of the spotlight."

"Who knows?" Melchior said. "So what's the trouble with Mrs. Meyer?"

"She's sleeping with the president."

Melchior shrugged. "From what I heard, you could open a rival to the Rockettes with the girls Jack Kennedy's bagged since he got in the White House."

"Be that as it may," Everton said, "none of the other girls are slipping him LSD."

Melchior didn't react for a moment. Then he leaned forward, retrieved his hat, and set it on his head.

"None of the other girls *is* slipping him LSD," he said, smiling beneath the brim of his hat. "None of the other girls *is*."

Chandler found it disconcerting to have to look up at Eddie Logan. The last time he'd seen him, Percy Logan's little brother had been as short as a walking stick and almost as thin. Outwardly at least, he'd become a man.

Logan attempted to keep a neutral look on his face, but a smirk flicked at the corner of his mouth.

"Well well well," he said as his eyes took in the whole of Chandler's book-lined cave. "How the mighty have fallen."

It had been so long since Chandler thought of himself as one of "the mighty" that Logan's words didn't really hit home. But the tone— especially coming from someone he still thought of as a pipsqueak— the tone stung.

"You must feel clever," Chandler said. "Vindicated. What's it been? Eleven years, three months, nineteen days?" There was an awkward pause after this figure rolled off Chandler's tongue. Something prompted him to give the rest of it. "And three hours. And thirteen minutes."

Logan's eyebrows twitched. "Jesus Christ, Chandler, we were kids. You don't think I've held a grudge for—how long? Eleven years, three months, eighteen—"

"Nineteen."

A bemused smile crossed Logan's face and he shook his head slowly. "If you want to know the truth, I was casing establishments for Naz when I saw you slumped over a martini at the King's Head. I guess I couldn't resist."

"'Casing establishments'? You were pimping her is what you were doing!"

"If the shoe fits—"

Chandler was up before he knew it. Had grabbed Logan by the lapels and, despite the fact that the former pipsqueak was now several inches taller than him, slammed him against the wall.

"How many other girls have you done this to? In how many other cities? Do you have girls skulking around bars in Greenwich Village and Georgetown, too? Maybe a little West Coast action?"

"Most girls think it's fun." Logan's voice was tight.

"Fun?!" Chandler's knuckles were white on Logan's lapels. "Your little bit of power's gone to your head."

"Nobody made Naz do anything she wasn't already doing. Least of all me. Or did she leave that part out?"

"Let him go, Chandler." Naz's hand was on his shoulder, and it seemed to Chandler that she wanted him to let go of more than Logan. He held Eddie's gaze for another moment, then released him. As soon as he stepped away, Naz put herself where he had been, and, though she didn't touch Logan, her manner made Chandler's seem benign by comparison.

"What did you *do* to us, Agent Logan? We have a right to know."

The fury pouring off Naz was so palpable that Logan seemed to shrink against the wall. "Well now," he said hoarsely. "That's the sixty-four-thousand-dollar question, isn't it?"

Chandler put his hand on Naz's elbow and drew her away from the wall. Logan relaxed visibly.

"Naz said there was some kind of drug in our drink."

Logan took a moment to smooth his lapels with hands that were still shaking slightly. "Lysergic acid diethylamide. LSD for short. Or acid, as some of its more visionary users are starting to refer to it. That was the base of the concoction anyway. But the boys in Technical Services are like chefs—always adding a dash of this and a pinch of that. Only they know what the final formula was. Naz was only supposed to give it to *you,* but I guess she was feeling adventurous."

"I don't care what it's called or what it's made of. I want to know what it *does.*"

Logan shook his head. "The real question is, what happened with you and Naz? Because I've seen dozens of different reactions—"

Chandler harrumphed here, and Logan colored visibly.

"—but I've never seen two people just stare into each other's eyes for nearly five hours as though they were reading each other's minds."

Naz and Chandler would have made bad spies: at Logan's last

phrase, they couldn't help but look at each other, then look hurriedly away. For the first time since he'd arrived, Logan smiled.

"O the subtlety!"

Naz cleared her throat. "There was—"

"Naz, don't!" Chandler stopped her. "You don't know these people. Once they get their claws into you, they never let go."

"Oh, I *know*, Chandler." Naz's bitterness was so strong that he had to step back from her. "But he's all we've got."

They stared at each other for a long moment. Finally Chandler nodded, and Naz turned back to Logan.

"There was a . . . connection. A mental connection."

"Huh," Logan said. "In spy school, they teach us that reluctant interviewees tend to understate the facts, often by eighty or ninety percent. If that statistic is true, then I'm guessing you guys experienced something like full-on telepathy." He snorted at the absurdity of what he'd just said, but Naz didn't snort, and neither did Chandler.

"Was that a possibility?" Chandler said in a level voice.

Logan just stared at him a moment, then shook his head as if to clear it.

"It depends who you talk to. Talk to Joe Scheider, he'll say don't be crazy, we're just trying to make a truth serum, a knockout potion, maybe our own Manchurian candidate. But talk to Allen Ginsberg, Ken Kesey, that lot, they'll tell you the sky's the limit. Telepathy, the astral plane, naked walks on the rings of Saturn." He looked between Naz and Chandler and shook his head again. "If you'd backed me into a corner and forced me to pick sides, I guess I'd've gone with the headshrinker. But there you go. Sometimes even the beatniks can be right."

Chandler nodded. "What's the Gate of Orpheus?"

Logan glanced at Chandler sharply.

"How did you—"

"I pulled it out of your head," Chandler said coldly, "when you were jerking off on the other side of the mirror."

Logan's cheeks turned bright red. His mouth opened, then closed.

"Jesus Christ." He shook his head incredulously. "Look, all I know—"

He broke off again, his jaw hanging open as the magnitude of what had happened settled into his brain. Nearly a minute passed before he took a deep breath and started speaking again.

"All I know is that some scientists have theorized the existence of a receptor in the brain. Just as certain people have unusually keen senses of smell or taste or rhythm, the hypothesis went, so other people might have retained some vestigial receptiveness to ergot alkaloids, which is what LSD is made from. Ergot's a fungus that affects most grains. It's one of those things like alcohol—its existence is so enmeshed with human civilization that most people have developed a genetic resistance to it. But, just as many Indians are especially susceptible to the effects of alcohol because they didn't evolve with it, it seemed possible that there might also be a population, albeit a much smaller one, similarly sensitive to ergotism. Even its proponents admitted that the possibility was remote, but the consequences if it proved true were so profound that the Company couldn't ignore it. We know the Soviets are conducting their own experiments, and we can't risk falling behind."

It was a moment before anyone spoke. Then Naz said:

"So how do we find out if Chandler possesses this receptor?"

Logan looked at Naz as if he'd forgotten she was in the room.

"We take a little road trip," Logan said. "It's time you two met LSD's fairy godfather."

Mount Vernon, VA
November 1, 1963

Melchior sat in the front seat of the battered Chevy he'd pulled from the garage beneath the Adams Morgan apartment. A hand-me-down from the Wiz, who'd driven it for half a dozen years, then passed it to his eldest son, then his youngest, then handed off what was left—rust held together by paint and prayers—to Melchior. You had to hand it to the good folks at General Motors: Melchior had hooked up the battery, and the jalopy started right up.

The radio was on. The speaker spat out angry white and defiant black voices calling one another names—nigger, redneck—in Bum Fuck, Alabama, or Shit Hole, Mississippi, the insults and epithets interrupted by hopeful or sentimental or otherwise naively wishful songs: "One Fine Day," "Be My Baby," "Blowin' in the Wind," along with the indecipherable but infectious "Louie Louie."

Outside the window, a big white house sat on the far side of a wide lawn. Picket fence, towering beeches, four Doric columns holding up the porch: the Wiz hadn't missed a detail in his colonial fantasia. Revolutions had been planned behind those paneled doors, assassinations, infiltrations, arms sales to ex-Nazis and Muslim extremists, yet it was hard to imagine anything more coming through them than a smartly dressed housewife with her arms around a pair of well-coifed children, the beaming face of a Negro maid looking over their shoulders.

Something was coming through the door now. Something as far from that dream of domestic bliss as it was from the equally unreal world of international espionage and covert ops.

Melchior could only look at it in bits and pieces. A bathrobe. A cane. Licks of gray hair sticking out like antennas from a mostly bald head. The Negro servant was there, though. A man, not a woman, guiding the shaking figure like a parent teaching a toddler to walk. A toddler with a bottle of bourbon in his right hand and a dark patch in the middle of his half-open robe. Melchior had photographed the bodies of thirteen schoolchildren killed by an errant rocket in the mountains of rural Guatemala, had picked up the pieces of a Company agent after the man walked by a Saigon cafe just as a shrapnel bomb went off, but he couldn't look at the Wiz. Not like this.

Instead he looked down at the seat next to him. A creased sheet of paper sat on the passenger's side. The blueprint had been through a lot in the past five days. There was a bullet hole in the upper-left quadrant, a few drops of dried blood in the lower left. The creases from the time it had spent folded in his shoe were so deep they'd rendered the diagram all but useless—that is, if you wanted to attempt to duplicate what had been drawn there. But you could see what it depicted just fine.

He looked up at the porch. The man in the bathrobe was talking animatedly to no one, gesticulating so wildly with his bottle that twelve-year-old bourbon splashed all over him. A part of Melchior wanted to walk up there and pour the whole bottle over the decrepit figure and set it on fire. The Wiz would have wanted him to do it. The Wiz would have put the lighter in his hands. But that wasn't the Wiz up there. The Wiz would've recognized his own car. The Wiz would have told him to get his ass up there and have a drink. Of course, the Wiz would have made him use the back door, but that was the Wiz for you: you could take the boy out of Mississippi, but, as the plantation house testified, you couldn't take Mississippi out of the boy.

Melchior looked down at the blueprint again. At the time, he hadn't been sure why he didn't give it to Everton. Oh sure, he was pissed off. But he'd been pissed off at the Company a million times before, over substantive issues, like the refusal to support the Hungarian uprising in '56 or the idiocy of sending fourteen hundred poorly trained men into Cuba on the heels of a wildly popular revolution. But now he knew that he could've never given the paper to Everton. Not even if Everton had shaken his hand and offered him the country's thanks and given him a corner office and a secretary who didn't wear panties. Because Melchior didn't work for Everton and he didn't work for the Company and he didn't work for the United States of America. He worked for the Wiz, and even after Drew Everton had stared at him like a Klansman looking at a black man with his dick in the lily-white pussy of Mrs. Jacqueline Bouvier Kennedy, Melchior would've still walked across that wide green lawn beneath the shade of the towering beeches and up the bluestone steps flanked by those Doric columns and handed that piece of paper to the Wiz. All the Wiz had to do was cock a finger at him, say "Git on up here, boy," as though he were calling his dog for dinner.

"Alterius non sit qui suus esse potest," Melchior said to the empty car. Let no man belong to another who can belong to himself.

The Wiz hadn't taught him Latin, but he'd taught him that phrase. But that wasn't the Wiz up there.

The Wise Men were on their own.

PART 2

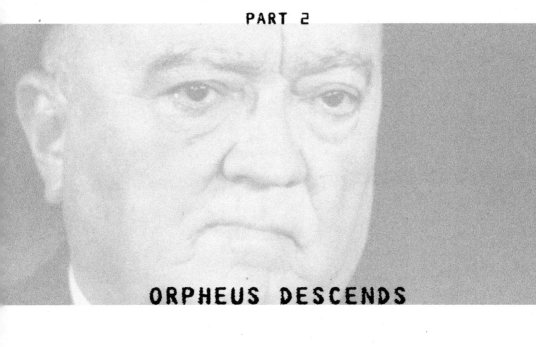

ORPHEUS DESCENDS

Maria Bayo trembled before the tall man in the gray suit. He wasn't a particularly big man—he was in fact as lean as a knife—and he'd done nothing to threaten the eleven-year-old. But there was something dead about his gray eyes and hair so blond it was the color of ice, and inside the gray suit his wiry body was taut as an icicle. Maria had never seen an icicle, but she thought it must be the worst thing in the world: water rendered hard as steel, and just as sharp.

"What is this barn used for?" the iceman said in heavily accented Spanish—the same Spanish used by the soldiers who wore uniforms with the hammer and sickle in their insignia.

Maria looked back at the car the iceman had driven her in. She hadn't wanted to get in the car with him, but she had wanted to get out of it even less when she saw where he was taking her.

"It's a mill, señor," Maria said, looking back at the car, gauging how long it would take her to run to it. "No one uses it since the revolution."

"There are tire tracks leading to the door, fresh bullet holes in the wall."

Long before the Communists came to power, Cuba's proletariat had learned to hide things from whoever was running the country. Whether it was a party official or tax man or sugar *hacendado,* the people in power made their money off the backs of the poor. But Maria was too scared to lie. Too scared to lie well anyway. Her brother had disappeared, and she was afaid she would disappear too.

"Maybe it was the American in the village. I never saw him in a truck, though."

"How do you know he was American?"

"He wasn't hungry."

The iceman nodded, then leaned close to her. "And how do you know it was a truck, if you never saw it?"

"N-n-no one from my village comes here, señor. The dogs guard it. They kill anyone who comes close."

"Dogs?"

"The wild dogs." Maria's head swiveled around, as if just mentioning the dogs could bring them. "They say the ones who guard this barn developed a taste for human flesh. Even one bite from them will make you sick."

Pavel Semyonovitch Ivelitsch paused. His men had shot four of the animals when they arrived this morning—mangy skin-and-bones wraiths with sores all over their bodies. The men said the dogs had stalked them as though they were a herd of deer or tapir. They'd found a couple of human skeletons, too. Ivelitsch had assumed the dogs were rabid. But now he was wondering.

"Maybe the man was in a truck with something like this in the back?" He drew on the ground, a complex arrangement of squares and tubes.

Maria shrugged. "There are many trucks, but usually they are covered. Farmers want to hide their produce from the inspectors so they can keep some for the black market."

"That is bad Communism."

"Yes, but good for their wallets, and their stomachs."

The iceman smiled, but at the same time he was using his shoe to rub out the image in the dirt. He moved his foot methodically back and forth until every trace of the drawing had been completely erased—so completely that Maria wished she hadn't seen it, because he clearly wanted it to remain secret.

Just then Sergei Vladimirovich Maisky came out of the barn, the wand of a Geiger counter dangling from his hand like a golf club. He took off his headphones and scratched his bald, sunburned scalp.

"Nothing, sir."

Ivelitsch had a hunch.

"Wave your wand over the dogs."

"The dogs, sir?" Sergei Vladimirovich was a thin, bookish man, and his lip curled in disgust.

"Humor me."

Sergei Vladimirovich walked over to the motley pile half hidden by some bushes. The carcasses hadn't begun to smell, but there were so many flies buzzing around them that they could be heard from twenty feet away.

Seeing the pile, Maria's eyes went wide with horror and she crossed herself. "You shouldn't have killed the dogs. They will only send worse next time."

Ivelitsch, who'd seen the mutilated corpse of her brother, thought perhaps the little girl was right, but he said nothing. He watched his man wave the Geiger counter over the grisly pile. After less than a minute Sergei Vladimirovich turned and ran back to Ivelitsch.

"You were right, comrade!" he yelled in Russian. "All of them! Trace amounts of radiation!"

Ivelitsch turned back to Maria. He squatted down, being careful not to put the knees of his suit on the dirt, and took one of her hands in his. It was a hot day, but his hand was as cold as the Arctic fields she imagined had spawned him.

"Do you know anyone who has been made sick by these dogs?"

Maria opened her mouth but nothing came out.

Ivelitsch squeezed her hand. Not enough to hurt. Just enough to press the chill to the bone.

"Listen to me, little girl. I am the man they sent to take the place of the dogs, and it will be much better for you and your neighbors if you tell me what I need to know."

Maria swallowed. "M-my uncle."

"Take me to him."

As part of the privileges of his first-class ticket, the tall young man in the gray suit was helped into his seat on the 10:27 Pennsylvania Railroad bound for New York City by an elderly Negro conductor decked out in full livery—brass buttons, gold braids, a flat-topped cap with a shiny visor. The conductor projected officiousness and obsequiousness in equal measure as he punched the young man's ticket, stowed his suitcase in the overhead rack, and laid his hat atop it. Finally he lowered the table between the man's seat and the empty one across from it and set a foil ashtray atop faux wood-grained plastic.

"Is there anything else I can do for you, sir?"

The conductor was already turning away, his uniform as square on his shoulders as a Marine's dress blues, and, although the young man would have liked an RC Cola, he only shook his head at the stiff fabric stretching across the man's retreating back.

At twenty-five, Beau-Christian Querrey couldn't have looked more like a G-man if he'd tried. Six-one, narrow waist, shoulders broad as a yoke; dark suit, white shirt, skinny black tie held in place with a brass clip. A buzz cut crowned the whole package, number one on the back and sides, three-quarters of an inch left on top. Though the effect was probably meant to be martial, there was something about his high forehead and wide, wondering eyes that made it seem like a little boy's first-day-of-school crew cut.

Despite outward appearances, however, he didn't *feel* like an FBI agent. Hadn't felt like one for the past year, since he'd been "promoted" from Behavioral Profiling to the Counterintelligence Program. But this latest assignment took the cake.

He sighed now, set his briefcase on the table, opened it. On the left sat a stack of folders held together with typewritten labels: MK-ULTRA and ORPHEUS, GATE OF. On the right sat a hardcover book: *The Man in the High Castle* by Philip K. Dick. The black cover depicted the flags of imperial Japan and Nazi Germany, as well as the tagline: "An electrify-ing novel of our world as it might have been." Since every novel was essentially a story of the world "as it might have been," this struck BC as a particularly pointless addendum, even for a work of science fiction. Nevertheless, in light of his morning meeting with Director Hoover, it seemed the less far-fetched of his two choices for reading material, and, sighing again, he placed it on the table, snapped his briefcase closed, and set it in the aisle beside his seat.

Before he could crack the cover, however, a commotion at the far end of the car distracted him. He looked up to see the Negro conductor with his hand on the shoulder of a large, suety figure in a wrinkled navy blazer. BC was surprised at the old man's boldness. They were still forty miles due south of the Mason-Dixon Line, after all, sixty by the train tracks.

"Sorry, son," the conductor said in a weary voice, "you got to ride in the lead car till the train reaches Bal'more."

The big man turned beneath the conductor's hand like a statue ro-tating on a plinth. You could practically hear stone grinding against stone as he pivoted on the soles of—BC wasn't sure *what* you'd call the shoes he was wearing. Some kind of woven sandals, the leather worn away almost to nothing. The man's dark hair had been brilliantined to his skull, but even so the distinctive ringlets were visible. His nose was thick, his lips full, his skin olive-colored, as they say, but an olive not fully ripened—if he *was* a Negro, as the conductor had assumed, he was a watery specimen of the race. But the more BC looked at him, the more he thought it just as likely that the man was simply a swarthy white fellow, in which case—

The conductor's eyes widened as he realized his error, and he shrank within his uniform. BC prayed the passenger would handle the situa-tion with dignity, but, given the man's appearance—not just the swar-thiness and slovenliness, but the flush that had turned his cheeks from olive to tomato—that didn't seem likely.

"*What* did you just say to me, boy?"

The accosted man's large, powerful frame outlined the conductor in wrinkled shadow. He tapped his finger into the side of the conductor's head hard enough to knock the older man's cap askew.

"I *ast* you a question, boy."

The conductor's head wobbled up and down as though his cap had grown too heavy for his neck to support.

"I'm sorry, sir. Here, sir, let me take your briefcase—"

"You touch my case and I'll break your arm, boy. Who the hell do you think you're talking to?"

"I'm sorry, sir. There's a nice seat—"

"Get outta my sight before I have you strung up behind the pump house so I can beat the black off your ass." The big man elbowed past the conductor and lumbered down the aisle.

Please, BC said to himself, don't let him sit—

"Goddamn uppity niggers." The man dropped into the seat opposite BC. Knees the size of cannonballs collided with his, bumping the fold-out table so hard the foil ashtray flew away like a flying saucer. The man slapped his briefcase on the table's quivering surface. "I blame Martin Luther King."

A pause while he spun the dials of the lock on his briefcase, a loud click as it snapped open. He opened the case and riffled through what sounded like a ream of wadded paper.

"What the hell are *you* staring at?"

"P-pardon me," BC stuttered. "I just—"

"And get me a goddamn rum toddy!" the man hollered over his shoulder. "Goddamn nigger calls *me* out in front of a respectable crowd of my peers, I need a drink, I don't care if it *is* ten thirty in the goddamn morning."

The briefcase snapped closed, and the man began setting out items on its scarred surface with ritualistic precision: an aluminum humidor sized for a single cigar; a box of wooden matches; and, instead of a cutter, a small, well-worn, pearl-handled pocketknife.

BC stole another glance at the man's face. Noted again the tinge of color. The full lips, broad nose, small ears, the tight curl of his hair. Really, it was anyone's guess.

"Sicilian." BC didn't see the man look up but suddenly his glittering black eyes were boring directly into BC's watery blues. "Mafiosi, *paisanos*, and the blood of Aetna. But no darkie."

Caught out, BC dropped his gaze. The man was sliding a cigar from the humidor as though it were some rare species of butterfly emerging from its chrysalis. BC noted the marque on the cigar's band: *La Gloria Habana*.

"I did a stint as muscle for a couple-a casinos in Havana back in the fifties," the man said. "Embargo or no embargo, there's no substitute for a fine Cuban."

The man opened his pocketknife forty-five degrees, unwrapped the cigar, placed it in the notch between blade and handle, popped the end off with a snap as quick and clean as the jaws of a caiman. It shot straight up like a jumping jack, came to rest on the man's closed briefcase, looking for all the world like a severed fingertip.

BC stared at it for a long moment, then looked up to find the man watching him, an amused, contemptuous smile playing over his thick, moist lips.

"Go on," he said tauntingly. "Smell it."

Biting back his revulsion, BC picked up the nubbin and brought it to his nose. A rich, deep, spicy scent went right past his nostrils to the back of his throat, and his mouth immediately filled with water. He wanted to swallow, but didn't want the man to see him do it, so he just sat there, the cigar-end resting beneath his nose, his mouth filling with saliva like a plugged sink with a leaky faucet.

The man tongued the end of his cigar until it glistened like a Tootsie Roll. Only then did he reach for his matches, light one (not on the box, but on the back of his thumbnail, which was as rough as an emery board), hold it a fraction of an inch from the cigar's tip. His lips sputtered like a landed fish as he sucked in a series of rapid inhales. Little rings of smoke erupted between each puff, till at length the cigar's cherry glowed red as a nickel pulled from a campfire. He took a longer drag, held it in his mouth a moment, then blew a single perfect smoke ring directly at BC. Though it dissipated before it reached him, it still seemed to BC that the ring slipped around his head like a halo, or a noose.

"So, Beau," the man said in a voice thickened by smoke and satisfaction, "where's J. Edna sending you today?"

BC's fingers twitched and the cigar-end shot up in the air. He opened his mouth, remembered it was full of saliva and sucked it down, choked, coughed, managed to get his arm up in time, ended up splattering the sleeve of his suit with a constellation of droplets that coalesced into a black wet patch the size of a beef cutlet. A fair amount of spittle had landed on his companion's briefcase as well and, after staring at it like a kindergartner regarding an incriminating pool of urine beneath his desk, BC pulled his sleeve into his palm and began wiping at it with slow, mortified strokes. Wool not being the most absorbent of fabrics, all this did was smear the saliva into long smooth arcs. It did, however, bring up a bit of a shine on the worn leather of the man's briefcase.

When the man finally stopped laughing, he nudged BC's briefcase with the toe of one of his worn sandals. The tag lay so that the address label was exposed.

If found, please return to:
Beau-Christian Querrey
c/o Federal Bureau of Investigation
Washington 25 D.C.

The man snickered. "I bet it says the same thing inside your underpants."

BC reached a hand down to turn the address label over, as if this could somehow remove its information from his seatmate's mind.

"Who do *you* work for?"

The man puffed on his cigar before answering. "Let's just say we're in related but tangential fields."

"You're CIA?"

The man's eyes widened. "Maybe you're not as green as you look."

Just then the conductor reappeared with the man's drink—the spy's

drink, as unlikely as that seemed. The conductor unfolded a napkin on
the table and set the drink on it. He had to nudge the man's briefcase
toward the window to do this, and BC could see that his fingers were
shaking, half retracted inside his gold-piped maroon cuff like the limb
of a frightened turtle. He put his hands behind his back after he set the
drink down, then stood there. The hot rum steamed on the table, giving
off an aroma of sugar and stale blood.

The CIA man picked up the drink, drained it in one long swallow,
set it back in its ring on the napkin.

"That was so good I think I'll have another."

The conductor paused, then picked up the glass. "Pardon me, sir . . ."

"I can't drink 'pardon me, sir,' and you can't feed your family 'thout
this job, so I suggest you hurry if you want to keep it." He paused just
long enough to make his last word gratuitous; then: "*Boy.*"

"Yes, sir. It's just that, sir, there's a, well, you see, sir, there's a
charge—"

"Hell's bells, boy, why didn't you say you was buying? Ask my friend
Beau here if he wants one too."

"Of course, sir. But that would be *two* drinks, sir—"

"It'll be three actually, countin' whatever Beau has. Now ask him
what he wants, boy, before you end up buying everyone in this car free
drinks from here to Pennsylvany Station."

It seemed to BC that the conductor shrank even more as he turned
toward him. He was nothing but a suit now, a pair of frightened eyes.

Before the man could ask, BC shook his head. "I'm all right, s-sir."

"Oh, I *like* that!" the CIA man said as the conductor scurried off.
"'S-s-s-s-s-sir.' Trying to show some *respeck* to the Negro people, even
though it don't come *nat'ral.*" The man leaned back in his seat, kneeing
BC's legs toward the aisle so he could stretch out his own. His accent,
which came and went with the conductor, shifted once again, from the
fields to the Big House. "Lemme guess," he said in the relaxed drawl of
a plantation owner, "you a Southern boy, but just barely. Maryland,
maybe DC proper. Maybe even Arlington. But no farther down. If you
was from farther down, you wouldn't-a stuttered when you said *sir.* You
wouldn't-a said it a-tall."

BC stared at the man, trying to decide what to say. In the end, manners won out.

"I'm from Takoma Park."

"Hell, you almost home then."

With a start, BC realized the train was moving. Had been for some time—they'd crossed the Maryland border already.

"Lemme guess. PG County? You got yourself a little bit of a race problem in PG, don't you? Darkies moving in, flatbed trucks loaded down with corn-shuck mattresses and pickaninnies. Your people get out in time? Hell, what am I saying? Look at that suit. Of course they didn't. Stuck with some big old row house, I bet, tall and narrow in the front but stretching way back to one-a them little kitchen gardens that don't get enough sunlight to grow anything besides beans and lettuce. Couldn't sell a place like that for ten cents on the dollar right now, what with the character of the neighborhood changing the way it has. Well, you couldn't sell it to a white family anyway."

The man's ability to read BC was a bit unnerving. There was a stunted apple tree in the back garden, but still.

He reached for his book and held it up as if it were a shield. "If you don't mind—"

"Wuzzat?" the man said, screwing up his face and squinting at the book as though it were a Polynesian totem or the innards of a Japanese transistor radio.

"It's, uh, a novel. A work of, um, 'alternative history.'"

"Huh. Not *too* redundant."

"Beg pardon?"

"C'mon, Beau. History's full of alternate versions, depending on who's doing the telling. What'd your momma call the Civil War?"

BC colored slightly. "The War of Northern Aggression."

"See what I mean? To good old-fashioned Christians like your momma, the war was all about common Yankees trampling on Southern pride. To Negroes like our overstepping conductor, it was about ending slavery. To Abe Lincoln, it was about preserving the Union. It's just a matter of who you ask." Without warning he snatched the book from BC's hands. "Lemme guess. J. Edna told you to look for 'anti-American content' so he can decide whether to put"—he glanced at the book cover—"Mr. Philip K. Dick on a watch list, along with Norman Mailer and Jimmy Baldwin and Allen Ginsberg and William S. Burroughs and Henry Miller and Ken Kesey and—stop me if I get one wrong. No? Jesus Chris, Beau, who do you work for? The FBI or the Library of Congress?"

"I'm looking for subversive content. Not anti-American."

"How in the hell can a novel be subversive? It's all made up."

"It can put ideas in people's heads."

"Well, golly, we wouldn't want to do that, would we?"

BC smiled tightly and held out his hand. "Still, if it's all the same to you, I think I'll get back to it."

"Get back to it?" the man scoffed. "You haven't even started it."

"How did you—"

"No bookmark. And if I know my Beau *Query*—and I think I do—I bet you got yourself a personalized bookmark that moves from book to book, and you never start a new one before finishing the last."

"My *name* is *Querrey*. Beau-Christian *Querrey*."

"Don't blame me for that. I only just met you." The man grinned. "C'mon. Show me the bookmark. *Come on.*"

Despite himself, BC snorted and reached into his breast pocket, pulled out a wafer-thin rectangle the size of a charge plate. It was made of ivory, however, rather than cardboard or plastic, and had a finely engraved image of—

"Why, that's just *too* poignant, ain't it?" The CIA man snatched the bookmark from BC's hand. "Huck and Tom rafting down the Mississippi. Poignant and pointed. Practically *on—the—nose*," he said, tapping his broad nostrils with the corner of the card. "Well, now, that's got a edge to it." He rasped the bookmark over the shiny stubble on his cheek. "Bet you use that to cut pages, too, don't you?"

BC would have snatched the bookmark from the man's hand, but it had belonged to his mother, and his mother had taught him not to snatch.

"But now lemme think here," the man said, scratching his face with the bookmark and staring at the book in his other hand. "Subversive content, sub-ver-sive con-tent. Why, that sounds like COINTELPRO work to me. So I gotta ask: what'd you do to get demoted?"

"Counterintelligence is one of the most prestigious—" BC stopped himself. This interrogation had reached an absurd pitch. Had the man researched him before getting on the train? And if so, why?

"See, only two kinds of agent end up in Counterintelligence: the ones who've served the Bureau long enough to prove to J. Edna that their first loyalty is to him rather than the law, in which case they're sent out to infiltrate whatever group's got his panties in a bunch—socialists, suffragettes, and of course the darkies—and the ones who're a little too independent for their own good. Maybe they open up a closed case to prove someone was convicted on faulty or, dare I say it, falsified evidence, or they call the local paper before they make a bust to make sure their picture ends up on the front page. The only thing J. Edna hates more than an open case is when a story about the Bureau mentions someone's name other than his. Of course he can't fire you for doing your job, so instead you get mustered out of—" He squinted at BC. "Organized Crime? Behavioral Profiling?"

"Profiling." BC sighed.

"And now you're reading weirdo novels looking for subversive content and taking long train rides to—well, I guess we're back where we started, ain't we? Where *are* you heading today, Beau?"

The man's read on his career was so accurate that BC had to laugh, if uncomfortably.

"At this point I'm pretty sure there's nothing I can say about myself that you don't already know, so why don't you tell me something: were you really in Cuba?"

The man's lips curled oddly around his cigar, and it took BC a moment to realize he was smiling.

"Would you like me to have been in Cuba, Beau?"

"I'd like you to be in Cuba right now."

A roar of laughter erupted from the man's mouth.

"D'you hear that, boy? He'd like me to be in Cuba right now! That's the best thing I heard since you called me a nigger!"

BC looked over his shoulder, saw the Negro conductor marching slow and steady down the aisle with a glass in each hand. He set the drinks down and scurried away, even as wet smoky laughter continued to burble out of BC's companion's throat.

"Let me explain the difference between an intelligence agent and a federal agent, Beau. See, a spy understands information's value isn't its accuracy, but how it can be deployed. The question isn't, Was I in Cuba, but, Can I make you *believe* I was in Cuba?"

BC couldn't help himself. He made a grab for his book, but the man was faster, held it above his head like a game of keep-away. But then, smiling, he tossed it to BC, who held it in both hands like a puppy for one embarrassing moment, then set it on the table.

The man sucked on his cigar and smiled wickedly. "What was his name?"

"Who?" BC said, although he knew what the man was talking about.

"The guy you got out of jail."

BC rolled his eyes. "Roosevelt Jones."

"Well, that answers my next question, don't it?"

"Yes." BC sighed. "He was a Negro."

The CIA man scrutinized him a moment, and then a broad smile spread across his face.

"You got your picture in the paper too, didn't you?"

BC had been waiting for the question. "Well, I couldn't very well get an innocent man out of jail and then leave a crime unsolved, could I?"

The CIA man laughed even louder than he had before. "Well, get a load-a you! I wouldn't-a thought you had it in you." Suddenly the man's voice leveled. "Well?"

Once again BC knew what the man was referring to; once again he pretended ignorance.

"Well what?"

"Yeah, you might be a good detective, but you're a terrible actor. So just tell me: did the Bureau manufacture evidence to convict Nigger Jones?"

BC steeled himself.

"No."

The man smiled again, but this time it was a mean smile. Mean, but not surprised, which only made BC's shame greater.

"Like I said, Beau: you're a terrible actor."

BC's eyes dropped, and there was the novel the director had given him that morning. He couldn't decide which was more absurd: the man sitting across from him, or the fact that he was being paid six thousand dollars a year to read a book.

Suddenly an idea came to him.

"Are you really CIA?" he said. "Or is this just some elaborate prank the director worked up to, I don't know, trick me into divulging Bureau secrets to unauthorized personnel?"

The man placed a spread-fingered hand on his chest, and for the first time BC noticed the hole under his lapel, just over his heart. "Did I ever say I was CIA?"

"Because if you *are* CIA," BC continued, "it seems like an awfully big coincidence that we're on the same train, in the same car, at the same time."

"Coincidental?" The man waggled his cigar like Groucho Marx. "Maybe even suspicious? Or just too good to be true? Who knows, maybe the Company sent someone to follow you up to Millbrook?"

BC opened his mouth, then closed it. This wasn't proof that the man was CIA, after all. He could still be the director's stool pigeon. He'd heard stranger rumors about his boss.

"So tell me, Beau." BC's companion was clearly enjoying his indecision. "What'd the director tell you about Project Orpheus? I'm guessing from your choice of reading material that he either told you nothing at all, or, even more likely, he told you *everything*, and you can't quite bring yourself to believe it, because then you'd have to admit to yourself that not only the Central Intelligence Agency but the Federal Bureau of Investigation is spending thousands—millions—of dollars on investigations that can only be called, well, stupid as shit. Pure science fiction," he said, tapping the cover of BC's book. "Truth serums. Brainwashing. Manchurian candidates even."

"*The Manchurian Candidate* is a novel," BC said, grabbing his book and staring down at the cover. *An electrifying novel of our world as it might have been.* He flipped the book open and pretended to read the first page, which happened to be blank.

"C'mon, Beau, I'm trying to help you out. Restore your faith in your employer. You don't think the director'd send an agent of the prestigious Counterintelligence Program all the way up to New York State to check out a bit of science fiction, do you? There's got to be something else involved, right? *Someone* else maybe? A VIP who has to be handled delicately? Lemme guess. He mentioned Chandler Forrestal? Told you how prominent his family is?"

BC did his best to remain impassive, even as he turned the page so violently he nearly ripped it. If this guy didn't work for the director, he had a bug in his office.

"Lemme save you the trouble of guessing. It's not Mr. Forrestal Director Hoover's worried about. It's Jack Kennedy."

Despite himself, BC giggled. "What, does he nip up there for the weekend in Marine One?"

"Gosh, that'd be fun, wouldn't it, albeit a misallocation of taxpayer dollars. But the truth is the president of the United States of America doesn't have to travel four hundred miles to get his fix. One of his girlfriends brings it to him. Now, how do you think the public would react if they found out, one, that the president has a squeeze on the side, two, that she's supplying him with a drug that has the potential to render the leader of the free world susceptible to mind control, and, three, that said drug is being tested by the Central Intelligence Agency—an organization that just happened to put together a private little war in Cuba a few years back that almost launched World War Three?" The man puffed on his cigar. "I mean, certain people might get a little worked up about that, don't you think? If not John Q. Public, then maybe Barry Goldwater or Nelson Rockefeller?"

BC could only stare at the man. One heard stories, of course. Rumors. Marilyn Monroe. But who wouldn't sleep with Marilyn Monroe? Even Jackie couldn't hold that against him.

"You seem skeptical, so let me give you a few more details. A few years back the Company tasked several agents with recruiting prostitutes as part of a project called Ultra. In exchange for not going to jail, the girls slipped their johns whatever drug the Company was investigating—LSD, psilocybin, what have you—and the supervising agent recorded the results on a movie camera. Ultra's pretty much fizzled out by now, but the practice lives on in Orpheus. Only this time it's not just hookers. See, the field agent in charge is one of those prep school boys, an entitled East Coast establishment prick, and just for kicks he shares his wares with his society friends, one of whom is Mary Meyer." The man paused to puff on his cigar. "She's the president's squeeze," he said, "in case you didn't put all that together."

BC continued to stare at the man. Finally he laughed. "You're your own worst enemy. Don't you know the first rule of lying: keep it simple, and keep it short."

"That's two rules," the man said. "And I ain't lying." All the mirth had vanished from his voice.

"I mean, good Lord. Isn't Mary Meyer Cord Meyer's *wife*?"

"Ex-wife."

"The man's number three or four at the—"

"At the good ol' C-I-of-A." The man's smile was not so much triumphant as vindictive. "Yes sir, Special Agent Query. You are the president's harem boy. You are John F. Kennedy's *eunuch*."

BC didn't know what was behind the anger on the man's face, but he knew it was a lot older than this train ride, and, despite the heat in the car, he felt a sudden chill on his sweat-dampened spine. He reached for his drink, took a big swallow before he remembered what it was. He wasn't a teetotaler, but he could count the number of alcoholic beverages he'd consumed on the fingers of one hand, and the rum entered him like a furnace blast. In a matter of seconds he felt sweat on his forehead, under his arms, trickling down the small of his back into the little gap where the waistband of his underwear (which had indeed been marked "Querrey," so that the Negro laundress his mother had used for more than twenty years wouldn't give her son's jockey shorts to someone else) pulled away from the cleft of his buttocks.

The thought of perspiration pooling in his underwear made BC sweat even harder, and the thought of his own buttocks made him blush like a high schooler pantsed in front of the whole school. He desperately wanted something cold to drink, but the only thing in front of him was a glass of warm rum. He looked at it, then looked at the man across from him, who was following BC's internal debate as if he could read his mind. Fuck it, BC thought, although he didn't think the word "fuck." He didn't think the word "it" either, since just thinking the word "it" doesn't make a lot of sense. He didn't think. He just reached for the glass and drank it all down.

The man across the table looked at BC for a moment, then, without taking his eyes from BC's, put his cigar out on the cover of BC's novel.

"My oh my. This is going to be a fun ride, ain't it?"

It wasn't.

Five minutes outside Pennsylvania Station, BC excused him-
self to use the lavatory. As he stepped out of the W.C., he noticed the
Negro conductor farther up the car, pulling ticket stubs from the tops
of seats. BC approached him, waited until the man had finished what
he was doing.

"Yes, sir?" The conductor didn't look at him.

BC had already pulled a pair of fives from his wallet—all the money
he had until the banks opened on Monday. "I'd like to pay you. For our
drinks."

The conductor unfolded the bills and handed one back.

"Keep it," BC said. "For the trouble." He tried to meet the conductor's eye but the man refused to look at him. "If there's a problem with
my companion. If he makes a complaint. I'd like to . . ." He didn't know
how to finish. "I'd like to speak in your defense. If I may."

The conductor continued to stare at the two bills in his hand.

"It's just that, well, how could I do that?"

"How . . . ?"

"How can I identify you?"

For the first time, the conductor looked up, and BC was surprised to
see that his eyes were filled not with fear or shame but fury.

"I *have* a name." The man's voice was so guttural that BC thought
he might actually bite him.

A glint of gold on the man's chest caught the agent's eye. BC Querrey, who had noted that the soles of the conductor's shoes were more
worn on their outside edges than the inside, suggesting an internal tor-
sion in the tibia, as well as the fact that the middle button of his jacket
had fallen off at some point and been sewn back on with yellow thread
rather than the gold that adhered the top and bottom buttons to the
placket, had not noticed that the man who had visited his seat thirteen
times in the past four hours was wearing a name tag:

A. HANDY

"Ah," BC said, or sighed. "Yes." Having seen the man's name, he now found it impossible to use it. "Well, if there's a problem, please don't hesitate to contact me." He handed the man one of his business cards even as, with a lurch and a hiss, the train came to a stop.

With a start, BC turned from the conductor and hurried down the aisle. He'd been so focused on making amends that he'd completely forgotten the train was reaching its destination. He weaved in and out of passengers, pardon-me-ma'aming and excuse-me-sirring his way with increasing speed, until he burst through the doors of his car. The seats were empty, the passengers queued at either end of the aisle waiting for the doors to open. It took only the briefest glance for BC to see that the CIA man was gone, along with his—i.e., BC's—briefcase.

BC ran to his seat. The only thing left on the table was the novel by Philip K. Dick, the half-smoked cigar sitting on top of it like a turd. BC noted that the book was turned toward his companion's seat and, flicking the cigar off it, he flipped open the cover. A folded, wrinkled piece of paper fell out, on which had been hastily scrawled:

> TELL MR. HANDY I SAID THANKS FOR THE DRINKS!
> OH, AND BY THE WAY: I AM BLACK.
> —MELCHIOR

The piece of paper was moist, as if it had soaked up some of the CIA man's—Melchior's—sweat, and BC unfolded it delicately, as much to avoid getting the moisture on his hand as to keep from tearing the paper. The diagram that emerged didn't make any sense at first. It showed a complicated mechanical device, possibly an engine of some kind. Most of the captions were written in what BC thought was a Cyrillic alphabet, but one English word popped off the page: "Polonium-210."

"Oh, my God."

BC grabbed his coat and hat from the luggage rack, swept up the book and paper from the tabletop—and, on impulse, the cigar butt too—and sprinted down the aisle. Before he'd taken two steps, the doors swished apart and people spilled out of the car like water through the opened gates of a dam. BC pushed his way through the crowd, his head darting left and right for a sign of Melchior—and then suddenly he was on the platform, and he pulled up short.

He stood there with his bundle clutched to his chest like a refugee as the bombers scream across the sky. The train shed of the nation's largest and busiest rail station occupied an enormous dusky cavern that receded into the distance on every side of him—acre upon acre of fretted steel columns reaching more than a hundred feet into the air and supporting a barrel-vaulted ceiling made of what seemed like millions of grimy panes of glass. At one end were a dozen arched tunnels disappearing into the bowels of the earth, at the other an equal number of staircases climbing two stories to the crowded concourse. But it was a cloudy day, and what little light managed to penetrate the filthy ceiling cast thick, oily shadows that confounded the eye, and on top of that at least two other trains were loading and unloading passengers: hundreds of people were pushing and weaving their way along the platform, ·nearly all of them shrouded in rain-darkened jackets and hats. BC's eyes flitted desperately from one to the next. Melchior had been carrying neither coat nor hat, and BC did his best to confine his search to the bare heads. There were only a few, but in the murky light every exposed head seemed uniformly dark. Any of the men could have been Melchior—or none of them.

He sprinted for the stairs at the end of the platform, ran into the station's world-famous waiting room. He didn't notice the immense coffered ceilings, the pink marble floors (muddied on this wet day, and stained with tens of thousands of footprints), the diffuse light streaming in through arched windows taller and wider than his house in Takoma Park. He raced across the waiting room—two blocks long and nearly half a block wide—up the stairs, out the front entrance. At least he didn't have to look for his car. A two-door coupé, mint green and shiny, individual raindrops glittering on its freshly waxed hood like a thousand slivers of glass, was parked directly in front of the main door, chaperoned by a nattily dressed young man leaning against a No Parking sign. He looked mightily pleased with himself.

BC ran up to the man, fumbling through the bundle of his coat to retrieve his wallet. He flashed his badge.

"Special Agent Querrey. Is this my car?"

"Nineteen sixty-two Chevrolet Corvair," the man drawled like a car salesman. "I'd roll the windows down if I was—"

BC pushed the man out of the way, threw his bundle into the passenger's seat, and—after pumping the gas too hard and flooding the engine and waiting five minutes for the plugs to clear—squealed down Seventh Avenue. Before he'd gone a single block the cabin had filled with noxious fumes coming in through the air vents, and he had to roll the window down.

He caught a last glimpse of the station's facade in the rearview mirror, five hundred feet of Doric columns stretching out like God's own picket fence. It really was impressive—more imposing than the biggest monuments in Washington—but he thought he remembered hearing talk of tearing it down. But in truth BC was less concerned with the possibility of New York losing its grandest edifice than with his own loss of a smaller piece of property. Not his briefcase: his bookmark, which, like his house, his name, and his sense of revulsion at the crude workings of the human body, he'd inherited from his mother. Thus are history's losses measured: eight acres of stone and glass and steel on the one hand; on the other, an ivory sliver no bigger than a driver's license. Both smudged from years of contact with human hands, and even more obscured by the shroud of sentiment that makes it difficult for us to see clearly the things we hold most dear. It would be the bookmark BC missed more in the years to come, Pennsylvania Station having played a significant role in the life of New York City but not in his.

But all that was in the distant future. Right now he had to get to Millbrook, to something Director Hoover had called an "experimental community" run by a Dr. Timothy Leary. He had no idea what was so important that both the FBI and the CIA had to send men to investigate. All he knew was that he had to get there before Melchior.

Chevy'd added an optional 150-hp engine to the '62 Corvair, but the Bureau'd clearly stuck with the 98-hp mid-range model. BC could've sworn the little engine cursed at him, and carbon monoxide spewed from the heater vents in visible gusts, but the little minx did what she was told. The posted limit on the Taconic was sixty-five; BC stamped both feet on the accelerator if the car dropped below ninety. He had to fight the Corvair's tendency to oversteer, a consequence of its unusual engine placement over the rear axle, and on top of that rush hour had begun. Despite this, BC covered the fifty-mile shot up the curvy, car-choked parkway in thirty-two minutes.

Once in Millbrook he had to find Dr. Leary's community—Castle or Castille, Castalia, something like that. The directions had been in his briefcase (along with the files on Project Orpheus), but even without them he had no trouble locating his target. At the edge of town he saw a large hand-painted sign in multicolored bubble letters:

YOU ARE ON THE PATH TO TRUE ENLIGHTENMENT (JUST TURN LEFT!)

Beneath that, someone had added in smaller but significantly clearer letters:

FREAKS GO HOME!

BC knew nothing about either the freaks or their detractors, but his initial reaction was to side with the latter, if only for their penmanship.

A mile down the road he came to an absurd fieldstone gatehouse, complete with a turret peaked like a witch's cap and something that looked a lot like a portcullis. Another half mile of curved driveway led to an enormous and extravagant building, a Lilliputian dollhouse swollen to Brobdingnagian proportions, with towers and gables and hundreds of feet of porch wrapping around the whole thing. Glasses and plates were strewn around the unmown lawn that stretched in front of it, along with a truly remarkable number of wine and liquor bottles, while a glowering pine forest encroached on the back. The dense trees, already losing their color in the failing light, made the giant house seem two-dimensional, as if you would open the front door and emerge on the other side of a theatrical flat. With the exception of the dishes and bottles and a few items of clothing, the place seemed to be deserted.

The Corvair sighed in relief when he killed the engine, and a moment later BC heard the sound of a distant jackhammer—woodpecker, he realized a moment later, and chuckled at himself. It had been a long time since he'd been in the country. The things of nature sounded like the things of man to his ears, when even he knew it should have been the other way around.

All at once he felt his shirt plastered to the small of his back, realized he was still sitting in the car with both hands glued to the wheel. Somewhat sheepishly, he opened the door. It was hardly better outside. A cool, cloying haze pressed wetly down on everything. Even the blades of grass sagged beneath its weight.

It was only after he was standing on the bent grass that he realized he hadn't wanted to leave the relative safety of the car. He was a boy of the suburbs. He liked trees and grass and birds just fine, but he liked them regimented, the grass mowed, the trees planted a uniform distance from one another, the birds regulated by local ordinance. But it was more than that. There was something unnerving about this place—something distinct from the humidity and the litter scattered over the lawn and the ragged curtains flapping from the open windows like a hydra's tongues. Something that had to do with the glowering pine forest on the far side of the house, which, like a painting by Magritte, seemed to suck up what was left of the sunlight even as each needle remained as sharply outlined as a syringe. The house was his immediate objective, of course (assuming these people hadn't taken to living in trees), but somehow he sensed that the forest was his ultimate destination. He cursed himself for getting sucked into Melchior's contumely instead of reading the files in his briefcase as he should have done. The scattered, spooky phrases Melchior had tossed around flitted through his head—"sleeper agents" and "psychological experiments" and "Manchurian candidates" and "mental powers." A few solid facts would have gone a long way toward easing his nerves. As it was, he was going to have to rely on his wits and—he squeezed his arm against his side, as if it might have disappeared with his briefcase—his gun.

The woodpecker drilled, paused, drilled, paused. There was a longer pause, then a bout of drilling so sustained that BC half expected to hear the crack of falling timber.

Centering his hat firmly on his head, he began to walk toward the porch. Before he'd gone five steps the front door opened. BC stopped short. So did the girl on the porch. BC wasn't sure why *she* stopped. He was wearing a normal suit, after all, whereas *she* was wearing a pair of denim pants that had been cut off all the way to the crease of her pelvis and—he squinted—yup, nothing else. He had to squint because the girl had exceptionally thick, long, dark hair pulled forward over her shoulders as in portraits of Lady Godiva. BC thought perhaps she was wearing a French bikini top. But no, her upper body was bare. The skin visible on the sides of her breasts was as evenly tanned as her arms, suggesting this wasn't the first time she'd walked outside so sparsely attired, and when she lifted her right arm to wave at him, her hair fell to one side and there, as full as an apple and brown as a piece of toast, was her breast.

The closest BC had ever come to seeing a naked chest was in the intimate apparel section of the Sears catalogs he hid in his bedroom closet. Their chaste airbrushed photographs of bullet bras made a pair of breasts look as geometrically pristine as side-by-side snowcapped mountains, whereas this was a sac of living, quivering flesh—not symmetrical at all, but gently sloped on the top and softly curved beneath. At the sight of it, BC's fingertips tingled and for some reason he found himself imagining how it would feel in his hands. Like a dove, he thought. Warm and soft, the heartbeat faintly palpable in his palm. Another man might have envisioned a less delicate animal, a more vigorous touch. Might have felt the tingle in a part of his anatomy other than his fingertips. BC, however, was a good boy, and he immediately averted his eyes.

But:

"Welcome! We're so glad you found us!"

And of course BC *had* seen naked women before. But these women had been uniformly dead, toes tagged, flesh an icy blue and bearing the marks of whatever had killed them, which rendered them both sexless and asexual—and of course silent. He hadn't realized a girl could speak with no clothes on and was unsure if he could—let alone should—reply. He stared mutely as the girl walked toward him as though she were as primly dressed and perfectly coiffed as Mary Tyler Moore greeting Dick Van Dyke just home from work. Her hair had fallen unevenly around her breast, and the nipple showed through the sparse strands, which somehow made it more prominent than when it had been completely uncovered.

The girl followed BC's gaze down to her breast, looked up again, smiled.

"Don't worry, come Monday you won't even remember how to tie that bureaucratic noose, let alone why you put it on in the first place."

It was incredible! She talked just like a girl in clothes. Fire didn't shoot from her mouth, the syllables were perfectly intelligible (although it took BC a moment to figure out "bureaucratic noose" referred to his tie).

"Shy, are we?"

She was right in front of him. Her hands were on his upper arms. BC braced himself, as though she were going to pick him up like a doll and toss him through the air. But all she did was raise herself on her tiptoes, her breasts pressing lightly against his chest with only the flimsiest layer of hair between them and his suit—which, as far as he was concerned, *was* his flesh—and then, lightly but lingeringly, she kissed him on the lips.

"Welcome to Castalia," she said, her voice huskier now, the welcome broader than it had been a moment ago.

"Jenny!" an amused but sharp male voice called from somewhere to the left. "Get away from that poor man. You're scandalizing him to death."

BC jumped back like a teenager surprised by the babysitter's parents. He turned to see a slim man rounding the corner of the house. Unlike the girl, his upper body was fully covered—by a long-sleeved yellow button-down whose loose tails winked in the breeze—but it wasn't immediately clear if he had anything on beneath it. He had a friendly, slightly crooked smile and bright blue eyes and unruly blond hair that was shedding its last respectable cut as quickly as the follicles would allow.

"We didn't expect you so quickly. You must have made great time."

"Ye-es," BC said experimentally. Everything seemed to be working. "Dr. Leary? I'm—"

"Oh, let's not stand on formalities." Leary used his clipboard to fend off both the name and the hand that came with it. "We just call the other one Puss-n-Boots."

"The other—"

"Or Candy Striper," the girl, Jenny, said, cutting him off.

"Ralph calls him Spooky, which is a little on the nose, but that's Ralph for you."

Jenny laughed. "And poor Dickie just calls him, and calls him, and calls him."

"Jennifer, please."

Jenny gave BC a once-over. "I think I'm going to call this one Lone Ranger. Because his face is a mask." She leaned forward to give BC a second, wetter kiss. "You're going to have a long life," she said to him quietly, "if you ever let it begin."

Both BC and Leary stared after her retreating form. "You think her tits are nice," the doctor sighed, "you should see the rest of her. That girl's vagina is so agile it could lace up a pair of jackboots and tie them with a sailor's knot."

"I . . ." BC didn't know what to say. "I don't know what to say."

Leary laughed aloud. "Makes you believe the old stories, doesn't it? That the best way to get information from a spy is via the intercession of a beautiful woman."

At the word "spy," something clicked in BC's brain, and he realized that Leary had taken him not as a guest but as a CIA agent.

Leary's blue eyes twinkled. "Believe me when I tell you that what I'm going to show you will make you forget all about Jenny."

He turned and hurried off—toward the back of the house, BC saw, and the dark forest beyond. BC hesitated, but the doctor was skipping along like a leprechaun. Taking a deep breath, BC set off after him.

"I want to prepare you for what you're about to see," Leary was saying when BC caught up with him. "It's going to be a bit shocking, and I don't want you to panic."

BC had heard this kind of line from countless coroners and county sheriffs, and in a slightly prideful voice he said, "I've seen many shocking things, Dr. Leary."

"No doubt you have, in your line of work. But that didn't stop Agent Morganthau from collapsing like Charlie McCarthy without Edgar Bergen's hand up his ass."

Morganthau? The name rang a bell, and then he remembered that the director had mentioned him in his briefing before he put him on the train. BC wondered if he and Melchior were the same person.

"Where *is* Agent Morganthau?"

"I left him with Forrestal and the girl in the cottage. The thing is, Agent, ah—I'm sorry, what did you say your name was again?"

Girl? Neither Hoover nor Melchior had mentioned a girl.

"Gamin," BC said absentmindedly. It was his mother's maiden name. "Who is—"

"Please, Agent Gamin." Leary's voice took on a sterner note. "Lecture first, questions after. Just listen for a moment."

After Melchior's rant on the train, the last thing he wanted to hear was another lecture. But he was too busy staring into the dark trees that were closing around them to protest.

"Now then. Our work at Castalia is concerned with the human animal's neuronal experience of the world around him. In layman's terms, his senses. If the conscious part of our brain had to process all the raw material our senses recorded, we'd end up so flooded with data that we wouldn't be able to walk upright or feed ourselves, let alone perform complex motor tasks like climbing a ladder or playing a cello or sculpting *The Gates of Hell*. Information must be excluded. Not just some of it: most of it. This process of selection starts from the moment we exit the womb and continues until death. It's so pervasive that we might just as well say life is a process of rejecting experience rather than accumulating it."

"Oh, um." BC wasn't sure how to respond to this. "Sure." The sun had disappeared behind the dense canopy now, along with the dilapidated mansion, and the early evening had stilled to an ecclesiastical gloaming. The feeling was only emphasized by the thousands of pitch-blackened trunks receding in every direction like the sooty columns of the Mezquita of Córdoba.

BC pulled up short.

"Something wrong?" Despite the shadows, the doctor's blue eyes twinkled, almost as if he was in on a practical joke being perpetrated at BC's expense.

"It's nothing," BC answered, and, when the doctor continued to stare at him: "A word popped into my head, that's all." Still the expectant stare. BC suddenly remembered the man's degree was in psychology. He disliked headshrinkers almost as much as he disliked Bohemians. "Mez-qui-ta," he said when Leary still refused to go on. He had to sound out the syllables like a child reading a strange word, because he'd never heard it before, let alone knew what it meant.

"Spanish for mosque," the doctor said as if reading BC's mind. He glanced at the trunks all around them. "The Great Mosque at Córdoba is famous for the hundreds of columns that hold up the prayer hall."

"Yes, of course." BC nodded. Still the doctor stared at him. "It's just that, well, I don't remember ever hearing that word before." It was more than that of course. He'd never heard of the Great Mosque itself, let alone knew what it looked like, and somehow he sensed that the doctor knew this.

But all the doctor did was nod, then turn and head deeper into the forest. Dark pines stretched farther than the eye could see in every direction, and, with a start, BC realized he had no idea which way the house lay. He swallowed his discomfort and hurried after Leary.

"For some time now," the doctor was saying when BC caught up with him, "psychiatrists have theorized the existence of a mental clearinghouse that sorts the information our senses gather into usuable and unusable categories. They refer to this clearinghouse as the Gate of Orpheus. You remember that Orpheus descended into the Underworld to retrieve his wife, Eurydice, who had been killed by a snakebite. After he failed in his task, undone by the same curiosity that killed Lot's wife, he returned to the surface, where he was promptly torn to pieces by the Maenads. This might seem like harsh treatment for a grieving widower, but the Maenads were servants of Dionysus, who was both dismembered and devoured, only to be reborn as an even greater god—a story that clearly inspired a certain young Jewish man running around the

Roman province of Judea half a millennium later. As Dionysus' high priest, Orpheus was said to possess mysteries culled from his time in the Underworld. Dionysus' Roman name was Bacchus, of course, and for the better part of a thousand years his followers claimed that the famed Bacchanalian orgies of drinking and sex and violence afforded glimpses into these mysteries.

"As with mythology, so with modernity: some contemporary psychiatrists have begun to search for what lies beyond the Orphic Gate in the human brain. No doubt you've heard the adage that we use a mere five percent of our mental capacity. This measure refers not so much to size as to functionality—mind as opposed to brain. It's my theory that the remaining ninety-five percent hides behind the gate, and if we can somehow find a way to open it, a universe of possibility will become available to us. Memories would reappear in crystalline detail. The unrepeatable sensation of our first coital orgasm, say, or the ambrosial taste of mother's milk. Our physical environment would acquire extra dimensions of sight and sound and smell and touch. Who knows, perhaps we might discover an ethereal bond linking all consciousnesses—the mental equivalent of a radio wave, needing only a receiver tuned to the right frequency to allow for instantaneous communication a thousand times clearer than mere words and gestures could ever convey."

It took BC a moment to catch up to the end of the doctor's speech—he stumbled on the term "coital orgasm," then fell flat on "mother's milk"—but when he thought he'd figured out what Leary was describing, he said, "Pardon me, Doctor. I was under the impression that your research was geared toward the creation of a—" He couldn't bring himself to say "Manchurian candidate" out loud. "It sounds to me as though you're referring to tele—tele—"

BC's voice broke off, though his mouth hung open.

"Telepathy," the doctor said, staring quizzically at BC's slack-jawed face. "And yes, Agent, ah, what did you say your name—"

"Querrey," BC said, completely forgetting the name he'd used a moment ago. His Adam's apple bobbed up and down as he swallowed audibly.

"Agent Querrey? Are you all right?"

"That depends. Are you seeing what I'm seeing?"

The doctor looked only at BC.

"Tell me."

"The trees," BC whispered.

"What about the trees?"

"They're . . . *rippling.*"

For the trunks of the pines had begun undulating like strands of seaweed. A small movement, to be sure, only a few inches in either direction, and so lugubrious that BC could almost hear the grain splintering along its fibrous length. A small, slow movement, almost imperceptible. But still. Trees. Rippling.

The light was completely gone now. Or, rather, the shadows had thickened until the quivering forest was midnight dark. The only light came from—

Came from—

BC rubbed his eyes, or thought he did. He wasn't sure if his arms had moved. At any rate, the building that had materialized in front of him was still there.

Bulky chimneys bookmarked the tiny structure; jagged fretwork gleamed like broken teeth against the shingles. Railings and balusters appeared to have been constructed from sinuous lengths of grapevine, and they slithered and danced around the porch like bark-covered lightning. In the bright light of day, the little building would have been nothing more than an overgrown dollhouse or gingerbread cottage. But lit only by daggers of moonlight—where *had* the sun gone?—it was a nightmare vision, full of dark omen.

A light flickered behind the curtained windows, a match-strike that quickly flared into lantern brightness. It bounced from one end of the house to the other like a goldfish leaping between fishbowls or a burning tennis ball hurtling from racket to racket or barrels of flaming oil launched by a pair of trebuchets from either side of an ancient city wall. The metaphors seemed to bloom in BC's mind of their own accord (along with words like "trebuchet," which he was sure he'd never heard before). With each volley the glow gained intensity—insanity—until it was nothing less than the superpowers hurling nuclear annihilation across the vastness of oceans. BC almost expected to hear screams coming from the cottage. He almost wanted to scream himself.

Suddenly a pillar of light filled the doorway and exploded over the porch. At first it was just fire. Then, impossibly, features came into focus. Arms, legs, a head. Slitted eyes and open mouth, hair flaming like a Klansman's torch. A witch? No. A boy. A burning boy.

No: a boy made of fire.

Like all seraphim, it was terrifying in its beauty and power. Something that didn't belong in the material world and shouldn't be seen with mortal eyes. Something that would kill you the way you might kill an ant—thoughtlessly, because it attached no importance to your existence, or heedlessly, because it didn't even see you.

BC's muscles tensed and twitched. He had seconds to decide: should he run, or welcome whatever message the boy brought? But was it attacking him, or merely fleeing the house? Carrying the truth, or carrying his death? A demon, or—please, God let it be *or*—an angel? He wanted to run, but terror held him rooted to his spot.

Somewhere far away from him, Timothy Leary was speaking to someone who wasn't quite there.

"You see why we thought this one was special."

Amid the rippling forest, the rusticated cottage was com-
pletely still. Yet somehow it was all the more frightening for that—a
clear indication that the building wasn't part of the phenomenon but
the source of it. It took all of BC's self-possession to mount the two
steps and walk across the narrow porch. The floorboards thumped solidly beneath his feet, the wrought-iron door handle was firm in his
fingers, neither hotter nor colder than the surrounding air; it didn't vi-
brate in warning over what lay on the other side of its portal. Even so,
BC couldn't bring himself to open it, and he turned to wait for Leary.
The doctor's eyes were on him, squinting, scrutinizing. The pantsless
professor is observing *me*, BC thought, as though *I'm* the anomalous
one. But any anger he felt was tempered by the trees dancing behind
Leary's back like a Greek chorus emerging from the wings to prophesy
the hero's fall. It was the sight of the trees that caused him to turn back
to the house more than Leary's prying eyes, and, squaring his shoulders, he rapped decisively on the curtained glass.

The only answer was a chuckle behind him.

"Agent Querrey? This isn't Thanksgiving dinner." And, sliding past
BC, Leary pushed the door open. The doctor started to walk into the
house, then stopped so suddenly that BC crashed into him.

"What the hell?"

For the first time, an element of fear entered the doctor's voice.

BC peered over Leary's shoulder. The first thing he saw was a red
handprint on the opposite wall. The print centered BC the way a track
on the forest floor centers a hunter. The rippling forest disappeared
from his mind as his eyes zeroed in on the bloodstain. The color was
dry but still bright, probably only an hour or two old, and thick, suggesting it was the hand itself that was bleeding—possibly from hitting
the wall—as opposed to the print of someone who'd touched a mortal
wound, then flailed around.

Leary was still frozen in the doorway and BC had to push past him to see the rest of the room. It had been torn to pieces. Tables, lamps, picture frames, all smashed to bits. Upholstery had been shredded, holes kicked in the walls, shelves broken in two, pages ripped from books. Almost all of the debris was stained with blood.

A strange whining noise came out of the doctor's throat.

"Wh-what happened here?"

BC ignored him. This kind of carnage was the work of a single disturbed mind, not a fight: not the haphazard destruction of bodies crashing into things, but the willful annihilation of a tormenting environment. The thousands of fragments of pottery were so pulverized they seemed to have been ground into the carpet by someone jumping up and down on them. BC was so sure of this last assessment that when he saw the ceramic shards embedded in the soles of a pair of shoes sticking out from behind the overturned sofa, his first thought was, I was right! Then he noticed the ankles sticking out of the other side of the shoes and, blushing slightly, rushed across the room. He didn't bother to draw his gun. There was something about the stillness of the shoes that told BC their wearer wasn't a threat to anyone.

He drew up short when he saw the blood on the man's chest. It wasn't the wound that surprised him—it was hard to see this kind of violence heading anywhere other than suicide—but, rather, the fact that the inch-wide slit was empty. A knife wound, not a gunshot. But if the man had killed himself, where was the knife?

"Is it—" Leary's voice caught in his throat. "Morganthau?"

BC wondered that himself, but he couldn't ask Leary. Still, the reversal in the two men's roles was complete. The blond doctor was quivering in fear, whereas BC felt focused and purposeful.

"I need you to call the local police. Ask them to send a car and an ambulance."

"There's no phone out here. I'd need to run back to the Big House."

"Then run."

Leary thudded off the porch and BC turned back to the man on the floor. He checked his pulse to confirm that he was dead, then grabbed a shredded cushion and placed it atop the pool of blood next to the body so he could kneel beside it. The chest wound was the only serious injury. The only other trauma was to the man's hands, which were swollen and scraped, covered in blood, paint, plaster. All of this reinforced the idea that he'd punched in the walls, but if he'd driven a knife into his own chest, there was no sign of the blade anywhere.

For the first time, BC turned his attention to the man's face. The victim was young, only twenty-two or twenty-three, with strong cheekbones and a jawline dusted with dark brown stubble. Even drenched in blood, however, his suit fit him perfectly, so well tailored that it hadn't ripped once during all his thrashing. It was even buttoned. There were faint bloodstains on his temples, but his freshly cut hair was still relatively neat, meaning that despite his distress the man had run his fingers through it to smooth it. Clearly, he was a man who took pride in his appearance. So why hadn't he shaved this morning?

All at once BC understood. The man had been here all night. He was guarding something. And even as BC remembered the name Chandler Forrestal—remembered Orpheus and the shimmering trees outside the cottage and the doctor's comment about "the girl"—he heard a thump above him, and realized he wasn't alone in the house.

He bit back a curse as he reached for his gun, ascended the stairs as quietly as he could. Someone must have heard him though, because a female voice screamed:

"Get away!"

BC made his way to the edge of the open door frame. There was a picture on the opposite wall, and its glass reflected most of the room. BC saw a bed with a male figure writhing on it, a girl leaning on the floor. Something gleamed in her stained hands.

"My name is Special Agent BC Querrey with the Federal Bureau of Investigation," he called loudly. "I want you to put down the knife and step away from Mr. Forrestal."

"Get away! Please! I beg you!"

BC didn't ask a second time. He stepped quickly into the doorway, his weapon leveled at the girl.

"Drop it!"

The girl screamed. The terror in her voice was so palpable that BC felt it wash over him like a wave. At the same time, he caught a glimpse of something flying at him from the right. He ducked, and a vase smashed against the door frame, spraying him with bits of pottery. He whirled but there was nothing there save a bureau pressed firmly against the wall. No one could have been hiding behind it.

"It wasn't me!" the girl screamed now, and BC whirled back to her. Her screams were unnerving—he felt almost as frightened as she was. He fought to steady the gun in his hands even as she waved the knife in hers. There was blood on the blade and handle, on her hands and clothes, too. Not a lot, though. BC knew how much blood spurted from a chest puncture. There should have been more.

"You have to believe me," she pleaded. "He killed *himself.*"

BC glanced at the man on the bed. He was drenched in sweat and writhing around, but appeared uninjured. He lowered his voice but kept his gun pointed at the girl.

"Is Mr. Forrestal injured?"

The girl's eyes went wide with fear and confusion. "I told him we'd taken too much, but he gave him more anyway."

"Who—Leary?"

"*Logan.* He came in last night when we were asleep. Used an eye-dropper. He got Chandler first, and the coughing woke me up."

"Logan? The man downstairs?"

The girl nodded her head convulsively. "I don't know how much he gave him. Thousands of times the normal dose."

BC wasn't sure how one got thousands of doses of a drug into an eyedropper, but talking seemed to be calming the girl down.

"LSD?" he asked, and when the girl nodded again, he said, "Every-one who comes here does so to take the drug. Why would you refuse?"

The girl shook her head. "We'd already taken it, and—" She broke off, shook her head. "We didn't understand what happened to us. Agent Logan thought Leary might be able to help."

"You knew Logan before?"

The girl suddenly snapped back into a panic. "He made me! He said he would go to the police otherwise! I had no choice!"

BC took a step closer. "I don't have any idea what you're talking about. But what you're describing sounds a lot like motive."

"Stay away!" The girl brandished the bloody knife in both shaking hands, but what BC noticed was the ring on her finger. A large ruby, its color deeper and richer than the blood that spotted her hands. He didn't know why, but it seemed to him that you would take off a ring like that if you were going to commit murder, or at the very least afterward.

"You have to believe me," the girl implored. "He stabbed *himself*. He couldn't take it."

"Take what?"

"I don't *know*. Whatever Chandler—whatever *he* saw."

BC glanced at the man on the bed. "What does he have to do with this?"

"I told him not to give Chandler any more acid, but he wouldn't listen! You have to get away."

Suddenly BC realized: the girl wasn't afraid *of* him. She was afraid *for* him. "You're trying to protect *me?*"

"He—" The girl gulped back the word. "It's out of control. You have to get away. Out of its reach. Until it wears off."

"But . . . but how did he—"

The girl screamed in frustration, so loud the man on the bed moaned. "Don't you see? Don't you *see?*"

And now BC did see: saw that the entire room had begun to shimmer like the trees outside. Only this time it wasn't just a hallucination. He could feel the floorboards warping beneath his feet.

"You have to run! *Please*. Before it's too late."

BC tried to hold the gun on the girl but the seesawing motion beneath his feet made it impossible. He reached for the wall but the wall was rocking too. Splaying his feet, supporting his right arm with his left, he mustered as much authority as he could.

"I'm sorry, miss. I have to ask you to put the knife down and step away from Mr. Forrestal. Until I figure out what's going on here, you're going to have to come with me."

The girl screamed, even as the bureau lifted up and flew across the room at him. He threw himself to the floor just before it hit the wall so hard that it smashed through, hung half in, half out of the melting bedroom in a cloud of plaster dust. A rain of random objects began pelting BC—books, lamps, pictures, little pieces of bric-a-brac that flew at him too quickly to make out. He squeezed himself into the corner behind a tall armoire and shielded his face as best he could. Glass exploded as objects crashed through the window over his head. This isn't happening, he tried to tell himself. It's just an illusion. A hallucination. It has to be. But he could feel glass and plaster and wood chips rain down on his hair and knew he was wrong. Somehow the man on the bed was throwing things at him without touching them. Throwing them with his mind.

Suddenly the girl screamed again. BC couldn't see her but he heard the difference in her voice: this was a scream of pure terror. A moment later there was a gunshot and she fell silent.

"Miss—" BC's words were choked out as the armoire he was leaning against suddenly tipped over and pinned him into the corner. His gun was knocked from his hands and his body was trapped in a low, painful crouch. His cheek was mashed against the wall so hard that it felt like his skull was going to crack. The little sliver of the room he could see began to blur as spots danced before his eyes.

"Is someone there?" he called, his voice a choked whisper. "Someone, please! Help me!"

There was a second gunshot then, and all at once the armoire fell off him and BC half stumbled, half rolled away from the wall. He wobbled toward his gun, but even as he reached for it he saw a large object hurtling toward him. He turned his head, had time to see that the object was a portable typewriter. A dark shadow filled the doorway, and the faint smell of cigar smoke, and then the typewriter smashed into his skull and the room went black.

The first thing he saw when he came to was a tattered lattice of sunset shining through the needles of the pine forest. There was something wrong with this picture, but he couldn't tell what it was at first. Then it came to him: the pine trees were solid now, their only movement caused by the breeze.

He sat up, wincing in pain. He felt the crust of dried blood on his face, looked down and saw a few drops on the front of his suit. Then he saw the car.

A Lincoln, flat, black, and rectangular, was slotted into the trees like a gigantic domino. He turned toward the cottage, looked first at the second-floor window to the bedroom where he'd confronted the girl and Forrestal. He stared at it a long time before accepting the truth of what his eyes told him: it was unbroken. Light shown through the drawn curtain, and dark shadows moved back and forth inside the room.

He started to stand and immediately felt a hand on his shoulder. He turned to see a stony-faced man sitting on a section of sawn tree trunk.

"I'm going to have to ask you to wait until the ambulance arrives, sir."

"I'm fine," BC said, and moved to get up again.

The man's hand was heavy on his shoulder, and BC sat down hard enough to send daggers of pain through his forehead.

"Sir, please. I'd hate to see you injured further."

BC squeezed his left arm against his side, confirming what he'd already suspected. His gun was gone.

"Who are you? What are you doing here?"

"The ambulance will be here shortly, sir. You should take it easy. That's quite a bump on your head."

BC would've shaken his head but it hurt too much. He turned back to the cottage, just in time to see a man back out the front door pulling something long, black, obviously heavy.

A body bag.

He dragged his burden across the lawn and stowed it in the Lincoln's trunk.

BC would've asked where he was taking the body, but he knew it was pointless. The man returned to the house and came out a few minutes later with a second body, then a third, this last one significantly smaller than the first two, and carried in his arms in a gross perversion of the *Pietà*.

"Lord have mercy. What have you done?"

The lights went off in the upper bedroom. As BC watched, the rest of the house went dark. The black-suited man scanned the ground, then got in the car. The engine started, the lights came on. Then a shadow filled the cottage doorway. Another dark suit, but there was something different about this one. It was bigger for one thing. Bulkier. More rumpled.

For some reason BC looked at the feet for confirmation of the man's identity. There were the sandals. When he looked up at the face, he saw that it was covered by a broad-brimmed fedora and a pair of mirrored sunglasses, as if the man was hiding his identity even from the people he worked with.

He was different now. The clothing was still shabby, ill-fitting, but there was nothing disheveled about the man himself. He was clearly in charge.

"Did you have to kill them? Mr. Forrestal? The girl?"

Melchior descended the steps and walked toward the car.

"Isn't it bad enough that you dragged them into your experiment? Did you have to shoot them when it went awry?"

A grin flickered over the corner of Melchior's mouth, and for some reason BC knew it was his use of the word "awry."

"Was Logan his real name?" he called as Melchior reached for a door handle. "Or Morganthau? His parents will want to know what happened to him. What about the girl? What was her name?"

Melchior pulled the door open. He paused a moment.

"She doesn't have a name," he said finally. "Not anymore. Give him back his gun, Charlie," he threw in, then got in the car.

The agent guarding BC handed him his gun, then the bullets that had been in it. Then he got in the Lincoln with Melchior and the other man, and, almost silently, the car pulled away over the pine needles. More out of instinct than hope, BC glanced at the rear bumper, but black fabric had been draped over the license plate, as though the car itself were in mourning for the three bodies it carried.

Maria Bayo's uncle had died by the time Ivelitsch reached him, but there were a half dozen other cases of radiation poisoning in the village. The epicenter was a small shed one block off the village's only paved road. Even without the Geiger counter Ivelitsch would have been able to find it: someone had painted the skull and crossbones on all four sides of the building.

"Readings are incredibly high, comrade," Sergei Vladimirovich confirmed. "Either the unit was damaged when Vassily Vasilievich stole it, or afterwards, when Raúl's man got it."

"Is there any other danger? Besides the leak, I mean?"

"You mean an explosion? No, comrade—" Sergei Vladimirovich broke off.

"What?" Ivelitsch demanded.

"Just a premonition. The thieves obviously stored the device here, but they moved it before we arrived. That means they knew we were coming. Next time they won't just stick it in a shed. They'll look for something less noticeable." Sergei Vladimirovich waved a hand, indicating the flat fields stretching beyond the village in every direction. "My guess is they'll bury it."

"And?"

"It's just that the water table's extremely shallow here, and porous as well. If this thing actually gets into the local supply, you could end up with hundreds sick, perhaps thousands."

"Your concern for human welfare is touching." Ivelitsch's voice would have raised the fur on a cat's back.

Sergei Vladimirovich surprised Ivelitsch. "I wasn't thinking of the villagers, comrade." He looked around the windblown shacks with almost as much distaste as he'd shown the pile of dog carcasses a few days ago. "An outbreak of suspicious cancers and birth defects is going to be hard to keep a secret, even in Cuba. If word gets to the relief agencies, everyone in the world will know what we're looking for."

"Well then. We'd better find the device before that happens."

Most of the sick people in the village didn't know anything. Ignorance, of course, is the Communist condition—in four years with the Czech secret police, Ivelitsch had been hard-pressed to find a single resident of Prague or Bratislava who knew his brother's wife's name, let alone whether his neighbor was an enemy of the proletariat—but even with a little cajoling the villagers stuck to their story. Ivelitsch ordered the sick to be quarantined and given tetracycline to combat the radiation sickness, which in most cases was fairly mild. The quarantine was more for his sake than the villagers', since it allowed him to interview each of the patients privately. Most of them knew nothing helpful, and Ivelitsch was beginning to lose hope—and patience—when finally he came to the last man. He'd been unconscious the first time Ivelitsch visited him, but was awake now, barely. The skin of his lips and nostrils and eyelids was pocked with blisters, and thin yellow mucus leaked from beneath his fingernails.

"*Favor,*" the man croaked, his tongue bulging from his mouth like a lizard's. "They said you had medicine."

There was a cane leaning across the arms of a chair, and Ivelitsch laid it on the floor before sitting down next to the bed. He pulled a pill bottle from his jacket and set it on the bedside table, just out of the patient's reach.

"I need information."

"*Favor. Se nada.* I know nothing."

Ivelitsch thought the man's response came too quickly. It wasn't an answer. It was a denial.

"An American in a truck. Dark like a Cuban, but big."

"*¿Gordo?*"

"Not fat. *Atlético.*"

The man turned his head toward the pills. The action triggered a cough, long and deep but hollow, as though he were almost emptied out.

"There was a man. He could have been American. He paid Victor Bayo to park it in his shed."

"What was in the truck?"

"He kept it covered."

"You would not be sick if you hadn't looked."

The man on the bed closed his eyes. For a moment Ivelitsch thought he'd lost consciousness. He was reaching for the cane to prod him when the man opened his eyes.

"I don't know what it was. Some kind of machine. As big as my sister's dowry chest. There was writing on it. Russian writing."

"How do you know it was Russian?"

"It was like the letters on the jeeps." A tiny croaking laugh. "Backward consonants and funny shapes."

"And what happened to it?"

"Someone came for the truck and took it away. Two days ago. He went east."

"The American?"

"No. Cubano. But the American sent him."

"How do you know?"

"He had keys to the padlock on the shed, and to the truck as well."

Ivelitsch nodded, and stood up.

"You did well to answer my questions. You saved your people much sickness." He grabbed the pill bottle and tossed it on the bed. "You might have even saved yourself. You are a lucky man."

Louie Garza waited for the Russian to leave before he took the first pill. Indeed, he was a lucky man. He only hoped the pills worked before the Russian figured out Louie'd sent him on a wild-goose chase, and came back for the truth.

The rain beating on the roof of his motel, coupled with the pain in his forehead, kept BC awake all night. It wasn't the drumming on the zinc sheets or the throbbing in his skull: it was the thought of all the evidence it was destroying. Tire treads and footprints melting into useless blurs; fibers, hairs, and other minuscule clues washing away; drops of blood dissolving into the soil. Any one of them might hold the key to unlocking what had really happened in the cottage—who killed whom, and how, and why. Morganthau, aka Logan. Chandler Forrestal, aka Orpheus. And the girl who, so far, had no name.

BC had looked at dozens of cadavers, stuck his fingers in knife and bullet wounds and probed nether orifices for signs of rape or cruder trauma. But never once had he looked a living victim in the face. Never once had he heard pleas for succor or mercy. And even though he knew she was incidental to this story, that Orpheus was the real star—or at any rate the chemical, the project that had made him—it was the girl who haunted him. Somehow he'd tricked himself into believing that victims acquiesced to their fate in the end. That the greatest crime was murder, not the horrible psychic torture that led up to it. But all night long the girl's screams echoed in his ears, and every time he closed his eyes he saw hers, wide with terror. Long after he'd forgotten she was dead, he remembered how she'd suffered when she was alive.

In an effort to get some sleep he tried to read *The Man in the High Castle,* the book Director Hoover had sent him north with. Among other things, the director expected a report Monday morning—assuming BC still had a job, of course. But he only got as far as the end of the second page. *How easily I could fall in love with a girl like this.* His cheeks reddened, the book fell from his fingers. He filled a rag with ice from the machine down the hall and put it on the bump on his forehead, then lay in bed listening to the rain wash away his chances of finding out what had happened to her.

The storm let up shortly after dawn. By the time the sun crested the

Berkshires he was stashing the Corvair a quarter mile from the front gate of the Castalia estate. A bone-chilling fog filled up the road, the lawns, the space between trees. The reduced visibility seemed to amplify what little noise there was—mostly BC, his shoes crunching over gravel, his breath whistling as he scaled the crumbling stone wall, and then his slip-sliding passage as he made his way up the slick hill toward the main house. Fog ribboned through the deciduous trees on this side of the house, and the ground was cushioned by layers of leaves and mulch. BC, punchy from his sleepless night but wired on two cups of bitter coffee, half felt that he'd stepped into another hallucination. He wanted to tell himself that was impossible, but after yesterday he wasn't sure he'd ever be able to say that about anything again.

There wasn't a light on in any of the main house's windows, and the building emitted a pervasive silence, as if its occupants weren't just asleep but unconscious, suppressed by the gargantuan structure until it chose to recognize a new day. BC skirted the wide lawns and made his way toward the pine forest. His chest tightened and he willed himself to relax. Forrestal was gone, he reminded himself. Orpheus was dead, and couldn't hurt him now.

The cottage came into view more quickly than he remembered. Without the interference of a shimmering hallucination, he could see it for what it was: a small building outfitted in the same combination of Bavarian and Catskill kitsch that decorated the Big House. He combed the yard first, but Melchior's team had been thorough. The only sign that they'd been there was the chewed-up ground itself. Inside, the rooms had the distinct look of a scene that's been gone through by professionals who don't care about covering their tracks. Books sat unevenly on the shelves from which they'd been taken and flipped through and hastily put back; drawers hung half-open, bits of clothing or paper peeking out; couch cushions bunched together like boxcars on a crashed train. They'd even pulled up the carpet, leaving it in a roll against one wall, and a couple of floorboards had been pulled up as well. BC had no idea if they'd found anything, but the one thing all this effort made clear was that the team hadn't known what was going on in the house before it arrived.

It wasn't until he unrolled the carpet that he realized the cleanup

team hadn't simply been searching for evidence: it had also been elimi-
nating it. A huge hole had been sawn out of the center of the carpet
where Logan's body had lain, ragged-edged, contemptuous even, as
though someone had hacked the blood-soaked portion out with the
same knife that killed Logan. BC looked at the walls again, realized
that all the bloody handprints had been scrubbed away. He was able to
find a couple of small stains in the carpet, but doubted there was enough
fluid in the fibers to get anything like a usable sample. Nevertheless, he
clipped the strands and dropped them into his pocket—his evidence
bags had been in his briefcase—then made his way through the rest of
the first floor, taking two or three more samples, but not really expecting anything to come of them. Only when he was convinced the lower
floor had been thoroughly exhumed did he make his way upstairs.

He'd meant to go through the ancillary rooms first, but the open
door lay just past the top of the stairway and he couldn't help but look
in. The bed had been stripped. Naked pillows lay atop the dingy white
mattress like seashells on a beach. A strong scent of bleach came to his
nostrils.

He stepped in. There was the bureau that had flown across the room
and slammed through the wall. It sat between two windows, not a nick
on it, and certainly none of the drawers were smashed into pieces; the
wall that it had crashed through was unmarked as well. The books and
lamps that had flown at him sat on shelves and tables, equally intact,
gleamingly clean. Could CIA have repaired the walls, replaced all of
the furniture? No, that was just paranoia—the kind of thinking that
dealing with CIA brought out in you. Somehow he had hallucinated
the whole thing. But how?

He looked at the armoire that had pinned him into the corner. It
stood a good three feet from the wall now, but when BC walked to the
far side, he saw faint scuff marks on the bare wooden floors. Someone
had made an effort to scrub them away—had gone so far as to fill them
in with wax. As aha moments go, it was small; but still, it was good to
know he hadn't imagined everything. Now BC saw a deep round dent
on the windowsill, flecked with black paint. He looked for the typewriter that had knocked him unconscious; it was missing from the
room. More evidence that not everything that happened yesterday had

been the product of his own mind. What was it his mother used to say? The devil mixes lies with truth to confuse you. An image of Melchior's smug pucker materialized in BC's head. Yes, he certainly did that.

BC crouched down in the corner. From this position, the armoire blocked his view of the door. Melchior could have stood there, assessing the room, formulating a plan: shoot the girl, then Chandler, then deal with BC. He shifted his attention to the bed. It sat exposed on top and bottom, barren of any sign a body had lain on it. But it was *too* barren. BC strode to the bed, threw the pillows off. The mattress was completely clean. I.e., no bloodstains. BC didn't care what kind of solvent the cleanup team had used, how hard it had scrubbed: blood always left a mark. Especially when it came from a gunshot wound, especially on white cotton ticking. And besides, the bed was completely dry, which meant the CIA team hadn't had to clean it. Which meant, finally, that there'd been nothing to clean off. He flipped the mattress just to be sure, but there was no blood on the bottom either.

But what about the girl? BC looked beside the bed. Immediately he saw a smattering of brownish red dots that had soaked into nicks in the old wooden bed frame. Scrubbed, but still visible. So she *had* been shot. There were no stains on the floor, however, and BC wanted to believe she hadn't bled a lot, that the wound hadn't been serious. But even if the bullet hadn't hit anything major, if it wasn't removed quickly it could easily lead to sepsis.

He put his hand on the wall. The plaster felt cool and slightly damp. It could've just been the humidity from the rain, or . . . He ran his fingers over the wall like a blind man reading Braille. It took nearly a minute to find it. A soft spot about eighteen inches above the mattress. BC pushed hard, and a bullet-sized hole appeared in the plaster. Now he knew for sure: whoever'd shot at Forrestal had aimed *above* his head. The body bag had just been a cover. The CIA wanted BC to tell J. Edgar Hoover that Chandler Forrestal was dead.

He pressed deeper, feeling for the slug. His fingertip bumped against something smooth and hard. He had to wiggle his finger to widen the hole so he could get it around the bullet, and when he pulled it out a chunk of wet plaster fell to the floor. A red gleam caught his eye, and he jerked his hand back as though it might be a lump of congealed blood. But of course it wasn't.

It was the girl's ring.

For a moment all he could do was stare at the dark ruby, wondering why Melchior had chosen to hide it here of all places. But then he realized: Melchior hadn't hidden it. He'd left it for BC to find. It was both a test and bait, and as BC picked it up and slipped it in his pocket he knew: he was hooked.

Just then a thump sounded from the lower floor—outside. The porch. A moment later the door creaked open, clunked quietly closed.

The bedroom was directly above the living room. If BC moved, whoever was downstairs would know he was here. All he could do was wait. He pulled his gun out. A part of him—it seemed to be centered on his trigger finger—prayed that it was Melchior. He would shoot him in the hip. He would cripple him, then beat the girl's location out of him.

For a long time there was no sound downstairs. It was as if whoever'd come in was as awed by the cottage as BC was. Then, slowly, steps marched toward the center of the house. The staircase. The person's tread was heavy, and BC couldn't help but imagine Melchior's large form moving through the living room. He sighted on the door and waited.

The steps mounted the stairs, slowing as they neared the top. BC knew the person was staring at the open door, working up the nerve to look in. He could almost hear him counting under his breath. Then, almost as if he'd been pushed, a man's form filled the doorway.

"Don't move!"

"Aaah!" Timothy Leary screamed like a frightened child and immediately collapsed on himself, covering his face with his hands. "Don't shoot, don't shoot!"

When Leary could walk again, BC took him downstairs, sat him on the couch (a cushion was missing, he noted now—the one he'd knelt on to keep from getting Logan's blood on his pants). Even after BC identified himself as an FBI agent, the doctor remained terrified, and his fear only increased when BC, hedging his bets, told him about the three body bags that had left the cottage.

"Chandler? Naz? Dead? Dear God."

"That was the girl's name? Naz?"

"Nazanin Haverman. She was Persian," Leary added, almost tenderly.

"Why was she even here? Was she Mr. Forrestal's girlfriend?"

BC felt almost jealous as he asked the question, but when Leary shook his head and said, "She was a prostitute," it was all he could do not to slug the man.

"What do you mean, a prostitute?"

"I only know what Morganthau told me. As near as I can tell, he made her give LSD to her johns in exchange for not having her arrested. She's been working for him for almost a year."

BC couldn't believe it. Even in her emotionally fraught state, the girl had looked like anything but a prostitute—and, as well, the idea that the nephew of the former secretary of defense would have to resort to whores beggared belief. But it also coincided with what Melchior had told him on the train yesterday.

"The girl called him Logan. Was that his first name, or . . . ?"

"We all assumed Morganthau was an alias, especially since he slipped up once and called himself Morganthal." A little smile flickered over the doctor's mouth, then quickly faded. "He was a little boy playing at being a spy. Logan could've been his real name, or just another alias."

BC was about to ask if Leary had ever seen Melchior before, but the doctor spoke first.

"Apparently Miss Haverman's father was what they call a CIA 'asset.' In Persia. He provided assistance during the revolution in '53, but was killed during the fighting, along with her mother and the rest of her family. Naz was barely a teenager then. The CIA brought her to the States and placed her with the Havermans, a wealthy Boston family. They even went so far as to adopt her, but she had trouble fitting in. Morganthau, Logan, whatever his name was, he alluded to the idea that her adoptive father might have behaved inappropriately. She was expelled from private schools up and down the East Coast for drinking and aggressive behavior and, ah, precocity. Morganthau told me he saw her name in a file when he was hired by the Boston office and decided to check up on her. When he found her, she was living hand to mouth, exchanging sex for cash or drink or whatever she could get. He seemed to think the arrangement he created was a step up for her. That he was helping her out." Leary shrugged. "It seemed to me he was obsessed with her. Even after he brought Chandler here, it was her he talked about. Her he was fascinated with." The doctor looked up at BC. "Just like you."

Even as Leary spoke, BC felt his hand in his pocket, fiddling with the ring that Melchior had left for him. It's not just me and Logan, he thought. Melchior was also caught in Naz's spell.

"I was going to get to Mr. Forrestal," he said brusquely, yanking his hand from his pocket. "It's just . . ." He shrugged helplessly. "I'm not really sure what to ask beyond, well, what *happened* yesterday?"

Despite the gravity of the situation, the smile came back to the doctor's face, and a look of awe gleamed in his twinkling eyes.

"It's easiest just to say it. Rippling trees. The Mezquita of Córdoba. Furniture flying across a room of its own accord. These images came from Chandler's head. Somehow he is able to broadcast his thoughts— his hallucinations—into the minds of the people around him."

An image of the burning boy filled BC's brain. "But there were other things. Things that came from *my* head. My past."

If anything Leary's smile grew bigger. "His ability seems to be related to the amount of LSD in his body. Seemed to be. Toward the end Morganthau was pumping him with thousands of times the normal dosage."

"But Miss Haverman said he administered the drug with an eye dropper while Mr. Forrestal was sleeping. How do you get thousands of doses—"

"You have to understand, Agent . . . Querrey?" Leary paused just long enough to remind BC that Morganthau wasn't the only young man who'd tried on an alias. "LSD is extraordinarily powerful. Doses are measured not in grams or milligrams but *micro*grams—one one-millionth of a gram. The threshold dosage is only about twenty or thirty mics. An eyedropper could contain enough acid to give everyone in Manhattan a buzz."

BC shook his head in confusion. "But LSD's been around for years.

I don't know much about it, but I know it's been used in quite a few psychiatric trials. And I assume you've taken it a few times. You don't have any mental powers, do you?"

"It's not illegal," Leary said quickly. "Just controlled. But no. No mental powers—yet." He sounded almost disappointed.

"Was it just the amount?"

Leary shook his head. "I don't think so. In fact, LSD has analeptic—stimulating—properties, and beyond a certain dosage it really should give you a heart attack. But this is the CIA. Who knows what they added to Morganthau's LSD? Who knows if it was even LSD at all?"

"And what does all this have to do with the Gate of Orpheus?"

Leary waved his hand. "You should think of the Gate as less object or organ than metaphor. Opening it was meant to lead to higher states of consciousness, not murder."

"You mean Morganthau?"

"Think how frightened you were yesterday. Imagine if that fear were amplified a hundred times. A thousand."

BC shuddered. "You think Mr. Forrestal killed him? Made him kill himself? With his mind?"

"I don't know," Leary said. "I don't know what happened here." His eyes flickered to the ceiling, to the stripped bedroom above. "And my sense is that now we never will. Unless . . ."

"Unless what?"

"Unless they make another one."

"Another—"

"Another Orpheus."

BC just nodded his head, but what he thought was: they don't have to make another Orpheus. Chandler Forrestal is still alive. And so was Naz, he thought, reaching for the ring in his pocket. But both of those facts could change quickly, unless he found them. And the only way he was going to do that was if he found Melchior.

The headlights on the the stretch Fleetwood went dark just before it pulled into the back parking lot of the Falls Church storage facility. Silent and invisible, detectable only by the glint of moonlight off chrome and glass and black lacquer, it sluiced across the empty asphalt like the lead ship of a naval battalion until it pulled up soundlessly in front of a lone man standing in the cone of darkness beneath a broken streetlight. A broad-brimmed hat further shadowed the man's face, but beneath it a nervous hand fiddled with a tiny hole in the suit jacket, under the lapel, over his heart. For the past thirty-six hours Melchior had been trying to make sense of what he'd experienced at Millbrook—the rippling trees, the objects that seemed to fly of their own accord—but as soon as he saw the car he forgot all that. He'd heard that Song was doing well, but not *this* well, and with a pang of embarrassment he wished he'd abandoned the affectation of Segundo's execution suit, or at least the worn-out sandals. Thank God today's socks didn't have any holes in them.

His regrets only increased when the tinted back window rolled down with a space-age hum, revealing a plush cavern lined with black leather, white silk, chrome accents—and a woman whose face, though familiar, still took his breath away. It had been almost seven years since he'd last seen Song. She was in her mid-twenties now—she'd been shady about her age even when he met her a decade ago in Korea. The features were still sharp, but they lacked the hollow, starved look they'd worn when Melchior first met her, had taken on a cast of polished onyx. The eyes were if anything larger and darker, but, though the anger was gone, it had been replaced by a hardness that was even more daunting.

Melchior couldn't help himself. He whistled.

Song didn't deign to look at him. "If you use the term 'Dragon Lady' in any context whatsoever, I'll have Chul-moo shoot out your knees. Now, what's so important that after seven years you suddenly need to see me personally, immediately, and at one in the morning?"

Well, *that* hadn't changed. Song had always been a no-nonsense type of girl.

"Actually, I was going to say that if I'd known you were going to turn out this pretty, I'd've never—"

"One more word and I'll shoot you myself."

"You're afraid I'll offend poor 'Iron Weapon' in the front seat?" Melchior glanced at the chauffeur. "Is he even old enough to drive?"

"His license says he is," Song said. "And he speaks no English, so the only person who will be offended by your banter is me. Let's cut to the chase: what do you need?" Song looked at Melchior for the first time, from the ragged sandals all the way up to the battered fedora, proffering an ironic smile that sent shivers down his spine. "And what do you offer?"

In return for services rendered to the United States government during the war in Korea, Song Paik—Song to her friends, Madam Song to everyone else—asked only that she be allowed to emigrate to America. Melchior had traveled to Korea with the Wiz when he was all of twenty years old, had recruited her himself. She was that one in fifty asset who neither disappeared behind the 38th parallel nor turned out to have been a Communist plant. She'd been fourteen or fifteen then, a slip of a girl, all angles and lines, with sunken eyes that burned with hunger and hatred. Like Melchior, she was an orphan, but unlike him she'd known her parents and witnessed their murder—and the murder of her brother, her nanny, and six more members of her extended family, not to mention countless friends and neighbors—at the hands of Kim Il-sung's soldiers. Melchior was pretty sure she'd've helped the Company even if the Wiz hadn't offered her U.S. citizenship. No one carried a grudge like a Korean. Of course he hadn't met any Persians at that point, so it was a qualified opinion.

In fact, after he and the Wiz had been in Korea for just over ten months, Douglas MacArthur made it clear he didn't give a shit about intelligence as long as he had tanks and bombers and 155-millimeter shells and napalm—God only knows what would've happened if he'd gotten his hands on the thirty-eight atomic bombs he'd requested. Never one to stick around where he wasn't wanted, the Wiz decamped for Persia to take care of Mohammed Mossadegh, dragging Melchior with him, while Song made her way to the States. Melchior kept tenuous tabs on her in the intervening decade. Though her presence in this country was legal, the rest of her activities appeared to be less aboveboard. He gathered that she'd tried a little bit of everything: smuggling, drug running, even espionage. Her primary source of revenue, however, was an exclusive brothel that offered every kind of Asian girl—Indian, Thai, Japanese, as well as more rarefied "varietals," as she called them, as though they were species of orchid—and whose regular patrons had come to include captains of industry and congressmen, along with a regular flow of intelligence agents from around the world, who came there for the information that was on sale along with the girls. Although the official line at the Company was that Madam Song's was allowed to operate unmolested because she funneled a large percentage of her income to organizations and individuals working for the overthrow of Kim Il-sung's regime, the truth was she'd taken her cues from the Company and kept extensive evidence—photographic and forensic—on the most sensitive visitors to her establishment. A nosy reporter might take her down one day (assuming she didn't have the goods on the paper's publisher), but no government agency ever would.

Melchior shook his head now. "The years haven't softened you, that's for sure. I need to move something," he said quickly, before she threatened to shoot him again. "Someone."

"Some who?"

"That's not important."

"Some where?"

Melchior chuckled. "Kind of far, actually. San Francisco. I'd take him myself, but I have some business to attend to first, and this is a priority."

"Seoul is kind of far. San Francisco is only six hours by plane, and I happen to have one."

Melchior resisted the urge to whistle again. "I see I called the right lady."

"You called no one. No one answered. Nothing will be moved. It just so happens that I enjoy visiting San Francisco. Usually I go in January, but I guess I can go in November this year."

"Understood."

"Sometimes when I'm in San Francisco I like to meet new people. Perhaps you know someone who could show me around?"

"In fact I do. He's a nice man. A doctor."

Song looked at Melchior skeptically. "I'm not looking for a husband."

Melchior laughed. "He's not that kind of doctor."

A pause. "Let me guess. One of the leftovers from Nightingale?" When Melchior nodded, she continued: "You want me to deliver someone to a Nazi scientist?"

"Ex-Nazi," Melchior said. "I haven't offended your sense of propriety, have I?"

"Assuming I ever had such a thing, I left it in Korea. I'm in America now, where the difference between right and wrong is a matter of dollars and cents. Why San Francisco? Aside from the fact that it's as far from Langley as you can get without leaving the country."

"I was in Laos for a few years, recruiting warlords to fight the Viet Cong."

"The Hmong," Song said, as though this were common knowledge. "Laos is not exactly in California."

Melchior did his best to keep the surprise off his face—fewer than a dozen people had known about his mission.

"The Company couldn't buy guns for them directly, so I helped them move some of their merchandise to market in order to finance the purchases."

"By merchandise you mean opium?" When Melchior nodded, Song said, "I thought it went to Marseilles, entered the U.S. through the East Coast?"

"Most of it. But I was able to funnel some to Frisco."

Song's eyebrows twitched. For the first time she seemed impressed. "You skimmed. And here I thought the Wiz had raised you to be a good boy."

"The Wiz never had anything against a little initiative."

"True." Song paused, and for the first time Melchior thought he saw a real emotion flicker over her face. "Have you heard anything about Caspar?"

Melchior had been just about to ask her the same question.

"Nothing," he said. "But I just spent a couple of years in Cuba, so I'm out of the loop. I assume he's still in Russia."

Song paused again, as if she was considering whether or not to tell Melchior what she knew. Then: "I saw him. In Japan, before he went to Moscow. The Wiz asked me to—"

"Check on him?" Melchior struggled to keep his voice level. "I never did like that part of the Wiz. I never liked that part of you, either."

Song's face went hard. For a moment Melchior thought he'd blown it. But then the condescending mask descended again, and Song's lip curled slightly as she looked Melchior up and down. "Whatever you skimmed from your opium scheme certainly didn't go on clothes. So? What do you offer me for delivering your guinea pig to the lab?"

Melchior looked at the Fleetwood, the furs, the expensively maintained cast of Song's skin. Even the boy in the driver's seat looked more like an objet d'art than a person.

"The, ah, continued goodwill of the Company?"

Song rolled her eyes. "Drew Everton, second and fourth Thursday of every month."

"Why, that dirty little scoundrel! I wouldn't've thought he had it in him." Although, really, of course he would: the only thing a Wasp enjoys more than hoarding his money is wasting it on a whore. Melchior's eyes flickered over Song's stole to the breasts beneath it. "I guess we'll have to call it a favor then."

A cunning smile spread across Song's face, though Melchior couldn't tell if it was a reaction to his gaze or the idea of having him in her debt.

"I guess we will."

Melchior nodded. "Dr. Keller will meet you at the airport."

"Keller." Song's eyes narrowed. Melchior was surprised. He'd thought Keller was his secret. "This is part of Ultra?"

"Everton can't keep his mouth shut, I see. But no, not Ultra. Orpheus."

"I don't know Orpheus."

Melchior couldn't tell if she was lying, but all he said was "Ultra's bastard child. You're about to meet him."

"Do I open the door? Or the trunk?"

"The trunk'll be fine." Melchior pulled a small black case from the pocket of his suit, opened it to reveal a syringe and a couple of vials. "He's sleeping. And if you want to get to Frisco in one piece, I suggest you keep him that way."

"In conclusion," J. Edgar Hoover's droning voice wound up, "the Review Committee, finding no evidence to support any of Special Agent Querrey's claims save for the single wound to his head, and having had the entirety of his account denied by both public and private sources at CIA, Dr. Leary, and all the residents of 'Castalia,' and having further found no substantiation of his assertion of an extramarital liaison between the president of the United States and Mary Meyer or of the possibility that the latter-named woman supplied the president with hallucinogenic pharmaceutical compounds, can only conclude that Special Agent Querrey was the victim of a hoax perpetrated either by Dr. Leary or perhaps by CIA itself, with the intention of discrediting this Bureau. In light of the smear that would have accrued to this Bureau if such a lapse in judgment on the part of one of its agents had become public knowledge—"

BC sat patiently, his eyes focused on the portrait of Jack Kennedy that hung directly above and behind the director, its plain wooden frame outlined by a larger pale rectangle, as if to say that the new president had a long way to go before he filled the space Dwight Eisenhower had vacated three years ago. BC had looked at this picture, or copies of it, countless times before, but now he found himself zeroing in on the private twinkle in the eyes, the too-wide parting of the lips, the eager, almost hungry set of the mouth: this was a lover's face, not a politician's. Marilyn Monroe. Mary Meyer. Who knew who else? And who knew what they were slipping into his drinks?

"—have no choice but to remove Special Agent Querrey from active service while his continued career in law enforcement is reevaluated. He will be placed on extended leave, with pay, until such time as we can decide what, if any, his role at the Bureau should be." Hoover looked up from his desk. "I want you to know I take no pleasure in this decision, Agent Querrey. You showed exceptional promise early in your career, but it takes more than intelligence to be an officer of this Bureau. But who knows? Perhaps, with time, and with a certain amount of soul-searching on your part, you can be rehabilitated."

Rehabilitated, BC thought. As though he were a drug addict. As though he'd asked to be promoted from Behavioral Profiling to COINTELPRO. The Review Committee's findings were hardly a surprise to him, and he felt no great desire to fight them. This case wasn't the Bureau's responsibility. It was his. Nevertheless, he thought he owed it to his career—and his conscience—to speak for the record.

"Three bodies left that cottage, Director Hoover." BC didn't bother mentioning his suspicion that Chandler and Naz were still alive, figuring that was the kind of circle-within-a-circle detail that would only make his account seem that much more far-fetched.

Hoover sighed. He closed the manila folder that contained the twenty or thirty sheets of paper that summed up BC's career, and, for the first time, looked at his disgraced agent. Four decades in office had erased any vestige of an inner self from the director's face, until only the public servant remained. The Bureau had replaced Hoover's blood with paper and his imagination with indexes, engulfing his once-lean features in a gelatinous form that seemed held together by the buttons of his shirt and the knot of his tie. His pale, almost neckless face spilled over the collar of his gray suit like foam spewing from the tip of a science-project volcano. His eyes blinked out of two folds of skin like myopic camera shutters. His voice was as impersonal as clacking typewriter keys. He took off his glasses, rubbed his eyes tiredly, put his glasses back on. Then:

"Have I ever told you the story of Amenwah, Agent Querrey?"

"*Three*," BC said insistently. "If you close the file on this case, who will bring their killer to justice?"

"Amenwah was an ancient Egyptian who lived during the time of the Ramesside dynasty, more than thirty centuries ago. He was accused of the most heinous of all crimes: stealing sacred artifacts from the tomb of Pharaoh himself. Because the objects in question couldn't be located, however, he was acquitted. Three thousand years later, when his tomb was excavated by modern archaeologists, the objects he'd been accused of stealing were found inside his own burial chamber. No crime goes unsolved forever, Agent Querrey. It might not be you who figures out what happened at Millbrook, but justice always wins in the end."

"Who will stop him from killing again?" BC said.

For a moment the director just sat there, not quite looking at him. Then, sighing slightly, he pushed his portly body out of his chair, buttoned his jacket, then turned and opened the curtains behind his desk. The view across Pennsylvania Avenue was of an old beaux arts theater, shuttered now, its sign removed, leaving it nameless and empty. It seemed to BC that the director gazed at the sight almost lovingly, his breath moving deeply in and out of his sagging belly, which strained at the button of his suit.

"The General Services Administration has just purchased this site for a dedicated FBI building. The initial plans call for nearly three million square feet of floor space to house over seven thousand employees. I'm sure one of them will be up to the challenge."

BC stared at the smudged outline left by the theater's sign. QUER— NO. ORPH.

Orpheum.

He sat up with a start.

"They won't name it after you, you know."

"Pardon—"

"You have to die first," BC said, and the viciousness in his voice shocked him. "They won't name it after you while you're alive. You'll never see the fruits of your labor."

Hoover's cheek twitched. BC didn't know what that meant, but he decided to take it as a victory.

"Associate Director Tolson will show you out of the building. I'd ask you to surrender your weapon to him before you leave."

At first he pretended it was just another night. He took the Metro to Takoma Station, went first to his boxing gym, did a half hour of calisthenics and another half hour on the bag, then accepted an invitation to spar with a high school boy in training for the Golden Gloves. He showered at the gym as he normally did, but then, instead of wearing his flannels home, found himself changing back into his suit. Even as he buckled his belt and knotted his tie and adjusted his (empty) shoulder holster, he didn't acknowledge what he was doing. Didn't ask himself why he strode past his house to the end of the block, didn't allow himself to wonder what the neighbors would think if they saw him walking up the sidewalk to the home of Gerry and Jenny Burton. Gerry Burton worked in the Department of Justice Building as an electrician, after all; there were any number of reasons why Special Agent Querrey might need to speak to him. He was a member of both the International Brotherhood of Electrical Workers and the American Federation of Government Employees, and he worked third shift to boot; as a consequence he earned nearly 25 percent more than BC did, despite the fact that he went to work in a pair of greasy coveralls.

The Burtons' home had been a carriage house until the owners converted it into a rental property, and as such was the smallest building on the block. BC's mother, who had engaged in the respectable practice of taking in boarders to make ends meet before BC started working, always said the conversion marked the beginning of the end of the neighborhood, although what she was really referring to was the fact that Gerry Burton—and his wife, Jenny, for that matter—were Negro.

BC didn't let himself think about that either.

Jenny Burton answered the door, a baby on her hip, two others screaming in the room behind her.

"Oh, hi, Mr., um, Query?"

"Please," BC said, then added something that would have made his mother turn over in her grave. "Call me Beau—"

"Gerry!" Jenny *pfft*ed a wisp of hair off her forehead. "Sit wherever's safe," she tossed over her shoulder—she hadn't actually invited him in—then disappeared into the kitchen.

A small square of parquet inside the front door gave way to a marginally larger rectangle of carpet whose color was indiscernible beneath a layer of children's toys. A boy and a second child of indeterminate gender, both around three years old, were playing a private version of Monopoly that involved acting out the characteristics of their various pieces.

"No, horse jumps over hat, you moron!" the one who was definitely a boy screamed.

There was a heavy footstep on the stairs. BC knew little of Gerry Burton save that he was a big man and, apparently, virile. In addition to the three children present, BC was aware of at least two more.

"Mom! Jack called me a moron!"

Burton's progress down the stairs was a series of groans, creaks, whines, and wheezes, though it was impossible to tell which came from him, which from the complaining treads. He appeared in the doorway, a dark robe pulled over his white T-shirt, and stepped with exaggerated care around the toys scattered on the floor.

"Evening, Mr. Query." Burton had a cautious, curious look on his face. Everyone in the neighborhood knew BC worked for the FBI. "Pardon the mess. Five kids, you know. Tiny house. Jenny does the best she can."

"Dad! Jack called me a moron!"

"Hush up, Lane. Can't you see we got company?"

BC steeled himself.

"I'm sorry to have to come to you in your home, Mr. Burton."

Burton squinted, his small eyes disappearing into his plump cheeks, as though he were reading BC's words rather than listening to him speak. After a moment he nodded, as if he'd reached the end of the sentence. "What can I do for you?"

BC took a deep breath. "As you know, an enormous amount of sensitive material passes through the Department of Justice Building, and it's vital that none of it be seen by the wrong eyes. I'm sorry to say that it's come to our attention that there have been several breaches in areas where you have been assigned."

In the silence after BC finished, one of the children screamed, "Car parks inside hat! In*side* hat! In-SIDE hat!"

"*Jack.*"

Apparently Jack knew this voice. He grabbed Lane and hightailed it into the kitchen.

"Agent Query?" Burton said when his kids were gone. "No one called me. This the first I heard about it."

BC smiled and nodded. "In light of your excellent record, the director felt you deserved the courtesy of a personal visit." As soon as he spoke, BC almost kicked himself. What was he doing, mentioning the director? As if J. Edgar Hoover would take notice of something this trivial.

"But I got Level 3 clearance, Agent Query. It was renewed less'n six months ago."

"My mother spoke very highly of you," BC said, though he had no idea why he was mentioning her either. "I'm sure you've done nothing wrong. Nevertheless, there have been breaches—minor breaches, but breaches nevertheless—" He broke off, tripping over the fact that he'd used the word "nevertheless" twice in one sentence.

"Is this about that thing with Ashley? Because, you know, me and the wife've already—"

"No, no, it's nothing like that. Look, Mr. Burton, I'm sure you've done nothing wrong, but until we can find out exactly what happened, I'm afraid I'll need to collect your ID badge."

"I'll call the office," Burton said, stepping toward the phone. "I'm sure it's just a misunderstanding. Ashley and me was just—"

"Mr. Burton!" BC tried to make his voice forceful, but it just sounded desperate in his ears. "There's no one to call. I'm in charge of the matter." He held out his hand and prayed it wouldn't shake. "Your ID badge, please."

Burton's feet shuffled back and forth until something squeaked beneath them and he started. He walked dazedly to a side table and retreived his badge, then gave it to BC with a fatalistic air, as if he'd always known his time would come. BC couldn't help but think of the conductor on the train to New York. Mr. Handy. Did every black man in America feel this way? As though his existence continued on sufferance only? But that in turn made him think of Melchior. No, he thought, at least one black man in America was unwilling to live on handouts anymore. Two, if you counted Dr. King. Oh, and Malcolm—

"Do you want to search the house or something?" Burton's somber voice broke into BC's reverie. "Cuz you'll see, we ain't got nothing to hide. We're honest people, Agent Query. We love this country. We wouldn't never breach security."

BC stuffed the badge in his pocket. "As I said, it's just an investigation, and, because of your close relationship to my mother, I'm going to handle it personally. In fact, I plan on returning to the office and clearing it up tonight. And I've made sure you'll be paid for the day. Think of it as a little vacation."

Burton sighed heavily and handed over the badge.

"Well, I wouldn't mind that. Be nice to sleep when it's dark out for a change." He stepped backward, and whatever had squeaked beneath him squeaked again. "God damn—I mean, gosh. Gosh darn. We're crammed in this place like the old woman in the shoe."

"Indeed," BC said. He lingered on the parquet.

"Is there something else, Agent Query?"

"It's pronounced *Querrey*," BC said. "And I need your uniform, too."

Melchior stared at Chandler Forrestal's body through the win-
dow of Chandler's makeshift hospital room like a father looking at his
first child in the neonatal ward. Asleep, Orpheus looked like nothing so
much as what he was: a twenty-eight-year-old white man with a face
that was a little old Hollywood, a little new: Gary Cooper circa *The
Virginian* crossed with the young star of *Splendor in the Grass,* Warren
Beatty. Even in a hospital robe there was something about him that
could only be described as dashing, however fruity that sounded. He
had that combination of hard muscles and soft hands that the children
of privilege possess; the only lines on his body were faint wrinkles
around his mouth from a lifetime of nervous frowning (although on
Chandler they looked less like wrinkles than dimples). Melchior had
read the files in BC's briefcase, so he knew about the money Chandler's
family had had and lost, the Wall Street and Beltway connections that
still leant a sheen to his name even if they'd long since evaporated. He'd
also read everything the Bureau's spies inside CIA had managed to ferret out about Project Orpheus, which pretty much confirmed what
Everton had said. Either they weren't telling him much, or there wasn't
much to tell. Whores. LSD. Unwitting test subjects and one-way mirrors. Putting aside the scandal that would erupt if the Mary Meyer-
Jack Kennedy connection came to light, it sounded like Ultra all over
again, and ten years of Ultra had produced nothing besides a couple of
Company Christmas parties that got out of hand. Certainly no one
seemed to have expected what Melchior had experienced at Millbrook
three days ago (although the thought of a telepathic president was
enough to make him chuckle). If he were the kind of man prone to self-
doubt, he might've tried to convince himself he'd dreamed the whole
thing up, rather than attempt to figure out how Chandler had managed
to project hallucinations into Melchior's head. But Melchior had never
been wrong in his life.

"So, Doctor?" he said, turning to the other man in the room. "You've had seventy-two hours with Orpheus, not to mention ten thousand dollars to kit yourself out with all manner of toys. What have you learned?"

Heinrich Keller was almost the definition of nondescript: of medium height, medium coloring, medium age, he seemed to fade away if you looked at him directly. But if you glanced at him out of the corner of your eye, half listened to the things he said, you caught a glimmer of something. A hunger. His nickname in the SS had been *der Anästhesiologe,* "the Anesthesiologist." Some people said it was because he put his interlocutors to sleep, but others said it was because he never, ever provided the same mercy to his subjects, no matter how much they begged or how loud they screamed.

"First of all," he said, his soft voice only mildly inflected by a German mad-scientist accent, "let's make sure we know what we're looking for. Have you confirmed what Agent Logan gave him?"

"I went through Logan's files as well as Scheider's, and everything else I could find about Ultra and Orpheus. Unfortunately, Agent Logan didn't survive his encounter with Orpheus, and it didn't seem prudent for me to ask Doc Scheider too many questions—"

"Because you told them Orpheus was dead," Keller said, a little smile twitching across his lips.

"Because it didn't seem prudent," Melchior repeated. "As far as I can tell, the only thing Logan had access to was pure LSD. A lot of LSD, but completely unadulterated. And he was spreading it around pretty widely too. Presumably if he'd been giving out some kind of altered or amped-up version of the drug, we'd have Orpheuses popping up all over the place—including the White House."

"So the president is safe," Keller said. "That still doesn't tell us much."

"That what's I hired you for."

"Indeed," the doctor said, and it was hard to tell if he was being ironic or ruminative. "So: it was difficult to do anything at first, since being around Orpheus when he's on LSD is disorienting, to say the least. However, it occurred to me that Thorazine, which has been used to bring people down from the 'acid trip,' might also protect the minds of the people around Orpheus when he's exercising his power. My surmise proved correct, and, after adding some Preludin to counteract the numbing effects of the Thorazine, I was able to make some progress with my observations. As near as I can tell," the doctor continued in his sibilant voice, "Orpheus externalizes LSD's hallucinatory effects. He pulls images from the unconscious minds of people around him and manifests them to their conscious senses."

"How do you know he's not making up the images himself?" Melchior asked, without looking away from Chandler. He lay unconscious on a hospital bed, an IV dripping into his arm, his ankles, wrists, and waist fastened to the bed by leather straps.

"Suffice it to say that he's produced some rather, 'ah, *singular* images during our time together." The smile flickered at the edges of Keller's mouth again. "However, I think Orpheus *can* manufacture images of his own, once he grows more accustomed to his new ability. But for now he's seems to be like a television, only able to broadcast external data. But there's more."

"Namely?"

"I said Orpheus's power is like a television: it can only broadcast what it receives. But the similarity is deeper: the person supplying the content—the other mind—can, once the channel is open, push thoughts into Chandler's head."

"And you know this because?"

Keller looked up from his clipboard, and this time the smile was broad and constant. Melchior was torn between the urge to vomit or hit him in the face. "The first time I gave Orpheus a dose of LSD and felt him in my mind, I panicked. When I am afraid, I imagine myself in the position of some of my past subjects. In their place. It was so real that if I hadn't locked myself in the room adjoining Chandler's, I am sure I would have killed myself as Agent Logan did."

A part of Melchior was dying to know in what position, exactly, the ex-Nazi had imagined himself, but Keller was still speaking.

"The second time I gave Orpheus the drug, I was more prepared. When I felt him feeling around in my mind, I pushed back, and for a few moments what I concentrated on is what manifested itself around me. It was hard to maintain focus, though, and the illusion faded after just a few seconds. But I think that if someone learned to discipline himself—"

"He could manipulate Chandler without him even knowing it."

"Exactly."

"It's very important that you keep this information from Chandler, Dr. Keller," Melchior said. "Presumably once he learns it, he can also learn to defend against it."

Keller nodded. "Of course, of course. Here," he continued eagerly, "take a look at this." He showed Melchior a couple of sheets of paper from an EEG printout. "This," he said, tapping a wavy line on the top sheet, "is Chandler's beta wave pattern after I gave him a combination of Thorazine and Valium to put him to sleep. And this"—the doctor pulled out the second sheet—"is Chandler's beta wave immediately after an LSD session, before I'd given him anything."

Melchior studied the two documents. "They look the same."

"Exactly! Chandler's nervous system seems to go into a kind of stasis after he's been given LSD. First there's an incredible acceleration—his heart rate reaches two hundred beats per minute, yet at the same time he doesn't seem to feel any cardiac distress. And the trip itself only lasts for an hour or two, even though the normal duration is anywhere from eight to twenty-four. And then immediately afterwards he appears to go into some kind of hibernation so that his body can recover."

"Hibernation?"

"Look," the doctor said, pointing at Chandler through the glass.

"At what?"

"His face."

Melchior looked. "He's a good-looking guy, Doctor, but not exactly my type."

"There's no stubble! It's been at least four days since he shaved, but his cheeks are completely smooth! Nor has he urinated or had a bowel—"

"I get the picture, Doctor. So, what next?"

"There are still a thousand tests to run. But I need a subject. Someone on whom I can gauge the extent and effect of Chandler's abilities."

Melchior looked back at Chandler for a moment, and then his gaze flicked to the right. To a second bed, accoutred with straps like Orpheus's, but empty.

"I was hoping you'd say that."

o   o   o

Chandler felt the needle's prick, the adrenaline entering his blood-stream. For the first time in days he became aware of his body, although it felt heavy, immobile, less flesh and blood than steel sarcophagus. Something flashed far off in the darkness that surrounded him, bright, fiery. The boy! The one who'd led Naz inside him, the one who had tried to save her right before she, before she . . . before she disappeared. He tried to follow but his legs wouldn't obey him, and almost as soon as he'd appeared, the boy winked out of existence. The adrenaline was coursing through his veins now, nudging, prodding, accelerating. *Wake up.* Chandler stared at the after-image of the fiery angel until the last glow died away, and then, reluctantly, he opened his eyes.

Strange, but he knew what the room was going to look like before he saw it. The unpainted drywall, the crooked asbestos tiles in the ceiling, the metal cabinetry. A typical examining room, sure, but he knew this particular one before he opened his eyes. Knew, for example, that there was a wastebasket in the corner behind him. Army green on the outside, black on the inside, rust on the bottom from a mop pushing against it a thousand times.

He turned. There was the can. But how did he know it was there?

"Welcome back to the land of the living."

Chandler jerked his head around even as a wheeled stool creaked up to the side of the bed. He knew he was tied to the bed but he pulled once anyway, felt the restraints bite into his wrists and ankles. A man in his fifties sat on the stool, graying blond hair combed back from a pinched, pale face, white coat draped over his shoulders. Chandler thought he was the one who'd spoken until he saw the second bed off to the right, the second man.

"Howdy," this man said. A big man, with olive skin and curly hair coming free from a layer of brilliantine. The shit-eating grin on his face seemed at odds with the fact that he, too, was tied in place.

"Who are you?" Chandler said.

"You'd be amazed how often I get asked that."

There was a clink, and Chandler turned to see that the older man had set a vial containing clear liquid on a metal tray. More to the point, he had a syringe in his hand, from which he was squeezing the air. A tiny bubble emerged from the tip of the syringe, and Chandler felt an ice cube of fear slide down his back. He pulled at the restraints again, uselessly.

"Where am I? What are you doing with me?"

"Settle down, Mr. Forrestal," the man on the bed said. "You're state property now, no point getting all worked up." He twitched one of his hands against his bonds. "Scratch my nose, would you, Keller?"

The man on the stool ignored him. Instead he wiped the hollow of Chandler's elbow with an alcohol swab. Chandler jerked at the chilly sensation, but of course his arm only moved a fraction of an inch.

"What are you talking about? And what in the hell have you done with Naz?"

"Miss Haverman is no longer of concern."

"I swear to God, if you've hurt her—"

Chandler broke off as the needle entered his arm like a sliver of ice, freezing the blood in his veins.

"What are—what—" It was hard to speak. Even his jaw seemed frozen.

"Relax, Chandler," the man on the bed said. "It's just a little acid. Well, not a little. About two thousand mics, which, if I understand these things, is several hundred times the normal dose."

Almost as quickly as the ice came, it thawed. Within seconds his blood was boiling. Beads of sweat appeared on his skin and popped like balloons, releasing vaporous genies. Already the room was starting to swim.

"You see it happens quickly," Keller said, even as he pulled a second syringe from his pocket. "Faster every time." Chandler expected him to inject the man on the bed, but instead he swabbed his own arm. "I give myself the Thorazine now," he continued, "lest I suffer poor Agent Logan's fate."

Chandler closed his eyes against the rippling walls, but the vision continued to dance behind his shuttered lids. Only—only it had shifted slightly. To the right. It was as though he was seeing the room through the eyes of the man on the bed beside him. When the man turned his head toward Chandler, he had the disconcerting experience of seeing himself with his eyes closed.

"Talk about *mise en abyme*," the man beside him said. "I feel like

I'm inside an Escher drawing. You don't know what you're missing, Doc."

There was a grunt and then a click as the door locked behind Keller. The sound echoed in Chandler's ears like cathedral bells, so loud that he almost missed the other man's question.

"How'd you kill him anyway?"

Chandler squeezed his eyes tighter, but still he saw everything. The man on the bed turned his head from side to side and Chandler saw the room swirl and melt before his eyes.

"Whoa. Heavy." The man's head continued to turn, the room fracturing into a kaleidoscope of colors and sounds. "Miss Haverman struck me as one tough cookie," he continued in a voice that was somewhat distracted, but not confused or overwhelmed. The only other person who'd reacted like that had been Naz—everyone else had been terrified, but this man was excited by what was happening. "But I'm pretty sure she couldn't've got the drop on Eddie, let alone stabbed him in the chest. And Leary Malarkey just ain't the type. Which leaves you. So fill me in. Did you really stab him? Or"—he turned back to Chandler, and once again Chandler saw himself repeat and retreat in an endless, diminishing stream of reflections—"did you use your *mental powers?*"

Chandler opened his eyes, turned to the man next to him.

"Please. I don't want this. Not anymore. Not *again.*"

The man's head jerked forward, back, as if he'd fallen asleep and snapped himself awake. His eyes widened, in fear at first, then wonder. "Jesus H. Christ. I have smoked some serious shit in my life, but this . . . !" He looked back at Chandler, wiggled his hands. "I told Keller not to let me out no matter how much I scream. Somehow I don't think he would anyway. So come on, Chandler. Do your worst. Show me how you got Eddie to kill himself."

But Chandler didn't know what he was doing, and all he could do was repeat his first question.

"Who *are* you?"

The man's eyes floated around the room, sparkling wildly, and a rapturous smile spread across his face like a miser opening the door to his vault and basking in the glow of his gold.

"Talk to me, Chandler. Is what I'm seeing what you're seeing? Is that how it works?"

Chandler thrashed at his bonds helplessly. He turned on his tormentor, shot daggers with his eyes. The man smashed his curly locks into his pillow.

"Yowza!" he said, wincing and laughing at the same time. "Fuck!" He shook his head gingerly. "Do that again."

But Chandler didn't know what he'd done. He stared at the man. His face—the man's face—glistened with sweat. Not as if he were scared or exhausted. No. It was a sexual sheen. The face of a man in a brothel. A Cuban brothel. A slender brown back bent over a pillow, a pair of buttocks thrust in the air, the man's face hovering over it. He saw it in all its disgusting detail, and he saw the man—Melchior, that's what he called himself—see him seeing it.

The smile on Melchior's face grew rapturous.

"What was her name?"

Again Chandler thought of Naz. That's what she'd said to him, in his apartment in Boston. What was her mother's name.

"Saba," he whispered. "A gentle breeze."

"You're not trying hard enough, Chandler," the man said, his voice turning ugly. "Tell me her *name*."

Chandler tried to shake the image of the naked woman out of his mind, but it wouldn't go. Instead it was joined by others. The mutilated body of a man, his skin covered with festering sores—no, not sores. Burns. Cigarette burns. A barn. Gunfire. A machine of some kind. Cracked seams, tangled wires. Was it a—

"Chandler! Concentrate!"

"Carmen," he whispered. "Her name was Carmen."

The man's eyes flashed wildly.

"Oh my fucking *God*. Can you see this, Keller? It's all there! Everything! C'mon, Chandler! Dig deeper! Show me how far it can go."

The man's excitement had a tang like a match lit under your nostrils. It was as if he wanted Chandler to see him in all his grotesqueness, to wallow in the filth of the things he'd done. But Chandler didn't want to see that. He didn't want to see anything, but he couldn't keep the images out of his head. So much violence, so many ways people had died. So many different kinds of people: black, white, brown, yellow, like a *National Geographic* issue devoted solely to war and misery.

Since he couldn't keep Melchior out of his mind—or keep himself out of Melchior's—he tried to push past those horrific images. Or, rather, before them. Before Melchior would have been old enough to serve his country. He was surprised how far he had to go. He knew Melchior was thirty-three, but though he pushed back a decade, a decade and a half, still, all he saw was war. There was another man in a lot of these pictures, an older round-faced fellow with an alcoholic nose and eyes that managed to be both jolly and mean at the same time. Frank. Frank Wisdom. The Wiz. He glowed in Melchior's thoughts like a father—like the kind of father you wanted to kill but, in killing, would become. Chandler followed this man back in Melchior's thoughts, all the way through his teens, through firing practice, language training, essays in coding and code-breaking and the hundred different kinds of stealth, and then suddenly he broke through to the other side.

BC didn't have time to wash Burton's uniform, so he sprayed it inside and out with Lysol. Not that it was dirty—and not that Burton was a Negro—but BC had never worn another person's clothing in his life, and the mere thought of sticking his legs where another man's had been brought goose pimples to his thighs. He wasn't sure how he was going to get the coveralls into the DOJ Building, though. The plan was to enter as Special Agent BC Querrey—it was unlikely anyone at the desk would have heard of his suspension—then become Gerry Burton somewhere inside. Should he put the uniform in a shopping bag? But why would an FBI agent carry a shopping bag into the Department of Justice Building, especially after hours? Should he carry a suitcase? But that would invite questions, and the answers could lead to rumors, and rumors had a way of getting back to Director Hoover. Then he realized: he could put the uniform in his briefcase! No one would ever think there would be *clothes* in a briefcase!

Then he remembered: Melchior had his briefcase.

In the end he used a valise that looked enough like a briefcase that he didn't think anyone would notice, and if they did notice he could just say it was his overnight bag (which in fact it was, and which he'd brought into the office more than a dozen times, but which seemed to acquire a suspicious sheen when he put someone else's clothes in it).

He waved at the guard when he went in. He didn't often work late, but often enough that no one was surprised to see him. What was surprising: the guard waved back, and smiled, too. It felt almost like a benediction.

At the elevator he punched the button for the fourth floor, as always. Once the doors were closed, however, he pressed three and got off there instead. The corridor was deserted, and he used Gerry Burton's key to let himself into the maintenance closet. He took his tie off but left the rest of his suit on, figuring it would help fill out Burton's voluminous uniform, which hung on him like a Santa suit on a scarecrow. He was just about to head out when he saw his shoes sticking out from the pant legs—pointed black wingtips so shiny he could see his face in them, even in the dim light. Definitely not janitor shoes. He looked about for a pair of galoshes or something, but, seeing nothing, grabbed a mop instead. It had been put away damp, reeked of mildew—BC was thinking that if he *did* work for the custodial department, he would have had to report someone—and quickly, before he could stop himself, he swabbed the slimy strands over his fifteen-dollar Florsheims, even turned the mop over and scratched at them with the rough wooden handle. Only when the reflection of his face was gone did he pull Burton's ID necklace from his suit and hang it over his head, and, taking a deep breath, he pushed open the closet door.

"Goodness gracious! You startled me!"

BC jumped so high he nearly hit the top of the door frame. A Negro woman, fifty or sixty years old but no bigger than a ten-year-old girl, stood just outside the door, a cleaning cart off to one side. BC had reached reflexively for his holster, which, fortunately, was empty, and behind the zipper of Burton's uniform to boot, so it just looked like he was pawing at his chest.

The woman stared at him expectantly, and he realized she was waiting for him to say something. What did janitors and cleaning ladies say to one another? The thought of Gerry Burton and "Ashley" popped into his head, and he felt a blush burn his cheeks. He opened his mouth, let whatever would come out come out:

"Shee-ut."

The woman chuckled. "No need to get nasty. I won't tell nobody. Now get on outta my way before somebody comes."

He took the stairs to the fourth floor. As he pushed through the door he stopped short. This was his floor. His hallway. Why hadn't he thought of it ahead of time? Anyone who saw him would recognize him instantly. Would wonder what in the world he was doing in a janitor's uniform. Why in the hell hadn't he waited a couple more hours before he came in, when he would be much less likely to run into someone he knew? As a detective, he knew this was why criminals get caught: they're so focused on the object of their crime that they forget the thousand and one things standing between them and their goal. He himself had caught a dozen men that way, in the year and a half he spent in Profiling before his transfer to COINTELPRO. He should have known better! But he was here now. There was nowhere to go but forward. He shoved his right hand in his pocket and wrapped his fingers around Naz's ring. He would let fate decide if he was meant to find her or not.

He trudged toward the director's office, letting his head hang and his shoulders hunch up around his face as much as possible. He should've brought some kind of cap. He should have mussed his hair, but really, there was no hair to muss. He'd kept his standing Wednesday evening appointment with the barber last night. Fortunately, even though he heard plenty of activity through open doors, the corridor itself was deserted, and eventually—he didn't remember the hallway being this long!—he found himself in front of the office of Helen Gandy, the director's secretary. He glanced up and down, then ducked in the open door. He started to close it, then, worried it might draw attention, went straight to the double doors that led to the director's office. He put his ear to one, heard nothing, took a six-inch metal ruler out of his pocket and slipped it between the doors, angled it back until it touched the tongue. Then, bracing himself, he leaned all his weight into the right door so that the lock's tongue emerged a fraction of an inch from its socket in the left. At the same time he applied pressure on the ruler, and it slid down the curve of the tongue just enough to push it into its housing in the right door. Without the slightest sound, the door slid open, and there it was:

The Vault.

The director's famed—and feared—personal files. Ten black metal cabinets, five on each side of the narrow hallway that led to the director's office. Yet the material they contained—compromising information on Hollywood stars, leading journalists and politicians, not to mention every president since Calvin Coolidge, who'd appointed Hoover head of the (not-yet-Federal) Bureau of Investigation all the way back in 1924—was enough to have earned their owner a forty-year sinecure as the nation's top cop. Though there were any number of more secure locations they could have been stored, the director insisted the cabinets be left here for all to pass through as they made their way to his sanctum sanctorum. The hubris was unbelievable. Ten filing cabinets containing enough material to ruin thousands of careers, bring down administrations and corporations and probably one or two governments. All of it guarded by the same kind of lock you'd put on a bedroom door.

An elevator dinged in the corridor. BC started, then stepped into the Vault quickly, pulled the door closed. Now it was just him and the files—standard-issue four-drawer Twenty Gauge cabinets with locks that could be picked by a hairpin, nail file, or, in BC's case, a ghost he'd made from an old padlock key.

BC scanned the cabinets. The drawers were labeled minimally: "A—*Ab irato*"; "BARKER, Ma—BIRMINGHAM, Ala." "CARTER, James—CIA." The file took up the entire back half of the drawer and extended into the next one, two, no, *three* drawers, a block of tens of thousands of sheets of paper the size of a bale of hay. BC stared at it in disbelief. It would take hours to search it all.

In fact, it took only minutes. J. Edger Hoover had made his name by proving that information is power, but only if you have ready access to it. In 1919, during the Palmer Raids, he compiled a list of more than 150,000 so-called "hyphenated Americans" (the phrase was President Wilson's), i.e., potentially subversive ethnic nationals with radical affiliations or sympathies; 10,000 were arrested, about 550 deported, including Emma Goldman (who, not surprisingly, didn't like the Soviet Union nearly as much once she had to live there). In order to achieve that kind of targeting precision, Hoover developed an indexing system that made it easy to move through his list quickly and efficiently, and, forty years later, his files were still as clearly—pedantically—demarcated. In a folder in the third drawer clearly marked "ORPHEUS, Project" BC found no fewer than six memoranda. The information itself was fairly banal. "Agent 'Ted Morganthau' (real name LOGAN, Edward), provided 5,000 micrograms LSD to HITCHCOCK, William for Millbrook colony ('Castalia') on 2/4/63"; "ALPERT, Richard, confirmed homosexual, which fact acknowledges openly; unlikely FBI can exploit"; and so on. But on one sheet of paper BC found what he was looking for:

9/3/63. JARRELL reports great activity at/interest in
Millbrook; SCHEIDER (See: TSS) believes LEARY might
have found Orpheus.

There were no other mentions of the name Jarrell in the Orpheus file, nor in the rest of the CIA section. BC locked that cabinet, then opened the drawer marked "Jackson, MS—KENNEDY, Joseph" and found a single entry under "Jarrell":

```
JARRELL, Charles. Ph.D. mathematics and biology
(1949), Columbia; M.D. (1954), Johns Hopkins. Assumed
identity "Virgil Parker" June 1956. Residence
established 117 New York Ave. N.W. July '56. Applied
CIA February '57. Approved May '58, placed in
Technical Services Section, Medical Engineering
Dept., under direct supervision SCHEIDER, Joseph,
July '59. Status: ACTIVE.
```

There was no further information in the Jarrell file nor, when BC checked, under Parker either. BC went back to the CIA file to check under Virgil Parker just in case, but all he found was a note to "See: JARRELL, Charles." It was a bread crumb, but it was his only lead out of the forest. Or, rather, back into it.

He was just about to leave when he stopped, went back to the files. "HARDING, Warren G.—HOOVER, Ivery." But there was nothing on Naz. He checked on Mary Meyer next, but, though there was a folder marked "MEYER, Mary Pinchot," the only thing in it was a note:

```
Contents removed for review, 11/5/1963. JEH/hg.
```

He'd just pushed the drawer closed when he heard a voice outside the door to the Vault. The first was familiar, although he didn't place it immediately. The second, however, was unmistakable.

"No, Clyde," J. Edgar Hoover said, "I think the intelligence is genuine."

New Orleans. A hot spring day in 1942.

The Evangelical Lutheran Bethlehem Orphanage.

A twelve-year-old boy, skinny as a fence post save for the mop of dark curls framing his round, dusky face, is shooting marbles with a group of other boys ranging in age from six to sixteen. He wins only one out of three tosses, but Chandler knows he's faking it. Roping the crowd in, working them up, making them think they have a chance. Deception came early to . . . to Melchior. So that really was his name.

Suddenly the boy looks up from his game. On his bed in the future, Chandler thinks Melchior is somehow looking at him. But no. He's watching a pair of men walk up the long narrow sidewalk that leads to the side yard of the orphanage. One is tall, with a soft-cheeked face that belies his fit frame: he isn't fat yet, but will be one day. The other is shorter, darker, walks with a slight limp. His beard is as sharp as Mephistopheles'. Melchior is sure the man knows this and courts the comparison. He looks like the devil. The devil in a light cashmere jacket and polished wingtips that seem as sharp as his beard.

But Melchior isn't as interested in the men as he is in their target: a child playing by himself in the grassless dust off to the side of the yard. A small-mouthed boy of three or four, his russet hair flecked with gold from long hours in the sun. He squats in his short pants as though he's shitting his drawers, but Melchior knows he is in fact drawing in the dirt. The same face over and over again: his father, who died before he was born. In the hierarchy of lost parents at an orphanage, this is a category unto itself, and even though the boy isn't really an orphan—his mother leaves him here Monday through Friday while she works, picks him up on the weekends she's not looking for a new husband—the boy still has a kind of totemic status. Like Jesus, he was born without a father.

The name comes to Chandler before he even realizes he is curious. Caspar.

Melchior has adopted Caspar in the way bullies sometimes adopt the helpless: this one and this one only will I protect. A large part of Melchior protects Caspar just for the many chances it gives him to fight—the child is so moony that older boys cannot resist picking on him—but there is some part of him that genuinely loves his charge. Loves him like a farmer loves his only hog, right up until the time he slices its throat.

The two men have reached Caspar. Melchior can tell from the way they approach him that they picked him out ahead of time. The bearded one takes notes in a spiral-bound notebook even as the tall man squats down in a kind of giant-sized replica of Caspar. He points at the picture in the dust. Melchior sees his mouth move, imagines his insipid question. *Whatcha drawing there, young feller?* He is pleased to see that Caspar's mouth doesn't move.

"Say, are you playing or what?"

One of the boys is impatient. One of the older, bigger boys. None of the smaller ones would dare question him in this way. Melchior turns, glances at the iridescent orbs scattered in front of the brick wall. Nine of them—his is the tenth and final shot. The farthest is a little more than an inch from the wall. He needs to shoot inside it to win.

He turns back to Caspar. The bearded man is talking to him now. Caspar has fallen back on his ass, looks up at the man as if transfixed. The man's beard cuts the air like a fang.

"I *said*, are you gonna—"

Melchior shoots without looking. The chorus of groans tells him he has won even before he turns to collect his money and marbles, then starts across the playground.

"I thought I told you not to talk to strangers."

Caspar looks up, scared at first, then brightening at the sight of Melchior. He points at his drawings.

"They was asking me about my daddy."

"You don't have no daddy. Now, run along."

Caspar stares confusedly between Melchior and the men. It is clear he wants to do what Melchior says, but the men are grown-ups. They trump him. He takes a half step backward, a half step forward.

"My daddy's in heaven."

The tall man stands, gives Melchior an amused, annoyed look. He seems to think the mere fact of his gaze will banish Melchior, and when the boy stands his ground, he says, "This here's none of your business, boy. Whyn't *you* run along?"

His accent is deep but not local. Southern but not city. Gentry, like the people whose house his aunt cleaned, before he got to be too much for her and she sent him here.

The bearded man looks not at him but at Caspar.

"Look at his face, Frank. See how torn he is—he doesn't know whether to obey his friend or us. He's trying to think of a way he can win both our approval."

"What are you guys, a couple-a perverts? Can't you screw each other instead-a little boys?"

The man called Frank whistles. He is entertained, but it is a nasty kind of pleasure—the kind the Romans took in watching Christians being mauled by lions and barbarians. Melchior knows immediately that not only will this man hit a kid, he'll enjoy it.

"You sure got a pair, don't you, boy? Got a mouth, too, and I don't like that. Now, hightail your ass outta here, or I'm-a stick my foot so far up it you're gonna taste shoe leather."

Melchior holds his ground. Gives the man a look that tells him if he hits him he'd better knock him *out*, because he *will* fight back.

"You been drinking," he says, "cheap shit, too," and turns on his heel. He walks not toward the orphanage but toward the withered live oak in the northern corner of the playground. His pace is steady, neither too fast nor too slow. The last thing he hears is Frank saying,

"The first thing we gonna teach you, son, is not to hang around with niggers."

Only when he reaches the live oak does he turn around. The bearded man has taken Caspar's hand and is leading him toward the gate. Caspar walks slowly, looking around in every direction. Frank has an impatient look on his face, like he just wants to kite the kid under his arm and get going. He, too, is looking around.

By now Melchior has retrieved his slingshot, and he pulls one of the marbles he has just won from his pocket.

"Timor mortis exultat me."

The words come to his lips unbidden, and he pauses with the marble in the pocket of his weapon. After his mother disappeared, the nuns had taught him to say the Office of the Dead as though she'd died rather than run off. The only phrase he remembered was *timor mortis conturbat me,* "the fear of death disturbs me," and that only because he'd come across a variation of it a few years earlier when he read *The Once and Future King: timor mortis exultat me*—"the fear of death excites me"—which warriors said before going into battle. He doesn't know why the phrase comes to his lips now, but even as he releases the first shot, he knows that it will stay with him for the rest of his life.

The marble catches the bearded man in the temple. He screams and falls to the ground. *Timor mortis exultat me:* it's not the warrior's fear of death that excites him, but his enemy's, and as Melchior watches the bearded man crawl like a scared dog behind a withered primrose, he thinks, Oh yes, he'll remember this sensation forever.

The man called Frank is reaching for the inside pocket of his coat like a heavy in a gangster movie, but before he can pull his hand out, Melchior's second shot catches him in the cheek. He staggers backward but doesn't fall or cry out. But he doesn't take his hand out of his jacket either.

"The next one takes out an eye," Melchior calls quickly, calmly. "Now, let go of him and get the hell outta here."

The bearded man is cowering behind the bush, but Frank is looking at the blood on his fingers with wide-eyed wonderment. A huge smile splits his face.

"You see that, Joe? He made that shot at twenty-five yards."

A prick in his arm; sludge filling his veins, his brain. A terrific weight that seemed to press down on him from inside and out at the same time. The room returned, fuzzy edged, its colors paled to duns and grays. Keller was pulling a syringe from his arm.

"Enough for today," he said.

As an irresistible fatigue sapped the energy from his limbs, Chandler's head lolled to the side. There he was: Melchior. His eyes were closed and his clothes disheveled and drenched with sweat, but a strange smile was plastered on his face.

Chandler's own eyes were drooping as Melchior's opened. He looked over at Chandler, his expression exhausted but satisfied, like a man who's just been serviced by his favorite whore.

"We gotta do that again," he said. *"Soon."*

There was nowhere to hide in the Vault, so BC ran into the director's office. It, too, was wide open. No closets, no nooks and crannies, not even a couch to scurry behind. The largest object in the room was the desk. If Hoover sat down, BC would be found instantly, but it was his only shot.

As he ducked behind the desk, he noticed the curtains on the window: thick blue muslin draperies that billowed all the way to the floor. Without giving himself time to think, he stepped behind the nearest one even as the key turned in the door to the Vault. As the curtain stilled around his body like a mummy's bandages, he remembered the director's story about Amenwah, although the truth is he felt more like Polonius. He hoped Hoover had left his sword at home that day.

The door opened and the director's voice sailed into the room.

"Well, we'll just have to put the squeeze on him tomorrow morning. A Junghans would be a rare prize indeed."

Junghans? The name rang a bell, but BC couldn't place it. German possibly, or Dutch, neither of which was the Bureau's province. Perhaps a smuggling ring? BC tried to concentrate, but it was hard, with the director's chair squeaking a few inches in front of him and dust tickling his nostrils. He bit back a sneeze. His hand was in his pocket, squeezing Naz's ring as though, like the Ring of Gyges, it could make him invisible.

A drawer opened, papers rustled. "Billy was telling me about a little place in Oak Hill the other day."

"Really?" the voice of Associate Director Tolson said. "The land of lawn jockeys and chipped chamber pots?"

"Billy says he found a John Pennington gravy boat there."

"No!"

"He says he did. I'll believe it when I see it."

"I once saw a Pennington butter dish with a group of Chinamen fishing for carp, or whatever they fish for in China. I tell you, you could practically hear the wind rustle in the reeds."

Now BC had to bite back a laugh as well as a sneeze. Here he was, a fly on the wall in the office of J. Edgar Hoover, and the director and his second in command were discussing gravy boats and butter dishes!

"Ah, here they are. Leave a note for Helen to order me another pair tomorrow, would you, Clyde."

"Already did." A pause, then: "Your dinner disagreeing with you, John?"

"What? No. Just"—an audible sniff—"someone used too much Lysol when they cleaned tonight."

A chuckle. "I'll have someone fired, okay, John?"

The chair squeaked as Hoover stood up. "Very funny, Clyde. I want them shot." A guffaw, then: "Come on, let's go home."

Footsteps receded across the carpet.

"So'd you hear about Caspar?"

"The friendly ghost?"

"Just came back from Mexico City. Spent a few days trying to get a visa to Russia."

"Didn't he just come back from there?"

"Last year."

"Interesting. I wonder what the Company's cooking up now."

"The Dallas office sent a man to his house twice, but he's been conveniently out both times, so they're going to pay him a visit where he wo—"

A sputtering motorcycle on the street below drowned out the director's voice, and by the time it sped away the door to the Vault had closed. BC waited a moment to make sure they were gone, then let out the biggest sneeze of his life.

Melchior did his best to relax on the flight back to DC. It was hard. His brain was whirring and whizzing around like clock parts spun free from each other, cogs, gears, levers, and arrows all floating free inside the vast cavernous space that was his mind. Because that's what Chandler had done. He'd made Melchior's brain real to him. Physical. Not physical like a bunch of cells, but physical like a space. A place. An underground city populated by memories so far gone that he'd forgotten he'd forgotten them. Chandler'd walked around his mind like a beat cop, poking his nose in this door, peeping through that window. Who knew how much he'd seen, how much he'd learned before Melchior, with a supreme effort of will, had been able to lead him to that particular memory. To the one event in his life he'd taken greater care to conceal than anything else. He suspected that he'd only half chosen it. That Chandler had gone looking too. For the thing that had turned Melchior into Melchior. Well, it certainly explained the narrative of his life. Whether it explained his character was anybody's guess.

And then . . . what? What the fuck had Chandler done? He'd made it *real* somehow. Melchior knew it had just been an illusion. But there was no way you could've convinced him of that while it was going on. He'd been twelve years old again, Caspar was four, the Wiz was still *compos mentis,* and Doc Scheider was still looking for guinea pigs to turn into zombies. But at the same time he was still Melchior, the thirty-three-year-old field agent whose two decades of experience changing identities the way other people change clothes had made him able to see this history as just another illusion, just another legend. He'd watched himself with an unparseable combination of hope and hatred, unsure which were his feelings now and which the feelings of the boy in the orphanage. And even as he raised the slingshot and fired at the Wiz, he couldn't decide if he was making the biggest mistake of his life. If he should have killed the man who stole his life—stole his life but gave him a new one in exchange—rather than impressing him with his marksmanship.

And now, like the Wiz, he'd made his own discovery. As assets go, Chandler was off the charts. There'd never been anything like him before, and if the information Melchior had gathered on Ultra and Orpheus was complete, there never would be again. It wasn't some new drug that Joe Scheider had cooked up that had turned Chandler into Orpheus and could create a legion of similarly super-powered soldiers. Logan had given the same cocktail to too many people for that to be true. No, it was something inherent in Chandler. Call it a gene, call it a receptor, call it the Gate of Orpheus, but if anyone else out there possessed it, the chance of that person getting hold of the kind of pure LSD that Chandler had been given was virtually nonexistent. All Melchior had to do now was figure out how to control him—though he had a pretty good idea how to do that. Because all the time Chandler had been poking around in his brain, he'd been looking for something. For someone. Naz. Melchior was pretty sure he hadn't found out what had happened to her, because if he had, he would have ripped Melchior's mind apart. Four days he'd known her, and he'd apparently spent several of those in a delirium. Yet the immensity of his desire was such that Melchior knew that as long as he could keep Naz's fate a secret, he could control Chandler. Melchior had bedded women on five continents, but he'd never felt a thousandth of what Chandler felt for Naz. She must have been something else in the sack.

It was funny that he hadn't seen what had happened to her though. He'd missed a few things, chief among them Melchior's real name, and Caspar's. Who knows, maybe it was because it'd been so long since he'd thought of himself as anything other than Melchior, or thought of Caspar as anything other than Caspar. Or maybe Chandler was so overwhelmed by his newfound abilities that he couldn't fully control where they took him—if Melchior's brain was a city, then it was a labyrinth on the order of Venice or Paris, and Chandler lacked a map and could only fumble about blindly, looking for beacons or signposts that stood out in the maze. That day in the orphanage was certainly a landmark. It was the day the Wiz gave him a chance at a life that mattered. But the name he'd had that day, that name hadn't meant shit. If someone called it out on the street, he wouldn't even turn around. Caspar, of course, still had to go by his real name, but it was a hollow symbol at this point, as unreflective of the man who bore it as the dog-eared copy of Marx he carried into boot camp.

The love, though. That had been real. Melchior had loved pale, pudgy, defenseless Caspar more than he'd ever loved himself, and, too, he knew Caspar's first loyalty would always be to him, no matter how much Joe Scheider fucked with his head.

If all was going to plan, he should've been back in the States, an American "defector" having been "doubled" by the KGB. He wondered if Drew Everton or whoever the hell debriefed him would put any more stock in his intel than they had in Melchior's, or if Caspar would end up out on his ass. In which case, who knows? Maybe the friendly ghost was looking for a new job.

The thought of Caspar reminded Melchior of BC. The two men shared a quality of naivete and misplaced trust in authority figures. He'd done his best to destroy Beau's faith in men like J. Edgar Hoover and John F. Kennedy during their train ride, but he doubted he'd succeeded. The young FBI agent was simply too much of a momma's boy, and it sounded like his mother had been a piece of work. But who knows what kind of effect Millbrook had had on him? Melchior couldn't help but wonder if BC had found the ring he'd hidden in the cottage wall, and, if so, if he'd taken the bait. In a way, Melchior almost hoped he hadn't, because if he did manage to track down Melchior, Melchior would have to kill him. BC may have been a suit without a soul, but he was no Drew Everton. Drew Everton was someone Melchior wouldn't mind killing. Not at all.

Just then a stewardess came down the aisle. She refilled his drink and plumped a pillow behind his head, leaning so close that Melchior could've bitten her tit if he'd wanted to.

"Do you need anything else?" the stewardess asked, then, almost reluctantly, added, "Sir."

"No thank you, darling," Melchior said, and anyone looking at his smile would've thought he'd already banged her. "I'm pretty sure I got everything I need."

Again the prick, again the swimming to consciousness. Chandler felt like a fish irresistibly drawn to a fisherman's hook yet thrown back each time for being too small. When would he be big enough to keep? Which begged the question: when would he be big enough to kill?

Keller stood over him with the usual array of tools. His movements were slow but precise, and Chandler knew even without trying to push into the doctor's brain that he'd dosed himself with Thorazine already. The drug turned Keller's brain into something soft yet impenetrable. Chandler had pushed at it last night but had never been able to get inside. Now, with the LSD gone from his system, all he felt was a staticky void where Keller's consciousness should have been, and, pulling once against his restraints, he closed his eyes and waited for the next shot. But this time Keller had something to say to him first.

"Mr. Melchior was nice enough to provide you with some company. I think you will find him very interesting."

Chandler opened his eyes, looked around the little room again. All he saw was Keller, preparing the shot of LSD as he had yesterday, the empty bed where Melchior had lain, the dark window beyond. But at the edge of his perception he felt a tingling. Not Keller's brain, but someone else's. A friable consciousness that seemed to crumble when he pushed at it, glinting like dust motes in a beam of sunlight. It was like no other mind he'd ever felt before. He found himself wondering if it was an infant's, or a monkey's. He was almost eager for the shot, to find out what kind of brain this was.

Keller injected him and left the room. A moment later light erupted from the other side of the dark window. A disheveled—decrepit—man stood in the middle of a room about the size of the one Chandler was in, though in lieu of hospital accoutrement it was filled with stacks and stacks of sagging shoe boxes. The man was clearly itinerant—his clothes bedraggled and filthy, his hair unwashed in so long that it hung off his head in tangled ropes an inch thick. A beard as coarse and matted as a sheet of felt covered his mouth and fell halfway down his chest. His features were so lost inside filth and hair that he could have been twenty-five or fifty-five.

A crackle, and Keller's voice came over a speaker mounted on the wall.

"This is Sidewalk Steve."

Chandler felt a flush spreading over his skin, knew it was from the amphetamines Keller had used to wake him up. But the itch underneath the flush was the acid, working its way toward his brain.

"Sidewalk Steve is a literary man, like you. He is a great fan of Kenneth Kesey."

The acid filled him with a nervous energy, and Chandler tried to fight the twitching in his arms. A pink slit had appeared in Sidewalk Steve's beard: a smile. His grubby fingers were snatching at invisible shapes in the air.

"*One Flew Over the Cuckoo's Nest* is a turgid example of solipsistic, nihilistic American romanti-romanti-romanticism," Chandler managed to spit out, doing his best to resist the insane images beginning to flicker into his consciousness from Sidewalk Steve's.

"He claims to have taken more than a thousand acid trips," Keller continued. "He is also a diagnosed schizophrenic. The line between reality and fantasy ceased to exist for him long ago, so if you're going to make an impression on him, you're going to have to try harder than you have before. Nothing you can pull from his mind will scare him. You will have to supply something of your own."

Chandler closed his eyes, which brought out Sidewalk Steve's visions more clearly. Polychromatic bubbles floated in the air around him. When he touched them, they popped, revealing naked, shockingly nubile pixies, who flitted away from his fingers.

"What about . . . an image of . . . your face?"

"Sidewalk Steve is a bad man. He needs to be punished."

Sidewalk Steve's brain was like a cross between a magnet and quicksand. It seemed to suck Chandler in and down, into a soup of chicken broth and breasts and rainbows. Chandler opened his eyes and concentrated on the bare wall in front of him, tried to pull his brain from Steve's.

"I—I don't understand."

"He has shirked his duty to class and country, just as you have. I want you to punish him the way you know *you* deserve to be punished. In return, Miss Haverman will not be harmed while she remains in custody."

"Naz!" Chandler felt his heart beat faster, and in the other room Sidewalk Steve jumped backward, as who knew what apparition appeared in front of him. "Naz is alive?"

There was a pause, and Chandler could have sworn he heard Keller curse under his breath.

"Is she alive?" Chandler demanded again, jerking uselessly at his restraints. "Where is she? You have to tell me where she—"

"I want you to show Sidewalk Steve how bad you think he is," Keller's voice practically shrieked from the loudspeaker. "I want *you* to devise his punishment. Do you understand me, Orpheus? Don't take something from Steve's mind. Make it up yourself, and show it to him."

"Where—is—*Naz?*" Chandler demanded, and in the other room Sidewalk Steve jumped again, whirled around, jumped back one more time, his hands batting at the air.

"The only way you will see Miss Haverman again is if you do as I tell you. Punish Steve, Chandler. Punish him as you deserve to be punished, and I will make arrangements for you to see Miss Haverman again."

"Please," Chandler hissed. "Don't hurt her. I'll do anything, just don't hurt her."

In the other room, Sidewalk Steve was swatting at the air, squinting and ducking as though a swarm of bees were buzzing out of the sky around him. He smacked at his skin, danced from one leg to the other as though snakes or crocs snapped at his legs.

"It's your fault we have her," Keller said implacably. "If you'd done what you were supposed to, you would've never ended up here. Never would have dragged Miss Haverman into it with you."

Keller's disembodied voice had acquired an echo, and an outline as well. Pink, puffy clouds came out of the speaker like particolored smoke. In the other room, Sidewalk Steve was tossing himself from one wall to another. The shoe boxes stacked in the room added their flimsy shape to whatever imagined terrors attacked him, and he grabbed them and ripped them to pieces, but whatever was attacking him wouldn't be kept away. His mouth was open, but no sound penetrated the window.

"Please," Chandler whispered, "don't hurt her."

"Oh, but she *is* hurting," Keller hissed through the speaker, the pink smoke coiling out like a serpent, "and it's all your fault. Now the only way for you to save her is to punish Steve. Create a hell for him and drop him in it. Do it, Chandler. Do it!"

"LET HER GO!" Chandler screamed, and from the other room came the faint echo of a reply.

"No."

But there was no stopping it now. It walked through the door of Sidewalk Steve's room like a flaming ghost. Chandler remembered it from Millbrook. From the cottage, right before Naz had been taken. The boy made of fire. But who was it, and why did it keep coming back? Was it friend or enemy?

But the apparition had no time for any of these questions. It swept Sidewalk Steve up in blazing arms and engulfed him in a corona of flames. Sidewalk Steve writhed in the inferno for two or three agonized seconds, then fell to the floor, his brain as blank as a freshly washed blackboard. Only his twitching fingers and feet gave any sign that he was alive.

But it wasn't quite over yet. The flaming boy turned toward Chandler and stared at him through the window. Its eyes were empty, dark sockets, its mouth an open, questioning O, but what it was asking, what it offered, Chandler had no idea.

"Who *are* you?" he whispered.

But the boy just stared at him for another moment, and then, sputtering like a pilot light, he disappeared.

The linoleum floor of the Salvation Army was coated with a layer of dirt that crunched beneath the soles of BC's shoes. A mildewy tang floated through the moist air, over which came the faint sound of Christian Muzak and the hum of innumerable fluorescent tubes.

BC had never set foot in a thrift store before and was amazed at how big it was—a gymnasium-sized space filled with clothes that had been worn by other people. Not just worn. Worn in. Worn out. Though the silver-wigged old lady at the counter assured him all the clothes were washed before they were put on the racks, BC saw innumerable sweat-stained armpits and yellowed collars and any number of faint and not-so-faint bloodstains. There was even an entire rack of used underwear: limp boxers and listless jockey shorts, their leg bands stretched and flaccid from being pulled on a thousand times, their flies sadly puckered from who knew what kind of fumbled or fevered gropings. Though BC felt that it was somehow violating the industry standard not to take a disguise all the way down to the skin, there was *no way in hell* he was putting on another man's skivvies.

Which still left him with the dilemma of trousers, shirt, jacket, hat. It was reasonable to assume Charles Jarrell's house was being watched— at any rate, it was not unreasonable to assume. And, too, he wasn't sure how Jarrell would react to a particularly G-man-looking G-man showing up on his doorstep. He might run, and BC would lose the closest thing to a lead he had to Melchior. BC had to get Jarrell to open the door. After that, he would worry about getting him to talk.

Many of the shirts had names sewn over the left breast—bowling shirts mostly, but also mechanic and gas jockey and repairman's uniforms, the thick, shiny threads of their embroidered names often in better condition than the threadbare garments onto which they'd been stitched. That was American job security: your name, on a shirt. You knew you were there for a while. The names flashed by like index cards until:

CB

Red letters, green background. But that wasn't what caught BC's eye. It was, rather, the words below the name:

Hoover Vacuums

How could he resist?

It took twenty more minutes to find pants that matched the shirt's green, a belt, a pair of battered shoes (he wasn't about to destroy another pair of Florsheims). But the real coup was the cap. It wasn't an actual Hoover cap, but it did bear the motto "Suck It Up." After waving it around in what was probably a futile effort to dislodge any lice eggs, BC tried it on, glanced in the mirror. But even through the healthy coating of dust on the glass, all he saw was a G-man in a goofy cap.

For some unfathomable reason the cashier had to record each purchase in a notebook.

"Pa-a-ants," she said, drawing out the word as she scrawled it into her spiral-bound notebook. "Twen-ty-fi-ive cennttssss. Shi-i-irt, twenty-five cents. Sho-o-oes, fifty. Ca-a-ap, fifteen." BC felt like a barbarian standing in front of a Roman tax assessor tallying up the worthlessness of his life.

The woman held up the belt, which, though not snakeskin, was every bit as wrinkled and cracked.

"I'll just give you that," she said. "Will that be all?"

BC was about to nod his head when he stopped.

"Just one thing. Where'd you get your wig?"

At 10:36 p.m., Keller made a final note in his log:

"BOTH SUBJECTS SLEEPING."

Sidewalk Steve had ripped hundreds of shoe boxes into confetti, which he'd burrowed inside of like a hamster or gerbil. There was some interesting theta wave activity on Chandler's EEG, which Keller suspected was some kind of deep dreaming: a fantasy taking place at a level before cognition, before consciousness even. Tomorrow the doctor would hook Sidewalk Steve up to the EEG to see if, as he suspected, Chandler was somehow able to produce his images in other people's brains, as opposed to a peripheral stimulation of the optic nerve. If that was indeed the case, they would be irresistible. You wouldn't be seeing them (or hearing them or feeling them): you would be *thinking* them, and your mind wouldn't be able to distinguish them from reality, no matter how fantastical they seemed. Fire would seem to burn you, bullets to pierce your skin. It was quite possible that Chandler could kill you with his thoughts—with your thoughts, rather, manipulated so that your body couldn't tell the difference between an imaginary knife in the heart and a real one. How Melchior'd come out unscathed was anyone's guess. "I'm used to living in a fantasy world" was all he'd said before he left, and, well, he was CIA. One was tempted to take him at his word.

But all that was for another day. Right now the doctor's brain felt stuffed with cotton batting. Conducting scientific experiments while on Thorazine was difficult to say the least. Among other things, he needed to see if he could add some kind of amphetamine to the Thorazine to improve his own functionality. But for now he needed to sleep. He could examine the data with a clearer head in the morning.

Chandler could feel Keller moving outside his room, but the doctor's brain remained closed to him. He was like a finger pressed against a taut scrim, discernible in outline only. But at least Chandler knew when he was there—and when he left.

He waited twenty minutes to make sure. Only then did he attempt to fire himself up again. It was difficult. He was so tired. All he wanted to do was sleep. In fact, he *was* sleeping. What he wanted was to be in a coma. But he had work to do. And it was the doctor who had shown him how to do it. It wasn't going to be easy, however. Not on him. And not on Sidewalk Steve either.

Deep inside his paper cocoon, warm, sweating, *safe,* Sidewalk Steve felt his body start to change. His muscles, grown slack from a diet of scavenged sugars and starches, began to firm, to bulk. His bones, soft from years without calcium or protein, hardened, lengthened. He had known the dark man and the mad scientist wanted to change what he was. He had thought they wanted to make him into a monster. But now he realized: they wanted to make him a hero. A superhero. A super soldier, to be precise.

Captain America.

He'd been Sidewalk Steve's favorite hero when he was growing up, not least because they shared a name, but also because Steve Rogers had been a bullied weakling like Sidewalk Steve, only to be transformed by the Super-Soldier serum into an avenging angel. Now he, Sidewalk Steve, would take up that mantle.

He wasn't sure how long he'd been in the stasis capsule. Several months, no doubt: it would've taken a while for the serum to achieve its full transformation of his body. But when the capsule's cover hissed open, Sidewalk Steve felt as though he was emerging from a single restful night's sleep.

He caught a glimpse of himself in the mirror mounted in the wall. His muscles bulged through his rags—a bit more Incredible Hulk than Captain America, but hey, this was a new era, right? Men in tights probably wouldn't be taken seriously by the average American.

Now, to get out of this cell.

The door appeared to be made from tempered steel. It looked like it wouldn't budge if a speeding truck rammed into it. But he was more than a speeding truck. He was Sidewalk Steve.

He slammed a foot into the center of the door. It rattled on its hinges like an alarm clock, but remained in place. The vibration traveled up the bones of his ankle. For one brief moment it felt painful—it felt like tibia and fibula were splintering along their seams—but then the sensation passed, was nothing more than a tingle, a tickle. He was Sidewalk Steve. He was indestructible.

Again he kicked. He felt the door give, just slightly. A small dent appeared in the steel sheet.

He set his mouth in a scowl of grim determination. This was going to take a while.

On the other side of the wall, Chandler heard the dull thuds of Sidewalk Steve's foot striking the door. He also felt the stress fractures in the man's ankle, the multiplying microbreaks in his tarsals. It took all his concentration to keep the image of the invincible hero front and center in Sidewalk Steve's mind, to suppress what would have been paralyzing agony as the bones of his foot and leg splintered and ground against one another.

It took fifteen minutes for Sidewalk Steve to kick down the door, which was in fact made of steel, but was fortunately hollow. When, finally, it buckled on its hinges, Sidewalk Steve's leg also buckled—or, rather, snapped just below the knee—but as he fell to the floor Chandler managed to switch the image in the vagrant's brain: he was a werewolf now. The full moon was shining down on him through a skylight, causing him to transform into his half-human, half-lupine state.

On all fours, Sidewalk Steve crawled from his cell. He sniffed at the locked door next to his, smelled the imprisoned damsel on the far side of the wall. He hoped his strange appearance wouldn't frighten the poor maiden out of her wits.

He didn't want to admit it, but his leg hurt. Well, heroes felt pain too, but they kept going anyway. That's what made them heroes.

Nevertheless, he trotted down the hall in the opposite direction. No need to kick down a second door if he could find a key.

The hall spilled onto a large open space crowded with tables piled high with lab equipment. He went from table to table until he found a set of keys that he picked up in his mouth, then galloped back to the other locked cell. Once there, he realized he needed a hand again, to open the door. As he transitioned back to his human shape the pain in his leg hit him. He wobbled, spots danced in front of his eyes, his spasming fingers dropped the keys.

Concentrate, Chandler! a voice screamed in his brain. He didn't know who Chandler was, but there wasn't time to worry about that. A damsel needed saving.

It took both hands to lift the key chain, and they were shaking so badly that it took a dozen tries before he managed to slip the right key into the lock. It turned. He pushed.

The door fell open and Sidewalk Steve collapsed on the floor. Chandler could just see the man's ruined right leg, the foot trailing off the ankle like a fish on a line.

The LSD was almost completely out of his system now, but he was still strapped to the table. If he couldn't get Steve to free him, all of the pain he'd inflicted on the vagrant would have been for nothing.

"Steve, please. You have to get up. You have to untie me."

On the floor, Steve moaned.

Chandler gathered his energy. He had seen the damsel in Steve's mind—a gypsy-looking girl with ridiculously large breasts bursting from her ludicrously low-cut blouse—but he didn't have the energy to sift for something more believable. He pushed. The walls melted into a mountainous vista, the hospital bed faded away, replaced by railroad tracks.

"Hurry, Steve!" the gypsy girl pleaded. "The train is coming!"

Steve lifted his head. When he'd pushed open the door, an image of the fire demon who'd attacked him earlier had floated before his eyes, but it was gone now. The damsel—a very masculine-looking damsel, with a jaw like Steve McQueen's—lay trussed on a pair of gleaming railroad tracks. He couldn't see the train but felt its rumble in the ground. He didn't have the strength to move, but he had to find it. Had to save her, even if she wasn't quite as pretty as he'd first thought. It was still his duty. His purpose in life.

He pulled himself up with his hands. Each moment was an agony. Spastic fingers pulled ineffectually at the ropes.

"Hurry, Steve!" the damsel called in her curiously deep voice. "Don't give up!"

But he could only free one of her hands. He looked up to see the train barreling down on them, then slumped atop the damsel's unfortunately flat chest. At least she wouldn't die alone.

"I'm sorry," he whispered, just as the train ripped through their bodies.

It took another ten minutes for Chandler to work himself free from the table. In the course of searching the factory-turned-laboratory, he found a bottle of morphine, and he shot ten ccs into Sidewalk Steve's arm in the hopes that it would keep him unconscious. He also found an ampoule of LSD, which he pocketed.

Melchior and the doctor might well kill Steve if Chandler left him here, so he hitched his hands under the unconscious man's arms and dragged him toward the door. For a big guy, he didn't weigh nearly as much as Chandler expected—and, as well, he, Chandler, wasn't nearly as tired as he thought he'd be after four days on his back. He suspected his freshness was somehow related to the changes LSD had wrought in him, but he wasn't sure how. After all, increased physical constitution and the ability to project images into other people's minds didn't seem to be related, unless there was some kind of physiological connection he didn't know about. It would have been fascinating to investigate, if it wasn't his own mind he was contemplating, his own body.

He lowered Sidewalk Steve to the floor to unlock the outer door and push it open. He'd just bent over again when something caught him in the small of the back. He heard it, actually, just before it struck, but couldn't dodge fast enough to avoid the blow. A sharp pain erupted in his lumbar spine, needles of pain strobed up and down his legs, and he fell head-to-feet on top of Sidewalk Steve. He had the presence of mind to roll, though, and the next blow—a baseball bat, he saw now—slammed into Sidewalk Steve's stomach. The homeless man was so drugged up that he barely flinched, but Chandler didn't have time to worry about him. His legs, still tingling from the blow to his spine, were sluggish as he pushed himself backward, but with each inch he felt the pain recede. The whole time his eyes never wavered from his bat-wielding assailant. A short Spanish fellow, with shoulders like softballs beneath his tight jacket. Chandler pushed at the guard's mind, but there was nothing: his reserves had been depleted, and, as well, he guessed that the guard had been dosed with Thorazine like the doctor, because Chandler didn't even sense the man's mind. This would have to be a physical fight. One on one—no, one on two, he saw, as a second guard, armed with a length of iron pipe, stepped into the door behind the first.

All this had taken a second, perhaps two. Now, as the thugs advanced toward him, Chandler held up his hands.

"I don't want to hurt you."

He was still sitting on the floor when he spoke, and all the two men did was look at each other and laugh.

"We was told that if you managed to get out, we could do everything short of killing you," the guard with the bat said.

"Three days we been hanging around," the second guard threw in, smacking his pipe against his palm, "just waiting to have a little fun."

"Please," Chandler said, looking around for something to use as a weapon. "You know this isn't right."

The room was filled with broken-down factory machinery too big to move, let alone use as a weapon, but here and there were a few beakers and test tubes and pieces of lab equipment. Rubber tubes, metal pans. Nothing resembling a scalpel.

The man with the bat lunged. Chandler rolled, avoiding a blow to the head—the guard had a generous idea of what he could live through—then shot his leg out, knocking his attacker's feet from under him. Even as he reached for the bat he noted how differently he and his assailant moved. The guard seemed ever-so-slightly slowed down. Chandler could almost believe it was the Thorazine making the man groggy, except he fell to the floor with the same slowness. Chandler's limbs, by contrast, darted from his body like striking snakes. He snatched the man's bat before he'd even hit the ground, used the fat end like a pool cue, slammed it into the guard's temple. At the last instant he pulled back slightly, afraid of shattering the man's skull, but there was still a sickening snap, and the man went limp on the ground.

Chandler whirled to face the second guard, bringing the bat up to protect his face. The pipe smashed into it close to the handle, and Chandler found himself holding four inches of splintered wood. Another inch and the fingers of his right hand would have been shattered.

"I thought you were told not to kill me," Chandler said, dodging a second blow, then a third. The guard aimed for his head every time.

"We're not paid enough to care," the guard said, swinging fiercely again—but carefully, Chandler saw. The man was making sure not to leave himself exposed as his partner had.

By now, Chandler's backward movement had taken him to the nearest table, and he put it between him and the guard. He tried to push the table but it was bolted to the floor, so he started grabbing objects and throwing them. His aim was good, but so was the guard's, and he smashed one beaker after another with his pipe, seemed almost to enjoy the spray of glass and liquids, smiling grimly through gritted teeth and slitted eyes.

"Best hitting practice I've had in a while."

"Yeah?" Chandler grabbed an alcohol burner, aimed right for the guard's strike zone. "Hit this."

Glass and liquid sprayed into the air in a sparkling mist. Chandler's fingers had already sparked a match on the slate tabletop. He threw it, and the air erupted in flames.

"My face!" the guard screamed.

The alcohol from the burner had mostly flown away from the guard, and his skin was nothing more than singed. But the flash had blinded him long enough for Chandler to leap the table and clock him with a fist to the jaw.

He stood there a moment, panting, not from exertion, but adrenaline. The whole fight had taken perhaps a minute. Finally he turned back to Sidewalk Steve, still sleeping on the floor.

"All right, Steve. Let's get you back outside where you belong."

Melchior got the call just after 3 a.m.

"I'm sorry to disturb you at such an ungodly hour. I'm trying to reach Thomas Taylor. Tommy."

"Sorry," Melchior mumbled. "Wrong number."

He dressed without turning on the light. Keller's use of the word "ungodly" meant the situation was urgent; a man's name meant the call concerned Orpheus; the addition of a diminutive meant something had gone wrong. It was just after midnight in San Francisco, which suggested Keller had been contacted by the guards. Either that or the doctor was working after hours. Neither scenario boded well.

Funny he should use the name Tommy, though. Melchior would have to ask about that.

Melchior had no doubt that anyone listening in would spot the call—the wrong number was a staple contact protocol. As a field agent with twenty years' worth of contacts, it would be easy enough for Melchior to explain it off as any of a dozen different people. No doubt the Company wouldn't believe him, and depending on just how suspicious they were feeling, they'd probably trace the call back to Frisco. But none of that mattered, as long as they didn't find out what was really going on before he took care of Keller's problem.

Melchior used the building's rear exit (whose light fixture kept mysteriously shorting out no matter how often the super repaired it) and hurried up the tree-shadowed street to the Chevy the Wiz had given him. He took four consecutive left turns to make sure he wasn't being followed, then drove randomly for eleven minutes before pulling over at the next pay phone he saw. He dialed the rendezvous number exactly thirty minutes after Keller had called his apartment.

"He's escaped!" the doctor screamed into his ear before the phone had finished its first ring.

Melchior swallowed his fury. He'd prepared himself for news of Chandler's death—Keller's time experimenting on Jews in concentration camps hadn't exactly left him with a delicate hand—but escape was unacceptable.

"What happened?"

"He got Steve to break down the door. Then he overpowered those thugs you hired."

Melchior wanted to know how, exactly, Chandler had gotten Steve to break down a steel door, but there wasn't time for that now.

"Did the guards say anything?"

"Only that Orpheus was very . . . unusual."

"We already know that."

"I mean physically. They said he moved with incredible speed."

"You're sure it wasn't the Thorazine?"

"I don't know, but . . ." Keller paused, and Melchior could hear the doctor's mind racing.

"What?"

"It's probably nothing. But assuming that the guards' perceptions were accurate, then their testimony suggests that Chandler's power is less mental than neuronal."

"In English."

"CIA theorized that the Gate of Orpheus would activate some specifically mental ability. But Leary felt the Gate was a processing station that would affect *all* the senses. He believed LSD didn't so much activate a dormant part of the brain as increase the central nervous system's ability to process stimuli that the senses weren't normally aware of."

"Once again, Doctor: in English."

"Chandler's ability to pull images from people's minds might simply be one aspect of an augmented ability to perceive sensory impulses. If that's the case, he can also see better, hear better, react faster than normal human beings. Who knows, he might be able to slow or increase metabolic processes to give himself extra energy when he needs it, or speed up his healing time in response to an injury. Certainly that would explain the hibernation effect that seems to happen when he's sleeping."

"Jesus. Are we talking Superman stuff, or what?"

"Well, given the fact that he wasn't able to break his restraints, I don't think we're facing a serious increase in strength. But he knocked two armed men unconscious in about forty-five seconds."

Melchior whistled, then stopped himself halfway through. A shadow had ducked behind the trunk of an elm halfway up the street. It could have been nothing. But if he'd been followed, the Company would dump the pay phone's call log and find the lab in San Francisco before Keller could clean it out—and thus discover that Chandler was alive, in which case Melchior would not only have to chase Chandler, but beat CIA to him.

"*Et in Arcadia ego,*" he whispered.

"What?"

"Nothing," Melchior said. "Listen carefully: I want you to go to checkpoint four. You'll find a phone number written on the bottom of the coin bank. Add seven to the odd numbers and nine to the even numbers. In the case of double digits, use the figure in the ones column. Do you have that?"

"Checkpoint four, seven odds, nine evens." One thing you could say about Nazis: they were good at taking direction.

"Good. Call that number. Say that you're a friend of the senator's and that you won't be able to come in on Friday. Is that clear?"

An excited tremor fluttered the doctor's voice. "It's the girl, isn't it? Miss Haverman? You didn't kill her after all."

"I'll call you at checkpoint five in twelve hours. If I don't call, assume the worst."

"What should I do about"—a little tremor of eagerness vibrated Keller's voice—"the guards?"

"Do your worst," Melchior said, and hung up.

He'd glimpsed the shadow twice while he gave Keller his instructions. Definitely a tail. Even worse, he was practically on top of Melchior's car. If Melchior walked back to the vehicle, he was as good as caught. But if he walked away, the tail would know he'd been made and would take off. And Melchior needed to find out what this was about—Cuba, or Orpheus, or if the Company was just watching him for the sake of watching him.

There was nothing else to do. He exited the booth and started for his car. He kept his hands out of his pockets to allay any suspicion he was reaching for a weapon, kept moving his head slightly, as though he were still looking out for anyone watching.

He'd picked a residential street to discourage gunfire. He guessed that the tail would circle the tree as he passed, come out behind him with his weapon drawn. If the tail just stepped out in front of him, he was caught. But . . .

He passed within a foot of the tree. He didn't see any movement. The tail was good. He'd kept the tree perfectly between him and his target. As soon as Melchior was abreast of the tree, he reached for his gun. It was out as he stepped off the sidewalk and began to loop around the tree.

A blur shot from the shadows. Melchior felt a sharp pain in his hand as his gun was kicked from his fingers, bounced off the hood of a parked car, and skittered into the street.

He didn't wait to see his assailant. He brought his hand down in a wide arc as fast as he could, let his attacker's momentum carry him into harm's way. His hand connected with the man's wrist before the rest of his body was visible. The man held on to his gun, though, and Melchior grabbed the wrist and smashed it into his kneecap. The man grunted in pain but still kept hold of his gun, and now his left fist was smashing into the side of Melchior's face. Melchior continued to pound the man's right wrist into his knee. After nearly a dozen blows the gun fell from the man's spasming fingers and Melchior kicked it under the nearest car. He jumped back, panting heavily, blood leaking down his cheek from a cut beside his right eye. Only then did he see his attacker's face.

"Hey, Melchior," Rip Robertson said in a voice that still carried a faint reek of Cuban rum. "Long time no see."

San Francisco didn't live up to the hype. For one thing, the fa-mous hills, so pretty in postcards and movies, were a pain in the ass to trek up and down, particularly in a pair of sockless loafers two sizes too big (Chandler's clothes were long gone, so he was wearing Sidewalk Steve's; the homeless man had turned out to have freakishly large feet). For another, despite the city's reputation for friendliness, not a single citizen had been kind enough to leave the keys in his or her car. Quite a few were unlocked—once, when Chandler saw a shadowed figure approach, he hid inside a Packard that must've dated to the forties—but even though he'd seen thieves and spies and adventurous teens hot-wire cars in any number of movies, he himself had no idea how to do it. You were supposed to reach under the steering column and produce a fistful of wires, but all he managed to do was bang his knuckles on the underpanel.

But one way or another, he had to get out of the city. Had to go east. To DC. A few scattered images he'd seen in Melchior's mind had told him Naz's fate was somehow connected to the nation's capital. A beautiful Asian woman in a long black car. A song—wordless, toneless, but somehow central to Naz's location. If only he'd been able to concentrate better! As disturbing as his new power was, he was going to have to learn how to use it if he wanted to find Naz. If he wanted to save her.

Meanwhile, though, he had no money. There were people he could call in Cambridge, but how to explain his situation? A prostitute working for the CIA slipped me some kind of experimental drug, and now I have mental powers? Oh, and a Nazi scientist held me captive, and I killed my best friend's brother? Somehow Chandler didn't think that was going to fly. And besides, wouldn't Melchior and his cronies be watching his closest friends? Listening in on their phones? Hanging out in front of their houses in repair vans outfitted with eavesdropping equipment? Who was to say they wouldn't kidnap the first person

Chandler called and threaten to hurt or even kill him unless Chandler surrendered?

None of which changed the basic facts. He was penniless. Nameless for all intents and purposes. Orpheus in the Underworld, looking for Eurydice, his only protection his song. His ability to melt men's hearts and minds.

He put a hand in his pocket, pulled out the vial of LSD. The inch of clear liquid looked like viscous water, yet it was enough to soften the solid shape of the world. He pulled the stopper from the vial, pressed his index finger to the lid, turned it upside down. He felt the spot of dampness fit itself to the grooves of his fingerprint as if the acid was the mirror image of his identity. He pulled his finger from the vial, looked at the glistening tip in the streetlight. It was hard to believe in the power there. But it was all he had to get him to Naz. He poured a dollop of clear liquid into his palm, then, screwing up his face like a five-year-old about to take a spoonful of cod liver oil, slurped up his medicine. Salvation tasted bitter, and he had to fight the urge to spit it out.

An hour later found him walking up the steep incline of Lombard Street. The world seemed to have a colored transparency laid over it, painting woodwork and masonry with a pulsing array of colors that might've been soothing had it not been so unnatural. Visions appeared in the windows, in the air, on the street—giant rabbits and lollipops and girls in pinafores, tanks, soldiers, mushroom clouds, a blizzard of books, a sudden riot of grapevine and pill bottles, a lone pterodactyl cruising silently down the urban defile. If he squinted, he could see through these apparitions, but it was easier just to let them roll over him. To trust that the world would continue to be solid even though his eyes told him he was walking on a crystalline lake over a bed of multicolored stones. No, not stones. Eyes, winking at him knowingly. The only thing he worried about was the return of the flaming boy. Chandler didn't know who or what it was, whose mind it had come from, but he knew he couldn't control it. Not yet. Maybe not ever.

A pinkish purple sea turtle swimming toward him slowly resolved into a massive mauve Imperial from the late fifties, before Chrysler scaled them down. An expensive car, immaculately maintained. Just what Chandler was looking for.

He felt for the driver's mind. He was as gentle as he could be—he didn't want the man, Peter was his name, Peter Mossford, to veer out of control when the road turned to water. Facts flitted past like flash cards. Mossford was fifty-two. Divorced. Was returning from an emotionally hollow rendezvous with the woman he'd foolishly left his wife for. Not that he missed Lorna—a shrew, born and bred—but he missed his boys. Mark, fourteen, still living at home with his mother, and Pete Jr., in his second year at Dartmouth. Mossford used to love to take Pete camping in the hills north of the city when the boy was younger—hell, when *he* was younger, before work left him too tired for anything on the weekends besides a steady stream of Scotch-and-sodas. What he wouldn't give to go back to the good old days, when his hair was still brown and thick and his sons didn't retreat to their rooms the minute he walked through the door, blasting their ridiculous jungle music on the hi-fis he'd mistakenly bought them in a bid to win their affection. When the city wasn't crawling with peacocky fellows like this one—a beatnik probably, "messed up" on Mary Jane, or who knows, maybe one of the fruits who'd started settling in the Castro. I swear, Mossford thought, it's not safe to let your kids walk the streets these days. Why, if that were Pete—

Mossford stepped on the brakes. Peered through the window. On the other side of the glass, his fair hair dappled in a ray of sunlight that shone on him like a spotlight, eleven-year-old Pete Jr. pantomimed rolling down the window.

"Hey, Dad," Chandler said as a blissful smile spread across Mossford's face. "Wanna go camping?"

It was too tricky to keep the image of Pete Jr. firmly fixed in his father's mind and at the same time convince Mossford that the western route out of Oakland was actually the road leading to the hills north of the bay, so Chandler let his chauffeur pilot the car as he wanted. Mossford spewed a stream of regrets to his son, apologies, pledges to do things differently. It wasn't right, Chandler thought. In the morning Mossford would wake up with the night's events pulsing in his brain more vividly than any memory, any dream he'd ever had, and how great would his sorrow be then? Life was hard enough already. One man shouldn't be able to do this to another. But the longing for Naz was too great, and he pressed on.

When they were safely in the deserted hills, the fantasy of Pete Jr. told his dad that he thought this place looked swell. Mossford parked the car, then went to the trunk to unpack the tent. Chandler couldn't bear to watch him go through the motions, a beaming smile on his face as he pounded imaginary tent pegs into the ground with an invisible hammer, so Pete Jr. said, "Look, Dad, I did it myself," and there before Mossford's eyes was a perfectly pitched pup tent. Mossford didn't question it, just as he didn't wonder how it had gone from a golden morning to a blustery night in the hour it had taken them to drive out of the city. Instead, father and son crawled into their respective sleeping bags for the night.

"Can we go fishing tomorrow, Dad?" was the last thing Pete Jr. said to his father.

Mossford pulled the imaginary zipper of his sleeping bag all the way up. "Whatever you want, son."

Chandler waited till Mossford was asleep before he lifted the man's wallet from his pants and got back in the car. He felt like a complete heel. He wanted to punish the people who had done this. Wanted to make them feel what Peter Mossford would feel when he woke up. But as soon as he had that thought, an image of Eddie Logan flashed in his mind—his face, contorted in terror, his own hand driving a knife into his heart to spare himself the horror that Chandler had put in his mind—and he knew that he'd already done much worse than what he'd done to Mossford.

It was a mean world, Chandler thought, and yawned widely. With or without mental powers, it was a mean, cold world. The mere thought of it exhausted him, and he struggled to keep his eyes open as he piloted Mossford's car on the rainbow ribbon of deserted highway. All he wanted was to find Naz and curl up with her and sleep forever, or at least until this nightmare was over.

The blade of Rip's knife glinted in the dim light. He appeared in no hurry to press the attack, and Melchior took a step back, slipping off his jacket. Rip was bending his right wrist tenderly, and Melchior suspected he'd fractured a bone or strained the tendons. Hard to stab someone when you can't close your hand all the way. After a moment Rip moved the knife to his left hand. That'll make things easier, Melchior thought.

"Tell me, Rip," he said as he wrapped his jacket around his right hand, "were you ever actually trying to kill Castro, or were you just there to keep an eye on me?"

"I'd tell you that you've got an inflated sense of your own importance," Rip countered, "but you're almost right. Killing Castro was the primary mission, but getting rid of you was the fallback."

"It wasn't the Cubans, was it? *You* ratted me out. I spent eight months in Boniato because of *you*."

Rip's smile caught the streetlights and glowed wetly.

"I'd've preferred killing you myself, but I'd been made and had to get out of the country."

The two men circled each other warily. Melchior suspected Rip wouldn't actually kill him unless he was forced to, since a dead man can't provide any information. He'd have to pull his blows, at least at first. That might be Melchior's only chance.

"So tell me. Does the Company know Orpheus is alive?"

"They do now. Jesus Christ, Melchior. You're Frank Wisdom's personal pickaninny. We always knew you was crazy, but a traitor? What gives?"

"It was the Company that betrayed the Wiz. Pushing him out of Plans, frying his brains to shit. My loyalty was to him. It still is. I'm disappointed in you," he threw in. "I'd've thought an old-timer like you would've known to bring a radio. Now I don't have any choice but to kill you."

Rip blinked. Melchior didn't wait for a second chance. He lunged. Rip went for him with the knife, and Melchior put his padded right hand directly in its path. A searing pain sliced across his knuckles but he ignored it, twisting the rapidly dampening jacket around Rip's wrist. The blood-soaked fabric tangled around Rip's weapon, tying him to Melchior, who kicked his right foot into the side of Rip's left knee. It buckled and Rip went down with a grunt. The tangled jacket pulled Melchior down on top of Rip, and he felt the knife drive deeper into his hand. At the same time there was a sharp pain in his right arm: in his panic, Rip was actually *biting* him. Melchior yanked his arm free. His elbow came down hard on Rip's nose, and the man's face vanished in a burst of dark blood. He brought it down a second time on Rip's Adam's apple, crushing it. The third blow, snapping the fallen man's sternum, was purely punitive—he couldn't believe the fucker had actually *bit* him.

Rip tried to suck air through his collapsed throat with a sound like greasy water going down a clogged drain. Melchior kept one eye on him as he untangled his bloody jacket. The knife had gone through the edge of his hand. Gritting his teeth, he pulled the blade out, then used it to cut a strip of fabric from the sleeve of his jacket and bound the wound. The whole time Rip gurgled and thrashed on the ground.

"It's a shame it had to come to this," Melchior said. "You're gonna miss all the fun." Then he stepped on Rip's throat to shut him up.

When Rip was finally still, Melchior just stood there, catching his breath, staring down at the dead agent. He was a little woozy from loss of blood, and his hand was starting to throb like a motherfucker, but at the same time he felt exhilarated. Another link between himself and the Company had been severed.

He pressed his foot into Rip's neck, felt the jelly of the dead man's Adam's apple spread beneath the thin sole of his sandal. He stared down at his foot for a long moment. Something about it bothered him. Then he knew. He plopped down on the grass, kicked off the sandals Segundo's men had given him when they pulled him out of prison, took Rip's shoes, and put them on his own feet. Pointy wingtips in shiny black leather. For a thug, Rip was a bit of a dandy.

Before he knew it, he was pulling Rip's pants off him, his jacket, his shirt. In full view of a dozen darkened houses and any cars that might happen along, Melchior stripped off the linen execution suit he'd been wearing for nearly a year and put on Rip's thoroughly respectable gray wool. He pulled his wallet and keys from his bloody jacket, tossed his old clothes in the backseat of his car, then walked up the block until he found a car with an unlocked trunk and stuffed Rip's nearly naked body inside. The corpse would probably start to smell in a day or two, and in another day or two, maybe longer if Melchior got lucky, someone from the Company would make the rounds of the morgues and put everything together. That was fine. Keller could erase any trace of the lab by then.

He drove a few miles out of his way to dump the knife in a trash can, then headed home. Before he went upstairs he threw his old suit and shoes in the incinerator in the basement, stood there in his new clothes watching them reduce to ash. It seemed to him that the last thing to burn away was the bullet hole over the breast of his old suit. A fantasy, he knew, the product of blood loss. But even so, the hole seemed to burn before his eyes, growing larger and larger and larger until it consumed the world.

All he needed to do now was get Orpheus back. But he wasn't too worried about that. He was pretty sure Chandler was going to come looking for him.

PART 3

ORPHEUS ASCENDS

Charles Jarrell took one look at the figure on his front porch, then pulled BC inside and slammed the door.

"Jesus H. Christ. Take that ridiculous thing off your head. You look like Phyllis fucking Diller." He looked BC up and down one more time, then shook his head. "Does he know you're here?"

BC pulled off the ratty wig and scratched his itching scalp. "Who?"

Jarrell kicked BC's mother's Electrolux hard enough to dent the motor's housing. "J. Edgar Vacuum, that's who."

"Oh, ah—no."

Jarrell opened his mouth, and even as a whiff of liquor-soaked breath floated BC's way he said, "I need a drink for this," turned on his heel, and disappeared.

He lived in a decrepit row house just a few blocks north of Capitol Hill, one of those DC neighborhoods that, forsaken by the nation's prosperity, seemed doomed to eternal poverty. But not even the boarded-up windows and beaten-up cars on the street could have prepared BC for the chaos inside Jarrell's house. The walls were covered with peeling paper whose color and pattern were completely obscured by a coating of cigarette smoke as sticky as creosote. Stacks of newspapers, five, six, seven feet tall, made a veritable maze of the floor, while the air was similarly partitioned by bolts—clots—of smoke. Despite the reek of tobacco, BC could smell the spicier tinge of alcohol and sweat beneath it. He'd heard the expression "down the rabbit hole" innumerable times in reference to CIA, but had never actually been *in* one before.

"Sit your fucking ass down, you're making me nervous," Jarrell said, returning from another room—or who knows, maybe just from behind a stack of paper. "This better be good, or I'll be mailing pieces of your body to Hoover for the next several weeks."

The newsprint- and nicotine-stained fingers of Jarrell's left hand were tucked into a pair of ice-filled lowballs and his right hand was wrapped around a bottle of rye. He filled the two glasses to the rim and shoved one across a stack of papers that served as a coffee table. BC sat down gingerly on a sofa mummified in what could only be described as ass-wrinkled newspaper. There were several dark kinky hairs on the pages. Given the fact that what hair remained on Jarrell's head was limply straight and gray, BC perched as close to the sofa's edge as he could without falling off.

"Well?"

"Mr. Jarrell—"

"Aw, Jesus Fuck!" Jarrell looked around as though someone might be hiding behind a stack of newspapers. "It's Parker! Virgil *Parker!*"

"Mr. Parker." BC shook his head helplessly. "I thought you'd been fired."

Jarrell smacked the side of his head, hard enough to make BC wince.

"Jesus, this really is amateur hour. I can tell by your ridiculous costume that you've at least *heard* of cover. So leap to the obvious conclusion."

"Ye-es. But you don't work for CIA under your real name. So why go to all the trouble of firing Charles Jarrell if it's Virgil Parker who's going to be hired by the Agency?"

For the first time, Jarrell chuckled. "Oh. Well. He really did fire me. Didn't like the way I dressed or talked or some shit. But then he thought better of it, sent me undercover." He waved a hand. "Enough background. What the hell are you doing here, especially if Hoover didn't send you?"

"I need to talk to you about Orpheus."

"Who?"

"Orpheus? Project Orpheus?"

"Never heard of it."

"A division of MK-ULTRA? LSD experiments—"

"Oh, *that?* Jesus, no one's mentioned that in a dog's age."

"But according to the director's files, you're the Bureau's liaison—"

"You broke into the fucking *Vault?* Sweet mother of God, you've got balls, I'll give you that. So look, CB—"

"BC actually."

"Yeah, I don't give a fuck. So look, CB-BC, there ain't many of us inside Langley, so we're spread a little thin. I'm the 'liaison,' as you so elegantly put it, on about forty different operations, projects, actions, and individuals at the Company. Orpheus or whatever the fuck you called it is about thirty-ninth or fortieth on my list of priorities."

BC felt his heart sink. Jarrell seemed as ignorant as he was crazy. "There was an incident," he said, a desperate whine making his voice sharp. "At Millbrook."

Jarrell's face softened slightly. "Is that where that nut job Leary set up camp? I can call someone in the Boston office, see what they know."

"Bureau? Or . . . Company?"

"Jesus Christ!" Jarrell practically screamed. "I—do—not—work—for—the—fuck—ing—Bu—reau. *Capisce?*"

BC nodded. "A Boston agent was involved in the incident."

"By involved, you mean died?" For the first time Jarrell perked up. "What the fuck happened?"

BC took a deep breath, then told the story as clearly as he could. Halfway through, Jarrell started drinking from BC's glass, and by the time BC finished he'd refilled both glasses and drained them as well.

"That is the craziest bunch of horseshit I ever heard—and I've heard some crazy horseshit in my life."

"I know it sounds unbelievable."

"I didn't say I didn't believe you. You strike me as a man incapable of telling a lie, as your pathetic attempt at a disguise makes clear. Whether or not you know the truth is another question. What'd you say the guy's cipher was? The swarthy fellow?"

"Melchior."

"Melchior, Melchior." Jarrell got up and began rummaging through the piles of newspaper, moving methodically from the living room through a wide doorway into what was probably the dining room, although it contained nothing but a maze of newspaper and boxes. As Jarrell worked his way through the stacks, BC noticed that colored slips of paper poked from them at various places—red, yellow, and blue flaps fluttering like pinfeathers. With a combination of fascination and re-vulsion, BC realized that the thousands of papers served as some kind of filing system, like one of IBM's room-sized computers. Only instead of punch cards, it was newsprint.

Now Jarrell pulled a classifieds section from a stack of paper. The ads were covered with hatch marks, and Jarrell's eyes flitted up and down the columns like a bookkeeper scanning accounts.

"Mother of fuck." He wadded the paper and tossed it on the floor. "You had yourself a run-in with one of the Wise Men."

BC's brow wrinkled. "The Magi? Melchior, Balthazar, and what was the last one called?"

"Caspar. And yes, those three. But also no. By which I mean no, you literal-minded dipshit. Wise Men is Company lingo for three agents Frank Wisdom brought in with him in '52."

"Brought in?"

"Wisdom was OSS during the war. Was one of the advocates for a permanent agency to oversee American intelligence-gathering activities as well as a direct-action division to follow up on that intelligence when more visible options weren't available."

"You mean covert ops."

"The Wiz more or less invented the concept. Legend has it that him and Joe Scheider recruited a couple-a three kids in his OSS days, was basically raising them to be spies—some spook story about sleepers and all that. In fact, now that I think of it, the program was pretty much the forerunner of Artichoke, Ultra, Orpheus, all that sci-fi crap. Anyway, the Wiz's recruits were known as the Wiz Kids at first—big surprise, right?—which later gave way to Wise Men, which in turn led to the idea that there were three of them—Melchior, Caspar, and Balthazar. According to legend, the goal was to place them in deep cover inside the Soviet Union, but Balthazar supposedly died during the course of his training, and Melchior was already too old—not to mention too dark—and ended up becoming the Wiz's field hand."

"And Caspar?" The name rang a bell, but BC couldn't place it.

Jarrell shrugged. "Who knows? Even odds says there never was a Caspar—that the whole thing was just a story the Wiz made up, or maybe even Melchior. At any rate, Melchior got a reputation for being a crazy fuck—among other things, he's repeatedly destroyed his own file, so no one besides the Wiz knows his real name or what he's been up to for the last ten or twenty years." Jarrell looked BC up and down in his vacuum repairman's uniform. "You, my friend, are one lucky son of a bitch."

BC ignored this.

"So how do I find him?"

"Melchior? Fat fucking chance. The Wiz had a nervous breakdown in '56 after the whole Hungary thing blew up. I guess he'd told the rebels that if they rose up against the Soviet Union, the U.S. would help them out. But Ike, you know, he'd already fought his war, plus he had an election coming up, and he wanted nothing to do with it. Thousands of rebels were pretty much slaughtered, and the Wiz took it hard. Ended up going for shock treatments and all that, never really did recover. They farmed him out to London, then finally forced him out entirely last year. Without his patron, Melchior was pretty much persona non grata. You'd hear stories. One day he was in the Congo, the next in Southeast Asia, then he was off to Cuba. They could've all been true or all been lies. But the one thing I can tell you is that he don't spend much time in DC." Jarrell paused. "Although, come to think of it, if he is here, you might want to check out Madam Song's."

"And she is?"

"Oh baby." Jarrell licked his lips like a teenager in the locker room about to describe the wonders of eating pussy. "Only the finest purveyor of female flesh on the Eastern seaboard. In addition to running an exclusive brothel, she also procures and supplies girls to mob bosses and politicians and other movers and shakers. Specializes in exotics—Orientals, Africans, niche-market cooz. She and Melchior were once 'linked,' as they say in the gossip pages, and there's a reasonable chance he's paid her a visit if he's back in town."

"For such a supposedly super-secret spy, his habits seem pretty well documented."

Jarrell shook his head at BC like a disappointed teacher. "You got to understand how the trade works. There's no such thing as a secret no one knows. Espionage is built on half truths, quarter truths, and lots and lots of lies. Every piece of useful information is attached to dozens, hundreds, of pieces of misinformation, and the best spy is the one who can sift through the bullshit to the truth. Part of it's what we call legend—the invented story that creates an operative's cover—and part of it's just aura, the mystique that Melchior cultivates in order to give himself more clout out there in spyland. I've probably heard more stories about the Wise Men than I have about my uncle Joe, but the difference is 99.9 percent of those stories are complete and utter fabrications."

"You don't have an uncle Joe."

"No." Jarrell smiled. "But Virgil Parker does."

"So what you're saying is that you have no idea if Melchior really even knows Madam Song, let alone if he'll have visited her."

"What I'm saying is that Melchior's name has been mentioned in connection with Song's often enough that there's probably something there. Whether they fucked once, or she's an agent herself, or just runs a really good brothel, is anyone's guess." Jarrell shrugged. "But yeah, that's about all the help I can give you."

"There is one more thing. A woman. I don't think she has anything to do with this, but—"

"Who?"

"Her name is Mary Meyer. She—"

"Yeah, I know who she is, and what she did. *Who* she did."

"She gave him LSD."

Jarrell shrugged. "So? He's already hopped up on more pain pills and antianxiety drugs than all the housewives in Arlington combined. What's one more?"

"She got the LSD from Edward Logan."

Jarrell chuckled. "Well, he doesn't appear to have developed any mental powers or turned into a zombie, so I think he's safe, for now."

BC stood up. "Well, thank you again." He couldn't help but ask. "Why did you help me?"

Jarrell poured himself his fifth or sixth whiskey before answering. He looked around the maze of newspapers with their colored markers, the myriad coded and recoded and decoded secrets they contained, then turned back to BC.

"I dunno. Because you found me, I suppose. Because you broke into J. Edgar Hoover's Vault. Anyone who can do that is obviously fairly good at what he does. He's also probably insane, but in a way I can identify with." He waved his drink at the stacks of paper. "I'd say it's better than even odds that you're gonna end up in a body bag like Logan, but still, I've always been a sucker for the underdog." He raised his drink to BC. "Good hunting."

A knock sounded at the door.

"Come in."

Chul-moo opened the door quietly, almost apologetically.

"The senator is leaving," he said in Korean.

Song didn't look up from her desk. "He had a good time?"

"Laurel says he gave her a gown from a French designer. Yves Saint Laurent. Garrison says she practically had him posing for the cameras. Also, the background check on Paul Ingram came up clean."

"If Paul Ingram is a Swedish businessman, I'm a Dallas housewife. Well, at least he's taken the time to build a good cover. Book him for Friday. Set him up with Njeri. If he's got any secrets, she'll beat them out of him. Is that all?"

"There was a call from San Francisco."

Song looked up. "Melchior's Nazi? What did he want?"

"He said that Melchior wants us to move the new girl."

"Move her where? The Mayflower? The Willard? Did he say why Melchior wanted her moved?" When Chul-moo shook his head, Song said, "If Melchior wants to foot the bill for different accommodations, he can call and tell me himself. Till then, she's staying here. Please make sure Laurel gets back to the residence. I'll see myself home."

"Of course." The tiniest of pauses. "Shall I check on her?"

"On?"

"The new girl?"

Chul-moo's expression hadn't changed, but the faintest note—of longing, pleading almost, had entered his voice. It was hard to imagine this knife of a boy asking for anything, let alone permission to visit a girl. Song had selected Chul-moo as her majordomo because his sexual taste ran to middle-aged white men, on whom he took great pleasure in exacting revenge for the destruction of his country (when Song got a client who particularly enjoyed being humiliated, she would send Chul-moo in instead of one of the girls; despite his youth, he was surprisingly learned in the ways of inflicting pain, whether lethal or remediable). Yet she could have sworn there was a note of genuine desire in Chul-moo's voice.

"That's not necessary. I'll be looking in on her myself."

"Of course." Chul-moo wasn't quite able to hide his disappointment. With a slight bow, he backed from the room.

Song remained in her office for another hour, reviewing the day's takings, monetary and photographic, and checking tomorrow's appointments, including an Iraqi Baathist who controlled nearly a third of that country's oil, and had helped to oust General Qasim in February after the latter established ties with the Soviet Union (Qasim himself had been a client here five years ago, just before he seized power). She'd contacted CIA to see if they were interested in incriminating photographs—the man's name was Saddam Hussein, and there was something about the set of his mouth that suggested he would get up to some *very* naughty things in bed—or if they wanted one of her more experienced girls to pump him for information, but the Company had turned her down, which suggested they were already working with him. That information was also valuable, although much trickier to sell, and she should have put out feelers to KGB to see if they were interested, but she was distracted tonight. For one thing, there was this Ingram fellow, whom she was pretty sure *was* KGB. For another, there was "the new girl," as Chul-moo called her. Song wasn't sure why she'd agreed to take custody of Nancy for Melchior, especially after she'd ferried Orpheus to San Francisco free of charge. It was a scenario with many possible drawbacks, including running afoul of CIA. Song was certainly not averse to risk-taking—you didn't build the kind of business she'd created without taking a few gambles. But it was hard to see the payoff in this deal with Melchior. Unless, of course, it was Melchior himself.

Meanwhile, there was the girl. Nancy. Song had never met someone quite like her. Someone so seemingly helpless, yet who incurred the aid of powerful forces wherever she went. One look at her and you wanted to protect her. No, that wasn't quite it. One look *from* her and you wanted to protect her. Take Chul-moo. He guarded her more fiercely than any of the other girls, and she didn't even work here. Well, not yet anyway.

Melchior'd told her that Nancy had worked as a hooker in Boston, but, unlike the girls Song hired, she didn't seem to have entered into her profession happily. She drank too much (although she hadn't touched a drop since coming to Song's), and practically radiated miserableness. But that morning, before Song left the residence, she'd stopped in Nancy's room, and Nancy had asked to work for her. Taken aback, Song had said she would think about it and get back to her at the end of the day.

She wondered about the call from Keller, though. If she had to guess, she'd say say that "Orpheus" had gotten away from the doctor and was on his way here. Well, let him come. From what she'd seen of him on the plane, he didn't look like much of a threat, and it was going to take more than one spurned lover to break into her house.

She closed her ledger now, stored it in the safe with the day's cash, headed for the residence. The Newport Place property was solely for business. She and the girls lived in a town house on N, directly behind the bordello and connected to it by a tunnel built with taxpayer dollars (although even the Company, who funneled her the money, didn't know of its existence). No doubt it was an extravagance, but it was a mark of Song's power, and she never failed to feel as though she were a queen striding the length of a great hall as she traversed the narrow cement chute. She had the palace, the imperial guard, a dozen ladies in waiting. All she lacked was a consort. If only he hadn't been wearing that shabby suit. And those *sandals*. Her lip curled in disgust at the very thought.

In the residence, she took the elevator to the fourth floor and knocked on her guest's door.

"Come in," a soft voice called.

This time it was Song who opened the door quietly, obsequiously even, as if she were the servant, the room's occupant the mistress. Nancy sat at her dressing table, her hair and makeup perfect, as if she'd been expecting the call.

"I just wanted to check in on you."

"I'm fine, thank you." Nancy pointed to a plate of ginger cookies. "Chul-moo came by earlier."

Song stared at the girl. What was it about her? She was lovely, no doubt about that. But Song trafficked in some of the most beautiful girls in the world and was unfazed by looks. No, there was something special about this girl. Something that made you want to soothe her. Protect her. Give her whatever she wanted. She was bewitching.

"I wanted to know if you'd thought further about your offer this morning."

"What is there to think about?"

"You're here as my guest. You don't have to work for your keep."

"I'm here as your prisoner," Nancy said, and even though there wasn't any acrimony in her voice, it still stabbed Song like a spear of ice in the guts. "But that's neither here nor there. Seducing people is simply what I do."

"I don't understand."

"Neither do I," Nancy said, and there was that curious helplessness again. Song wanted to wrap her arms around the girl—and the last person she'd hugged had been her brother's murdered body. She knew she should refuse Nancy's request. But she also wanted to know what would happen if she said yes.

"You're Persian, no?"

Nancy nodded.

"Do you happen to speak Arabic by any chance?"

"Some. It's rusty, though."

"I have an Iraqi gentleman coming in tomorrow. I'm sure he'd appreciate not having to bring a translator into the room."

Naz looked at herself in the mirror. She brought the brush to her hair, then put it down again—a tacit acknowledgment that the face that looked back at her was already perfect.

"He won't be disappointed," she said quietly.

"No," Song mused. "For some reason, I don't think he will be."

It was almost true: clothes make the man. Just as the maid in the Department of Justice Building had taken a clean-cut white fellow in a soiled uniform ten sizes too big for an electrician, so did the residents of Dupont Circle take BC for one of them: a man of the world, of power, influence, prospects—and sexual needs.

He paused before the double doors of the Newport Place town house: a sheet of plate glass sandwiched between an ornately curved wrought-iron scroll without and golden gossamer curtains within. The curtains were just thick enough to obscure the view inside but still thin enough to allow a globe of soft yellow light to illuminate the porch, whose upper landing was shaded by a delicate tangle of wisteria. And there, reflected in the gold-backed sheet of glass, stood the new, improved BC Querrey. Beauregard Gamin, at your service, ma'am.

Or, rather, madam.

"Song won't be fooled by cheap imitations," Jarrell had told BC. "You go to her house, you wear bespoke or nothing at all." He'd given BC the name of a tailor on Wisconsin Avenue in Georgetown. Told him to order two suits, one in a simple charcoal twill, the other in a shiny black. "Tell him to widen the lapels a bit on the charcoal, cut the trousers a little loose in the ankle—say, 1960, 1961 at the latest. You want it to look like you've had it for a while. The black should be mod—one-inch lapels, stovepipe legs. The jacket should fall just above the bottom of your ass and the trouser cuffs should expose a good inch of sock when you're standing up. Trust me, Song's business is appearances. She'll notice."

BC had regarded the disheveled man delivering such specific sartorial advice with more than a bit of skepticism. "How much is this going to cost?"

"The suits are going to run about a hundred each," Jarrell said, and

BC fought back a gasp. "But first-timers at Song's have to pay a cool grand just for the privilege of saddling up. After that it's two hundred and fifty dollars a ride." He'd looked BC up and down in his thrift store costume. "You can put your hands on that kind of cash?"

For some reason an image of Gerry Burton flashed in BC's mind. "I'll get it somewhere."

An Asian boy answered the door. He wore a plain black suit, not quite livery, and despite the fact that it fit him loosely, and that he couldn't have been more than sixteen or seventeen, he still managed to project an aura of barely contained strength and menace.

He neither spoke nor stood aside, just looked at BC as if he were stripping off the newly minted threads and seeing the naked, quaking man beneath.

BC took a moment to hear his grandmother's rolling drawl in his mind. Then:

"Good evening, sir. Is there any chance Madam Song is at home on such a beautiful night?"

The majordomo continued to stare at him blankly. Finally, after BC was about to repeat the pass phrase, he moved aside. BC took a step forward, only to be stopped by an arm that, however thin, still felt as hard as an iron bar. The boy flicked BC's arms away from his side, and nimble, pincer-strong fingers squeezed each limb from wrist to shoulder, patted the outside of his jacket, then reached inside. BC felt the boy's hands on his chest, his ribs, his waist.

"The only man who usually touches me this way is my tailor," BC drawled.

The boy used his foot to nudge BC's legs apart, knelt down and gave each leg the same thorough going over. At the end he brought his hand up sharp at BC's inseam, let it sit there a moment longer than BC was comfortable with. He looked up at BC with a little smile on his face.

"No weapon," he said, standing up. "Suit nice though."

"Thanks," BC said. "I had to sell my momma's house to pay for it."

o   o   o

"Security consists of three men," Jarrell told him. "The majordomo will answer the door. Lee Chul-moo. Don't let the baby face fool you. Song picked him up off the street in Korea. He's supposed to be versed in all those kung fu–sumo wrestling maneuvers."

"Kung fu is Chinese. Sumo is Japanese."

"Let's just say that he can rip your legs off and beat you to death with them. Once past the front vestibule, you'll see a staircase directly ahead of you. There's a security booth in the room below it. It's manned by a single guard who monitors the closed-circuit cameras installed in each of the guest rooms. For the past couple of years it's been a guy named Garrison Davis. He's more of a gadget geek than Chul-moo, but you can expect he'll be packing. No one knows where the third man is stationed, but you don't need to worry about it. If you catch a glimpse of him, chances are it'll be the last thing you ever see. And then of course there's Song."

Chul-moo led BC past a large parlor to the end of the hall, where he knocked on a closed door. The door opened on a small office. The parlor-height ceilings were taller than the room was deep, and a single coffin-shaped window, heavily draped, added to the cloistered feeling. A series of framed sketches depicted Victorian women holding little frilly dogs in their laps. The rest of the furniture was similarly proper—female but not feminine, cool but not cold—without a hint of the Eastern, let alone the harem. Just like the woman sitting at the small escritoire.

"Song does a lot of business with the intelligence community. Because your entrée is coming from me, she'll immediately have a scenario in mind, namely, that I'm going to try to blackmail you into performing services for the Company. I suggest a munitions cover—bullets perhaps, or handguns. Nothing too fancy, but something the Company might be interested in acquiring at a discount. So in addition to the money she takes from you, she'll be looking at a substantially larger payment when she sells me the copies of the film footage of you and one of her girls. That said, she can smell bullshit a mile away. She wouldn't have gotten where she is otherwise. You're a young, good-looking man and, as far as she knows, quite wealthy. Obviously you don't need to resort to prostitutes. In order for you to gain her trust, you're going to have to convince her that you're not just another pussy-hound. You're a connoisseur of tail. You've had the starlets, the debutantes. Now you want the kind of girls you can't get back home in Georgia or Ole Miss or wherever you decide to hail from. The kind of girls who do the kinds of things that, well, no respectable girl would do."

"Things—"

"Choose your kink," Jarrell said with a wicked gleam in his eye. "And if I were you, I'd seal the deal, if you know what I mean. You're forking over twelve hundred and fifty dollars. Might as well get your money's worth. And believe me, Song's girls are worth it."

Because she was Asian, and because she ran a bordello, BC had pictured something a little more exotic. A kabuki girl or whatever they were called. A geisha. A dragon lady. Instead he found himself facing a demure, almost prim woman in a dun-colored herringbone suit lightened only by a bit of pale fur at the end of the three-quarter-length sleeves. Her black bouffant was the spitting image of the First Lady's, and she'd shadowed her eyes in such a way as to minimize their epicanthic fold. Her accent was similarly Americanized, her vowels as flat as a Midwesterner's, her consonants as firm as her handshake.

"Mr. Gamin." Song didn't stand, but let her hand rest in BC's for a moment, not limply but delicately: the clothes offered a masculine front, the handshake gave a feminine finish. BC felt weak in the knees. "Please, have a seat."

BC did his best not to plop into one of the spindly cane chairs opposite the desk. He wasn't sure what he expected. Some small talk perhaps. Questions about his background. But Song was all business.

"Tell me what you like in a girl."

An image filled BC's mind: his mother, inspecting his appearance before she let him leave the house each morning, from the time he went to kindergarten all the way through his first days at the Bureau. A sharp, calcified nail would repart his hair ever so slightly to the left or right of where he'd combed it, and her cold fingers would smooth it off his forehead. He knew she didn't mean to seem critical, that it was just her way of finding an excuse to touch her son. But still, he had to fight off a shiver as he remembered the chill of her fingers running over his scalp.

"Warm hands," he said quickly, then threw in a bit of a smirk, hoping that would make the comment seem more lascivious.

Song waved his words away with an impeccably manicured hand. Though he'd shaken it less than a minute ago, BC couldn't remember whether it had been cold or warm. He guessed that it could be either, depending on her inclination. Something told him it would be frigid for him.

"Be more specific. All of our girls have a uniform body temperature."

An image of Naz filled BC's mind. Her eyes flashed in his. Deep, dark, full of fear, but also fiercely protective, as she hovered over Chandler's delirious body in the Millbrook cottage.

"I've always liked a girl with dark eyes," he said, his shyness only half feigned. "Dark hair. Dark . . . skin."

"Exotic or domestic," Song said, as though she were referring to automobiles or beers.

"I'm afraid I don't quite take your meaning."

"Something like me," Song said, with the slightest hint of mockery in her voice—as if the man on the far side of the desk could aspire to a woman like her. "Or something like your ancestors owned?"

Jarrell had called him yesterday.

"Jesus Christ, it took me forever to track you down."

"I'm sorry, I sold my house to pay for those suits."

"You *what?*" Jarrell exclaimed. "Never mind. Okay, first off, I asked around about Mary Meyer. The thing with the president seems to have been over for a while, so I think she's fine."

"And secondly?"

"She's at Song's."

"Mary Meyer is at a brothel?"

"No, you idiot. The girl. Haverman."

"What? How do you know?"

"Your description of her was very . . . memorable." There was a leer in Jarrell's voice, and BC found himself wondering if Jarrell had done more than look.

"What's she doing there? Is she a prisoner?"

"As far as I can tell, she's working."

"As . . . ?"

"It's a brothel, BC." Again the audible leer. BC was glad Jarrell was doing this over the phone, or he was sure he'd've slugged him.

"Why would she do something like that?"

"I'm a spy, not a prosecutor. I don't need motive. Just facts. But don't try anything stupid."

"Stupid?"

"Don't try to rescue her, BC. You'll just get the both of you killed."

"Mr. Gamin?" Song prompted.

"I was thinking something Latin. Or not quite Latin."

"Not quite Latin?"

BC didn't want to be too clear, for fear of seeming too obvious.

"I like Latin features—dark hair, petite frame, curvaceous figure."

"Are you a lover or a dressmaker?"

BC hoped the room was dark enough to conceal his blush.

"I like the look. I just don't go for the Latin temperament. Especially in a girl. It's a little unrefined for my taste. Too forward for a Mississippi boy like me."

"You prefer something more submissive."

"I think I would say quiet. Respectful."

"Quiet." The word seemed to strike a chord with Song.

"Like Natalie Wood," BC said, not quite sure where the name came from. "In *Splendor in the Grass.* But before . . ."

"Before she was ruined." Song nodded. "You shouldn't be so coy, Mr. Gamin. There are no taboos here."

"Must be the Southerner in me, Miss Song. We speak delicately of ladyfolk back home, even when they're professionals."

"Nancy is not to everyone's taste," Song continued, ignoring him, "but her devotees are quite passionate about her charms. That leaves only one remaining detail."

"I assume you mean the money."

Song offered him a slight smile. "We speak as delicately of such matters around here as you do of girls, Mr. Gamin."

"In case the walls have ears?"

Song didn't answer, and BC reached for his new wallet—a gorgeous billfold made from butter-soft caramel-colored leather. It was stuffed with hundreds, and he counted out thirteen as though they were singles, handed them over with a smile.

"Momma always said you get what you pay for."

"Trust me," Song said, "even your mother will agree you're getting your money's worth." She pressed a button and BC heard the door open behind him. "Chul-moo will take you up."

She didn't offer him change, and BC didn't ask for it.

The town house was four stories tall, and Naz's room—if Nancy was in fact Miss Haverman—was on the top floor. BC's heart sank with each ascending flight. How was he going to get her out of here? Because he knew that's what he was here to do. Melchior could wait, and Chandler, too. He touched the ruby ring in his pocket, imagining the glow in Naz's dark eyes when he slipped it on her finger.

But he was getting ahead of himself. There were other questions to address first, not least of which was how Naz had ended up actually working in Song's establishment. Jarrell hadn't made it sound like a place where the girls were forced to do anything. Indeed, he'd suggested that competition to get into Song's was fierce, given that two or three years here could set a girl up for life. The fact that Naz would volunteer for such a fate so quickly after her experiences in Boston and Millbrook didn't speak promisingly of her stability. The only thing harder than getting a girl out of this place would be getting a girl out of this place who didn't want to leave.

On the top floor, Chul-moo paused in front of a closed maple door varnished to mirror sheen. His knuckles rapped on the wood with surprising delicacy, and then he turned the latch, opening the door a quarter inch. He stared at BC as the detective walked into the room, his expression inscrutable yet somehow mocking at the same time. Then the door closed between them, and BC was alone in a small but opulent sitting room furnished with French country antiques upholstered in dove gray damask. Through a silk-curtained archway he glimpsed the foot of a bed that, from the hand-stitched lace border of its bed skirt to the delicate embroidery on the bedspread, was the model of feminine chastity.

A deep wingback chair was angled so that all he could see was a soft wave of dark hair, the supple length of a single silk-covered calf.

"Come in, Mr. Gamin," a female voice said, as soft as Song's had been hard, as far removed from the frantic screaming at Millbrook as it was from the revolution Timothy Leary said had taken her parents. Yet it was unmistakably her.

BC stepped all the way into the room and closed the door. The fact that Naz knew his alias told him that there was an in-house phone, confirming Jarrell's report that the establishment was as wired as Langley. Not sure if he was being watched but taking no chances, he tried to seem as though he was merely admiring the décor as he scanned the room for the probable location of microphone or camera. Then Naz stood up and BC forgot about all that.

For a moment he thought he'd been mistaken. It wasn't her. It couldn't be. This girl was so calm, so inviting. A pale violet dress rolled over the curves of her body from her neck to the tops of her knees, cinched in at the waist to accentuate the swell of hips and bosom. She offered him her profile for a moment, then turned slowly, giving him the rest of the view.

The last time he'd seen her face, it had been twisted in anguish, the hair wild, the skin flushed. Now it was serenely composed, a rich dark amber that sucked up the light and radiated it back with a coppery glow. A hint of green shadow framed her eyes, and her lips had been painted plum. In twenty-five years, BC had never seen a girl in anything other than red lipstick, or at any rate never noticed a girl in anything other than red lipstick. He found himself biting his own lips, wishing they were hers.

If she recognized him, she gave no sign.

"Good evening, Miss—"

"Nancy," she said quickly, then walked to him, laid her arms delicately on his shoulders, turned her face to his. Her mouth was so close that BC could feel the heat coming off her lips. He was about to kiss her—for appearances' sake, of course—when she spoke in a voice as cold as ice.

"You shouldn't have come."

BC pulled her closer, felt the tenseness of her muscles beneath the softness of her dress. "Don't worry, I'm going to get you out of here."

Naz ran her cheek softly against the side of his face. "You stupid boy," she hissed into his ear. "I'm not going anywhere."

Thirty hours after he escaped from Melchior and Keller's San Francisco lab, Chandler woke up in the stolen Imperial in the middle of the Utah Salt Flats. He had been out for eighteen hours—eighteen hours and twenty-two minutes—the knowledge of which was almost as disturbing as the time itself. But, just as on the morning he woke up in Cambridge after sleeping for five days, he felt refreshed rather than disoriented. Unsettled, sure, but not hungry or stiff. He didn't even have to take a leak. His cheeks and chin were virtually as smooth as they were the last time he'd shaved—eighteen days ago. His hair hadn't grown, his fingernails seemed freshly trimmed, even his damn underarms smelled dewily fresh. It was as if he'd stepped out of time itself.

A car went by then, slowing as it passed the shouldered Imperial before speeding away on the empty road. With a start, Chandler realized that if the CIA was looking for him, it would probably check the most direct routes between San Francisco and DC. He started the car and at the first opportunity veered south. He ditched the Imperial in Salt Lake City for a Nash, then swapped that for a battered 1950 Bel Air north of Flagstaff, where he finally worked up the courage to turn east. A white Chrysler followed him for the entire 250 miles between Holbrook, Arizona, and Albuquerque, New Mexico, and Chandler had to keep reminding himself that there was literally nowhere for the Chrysler to turn in the vast stretch of empty desert. Still, it took all his will not to veer south again. By that point he realized it wasn't the CIA he was running from as much as it was himself—from this new version of himself, unchanged on the outside yet completely different under the skin. The only thing that kept him going east, that kept him from driving into Mexico, or into the Gulf of Mexico for that matter, was the thought of Naz. Whatever his ultimate fate, he had to see her one more time. Had to make sure she was safe. And the only way he was going to do that, he knew, was if he took stock of his new abilities. Found out exactly what he could do, and how best to use that power to get Naz away from Melchior.

The Bel Air was running on vapors by the time he pulled into a Phillips 66 in the middle of Texas pastureland. While the pump was ticking he washed the windshield and checked the oil and water, but as he worked he stared absently out at the empty horizon. Fallow fields surrounded the station on all four sides, green-brown grass covering the land from horizon to horizon like a planet-sized bedspread. The only interruption in the emptiness was the station and the two blacktop roads that crisscrossed in front of it, but there must've been a town nearby, because the east-west road sported a fairly steady trickle of traffic. This was as good a place as any, he told himself as he replaced the nozzle in the pump. He had to do it sometime.

He sauntered into the office, smiled at the gas jockey, a small Mexican-looking fellow. Chandler waited till the man was finished counting change for one of the other cars; then:

"Do you have any NoDoz? Or Vivarin?"

"Long drive ahead-a ya?" The gas jockey pulled out a half-empty box of caffeine pills and, when Chandler scooped up four packages, let out a sharp whistle. "Real long drive."

"Gotta get there in a hurry," Chandler said. "I've been dawdling."

"Caffeine'll speed *you* up. Not much's gonna help that ol' jalopy out there. That'll be three seventy, including gas."

Chandler pulled a wrinkled single from his front pocket, and even as he flattened it on the counter he let his mind relax. Because it was like that now—not working to get into someone else's mind, but relaxing, to lower the barriers that kept other people out. In the past four days he'd come to realize that the fundamental root of his power was present even when there was no drug in his system, that he could even conjure tiny illusions if all he was doing was augmenting an object that was already there. Like, say, the addition of a couple of zeroes to a one-dollar bill.

"Criminy, mister. Ain't-cha got nothing smaller? You're gonna clean me out."

"Sorry." Chandler didn't meet the man's eyes (he'd done that to a gas jockey in Utah and the man had had the disconcerting experience of seeing his own face on Chandler's body). Little flashes flickered in and out of his mind: a fat boss with a greasy merkin of fake hair pasted to his bald pate, a pregnant wife with ankles swollen to the size of milk bottles, a couple of Spanish words: *lechuga, miércoles*. He kept his breathing steady as the gas jockey pulled three twenties from the till, two tens, two fives, four singles, a couple of dollars in silver. He was about to count out the thirty cents in pennies when Chandler told him to keep it. He shoved the money in his pocket—his billfold already bulged with more than three hundred dollars—then headed back out into the Texas sun. As he climbed into the Bel Air he looked around again. Not a house or building in sight. Just the pastures and the two lonely roads and the trickle of cars. He drove about a quarter mile south until he reached a small field that seemed to serve as a used-car lot, then stopped the car.

For a long time he just sat there, gripping the wheel as though it were the bar of a roller coaster and if he let go he would go flying into space. Then, abruptly, he reached for the vial he'd taken from Keller's lab. He'd dipped into it sparingly over the past six days. Among other things, he'd noticed that using more than a few drops seemed to burn up all the energy in his body, and one time, after he'd spilled a dollop of the clear liquid on his palm and licked it up, he'd tripped for just under three hours, then slept for more than twenty. He thought he might be able to counteract the latter effect with a jolt of something—Benzedrine, cocaine, or just a lot of caffeine. Hence the NoDoz.

He took the caffeine pills first. A whole package, washed down three at a time with half a bottle of flat Coca-Cola. After a few minutes he felt a little jittery, but that could've just been nerves. After a quarter of an hour he started to twitch. His breath came fast and hollow, his chest felt tight.

He looked down at the vial in his shaking hand. He'd caught glimpses of it in Keller's mind, knew it contained about ten thousand doses of acid. It was still more than half-full.

He took a deep breath.

"Down the hatch," he muttered aloud, and tossed back the contents of the vial like a shot of whiskey.

He closed his eyes, as best he could anyway. There was so much caffeine coursing through his bloodstream that his eyelids were spasming, and he could feel his heart pounding against his ribs.

It happened fast now. Less than five minutes after he swallowed the acid he was hallucinating behind his closed eyes, and less than five minutes after that he'd moved past the hallucination stage as his body did the extra thing it did, turned the acid into some new chemical that in turn turned his brain into a giant radio antenna.

When he opened his eyes, there was the by-now familiar scrim, faint objects—today it was mostly ribbons of color, vivid but translucent—wafting over the real world, but if he concentrated on something—say, the modernist wedge of the gas station in the rearview mirror—it emerged in sharp relief. There were faint whispers, too, so real that he even turned and looked in the backseat until he realized they were coming from the minds of the people back at the station. *Hurry it up, buddy,* he heard someone think, and he decided to take the suggestion to heart.

He got out of the car and walked down the center of the road like a gunslinger in an old Western, getting ready to push through the swinging doors of a saloon and shoot the place up. *Rollin', rollin', rollin' . . .*

The gas jockey was back outside, moving slowly but efficiently between the vehicles. Joe Gonzalez, Chandler learned now, the information absorbed as effortlessy as sight and sound. That was the gas jockey's name.

There were four cars in the station. Chandler could see five, possibly six shadows in the cars. But if he ignored the evidence of his eyes, he could tell that the four vehicles held seven occupants—there was a baby in the backseat of the Chrysler driven by Mae Watson and her spinster sister Emily. The baby's dreams were little flickering flashes of color, and it was these Chandler let out first. Orange and yellow lights began to pulse across the empty fields.

"Fireflies," Dan Karnovsky, sitting alone in the Buick behind Mae and Emily, mused to himself. "Nice tits," he added when Mae leaned out of the car to tell Joe Gonzalez to check the air pressure in the tires.

But Chandler didn't just want to pull images from other people's minds. He wanted to see if he could make something himself. It was hard to isolate. Between the hallucinations and the bits and pieces of other minds, his own thoughts were hard to find.

Concentrate, Chandler!

Mae turned to her sister.

"Did you say something, sis?" About my breasts, she added, but silently.

"Huh?" Emily said, but Mae didn't hear her.

Neither did Chandler.

Push, he said to himself, and screwed his eyes shut. *Push!*

In the Watsons' Chrysler, Baby Leo woke up crying.

Joe Gonzalez, pulling the nozzle from Jared Steinke's Dodge, stopped dead in his tracks. Fortunately, the handle he was holding was closed, and only a few drops of gasoline spilled on the stained concrete. But Joe didn't see them because he was staring at the sky.

"Dios mío."

A flash of light was tearing a hole in the air above the crosshairs of the intersection. Silent, smokeless flames belched skyward, but instead of dissipating into the atmosphere they remained tightly knitted together like bolts of lightning emanating from a single dense thunderhead. In a moment the figure had taken shape. The legs, the arms, the head. The open eyes and mouth. He wasn't a boy now. Not anymore. He was a warrior. A messenger from God. A roiling, fiery seraph more than a hundred feet high.

A Ford on the highway veered sharply to the left and bucked through the shallow drainage ditch and through a barbed-wire fence.

Chandler opened his eyes, looked at the figure in the sky with as much disbelief as the eight people in the gas station (and Wally O'Shea, the driver of the Ford, which had skidded to a stop in the middle of a fallow pasture). First Millbrook, then San Francisco, now Texas. It was as if the seraph was following him, as if he was trying to tell him something.

"Who *are* you?" he demanded, even as the figure turned to look at him, its mouth open, silent, desolate, yet mocking at the same time. "Go away!" Chandler screamed. He waved his hands at the flaming figure. "Leave me alone!"

But the figure lingered on, the flames of its body so bright they cast shadows for what seemed like miles in every direction. An arm lifted from its side, raised up, pointed. As if to make sure there was no mistake, it reached out and out and out till it was inches away from Chandler's face. Though it was easy to see the finger as some kind of accusation, Chandler saw it more as a summons, a selection: a heavenly version of Uncle Sam's "I Want You."

"No!" he screamed at the warrior. "I refuse! I do not accept this responsibility!" He swatted at the finger like a cornered kitten swiping at a rabid Saint Bernard. "Go away!"

And just like that, the warrior disappeared. No flash, no flicker, no poof. It was simply gone, leaving Chandler alone at the edge of the parking lot with eight pairs of terrified eyes staring at him. For a moment there were only the screams of Mae's baby, and then Joe Gonzalez coughed.

"¿Señor? ¿Eres el diablo?"

Naz led BC in a slow two-step around the sitting room. She'd put a record on the turntable, and quiet jazz wafted from hidden speakers, but her fingernails bit into BC's shoulders like an eagle's talons, as though she wanted to rip him apart.

"Don't you understand?" she hissed into his chest. "That man will kill him."

"His name is Melchior," BC whispered into the dark waves of Naz's hair, "and I don't think he will. Chandler's too special."

"I've thought this through," Naz insisted. "The only way he can get Chandler to obey him is if he threatens me. But if I escape—if Chandler finds out I've escaped—he'll refuse to do what Melchior tells him to. And then Melchior will kill him."

"But how would Chandler find out you got away? Melchior would never tell him."

"Trust me. Chandler will find out."

Naz's tone discouraged further questioning, but BC knew what she was referring to. The reason he was here. The reason Chandler had been taken in the first place. Orpheus.

"Melchior's no amateur. Neither are the people he works for. They'll experiment on Chandler till they find out how his power works, how they can duplicate it. Once they've created willing subjects, they'll dispose of him. Believe me, you risk more for Chandler, as well as yourself, by waiting."

"There are risks no matter what we do. That's what happens when these people start to meddle in your lives. Believe me when I tell you, it will be easier for Chandler to find me than for me to find him."

"I spoke to Dr. Leary, Miss Haverman," BC whispered. "I know about Persia. About your parents and Mr. Haverman and the way Eddie Logan blackmailed you into giving people LSD. But you can get away from them. You can take them down, if you go public with your story, rather than try to beat them at their own game."

Naz gasped, and had to bury her face in BC's chest to conceal it. He felt her breath through the mercerized Egyptian cotton of his shirt. For a long moment there was just the soft croon of a saxophone, the cool thump of an upright bass. Then Naz stepped back from BC, holding on to his hands, and offered him a full view of her body.

"This way, Mr. Gamin."

BC instinctively went toward the door, but she pulled him in the direction of the bed.

"Miss—Nancy?" BC did his best to keep the confusion off his face.

Naz walked backward into the bedroom, leading BC as though he were a toddler.

"The camera is directly behind me," she whispered. "In the clock on the mantel. You're going to take your jacket off, then your shirt, then your pants. Toss them any which way. Then take my dress off me, and toss it over the clock."

"Why—"

"If you covered the camera with the first thing you took off, it would look too convenient. And please. Try to look lustful rather than constipated."

She released his hands and twirled across the floor as lightly as a music-box ballerina. Her beauty made it easier. Her beauty and her laughter and the way the dress spun away from her when she moved, only to settle all the more tightly over her curves when she stilled. BC almost believed she really was trying to arouse him. When he licked his lips, he wasn't acting.

He loosened the button on his jacket, let it fall from his shoulders, and tossed it across the room (he couldn't bring himself to toss it on the floor, however, and aimed for the wingback chair instead). Naz shimmied forward to loosen his tie, then pulled it off his neck as she shimmied backward. She ran the silk over her cheek and tossed it aside.

The look on her face was pure, the sexual energy palpable from five feet away. BC's fingers fumbled with the buttons of his shirt. He'd never undressed in front of a woman besides his mother, and not even that since he was three years old and his mother taught him that his private parts included everything between his neck and his knees. The only thing that made it possible was the look on Naz's face. The parted lips, the open stare. It was obvious that this beautiful creature knew everything he didn't. That she could give him the things he'd always been too embarrassed to ask for.

His shirt slipped from his shoulders. He flicked it with his wrist and it glided like an owl for a few feet before pouncing on one of his shoes. He didn't remember kicking the shoe off, but there it was. He kicked the other one off now. Italian leather, hand-stitched, with hard soles that thumped on the floors like drumsticks. They'd cost him the equivalent of a month's salary, and here he was tossing them off like sweaty sneakers.

It seemed necessary to remove his belt before he took off his pants. It slid out of the loops like a snake from its hole, the thin silver buckle glinting like a flickering tongue. Then the buttons of his fly. There were five of them, and he undid them all. Naz's eyes never left his, yet somehow he felt that her attention was focused on his groin, slowly coming into view.

Naz nodded. BC let go of his pants and they fell like a stage curtain. He felt the cool air of the room on his legs, felt the hair horripilate from calves to the nape of his neck.

For the first time another look entered Naz's eyes.

"Beau?" she whispered—she was using his alias, but what he heard was Melchior's mocking "Beau" on the train between DC and New York, and the disjunction enflamed BC. He took Naz by her bare, cool, thin shoulders, pressed her against his body in an embrace that was equal parts lust and power and contempt. He smashed her lips with his own, forced his tongue into her mouth. For a moment there was nothing, and then she was kissing him back, pulling him to her as hard as he was pulling her to him, and that's all there was for a minute or a lifetime, BC had no idea, until Naz's hands loosened on his shoulders, her mouth softened, her tongue retreated. Her sudden lassitude seemed to infect him, and he let go of her in confusion. Her eyes were looking down, at his feet, a pair of half-inflated circus balloons in their gaudy silk socks, at his crotch, equally painted in bright silk boxers, and equally flaccid.

"I—I didn't know."

BC wanted to hit her then, to wipe the look of pity off her face, but he wanted to hit himself even more. Wanted to turn and run from the room with his clothes clutched to his chest like a spurned lover. But it wasn't Naz who had rejected him. It was he who had rejected Naz. At any rate, his body had. His body, which never failed him in any other situation—be it boxing or gathering evidence at a crime scene or holding up a suit of clothes and making them look like a man—this body had rejected Naz's flesh like a finicky cat turning up its nose at a saucer of cream. Before he could do anything, though, Naz turned around. Oh, she was a consummate professional. She could make the bones of her skull and shoulders seem as soft and alluring as her cheeks, her lips, her breasts. But even BC knew it was all just for show now.

"If you would help me with my zipper, Mr. Gamin."

It could have been the zipper on a body bag for all the tenderness BC showed. The violet fabric parted, revealing the white silk desert of her slip. Naz turned, steadied herself with one hand on his implacable shoulder, and stepped out of the dress, which BC held by both collar and hem, as though it were a flag that couldn't touch the ground.

She was clothed only in her slip and stockings now. BC held the dress in his arms for a moment more, then, without looking, he tossed it over the camera.

In a flash Naz was on him.

"I'm going to press the trouble button." The coldness of her hiss shocked him, but it also brought him back to his senses. "They're supposed to send up both men. Chul-moo, the majordomo, and Garrison, who works—"

"The surveillance booth," BC finished for her. "And the third man?"

"I didn't know there was a third man."

BC scanned the room, then, still in his skivvies, headed toward the bed.

"What are you—"

A faint *crack* cut Naz off as BC wrested the ball off the top of one of the bedposts. He tossed it to Naz, then wrenched off a second for himself. It was about the size of a croquet ball and made of solid walnut, but using it would mean getting close to Chul-moo's sinewy arms, not to mention Garrison's gun. That left the mysterious third man, if he showed himself. And Song, of course.

"I don't know if I can hit a woman," BC said to Naz.

"Leave her to me," Naz said. Her knuckles were so white around the ball that BC was surprised it didn't shatter in her grasp.

The arrayed faces in the filling station stared at Chandler with a combination of fear and revulsion. He stared back, unsure of what to do. He glanced at his car. It was farther away than he'd realized. Somehow he thought running would only make things worse.

"M-mister," Emily said. "Did you do that?" She pointed to the empty air over the intersection.

Without thinking, Chandler changed his face. It was an instinct. He didn't know where it came from. But in the fraction of a second that it took him to turn back to Emily, a stranger's features floated up from the depths of his mind and covered his own. He couldn't see it himself, of course. But he could see it in the eyes of everyone looking at him: the sharp chin, the tiny smirk, the eyes, amused and scared at the same time.

Melchior's friend from the orphanage. Caspar.

Chandler pushed the image into the minds of everyone in front of him in the hope that it would erase his own face from their memories. He saw them wince, and thought he could probably do more damage if he wanted to, but he had no desire to hurt them. *Leave!* he told them, pushing the word into their minds as hard as he could. *Go away!*

Instead of leaving, Jared Steinke got out of his old Dodge pickup and opened the handmade toolbox straddling the bed. Chandler saw what Jared was going for even before he pulled it out: a double-barreled shotgun, fully loaded. Jared had been planning on getting a head start on pheasant season, which officially opened Thanksgiving Day.

"Jared," his mother screamed from the passenger seat—he'd been taking her to the hospital in Wichita Falls to get her diabetes checked— "Jared, get back in this car right now!"

Joe Gonzalez, seeing the shotgun in Steinke's hands, turned and trotted toward the filling station office. It might've looked like he was running for cover, but the pistol beneath the cash register burned brightly in his mind.

Jared Steinke raised the shotgun to his shoulder.

"The Lord is my shepherd, I shall not want—"

He was squeezing the trigger when the ravens swooped down on him and he jerked the rifle up just as it fired. The glass of the Phillips sign exploded in a shower of sparks.

Chandler hadn't seen the new Hitchcock movie, but Emily had, and it was her mind that gave him the ravens. He made just a pair at first, but then he added a dozen, two dozen more. A cloud of birds spiraled down on Jared Steinke like an avian tornado and Jared stumbled backward but refused to drop the shotgun. The pain as the ravens' dagger-like beaks and razor-sharp talons slashed his skin felt so real that Chandler was surprised Jared wasn't actually bleeding.

Now Joe Gonzalez was running back out of the office, pistol in hand. He fired at the ravens attacking Jared Steinke, who was standing right next to the number three pump. On the third shot he nicked the hose and dark gas began spewing over the concrete.

"Mae," Emily said to her sister, "if you want your baby to live to be baptized, you best drive *now*."

Jared Steinke, as frightened by Joe Gonzalez's shots as he was by the ravens, began firing wildly. The first shot caught Dan Karnovsky full in the chest as he was getting out of his Buick. The second shot blew apart the number one pump, and more gas began spewing onto the concrete. Already an area the size of a backyard swimming pool had been transformed into a black mirror, reflecting Joe and Jared and Jared's mother ducking out the driver's side door of Jared's truck and scampering across the glassy surface of the gasoline like Jesus walking on the water. Chandler saw none of this. He was concentrating on the ravens, trying to drive the crowd away. His head ached with the effort, and he could feel the sweat running down his spine.

There was a cough and a backfire as the engine of Mae Watson's Chrysler caught. Gasoline sprayed from beneath her tires as she sped toward the filling station's exit.

"Go, sis!" Emily hissed at her sister. She had seen *The Birds* seventeen times. She knew how this scene ended. "Go, go, go!"

Chandler felt her panic, pushed it into everyone's mind even as he felt his own mind wavering. It was too much. Energy was draining from him like the gas pouring from the pumps—not just the power to conjure and hold his hallucinations, but the simple strength to stand. The ravens were flickering in and out like a rolling picture on an old TV, and he knew he couldn't keep them going for much longer. He could feel the chemicals burning up in his body like a V8 with the pedal pushed to the floor. It was a matter of seconds, not minutes, before he ran out of gas, and who knew how long after that he'd be able to stay conscious.

Janet Steinke was halfway across the parking lot when Mae Watson's Chrysler, still spitting up a fine mist of gasoline, passed underneath the shattered Phillips sign, which was shooting out the occasional spark like a dud firecracker. A moment later the air turned orange as the mist ignited. In another moment the gas on the concrete caught, and the pool was transformed into a lake of fire.

Joe Gonzalez was just out of reach of the flames, and he turned and ran for the shelter of the office. The Steinkes weren't so lucky. Mother and son caught fire almost instantly. Janet Steinke tripped and fell and lost consciousness, thus saved the horror of feeling the flesh burned off her bones like the charred husks of barbecued corn, but Jared was too hopped up on adrenaline to pass out. The flames engulfed his gasoline-saturated clothing, and in seconds he'd been transformed into the living manifestation of the image that Chandler had placed in the sky less than a minute before. Only then did Jared start to run.

He ran straight for Chandler, the shotgun still in his hands. When he was halfway across the burning gas the last two bullets in his gun exploded, but by then all the nerves in his skin were dead and he didn't feel it. His lips were gone, his nose, his eyelids. His eyes had started to melt, so he couldn't see anything. Not with his eyes. But in his mind—in what was left of it—the image of Satan's demon burned brighter than the flames engulfing his body, and he ran straight for it.

Chandler stood there and watched him come. All he'd wanted to do was test his power, and now—now two people were dead, and a third about to join them. And him, too—he was going to die if the flaming form of Jared Steinke managed to reach him. But all he could do was stand there and watch death hurtle toward him just as BC had.

BC? Who was BC?

He was saved by the explosion. The flames seeped into the underground tanks, and a fireball blew the pumps and the four cars and the canopy that covered them fifty feet into the air. The shock wave picked up Jared Steinke's body and threw him over Chandler like the angel of death he so resembled, and knocked Chandler ten feet back on his ass. The column of fire shot more than a hundred feet in the air, looking for all the world like a miniature atomic explosion. Red flames and black smoke etched concentric rings in the colorless Plains sky.

For a long time Chandler lay there, unsure if he was dead. The only minds he was able to feel were Joe Gonzalez's, running more or less due east away from the station, and Wally O'Shea's, the driver of the Ford that'd crashed into the pasture, who was hightailing it in the opposite direction.

He staggered to his feet. His head was throbbing and his body hurt almost as much. He felt like he'd just tried to stop the entire offensive line of the Yale Bulldogs, which wasn't a particularly good football team (neither was Harvard's when you got right down to it), but still. He was aching. He set off slowly down the road toward his car, spots dancing in front of his eyes as he struggled to keep them open. So much for the caffeine pills. He was so tired it was painful, but it was a bit of a blessing, too. Otherwise he'd have had to contemplate what he'd done.

He'd killed three people.

Not directly, maybe. But if he hadn't been experimenting with his newfound abilities, there was no doubt they'd still be alive.

All his life he'd run in the opposite direction from his uncle's world, his uncle's wars, because he didn't want anyone's blood on his hands, and now three people were dead because of him. He was a soldier, willing or not, of the United States of America, which happened to be the enemy as well. His general was named Melchior, and so was his adversary. And Chandler was going to find him and kill him and rescue Naz, and then—

And then he was going to kill himself, and save the world—save himself—from whatever it was he'd become.

A knock, a rattled doorknob. The sound of a bolt thumping into its housing. The door opened halfway, and Chul-moo bounded into the room.

"Miss Nancy? Where—"

The newel ball smashing into the side of Chul-moo's head made a muffled crack like a tree branch breaking inside a thick shroud of ice. Even as the boy crumpled to the ground, the door smashed the rest of the way open. Naz, who'd been standing behind it, was sent flying. Her hand cracked against the wall and the ball fell from her fingers and disappeared beneath the bed. Garrison stepped over Chul-moo's form, his revolver already drawn, then stopped when he saw who he faced.

"Nancy?"

His voice was confused, but then a light went on in his eyes. He whirled, just in time for BC to smash his own newel ball into Garrison's forehead. The guard seemed to freeze in place, his fingers still holding his gun, until BC whaled him a second time, and he fell on top of Chul-moo.

BC dropped the ball, was reaching for Garrison's weapon when a voice came from the hallway.

"Back away from the gun."

He looked up. Song stood just outside the door, pistol in hand and aimed at his head. She advanced as he retreated, retrieved Garrison's weapon and tucked it into the waistline of her skirt like a demurely dressed Annie Oakley. Before she could do anything else, though, Naz spoke.

"You *bitch*."

Loathing dripped from her voice like venom. BC could feel the hatred roiling off her in palpable waves. Song actually shuddered, as if she'd been struck.

"Nancy?" Song turned halfway, trying to look at Naz without losing sight of BC. "I don't understand. You volunteered. You—you *insisted*."

BC couldn't figure out what was happening. A despair as great as any he'd ever felt had gripped his brain and body. It was like his father's death and mother's death and his demotion from Behavioral Profiling to COINTELPRO had all been mixed with liquid nitrogen and poured into his veins, freezing him in place. If he'd had a knife in his hand, he would have stabbed himself, just to end the suffering. Just like—

Just like Eddie Logan.

He stared at Naz. Her hands were balled into fists, and she took tiny steps toward Song, heedless of the madam's gun, which was trained directly, if unsteadily, in her direction. Despite the whiteness of her slip, she seemed like a demon from hell. Her hair had come loose and radiated out from her head in inky waves, and her eyes were two dark coals burning into Song's body.

BC turned to the madam. Whatever he was feeling, it was obvious she was feeling something a hundred times worse. Her normally taut body had gone slack and the gun dangled from her twitching fingers. She pressed her left hand against her temple.

"Stop it," she begged. "Stop it, please, stop it!"

In the depths of his own blackness, BC recognized what he was feeling as the same terror that had gripped him at Millbrook. He'd thought the fear had come from the disorienting hallucination radiating from Chandler's brain, but now he realized the feelings, if not the images, had been coming from *Naz*—

—who was trembling, he saw, nearly as much as Song. Sweat beaded her face, and she grabbed a chair back for support. Whatever she was doing, however she was doing it, it was costing her dearly. BC knew he had to act.

"Here!" he yelled, staggering to his feet. He needed to draw Song's aim. She jerked in his direction, squinting in an effort to concentrate, but BC was faster. He knocked her wrist to the side as she squeezed the trigger and a hole appeared in the floor.

BC fixed Song in the eye. "I apologize, ma'am," he said, then decked her with an elbow to the—

But Song wasn't there. In the half second it had taken BC to move, she'd recovered, ducked, and now he felt her heel in the small of his back. He went reeling forward and sprawled on his stomach. He rolled over to see Song bringing the gun up to aim.

"No!"

BC and Song whirled in Naz's direction, just in time to see Naz's arm flash. The wooden newel ball was a blur in the air until it slammed into Song's temple and she fell to the floor.

Sounds of commotion were coming from the rest of the house, but Naz's screams were louder, as she fell on Song and began beating her with her fists.

"If he's dead, I'll come back for you! I'll make you suffer in ways you can't even imagine!"

"Miss Haverman!" BC pushed through the waves of fury rolling off her to grab one of her wrists. "We need to go."

Naz looked up wildly, her teeth bared in a snarl, and BC fell backward as if he'd been struck. Then Naz's eyes cleared and her face softened.

"Agent Querrey?" She seemed surprised to see him in the room, in his underwear. Especially *that* underwear.

BC shook his head. "It's just Mr. Querrey now."

Naz shook her head dazedly. "I'll get your pants."

They dressed quickly. BC checked the hall for the third guard, but all he saw was an open door to one of the bedrooms. A half-naked man peeked out, saw the gun BC had taken from Song, and ducked back inside. BC motioned to Naz, and they went for the stairs.

He heard Naz's "Oh!" just before a blow caught him squarely between the shoulders. He slammed against the spindly banister, which broke beneath the impact, and he fell half a floor to the stair treads and rolled the rest of the way down. He had the presence of mind to hold on to his pistol, which turned out to be a mistake—he squeezed so tightly that it went off and a bullet whizzed by his ear. He dropped the gun just as he smashed into a pedestal table at the bottom of the stairs. An enormous vase flew into the air, narrowly missing BC's head before smashing into the floor.

His attacker was on him before he'd stopped moving. Like Chulmoo, he was Asian, but full grown: tall, muscular, and very, very fast. He seemed to fly down the stairs, grabbing a pair of broken banister railings as he went and brandishing them like swords.

BC felt a momentary surge of relief—at least the man didn't have a gun. Then the guard began hitting him with the railings—in the legs, the torso, the arms, each blow stinging as sharply as a whiplash. The guard caught him with a blow to the side of the head and then a foot slammed into BC's ribs, sending him flying back over the table.

The guard leapt after him, but slipped on the pieces of broken vase all over the floor. It was the closest thing to a break BC had caught. He grabbed the fallen table by its central leg and held it in front of him like a shield. It vibrated beneath the guard's blows as BC attempted to shoo him back like a matador facing down a bull.

Suddenly the guard dropped the pair of railings and grabbed the edges of the tabletop. BC braced himself, expecting the man to push, but instead the guard spun it so rapidly that the feet at the base of the table spun like propeller blades, smashing him on the chin. Stars flashed in BC's eyes and he went down hard on the ceramic-covered floor. The guard kicked at his ribs, and BC barely managed to roll out of the way. He felt ceramic shards cutting into his suit, and for some reason this made him angrier than anything else.

"Do you *know*"—he panted, rolling down the hall to avoid the guard's kicks—"how much I *paid*"—still rolling—"for this *suit?*" His fingers clutched at the shards, and finally he managed to grab one. He flung out his arm to stop himself, braced himself for impact, and felt the guard's foot slam into his abdomen. A bolt of lightning stabbed through his body. As the air rushed out of his lungs he threw everything he could into a single blow, jamming the shard into the guard's femoral artery.

The guard staggered backward, the piece of ceramic protruding from his thigh. At first BC wasn't sure he'd managed to stab deeply enough, but then a dark stain plastered the man's trouser leg to his skin. Within seconds blood was seeping from beneath the man's cuff and pooling around his shoe.

Wincing as he struggled for breath, BC leaned heavily against the wall and pushed himself to his feet. He lifted his arms, and another bolt of lightning sliced through his chest. He didn't know if he had the strength to hold his arms up, let alone throw a punch, but the guard was still standing. BC had no choice. Warily, wheezingly, he advanced.

The guard took his own halting step in BC's direction, but it was clear that his injured leg wasn't going to hold his weight. For a moment the two men just stared each other down. Then the guard shrugged and reached into his jacket and pulled out a long knife.

He smiled, not so much wickedly as triumphantly, as he raised it above his head to throw.

Before he could, however, a shot rang out, and he pitched forward. BC looked up the stairs as Naz descended. There was a spot of blood on her lip, but otherwise she seemed unhurt. Unhurt, but exhausted. She clutched the banister, and on the penultimate step she stumbled. If BC hadn't stepped forward to catch her—the pain in his ribs was as bad as when the guard had kicked him—she would have fallen to the floor. For three long breaths she leaned heavily on him, then recovered enough to stand on her own.

"That—upstairs," BC said, taking the gun from her trembling fingers. "Is that what happened at Millbrook? To Eddie Logan?"

Again he felt that sudden connection, not of sex or rage this time, but an empty sorrow, as of a bucket striking the bottom of a well whose water has long since dried up.

"Everyone who knows me ends up dead or gone," Naz said in a muted voice. "My parents, Agent Logan, Chandler. I hope you fare better, Mr. Querrey."

BC did his best to smile. "I have something for you." He reached into his pocket for the ring he'd been carrying around for the past ten days, then stopped when Naz's eyes went wide with horror. She grabbed BC's arm and pulled herself right next to him.

"Tell Chandler," she hissed just before BC's head exploded in a shower of sparks. "I'm *pregnant.*"

Pavel Semyonovitch Ivelitsch exchanged the brass lamp he'd hit BC with for a pen he pulled from his pocket, which, when uncapped, revealed not a nib but a needle.

"Everyone seems quite interested in you," he said, pressing the needle against Naz's suddenly pliant arm. "I think it's time we found out *how* interested."

"I don't understand how you let this happen!"

Melchior's growl practically rattled the paintings off the walls of Song's office. Although maybe it was just his feet: the shoes he'd taken from Rip came down so heavily on the small Persian carpet that it seemed he was trying to grind it to dust.

Song sat at her desk, rubbing a knot on the side of her head. Melchior could tell from her pout that she was pressing hard enough for it to hurt.

"I suspected the man was KGB. Now I know."

"And this one's FBI." Melchior jerked a thumb at BC. "I thought you said your establishment was secure, yet somehow you've managed to run afoul of the three largest intelligence and law-enforcement agencies in the world in the space of a single night."

"Maybe if you'd told me what I was dealing with—"

"A mentally unstable twenty-three-year-old prostitute with a drinking problem? I thought you were supposed to be able to handle things like that."

"Nancy—"

"*Naz.*" BC spoke for the first time since Melchior had shown up. He lifted his head slowly, a lump the size of a dumpling visible through his high-and-tight. "Her name is Naz."

"Another thing you didn't tell me," Song said to Melchior.

"What other thing?" Melchior demanded again. "*What* didn't I tell you?"

"She . . . did something. I don't know how to describe it."

"Yes, you do," BC said.

Song and Melchior both turned to him.

"She made you feel bad," BC said. "So bad you wanted to kill yourself." BC looked up at Melchior. "Just like Eddie Logan did."

"Who's Eddie Logan?" Song asked.

"He was a CIA agent," BC said.

"If you don't shut your fucking mouth, I'm going to—" Melchior broke off, walked the two steps to BC's chair, and backhanded him across his bruised skull. "Shut *up*."

"You sent a fugitive from CIA here without telling me? Good God. I almost set her up with Drew Everton. It's amazing KGB got her before the entire Company came down on this place. What the hell were you *thinking?*"

Melchior glared at BC for a moment before turning back to Song.

"I was thinking . . ." He shook his head. "I don't know what I was thinking. My stateside contacts are thin. You were all I had."

"I don't mind that you turned to me. I mind that you didn't fill me in. Do you think I would have let her out of the residence if I'd known CIA was looking for her, let alone KGB?" She paused. "Melchior, you have to tell me what you're doing. Not just with Naz." Her eyes burned into his. "With Orpheus."

Song's face was inscrutable. Was she trying to help him, Melchior wondered, or herself? He didn't know. And what did he want from her anyway? Assistance, or something more?

What the hell was he doing? Risking his life to squirrel Orpheus away from the Company, and then Cuba, too. If only Chandler hadn't disappeared. If only it hadn't been Rip the Company sent after him. If only KGB hadn't entered the fray. He could have handled one thing at a time: Song, or Naz, or Chandler, or Cuba. But all of them, all at once. It was too much.

"Melchior," Song said again. "Are you going—?"

"Don't say it!" He jerked a thumb at BC. "We have to get rid of this one first."

Song's eyebrows flicked, just once. "Killing FBI agents? You *have* come a long way since the last time I saw you."

"Believe me, there's nothing I'd like to do more than drill Beau here through the eyes, but that's the kind of heat I don't need on top of everything else. But don't worry, there are other ways to take care of him—ways he'll enjoy a lot less than death." He pulled a vial from his pocket. "How's Garrison's head? Can he work a camera?"

Song paused a moment, then smiled. "I think he can manage."

o   o   o

An hour later, Song and Melchior stood in the open archway between Lee Anne's sitting room and bedroom. The only sound in the suite was the clicking of a camera shutter and a faint, confused moaning.

On the bed a headless, naked male torso and a pair of well-muscled legs stuck out from beneath Lee Anne's large firm buttocks and wild mane of hair. BC's skin seemed even whiter against Lee Anne's chocolate brownness, and his moans echoed out from her nether regions.

"What did you give him?"

"A combination of things. LSD, coupled with methamphetamine to keep him awake, and six shots of Scotch to make sure his breath smells extra sweet when the cops find him."

"I hope you didn't raid my private supply. It costs fifty dollars a bottle."

"It costs someone fifty dollars a bottle. I doubt it's you."

"The LSD seems to have had a *suppressing* effect on him."

Melchior chuckled. "Somehow I don't think it's the drugs that're keeping BC's little soldier down."

"How's this?" Lee Anne's back was arched so that her ass peeked out from beneath the feathered hem of her negligee, and her breasts sat atop her brassiere as though on a shelf.

"You look great, baby," Melchior said, "but we gotta see his face. Scoot down his chest a bit."

"Naz?" BC said when his mouth was uncovered. His hands fumbled at Lee Anne's breasts. "I'm sorry, they're just so"—he shook one up and down—*"bouncy."*

Song stiffened at the mention of Naz. "There's something about that girl."

"You should meet her boyfriend."

"Orpheus?"

Melchior waved the question away.

"Let's finish this first."

"Actually," Song said, "I'm more concerned about this." She reached into her pocket and pulled out a piece of paper, handed it to Melchior.

TELL MELCHIOR I KNOW ABOUT CUBA.
—P.S. IVELITSCH

Melchior crumpled the note in his hand. "Fuck."

Song waited. Then, when it was clear Melchior wasn't going to be more forthcoming: "Can I offer some advice?"

"Shoot."

"You need an organization."

"To do what?"

"To do what you're doing."

"Don't say it."

Song turned him away from the bed and made him look her in the eye.

"Melchior," she said. "You're going rogue."

Melchior was silent a long time. He looked down at the crumpled piece of paper in his hand.

"Fuck," he said again.

Song surprised him then. She put her hand on his shoulder, turned her face to his. Somehow the little knot on the side of her head made her that much more attractive.

"Yes," she said. "Let's."

"Flip him over," Garrison was saying as they left the room. "And hand me that newel ball. He thinks popping me upside the head was painful, but it ain't nothing to what it'll feel like when I stick that piece-a wood where the sun don't shine."

It was easy to climb the snake ladder once you set your mind to it.

He'd been afraid the snakes were going to bite him, but soon enough he realized they couldn't—if they opened their mouths the ladder would come apart and the snakes would fall to their deaths in the canyon below, which was inexplicably filled with camellias. Camellias made from cut glass.

Well, a lot was inexplicable really. Like why he was climbing a snake ladder, or why it led to a giant nest woven of tubes and wires, or why there was a baby sitting inside the nest.

His baby.

His and Naz's.

He wasn't sure how they'd made a baby, since all he'd done was squeeze her breasts—which had been much larger than he'd thought they'd be, and browner, too—and he was a little surprised their child was still an infant, since it had been almost three centuries since the last time he'd seen her. But he didn't worry about that, just as he didn't worry about why the infant was the size of a rhinoceros. It was his baby—his and Naz's—and it was calling him. He had to go to his son.

He himself had grown so old that his wrinkles had turned to scales. Well, less snake scales than lizard skin. His fingernails had grown into claws, and his hair had been replaced by a dorsal ridge that extended from the top of his head to the tip of his tail, which hung down several feet lower than his legs. He didn't remember when any of these changes had occurred, but he accepted them at face value because they were what he saw when he looked in the mirror, or when he closed his eyes for that matter. There were mirrors inside his eyelids now, and they reflected him more perfectly than any looking glass ever had.

He was nearly at the top of the ladder now. The snakes hissed and writhed in his grasp, but none bit him. For all he knew they were his friends and not his enemies. It was hard to tell these days.

He glanced up. The tubes and wires and plates of soldered steel that made his son's nest were familiar for some reason, although he couldn't remember where he'd seen them before, and even though they weren't transparent he could still see the boy's shadow through their tangled mass. His chubby legs splayed in front of his torso, his pudgy arms batted at the air. The nest itself was huge. As big as a pile of towels in the laundry room of a prison. Given the size, the boy must be seven, eight feet tall. BC wondered if he had been born this big or grown to this size. It would have been a painful delivery for Naz.

He reached the lip of the nest sooner than he expected, toppled over the edge into its hollow cradle. The boy was even bigger than he'd imagined. Eight or nine feet tall from the bottom of his diapered rump to the wisp of hair on his otherwise bald head, which was easily five feet in diameter. Except . . . except the head wasn't a head.

It was a bomb.

An old-fashioned bomb, perfectly spherical, with two chalk circles marking the boy's eyes and a single line stretching from ear to ear for a mouth. The coil of hair growing from the head was actually a fuse, and the fuse was burning. For some reason its glowing end reminded BC of the tip of a cigar, but before he could figure out why, the fuse reached the bomb with a little *pfft* of smoke.

BC braced himself, but all that happened was that the mouth opened with a clockwork whir, revealing row after row of slimy, sharp teeth and a sulfurous glint coming from the back of its throat. BC squinted. It was Naz's ring.

Tell Chandler, the mouth said, opening wider and wider.

"Tell him what?" BC said.

Tell him about me, the mouth said, and then, darting forward, it swallowed him whole.

The beat cop who found BC on the corner of Chesapeake and Seventh Street SE nudged the moaning man with his foot.

"Buddy? You okay?"

He rolled BC over, and a wave of whiskey-soaked breath bathed his face. Underneath it, though, the officer smelled something sweet and smoky. Marijuana. And a large dose of urine as well. The bum had pissed his pants.

"Fuckin' beatniks," he said, and this time his toe caught BC squarely in the jaw. "Let's go, buddy. It's into the tank with you."

As he hoisted BC onto his shoulder, a picture fell out of the bum's expensive-looking jacket. It took the officer a moment to sort out the tangle of legs and arms—he counted six of the former, but only five of the latter. He hoped the missing limb had merely been cropped from the frame.

"A pervert, too, huh? What the hell is this world coming to?"

When they finished, Melchior said, "That proves the old axiom that the boss should be able to outperform any of her employees." In case Song had missed the point, he added, *"Wow."*

Song lit a cigarette, took a drag, passed it to Melchior.

"As I was saying earlier," she said in a voice that gave no hint of the ripe smell that hung in the room, "you need an organization."

Melchior sucked on the cigarette, held the smoke in his lungs just to the point of discomfort, then exhaled.

"This conversation requires clothes."

"So," Song recapped after Melchior had told her everything that had happened since he'd returned to the States. "Orpheus in Frisco. Naz in DC. And something"—she looked at Melchior significantly—"in Cuba. You entrusted them all to freelancers and look what happened. You've lost at least two assets, and, depending on what Comrade Ivelitsch meant by his note, possibly all three."

"He wouldn't have left that note if he'd found it."

Song rolled her eyes.

"I know it's a bomb, Melchior."

"What's a bomb?"

"I told you. Drew Everton, second and fourth Thursday of every month."

"He doesn't believe me when I tell him there's a nuke in Cuba, but he tells—"

"Focus, Melchior. We're talking about Ivelitsch. He wouldn't have left that note if he was acting with KGB approval."

"What are you saying?"

"I'm saying he's testing the waters, just like you. Looking for an excuse to go freelance."

"And what's that mean to me?"

"He's going to call. My guess is he'll make a perfunctory effort to turn you. I want you to counteroffer. The two of you pretend to work for KGB to take advantage of their resources, but in actuality you form a new, independent organization."

"With you as a partner, of course."

"Let's face it, Melchior. If someone didn't kick your ass, you'd still be carrying around a slingshot."

"Oh, I'm pretty sure I'd've graduated to a shotgun by now." Melchior chuckled. "And what's this new organization stand for anyway? What is it supposed to do?"

Song made sure Melchior was looking at her before she spoke.

"Anything you want."

Even before Chandler opened his eyes he had a sense of him-
self in a moving vehicle. This was strange, because he was also lying
down. The first thing he saw was a ceiling of tufted white silk a scant
eighteen inches above him, stained here and there from old drips. Two
rows of windows flanked either side of the long, narrow compartment,
covered by drawn curtains.

It hit him. He was in a hearse.

He was dead.

A voice chuckled somewhere in front of him.

"Back among the living?"

Chandler rolled onto his stomach—he wasn't tied up, which all by
itself was a good thing—and he wasn't in a coffin either. An even bigger
plus. The rearview mirror was angled so that the driver could see the
bed of the hearse. Chandler could see the driver as well: a white man, a
few years younger than him. His haircut looked military, but his black
suit was almost rakishly mod, the lapels barely an inch wide, the tie
equally narrow.

Suddenly the memories crashed down on him. Running from the
Phillips station, the smell of smoke in his nostrils, roasting flesh. He'd
barely made it to his car before passing out. It was three hours before a
Highway Patrolman inspected the vehicle. Chandler remembered the
sound of the billy club tapping the window, a voice calling through the
glass, the door opening, the cop shaking his shoulder, the twenty-
minute wait for the ambulance to arrive and the forty-five-minute ride
to the hospital and the battery of tests the doctors had performed on
him—tests to which he had remained unresponsive, even as he recorded
everything that was happening through the eyes and ears of the people
around him. He'd spent a day in the bed—twenty-three hours and

fourteen minutes—and then this man had arrived and taken him away; they'd been on the road for almost twenty hours.

He looked back at the face in the mirror.

"Agent Querrey?"

A look Chandler had only ever seen in religious frescoes and Cecil B. DeMille movies came over the FBI agent's face. A look of beatific gratitude, as if Chandler were an angel confirming BC's election among the holy.

"Orpheus," BC whispered.

"No," Chandler said. *"Chandler."*

They set up camp at the Star-Lite Motor Lodge, just across the highway from the Bowl-a-Rama, which, according to the hotel clerk, was the only place still serving food within a twenty-mile radius. BC loaned Chandler one of his new suits—burgundy sharkskin, black piping over the pockets, a tapered waist that made Chandler feel as though he wore a corset—but it beat the tattered remains of Sidewalk Steve's clothes, not to mention an open-backed hospital gown sans skivvies. He squeezed his feet into a pair of Italian loafers—BC was about an inch taller than him but had rather small feet—and, feeling like a cross between a Mod and Little Lord Fauntleroy, followed the detective across the highway to the bowling alley.

"Lucky it's not league night," said the pin monkey, who could've been the twin of the clerk at the motel, if not the same person. He handled BC's and Chandler's dainty shoes like newborn kittens, slotting them into cubbies as though putting them in a sack to drown, then gave them mimeographed paper menus. "Y'all have to circle what you want. Chang don't speak no English." Ten minutes later, they were seated at a small Formica table at the head of a lane, paper napkins spread over their laps and tucked inside their collars, Chinet plates mounded with rice and glutinous-looking foodstuffs set between.

"Chinese food in a bowling alley in West Virginia," BC said. "Go figure."

Chandler wasn't particularly hungry, but (semi-) solid food was enough of a novelty after two weeks of a mostly intravenous diet that he shoveled down the greasy but flavorful fare.

"So," he said between bites, "how'd you find me anyway?"

BC looked at him quizzically. "You really don't know?"

Chandler didn't understand at first, then got it. "It's not like a radio. Things don't just come to me. Or, rather, it *is* like a radio, but it has to be plugged in first. Switched on."

"You mean LSD?" BC said even as he reached into his pocket, brought out a folded piece of newsprint. It was the cover of one of those supermarket tabloids specializing in Hollywood gossip and alien abductions and divine—or demonic—apparitions.

THE DEVIL IN DALLAS?

The headline was a bit misleading, given that Chandler'd been 250 miles north of the city, and the burning boy, despite his flame-engulfed body and gargantuan size, was clearly human, and adolescent to boot.

Chandler stared at the artist's rendering, which was remarkably accurate, save for the snarling face and the horns jutting from the forehead. Then he noticed the insets at the bottom of the page, the photographs of Dan Karnovsky, Janet and Jared Steinke, and pushed the paper away. The two men finished their food and sipped at their beers until Chandler, not knowing what else to do, stood up and grabbed a ball.

"Loser pays for dinner?"

BC shrugged. "Take off that jacket first. I don't want you splitting the seams."

Chandler was only too happy to comply, although the shirt underneath, a dark green number with French cuffs, was only slightly less form-fitting. He'd bowled maybe a half dozen times in his life but understood the principle. It was all in the wrist, as everyone said. He lined up his shot, took two steps, swung the ball in a pendulum arc, and released it with a sharp quarter turn. The ball shot toward the right edge of the pyramid of pins, waiting like penguins staring down a polar bear, but Chandler could see from its marbling that it was twisting counterclockwise, and slowly it began to list to the left. It hit between the 3 and 6 pins, demolished the entire stack in a fraction of a second. As the grate swept the still-quivering pins away, Chandler turned back to see BC eyeing him querulously.

"I think I've been played."

Chandler couldn't quite keep the grin off his face. "Didn't know I had it in me."

Since the game was a pro forma affair—BC rolled a respectable 182, but Chandler knocked strike after strike on his way to a perfect 300—and because they were running from the CIA—running from them, yet running after them as well—they started to talk.

"You've got to admit," Chandler said, "it really is a bizarre organization. It invests enormous amounts of money and manpower into every possible way of achieving a goal—psychic aptitude studies, chemicals to create superheroes, disinformation campaigns and covert armies and assassination plots—and yet, where's it gotten us? They couldn't keep the Rosenbergs from stealing our nuclear technology and selling it to the Soviets, they didn't discover Khrushchev's missiles in Cuba until they were already there, and they can't keep Communism from spreading like wildfire across Asia and South America. I mean, *something's* not working."

BC let out a little chuckle when Chandler finally came up for air. "You've given this some thought."

"It's not thought as much as it's breathing. My uncle was one of the architects of the agency. When I stayed with him at his house, people would discuss nuking the thirty-eighth parallel over breakfast and trading Poland for East Berlin over lunch. I was supposed to follow in his footsteps, but my best friend, Percy Logan, went to Korea at seventeen and was dead a month later. Then Eddie . . ." Chandler shook his head. "I've spent my entire adult life running from that world, yet somehow all I managed to do was run straight into it."

"I think it's fair to say that it ran after you," BC said, then added quietly, "About Eddie . . ."

Chandler's eyebrows shot up.

"I'm just wondering if you know what happened at Millbrook. I mean, if you know how he actually died. That is, do you think it's possible Miss Haverman—"

"Naz had nothing to do with Eddie's death!" Chandler said vehe-mently. He jammed his finger on the pictures of the people who'd died in Texas. "*I* killed him, just like I killed these three. The *Company* killed them, using me as the weapon."

BC glanced nervously at a couple of polyester-shirted men two lanes over, who'd turned at Chandler's exclamation and were staring at them with confused, slightly hostile expressions.

"It's okay," Chandler said, following BC's eyes. "They just think we're fairies."

"Did you . . . ?"

Chandler shrugged his emerald shoulders. "I didn't have to read their minds to figure that out."

BC colored. "But you will admit Miss Haverman is an unusual girl. When we were at Madam Song's, I felt something. Something I've never felt before. Not because it wasn't my emotion, but because it was Naz's."

"What are you trying to say?"

"I think you weren't the only person changed by the drugs Agent Logan gave you."

"Oh, Jesus." Chandler looked more distraught than when he'd no-ticed the pictures of the people who'd died at the gas station. "Does Melchior know?"

"I'm not sure. Song was there too, but I don't know if she under-stood what was going on."

Chandler smacked the ball in his hands. "What the hell does he *want,* anyway?"

"I don't think he knows," BC said. "But it's obvious he's angry and frustrated, and now fate's thrust you into his hands and he sees an op-portunity. He might end up destroying his life rather than saving it, but in either case he's going to take a lot of people down with him."

"So tell me again why we're going after this guy instead of running far, far away?"

"Because he's the closest thing to a lead we've got to Naz."

"Oh right," Chandler said. "Naz."

At the word, something clicked in BC's brain. A flash of light, a whispered voice. *Tell Chandler I'm pregnant.*

"BC?"

BC stared at Chandler's face, at the desperation there, and couldn't bring himself to say anything. Chandler already had enough to deal with. Naz could tell him herself, when they rescued her.

Suddenly he felt a curious sensation, like the beginning of a tension headache. It felt as though someone had slipped his hands between BC's skull and his brain and begun to squeeze, and squeeze, and squeeze. Chandler's eyes had narrowed to slits and his lips were white with effort.

"Chandler," BC said hoarsely. "Don't." But if Chandler heard him, he didn't acknowledge it.

The pressure in BC's head wasn't painful as much as it was weird, and wrong. You shouldn't feel someone else touching your brain. It took all of BC's strength to lift up his hand and put it on top of Chandler's. *"Don't."*

And just like that it was over. Chandler's face relaxed and his shoulders slumped slightly. BC's head felt light as a balloon. He peered at Chandler, trying to tell if he'd seen anything, but it seemed pretty clear he hadn't.

"I'm sorry. I shouldn't have done that."

"That was . . ." BC shook his head gingerly. "I don't know what that was, but I wouldn't want to feel it when you're juiced up."

"Speaking of which," Chandler said, "I don't suppose you have any?"

BC shook his head. "The easiest thing would probably be to go to Millbrook. Wait. Leary said he had a partner. Alpert. Richard Alpert. He goes on regular buying runs to Europe. Flies in and out through Idlewild, usually stays with Billy Hitchcock's sister in New York City."

"What if he's not around when we go looking for him? Millbrook's only a few hours on from New York."

"Yes, but if Melchior's watching anything, it's going to be Leary's place. If we don't manage to find Alpert, we can decide if it's worth risking a trip upstate."

"It sounds like we have a plan then." They sat quietly for a moment, and then Chandler drained the last of his beer. "Last frame?"

"Be my guest."

Chandler picked up his ball, rolled three more strikes, and then the pinsetter laid BC's final frame. In a hurry to get the evening over, BC fired off his shot too quickly, handed himself a 10–2 split. It was hard not to see the two pins as emblematic: Melchior and Naz, too far apart to get both at once. You had to connect with one and hope that would get you the other. It could be done, he told himself. All you had to do was aim right.

He picked up his ball. This time he spent a good minute lining up his shot. But just as he released it he heard Naz's voice again—*Tell Chandler I'm pregnant*—and the ball sliced down the alley right between the two pins, and BC realized that sometimes when you go after two targets, you don't get either.

It was a wet day, and Union Station's cavernous waiting room was filled with squeaks and squeals as rain-soaked commuters hurried to make their trains. It'd been raining the day he met BC, too, Melchior remembered, and he couldn't help but smile as he thought about how he'd messed with the poor G-man's head. My God, he'd never met a squarer peg in his life—the starched-and-stuffed embodiment of the Eisenhower generation, so naive that he didn't suspect that virtually every law, value, and custom he was paid to uphold was being flouted by the man he worked for. He wondered how ol' Beau was doing these days. If his meeting with Melchior hadn't fucked him up but good, then his encounter with Orpheus surely had. No doubt he was doing his best to forget he'd ever met either of them. . . .

But he had more important things to think about. Namely, his meeting with Pavel Semyonovitch Ivelitsch. Melchior'd arrived a half hour early to case the station, and now he sat in the middle of a central bench, scanning a paper while he waited for the Russian to show. Race dominated the headlines. Martin Luther King was still riding the success of August's March on Washington, and there was even talk that he was up for the Nobel Peace Prize. In Mississippi, a voter registration drive for Negroes had been broken up by whites whose numbers included uniformed police officers, while a similar one in rural Georgia had persisted despite trash, rotten fruit, and bottles being thrown at the participants. Publicity-hungry congressmen called press conferences to discuss their position on the president's Civil Rights Bill—vitriolically against, bellicosely for—but it had yet to actually reach the floor, since insiders felt there weren't enough votes to pass it. Beyond that, there was a smallish article on the continuing chaos in Saigon following Diem's assassination, and a sidebar on JFK's upcoming trip to New Orleans and Dallas as part of the long windup to the '64 election.

"The *Post?* I thought they got their stories from you, not the other way around."

Melchior finished the sentence he was reading before looking up.

"I'd say it's more a question of give-and-take." He placed the newspaper on the bench to his right, patted the space to his left. "Comrade Ivelitsch. Please, take a seat."

Ivelitsch smirked as he sat down.

"You Company men and your protocol. Seat a potential target to your left so you can shoot him without removing your weapon from its shoulder holster, while at the same time placing him in the awkward position of having to draw and turn."

"Given the fact that you're left-handed, that strategy would be only half-effective. Also, since my objective is Naz's recovery, killing you ranks rather low on my list of priorities—at least for this meeting."

From the corner of his eye, Melchior saw Ivelitsch pretend to look around. He knew full well the KGB man had cased the joint as thoroughly as he had himself.

"And the beautiful Madam Song? Will she be joining us today? Or any of her associates?"

"She's shopping for a replacement lamp for the one you broke. Charles Rennie Mackintosh. I'm sure that seems hopelessly bourgeois to you, but apparently it was quite expensive."

"On the contrary. Even a Communist can appreciate the need for domestic comforts. The Russian winter is long, dark, and cold. You should spend more time with her, Melchior," Ivelitsch continued. "Aside from the fact that the girls in her house are even more beautiful than the antiques, she's a clever girl. She could teach you a few things."

"Such as?"

"The need for an organization. Going rogue requires a flight of inspired lunacy. But going solo is just insane."

Ivelitsch's words were so similar to Song's that Melchior wondered if they were conspiring together. But he managed to keep his face and voice impassive.

"And what makes you think I'm going rogue?"

"Rip Robertson's corpse for one thing. And Orpheus for another."

Melchior tapped the paper. "Rip's death hasn't made the news, so I take it this is your way of telling me you've got a man inside CIA. However, I was just batting cleanup on Orpheus, so whoever your man is, he's only getting half his facts."

"Our man is Stanley."

"Stanley?" Melchior did his best to keep his voice level. "The mythical mole who penetrated MI-5? He's the British version of the Wise Men."

"He's Kim Philby, and he's every bit as real as the Wise Men. He has lunch several times a week with James Jesus Angleton whenever he's in DC. After three or four gimlets, there's very little Mother won't tell his old friend."

This time Melchior made no attempt to hide his surprise. "Why in the world would you tell me that?" he said, although he knew there could only be one answer. "Philby's been missing since January."

"He's in Moscow, drinking all the vodka his liver can stand. Now, turn around, you half-caste moron, before you attract attention."

Melchior looked forward again. He stared at the shrouded faces of the wet commuters, wondering if any could even begin to imagine what was happening while they raced toward their trains.

"You're rogue too," he said, and again wondered if Ivelitsch and Song were in cahoots—it seemed like an awfully big coincidence (the very thing that BC had said about Melchior's presence on the train, come to think about it) that she would ask Ivelitsch to turn against KGB when, in fact, he already had.

"I prefer the term enlightened," Ivelitsch was saying now. "The Cold War is a lose-lose scenario. The United States and the Soviet Union can't make a serious move without risking nuclear reprisal. They put on frivolous headline dramas like the Cuban Missile Crisis or mount expensive but largely pointless proxy wars—the Baathists versus General Qasim in Iraq, say, or Movimiento 26 de Julio in Cuba, the North and South Vietnamese—and send them to the slaughter. What's needed is a smaller organization, more nimble, more obscure, free of the restraints of dogma and politics that neither side actually believes, let alone adheres to."

Melchior flicked a picture of President Kennedy shaking hands with Martin Luther King on the cover of his paper.

"I think both of these men would disagree."

Ivelitsch looked at the two beaming faces as if he couldn't tell them apart.

"As a Negro, Reverend King leads the only American manifestation of a phenomenon so common in the old world, namely, the remarkable tenacity of ethnic groups to resist integration into the modern hetero- geneous state. His idealism is tribal, which makes it resistant to com- promise, but also confines it to his own constituency. The last I checked, Negroes made up about ten percent of the U.S. population, which is a number that means more to retailers than pollsters. President Kennedy, by contrast, wants to have it both ways. His optimism is ridiculously naive—ridiculously American, one wants to say—but his cynicism is Irish to the core. He's trying to appease everyone—the hawks and the doves, the businessmen and the beatniks, the New Men and the Ne- groes. In the end it's going to be the death of him."

Something about Ivelitsch's use of the word "death" suggested it wasn't a euphemism.

"Lemme guess," Melchior said. "The mob. Johnny Roselli? Jimmy Hoffa? Sam Giancana maybe? Pissed off that Bobby isn't giving them quid pro quo for Cuba?"

Melchior's tone was joking, but Ivelitsch responded to it seriously. "Have you heard anything specific?"

"Let's just say that if you want to get away with knocking off the president of the United States, you probably shouldn't go around telling everyone that that's what you intend to do. Have *you* heard anything?"

Ivelitsch shrugged. "Mafia men dislike Communists even more than they dislike Kennedys. But if and when it happens, we need to be ready to take advantage of the chaos that will surely follow. Until then, there's the question of Orpheus, and, of course, the bomb. We need to get the former out of the country, the latter in."

Melchior could only shake his head at Ivelitsch's candor. The man was working as hard as possible to prove his break from his employer. Either that or he planned on shooting Melchior as soon as he found out what he wanted to know. Of course, Melchior was considering the same thing, assuming he could get Ivelitsch to stop talking about U.S. politics and tell him where the hell Naz was, or what he wanted for her return.

"So," he said, moving the conversation in that direction. "Where do you propose we move Orpheus? With Miss Haverman?"

"Is that her name?" Ivelitsch said. "A lovely girl. Beguiling, I have to say. I can see why she'd have such a hold on Orpheus."

"How much do you know about that?"

"Rather less than you, I think," Ivelitsch said. "Edward Logan's records on Project Orpheus seem to have disappeared from the Boston office. Ditto Joe Scheider's from Langley."

"I wouldn't know anything about that," Melchior said.

"I didn't think so," Ivelitsch said, smiling wryly. "At any rate, Miss Haverman is enjoying the comforts of one of the luxury suites in the basement of the Soviet Embassy for the time being. As for Orpheus, I think he'd be better off in the Soviet Union."

Melchior snorted. "Putting aside the fact that that is the stupidest idea I've ever heard, I thought you were leaving KGB?"

"Why would I do something like that? KGB has access to the kind of money and manpower you and I could never raise, at least in the short term. And unlike you, I've been nothing but a model citizen my entire career. My superiors have no reason to suspect me."

"If only they could hear this conversation," Melchior said. "All right then. Orpheus to Russia. And the bomb?"

"We haven't found it yet, but you have to realize that it's only a matter of time. It's leaking—badly. A dozen people have already fallen ill. It's a trail of human bread crumbs. You need to tell me where it is so I can send someone to fix it before the Cubans or my team find it or, even worse, it's no longer good for anything."

"And then you look the other way while I move it again?"

"We move it here."

"Here . . . ?"

"To the States. We can bring it in through the Keys or New Orleans or even Houston."

"And then what? We blow up the White House? The Empire State Building?"

"Don't be stupid, Melchior. You can only blow up a bomb once. But you can threaten to blow it up forever, or at least until people no longer believe you, at which point you can always sell it."

"Or actually blow it up."

Ivelitsch smiled. "Or actually blow it up."

Melchior shook his head. "I don't know if you're crazy or insane."

"Those words mean the same thing."

"And you'd have to be crazy insane if you think I'm going to tell you where either Orpheus or the bomb is. But in any case, we're going to have to settle this question another day. We got company."

"I love it when you go working class. It's almost as charming as your autodidacticism. I assume you mean the gentleman at two o'clock. Navy pinstripe, rep tie."

"Andover. Nice catch. But I was actually referring to your man. Seven o'clock. Gray suit, poorly fitted."

"Sartorial socialism at its finest. What gave him away?"

"He's doing the crossword and he keeps saying *'Blyat'* under his breath. Russian for 'whore,' as I recall."

"Well, that's a good enough reason to kill him, I suppose, although he also has a habit of singing 'The Internationale' at three in the morning after he's polished off his nightly bottle of vodka."

"I'd practically be doing you a favor." Melchior's chuckle faded into the vast open space of the waiting room. "We have to kill them, don't we?"

"For my sake, no. KGB knows of the work you did for Raúl, so it was easy enough to convince my superiors that I was meeting you to see if I could turn you. But you're already under suspicion, and if word gets back to Langley that you spent a half hour chatting with a top Soviet operative—"

"You flatter yourself."

"—it will look bad. Angleton already suspects you're working for the Castros, and Drew Everton can't be too happy about the fact that you apparently killed Orpheus rather than recovering him, and then there's poor Rip. At some point they're going to call you in for a meeting, and you'll be lucky if you get out before Kennedy loses the election next year."

"You know more about my career than I do. Okay then. How do you want to play this?"

"Attempt to take me into custody. The commotion will bring Ivan into the fray, during which I'll escape and Ivan, alas, will die. I'll go for rep tie, but if I fail, he'll at least report that you attempted to apprehend me."

"So you're saying I have to kill Ivan solely on the chance that you miss Andover? You're a cold-blooded bastard."

"Remember the bad singing."

"Andover won't be alone. Not after Rip."

"Have you made his partner?"

"Not yet, but he'll make a move during the fight. Keep your eyes peeled. Oh, and—"

"Yes?"

"This one's for Song."

Melchior drove his elbow into the side of Ivelitsch's face. He wanted to surprise him to make it look real, in case the watchers did get away, and he also wanted to let him know who was going to run this partnership, should it survive its first test. There was a snap—probably not a broken jawbone, but maybe—and Ivelitsch rolled to the left. The two men fell to the floor, briefly out of sight of the KGB and CIA agents.

"We've got to switch guns," Melchior hissed.

Ivelitsch had to pop his jaw before he could speak. "What?"

"Forensics needs to find Makarov slugs in both Americans."

"Good point," Ivelitsch said. He swapped guns with Melchior, but before he got up he grabbed Melchior's arm.

"For this to work everyone who knows you has to die. Frank Wisdom and Drew Everton and—"

"I understand."

"*Everyone,*" Ivelitsch said. And then: "Say it."

"Say—"

"You know."

Melchior rolled his eyes.

"*Timor mortis exultat me.*"

"If I were a girl I'd kiss you," Ivelitsch said. "But since I'm a man . . ." He smashed his forehead into Melchior's nose.

The Russian was up first, the magnum he'd taken from Melchior already level. A woman screamed before he fired the first shot, which only missed Melchior because he rolled behind the bench. He knew Ivelitsch *would* shoot him if he got the chance. This was a test, for both of them, and it was pass or die.

As Ivelitsch had predicted, Ivan was in motion. The second KGB man didn't seem to realize that the two fighting men were aligning themselves so that—

Ivelitsch aimed, and Melchior threw himself to the floor. He heard the shots, turned to see Ivan falling backward with two dark holes in his chest, a last silent *"Blyat!"* passing his lips. Melchior jumped up a few yards to the right of his former position, gun already aimed. He could have sworn his shot grazed Ivelitsch's back. It caught Andover in the meat of his left shoulder. He staggered backward, but he was also reaching into his jacket for his weapon.

Melchior took a second to aim. If he missed, if Andover got away, it was all over before it began. His second shot blew the fedora off what was left of the agent's skull, but Melchior was already scanning the crowd before the hat hit the ground.

He saw what he was looking for halfway down the station: a man moving quickly but calmly amid the frenzied crowd, heading for the front exit. Something flashed in the man's hand. Not a gun. Worse— car keys.

"Mashina?" he called out.

"Nyet," Ivelitsch yelled back, still squeezing off shots as he made his way toward the gates, where, presumably, he'd hop a train as it pulled out of the station or escape through the tracks. The Russian was making this a little *too* real. Melchior had to duck and zigzag his way across the waiting room, all of which let the second Company man get farther away. When he'd finally put enough people between himself and Ivelitsch's gun, he stood up straight and ran for the front exit. The Company man was already outside. Melchior spotted him getting into the driver's seat of a taxi parked in the rank of livery vehicles on Massachusetts Avenue.

There were two tickets under the windshield wiper of Song's bathtub Porsche. Melchior would've preferred a Catalina or a Fury or even a Corvette, but Song had assured him the 356 would get him where he needed to go. He'd had to leave the top down because the car was too damn small for him otherwise. He vaulted the door, slid his legs under the steering wheel, jerked the choke, pumped the gas, turned the key. The Porsche whined like a half-grown lion cub.

The agent didn't seem to have seen Melchior leave the station. He pulled his taxi onto the semicircular road that would give him access to Columbus Circle and a half dozen streets. Melchior pulled into the one-way drive's exit to cut him off, weaving in and out of the heavy afternoon traffic. The agent spotted him and jerked the taxi over the curb, tearing across the strip of park that separated the station's access road from Columbus Circle. He barely slowed as he shot across eight lanes of traffic, heading straight for Delaware Avenue.

Melchior was acutely conscious of how tiny the Porsche was as he followed—not just because his left knee slammed into the underside of the console every time he shifted, but because all he could see were the enormous grilles of Fords and Chryslers and Chevies closing in on him like a pack of Saint Bernards. He shot onto Delaware, straight toward the Capitol, less than a hundred feet behind the bright yellow Crown Vic. At that point Melchior had to give the little car its due. He punched it and it sprang after the taxi as though a leash had snapped from its collar.

Melchior sent a couple of shots through the taxi's rear windshield. Glass exploded into the air, and he had to duck behind the twelve-inch-high windscreen of his own vehicle as the flak sliced into his car. The taxi fishtailed wildly, then straightened out. The agent slammed on the brakes, and Melchior had to jerk the wheel to the left to avoid slamming into the taxi's trunk. The agent squeezed off a shot over Melchior's windscreen even as he jerked the taxi to the right and veered onto Constitution—toward Federal Triangle if he continued straight on, or, even worse, the White House if he turned onto Pennsylvania. There were still no sirens behind them, but it was hard to imagine anything less than a flotilla of armed vehicles if two cars shot past 1600 firing at each other. Melchior had to end this now.

He screeched onto Constitution, narrowly avoiding a panel truck. Again he floored it; again the roadster responded. There were a dozen car lengths between him and the Crown Vic, then there were six. Three. As they flew across Third Street, Melchior pulled up on the taxi's left flank. The agent was cranking the wheel with both hands to make the turn onto Pennsylvania. Melchior put a shot in the man's ear and when the agent released the wheel, the car skidded, hit a curb, then turned ass over nose onto the road, crushing the cabin beneath the chassis. If the agent wasn't dead before the car flipped, he was dead after.

Melchior looked forward—just in time to see a truck cross perpendicularly in front of him. He was going sixty miles an hour. There was no missing it. He threw himself onto the passenger's seat. The 356 shook and glass exploded all over his back as the car's nose went under the bed of the truck and the windscreen was ripped off its struts. There was a moment of vibrating darkness and then, somehow, Melchior was through. He'd gone right under the truck.

He sat up, shaking glass out of his hair, then jammed the car onto Fourth Street. Still no cops—God bless America. Two cars exchanging shots a quarter mile from the White House, and not a police cruiser in sight. President Kennedy needed better security.

He ditched the car in a garage Song had told him about "just in case," then turned the Wiz's battered Chevy toward Langley. He'd just shot two Company agents. It was time to turn himself in.

"Once I destroyed a man's idea of himself to save him."

"Beg pardon, sir?" The Negro elevator operator seemed anything but interested in what the curiously dressed white man had to say.

"Oh, nothing, nothing," BC said. Then, thinking he'd better try out some beatnik jargon: "Just some jive by this cool cat of a poet someone turned me on to, Frank O'Hara."

Without doing anything more than lifting one eyebrow, the elevator operator managed to convey the idea that if the man in the car was what lay in store for the beneficiaries of Civil Rights, he'd just as soon remain a second-class citizen.

"I'm sure I don't understand, sir." He stopped the car and pulled open the polished wooden door. "Fifteenth floor, sir."

BC had been able to track down Richard Alpert at the home of Peggy Hitchcock—sister of William, owner of the Millbrook estate. He insisted on going alone. Chandler didn't put up much of a fight, which didn't really surprise BC. He'd noticed that being around people made his charge visibly uncomfortable. No doubt part of this had to do with the fact that Chandler had become different from everyone around him, but BC suspected Chandler'd been a loner even before his transformation. He said he was more than happy to sit in the hotel and watch television. "That new guy on *The Tonight Show.* Carson. He's no Jack Paar, but I like it when he puts on the turban." He paused. "Are you going to bring your gun?"

BC just looked at him drolly. "Guns are so uncool, man."

There was a mirror just outside the elevator, and BC took a moment to inspect himself. To remind himself who he was supposed to be. He'd done rather well, if he said so himself: black turtleneck covered by a long vest in some peasant-looking striped fabric, paint-spattered chinos and battered work boots, all courtesy of a Village thrift store. The coup de grâce, though, was a dark wig that fell almost to his shoulders. It could have come right off the head of Maynard G. Krebs. A suede headband held it in place and gave BC a bit of a Comanche look besides.

To further solidify his performance, he'd spent the afternoon in a dusty bookstore reeking of marijuana smoke, culling bons mots from the likes of Allen Ginsberg, William S. Burroughs, and Lawrence Fer- linghetti. The only one he remembered, though, was the line from O'Hara's poem (entitled simply "Poem," as if to justify its presence on the same bookshelf as Shakespeare, Milton, and Donne): "Once I de- stroyed a man's idea of himself to save him." As BC regarded the un- shaven, floppy-haired stranger in the mirror, he felt he understood exactly what the poet meant.

Hitchcock lived in a sprawling apartment on Park Avenue, a laby- rinthine complex of large high-ceilinged rooms stuffed with Asian an- tiques, African sculptures and textiles, and modernist canvases covered with squiggles and smears and clumps of things BC thought belonged in a trash can rather than on a posh apartment wall. Not that he was able to get a good look at any of them, for, in addition to the expensive objects, Peggy Hitchcock's home was also stuffed with people. Though it was a Monday night, "the joint was jumping," as the person who opened the door said to him. Industrialists and beatniks, socialists and hipsters, starlets, jazz musicians, and artists thronged the rooms, crystal tumblers full of gin or vodka or bourbon in one hand, cigarettes of to- bacco or cloves or marijuana in the other, and all of them, male and female, white, black, and indeterminate brown, *loved* BC's outfit.

"Nice threads, my man."

"Looking fly, white guy."

"Way to work it *out.*"

BC had never been in an environment where people were so open about their desires. Women in acres of chiffon or inches of polyester stared at him openly, as did more than a few of the men. Normally such overt sexuality would have made him uncomfortable, but the drink that'd been thrust into his hands the moment he walked through the door had calmed him, and he thought he might also be getting some- thing he'd heard referred to as a "contact high" from the layers of sweet smoke in the air. BC used the smoke as his pretext for conversation with various persons, gradually honing his dialogue from "Pardon me, but can I ask where you procured your marijuana cigarette?" to "Any idea where I can score something stronger, dig?" which, after half a dozen tries, finally hit paydirt.

"Did someone mention scoring?"

BC turned to see a pale woman with dark hair pulled straight off her face and held in place by a large silver comb etched with some sort of Indian scrollwork. Despite the lack of hairspray or makeup (aside from some elaborate paint around the eyes, which gave her face the look of an Egyptian death mask)—not to mention the slim trousers and button-down blouse she wore—her extreme thinness and pinched tones, along with the emerald nugget on her right hand, gave her away as a member of the aristocracy.

"Miss Hitchcock," he said, taking a chance. He decided to drop the beatnik pose and revert to his Southern accent. "I'm so glad we've finally run into each other!"

"Have we met?" Peggy Hitchcock said, looking, in the manner of one whose every social interaction is cushioned by millions of dollars, completely unconcerned that she might have forgotten an acquaintance's name. "I don't seem to recall your face, or your accent for that matter. Southerners are as common as dodos around here, if not *quite* as funny-looking."

BC had no idea how to take this, and decided to pass over it. He extended his hand.

"Beauregard Gamin. We, that is I, am nothing more than a gate-crasher. I was at the Blue Note to see Miles blow"—BC had in fact read a review by Nat Hentoff of the performance in the *Village Voice*—"and a pretty hep character mentioned your pad was *the* place to meet the coolest cats in town."

"The coolest cats, you say?" Hitchcock's eyebrows went up in amusement. "I think Miles is in the library. I tried to get him to play, but he's having more fun standing around the musicians and intimidating them."

BC had assumed the faint sound of jazz in the apartment came from a hi-fi. He was impressed, and showed it.

"Back in Oxford, Mississippi, where I come from, the only Negroes we ever let indoors wore livery." He glanced at a beautiful Negress who had her arm around a bearded white man. "You can't imagine how exciting this is for me."

"Change will come to the South just as it has to the North. If it's not Martin Luther King, it'll be Mary Jane."

"A wonderful girl! I hope to meet her one day!"

Hitchcock looked at BC sharply again. "So, did I hear you say you were looking for Richard Alpert before?"

"I've heard that he traffics in, how shall I put it, mind-opening experiences?"

Hitchcock was silent for so long that BC was sure she was going to throw him out. But finally she laughed and said, "My God, Mr. Gamin, you practically sound like a G-man. Just call it acid, please."

BC lowered his eyes modestly. "Pardon me, Miss Hitchcock. It must be that Southern reserve."

"I'm from New England. From my point of view, you're all flatulent windbags."

"I, ah . . ." BC had never spoken to a woman who was so matter-of-factly rude. "I believe flatulent windbag is redundant."

Hitchcock threw back her head and laughed the kind of laugh that would have caused BC's mother to stab her in the throat with a kitchen knife.

"Oh, you are a *hoot*, Mr. Gamin. You hold on. I'm going to see if I can find Dickie. Don't hesitate to grab him if you see him. Big guy, thick beard, rather less hair on his head. Black turtleneck with a gold medallion on his chest."

BC waited fifteen minutes before he realized Hitchcock probably wasn't coming back, and then began to make his way through the apartment in search of her. He'd just finished his second revolution when he turned and collided with a large, solid man. Coarse strands of beard rasped across his lips and he felt something hard strike his chest. A pair of hands landed on his hipbones, pushing him back a few inches, then held him there.

"Easy there, young fellow," a soothing voice, mildly redolent of anise, breathed into his face.

BC wanted to step back, but the hands on his hips rooted him to the spot. He looked up into a tangle of black beard, liberally laced with gray. A pair of warm brown eyes sat atop furred cheeks, glinting at him like a benevolent bear's.

"I, uh, that is, pardon me . . ."

"Do we know each other?" the man said, still holding BC in place. A big cavey warmth radiated from his chest and stomach.

"No." BC's eyes fell to the gold medallion dangling from the man's throat. "That is, are you Richard Alpert?"

A smile appeared in the beard.

"As long as you're not a federal officer or vice cop, I am."

He laughed, and the shaking was just enough to dislodge his hands. BC stepped back.

"My name is Beauregard Gamin." BC stuck out his hand, which Alpert took in both of his and held softly but firmly, as though it were a wild bird. "I was hoping to meet you."

"And what have I done to earn the attention of such a handsome young peacock?"

BC grinned in spite of himself, smoothing the front of his vest.

"I heard that you, that is, it's my understanding—"

"Oh, are you the Southern gentleman Peggy mentioned? Goodness, she didn't do you justice."

"Do you think you can help me out?"

Alpert smirked. "It's my mission in life to help out men such as yourself. Open your mouth and say aahh."

BC blushed. Before he could say anything, however, Alpert laughed and said, "Just kidding. Follow me."

He led BC into a nearby bedroom where two—no, three—legs protruded from a pile of jackets. He reached into a pocket and pulled out a wax paper envelope, peeked inside. BC saw something that looked like a sheet of perforated paper. Alpert tore off a stamp and held it up between two pinched fingers.

"Now then—"

"Actually, I'd prefer to take it with me if I can." BC looked around the messy room. "I've heard that setting plays a vital role, and I'd prefer something more familiar. Intimate."

On the bed, the big toe at the end of one leg scratched the ankle of one of the others with a sandpapery sound.

Alpert frowned. "A guide is every bit as important as setting, and I'm leery of leaving you alone for your first experience. LSD is an extremely powerful drug."

"So I've heard," BC said drily.

Alpert deliberated with himself, then shrugged. He reached into a pocket and pulled out a somewhat battered card, slipped it into the envelope with the acid, and pressed it into BC's hand. Once again, he refused to let go.

"These are my numbers. I want you to call me at any time—before, during, after." He squeezed BC's fingers. "Perhaps I can lure you to Millbrook for a more in-depth experience."

"Millbrook?" BC felt his hand sweating inside Alpert's furry paws. "Miss Hitchcock has a house there, doesn't she?"

"Her brother, Billy. It's quite a special place."

"Well, if this is everything people say it is, no doubt I'll want a second experience."

"Oh, don't take all of this at once! You'll be jumping off rooftops thinking you can fly!"

It was another fifteen minutes before BC could get away from Alpert, and even then it took a gaggle of floppy-haired boys and girls to drag the big man away. BC tucked the envelope inside his jacket and headed for the hall. But at the top of the stairs he was stopped by a tall, sturdy-looking man in a bland gray suit. The man opened his jacket just enough to show BC the butt of his pistol.

"Whoa, man," BC said. "Guns are so uncool." He smiled, but the man didn't get the joke.

"I hope you will come without a fuss, Agent Querrey."

BC heard a trace of an accent. There was nothing particularly Russian about it, yet somehow BC knew the man was KGB. As casually as possible, he turned and looked toward the other end of the hallway. Another gray-suited man waited there. He had a softer face than his companion, with shoulders like ham hocks and a scowl curling his pudgy lips.

BC turned back to the first agent. His eyes traveled up and down the gray suit disdainfully.

"You could have at least dressed the part."

Melchior was sitting on a bench in Fort Washington Park when Song's Cadillac pulled up, a newspaper flapping in his hands in the breeze coming off the Potomac. He looked up with a tired smile on his face as the whiplash form of Chul-moo opened the back door, then frowned when he saw Ivelitsch step from the car. The Russian scanned the surroundings, then pulled his hat lower on his head and reached back to hand Song out of the car with a familiar air Melchior didn't like *at all*.

"What is this, the prom? Jesus Christ, Song, why don't you just pick him up at the Soviet Embassy next time?"

Song turned up the fur collar of her coat against the breeze. "Relax. We made sure we weren't followed."

"I'm kind of surprised to see *you* here actually," Ivelitsch said.

"You don't sound happy about it," Melchior replied. *"Actually."*

"I don't know why you went in in the first place. The Company suspects you of murdering three agents, after all."

"It was the only way to divert suspicion," Melchior said.

"You must have an amazing amount of confidence in your ability to bullshit. Especially with someone like James Jesus Angleton."

"It was just Everton," Melchior said, glaring at the Russian's smug, well-rested face. "Mother was out of town. I've never had the privilege of meeting him, which he'll thank me for one day." He held up his hand when Ivelitsch started to speak again. "Look, I don't have the time or energy for chitchat. It's been more than a week since Chandler escaped, and he's bound to show up soon. I want to know where Naz is. Without her, we have no way of controlling him; and without him our ace in the hole is gone."

Ivelitsch glanced at Song before speaking. "I have men watching Millbrook and the Hitchcock woman's apartment in New York City. If he shows up, we'll handle him. I'm beginning to think Orpheus is a distraction. We have bigger fish to fry."

"I'll have Keller give you a test flight when we get him back. Good luck to your men, by the way."

"If he's as powerful as you say, what's to stop him from plucking the secret of Naz's whereabouts from your mind? Isn't it safer if I *don't* tell you where she is?"

"I have to agree with Pavel," Song said, a little too quickly for Melchior's taste. "The fewer people who know Naz's location, the better. And she needs to be far enough away that if Orpheus does manage to ferret out her location, we'll be able to move her before he can get there."

Melchior looked between the two of them with suspicious, tired eyes. "How far, *Pavel?* Russia?"

"It would be difficult to get an unwilling girl on a plane to Moscow, at least in Washington. Perhaps from another city. If we could get her on a boat to Cuba, we could handle the transfer from there much more easily."

"I have contacts in a few coastal cities," Song added. "Miami, New Orleans, Houston . . ."

"Jesus Christ, I wasn't *serious.* You really want to send Naz to the fucking Soviet *Union?*"

This time it was Song who looked at Ivelitsch before answering. "We should at least get her away from Washington. Then, if we decide we need to move her out of the country, we can."

"In the meantime, we have something else to deal with—namely, the real reason why you were released last night. It's not because you managed to explain your way out of trouble. Everton let slip on his last visit to Song's that you're going to be sent to Dallas to retrieve an agent—"

"It's Caspar," Song cut in.

"*Caspar?* What the hell is he—no, wait." Melchior turned back to Song. "I thought you said Everton came in on the second Thursday of the month. That was almost a week ago."

"The Company decided to send you when they found Rip's body," Ivelitsch said smoothly. "Angleton's pretty sure you killed him. He thinks Raúl doubled you in Cuba."

"If he believed that, why didn't he have Everton hold me when I went in last night?"

Ivelitsch sighed as though he were trying to explain quantum mechanics to a three-year-old, or a German shepherd. "Are you familiar with Anatoliy Golitsyn?"

"The KGB officer who defected in '61? What about him?"

"Mother was convinced he was a KGB plant, and he was a little, shall we say, zealous in his attempts to get him to confess. If Golitsyn went public with the details of what was done to him, it would be very embarrassing to the Company, especially on top of the flak it's taken over the Bay of Pigs and the Missile Crisis. He apparently commanded a healthy settlement as hush money, and Drew Everton doesn't want something like that happening on his watch. So rather than do anything excessive in-house—"

"They want Caspar to kill you," Song said.

Maybe it was because he was so tired—that pinhead Everton had kept a light shining in his face for twelve straight hours—but Melchior's mind filled with an image of Caspar at four years old, looking up at him with trust—love—in his eyes. He saw Caspar at six, eight, ten, twelve, the love steadily replaced by a dead smirk as he attempted to maintain some sense of self while the Company put him through the wringer. Finally Caspar at eighteen, on leave from the Marines. "They're sending me to Japan," Melchior remembered him saying, both hands wrapped around a glass to keep them from shaking. "I guess it's finally starting."

"Melchior?" Song's voice cut into his thoughts.

Melchior shook himself. "Last I heard, the Company'd got Caspar stationed at Atsugi. The idea was that he would stage a defection, then buy his way into KGB with secrets about the U2 program. Although, after Powers, the cat was pretty much out of the bag."

"That was four years ago," Ivelitsch said. "Caspar arrived in Moscow in October 1959. Of course we suspected him of being a Company operative. Who in his right mind wants to move to the Soviet Union? We spent months trying to crack him, but he proved intractable. This seemed less due to any fortitude than simple instability. Caspar"—Melchior found it telling that Ivelitsch chose not to use Caspar's real name, since neither he nor Song had—"suffered from paranoia and delusions of grandeur and general confusion about who he was and what he believed in. He started calling himself Alik for some reason—his wife didn't even know his real name until after they were married."

"He got *married?*"

"A whirlwind romance," Ivelitsch said wryly. "Less than two months passed from the day they met until their nuptials."

"Hmph," Melchior said. "That doesn't sound convenient *at all.*"

Ivelitsch didn't respond to Melchior's innuendo. "When Marina became pregnant, Caspar requested to return to the United States. He said he was 'disillusioned' by Communism."

"If everyone who felt that way was allowed to leave the Soviet Union, the country'd have fewer living inhabitants than Pompeii after Vesuvius blew its top. Lemme guess, you let him take the wife, too? Because she was pregnant."

"Ultimately we decided it was easier letting him leave than watching him all the time. As soon as he got back here, he immediately resumed his pro-Communist persona, and became a very visible supporter of the revolution in Cuba—even as, behind the scenes, he made connections with several persons involved with CIA's program to assassinate Castro, including some associates of Sam Giancana."

"Giancana, huh?"

"Do you know him?"

"Let's just say his name keeps coming up."

"Melchior," Song said, "Caspar wouldn't—couldn't—kill you, could he? After all you've been through?"

Melchior shook his head. "I dunno. It's been a long time."

"CIA feels Caspar's behavior has become alarmingly erratic," Ivelitsch said. "Angleton suspects we might have doubled him even."

"Golitsyn, me, Caspar. Is there anyone Angleton *doesn't* think is a double agent?"

"Yes. Kim Philby." Ivelitsch chuckled, then went on. "At any rate, Caspar's involvement with Giancana is entirely self-initiated. Last month he even tried to get a visa to Cuba, presumably to make an attempt on Castro's life. And the Company's pretty sure he was the person who took a shot at William Walker back in April."

"Walker's a fascist, Castro's a Commie," Melchior said. "And Kim Philby's in Russia."

"Scheider thinks Caspar—" Ivelitsch broke off. "What?"

"I said, Kim Philby's in Russia."

"What's your point?" Ivelitsch said coldly.

"My point is, you said yesterday that Philby was your mole inside CIA. But he's been in Russia since January, which means there's no way Angleton could have told him he wanted Caspar to kill me. Which means you got the info from someone else. I'm guessing it was Caspar himself."

"Pavel?" Song said. "What's he talking about? Did you turn Caspar?"

"Yes, *Pavel*," Melchior sneered. "Did you double him? Or is he playing you? Because if the Company's got a file on you, then this partnership is *over*."

Ivelitsch didn't say anything for a moment. Then: "You'll have to ask him that yourself. When you see him in Dallas."

"Cut the bullshit, comrade. I need to know the truth before I see Caspar. Has he been in regular contact with KGB since he came back from Russia?"

"Of course we tried to recruit him," Ivelitsch said exasperatedly. "But Caspar's so confused that he can no longer distinguish between legend and reality. He may well think he's working for KGB. For all I know, he'll tell you we have dinner once a week. But the simple truth is that he's too crazy, even for us."

"So what you're saying is that I should believe Caspar if he tells me what you want me to believe, but if he contradicts you, it's just a delusion. You'll understand me if I find that unsatisfactory."

"I'd worry less about who he's working for than if he's going to shoot you. After his failure in the Soviet Union, he needs to do something that'll prove his worth to the Company—it doesn't matter if he's doing it out of loyalty to the U.S. or the Soviet Union. You'll still be dead."

"And so will he," Song said. "The Company will tip off FBI, who'll pick him up for murder, and six months later he'll end up in the electric chair. And that's the end of the Wiz Kids."

Melchior glanced at Song, but he was thinking about Caspar again. About the last time he'd seen him, in a geisha bar outside the naval air base in Atsugi. Just before they parted, Caspar had pulled Melchior aside. "Promise me you'll get me out if they brainwash me."

"Get you out—"

"*Take* me out," Caspar corrected him. "I don't want them to turn me into something I'm not." Such a statement begged the question: what was Caspar? But Melchior hadn't had the heart to ask it. "Promise?" Caspar had said. "I promise," Melchior had said, and somehow they both knew he was going to break it.

"Melchior?" This time it was Ivelitsch who pulled him from his reverie. Melchior shook his head to clear it, but Caspar's face refused to go away. He stood up so abruptly that his newspaper fell to the ground and a few pages fluttered away in the breeze.

"I have to go to Chicago. We'll deal with Chandler and Naz later."

"Chicago?" Ivelitsch called after Melchior's retreating form.

"You want the bomb to come to America," Melchior called back. "I'm going to get it here, and take care of Caspar at the same time."

Ivelitsch turned to Song. "I don't understand."

Song put a hand on Ivelitsch's knee to keep him from getting up. "I don't either," she said, staring after Melchior. "But Chicago is Giancana's home base."

"Ah," Ivelitsch said.

Song pointed to the dateline on the paper, and for the first time Ivelitsch noticed that it was the *Dallas Morning News*. It took him a second to figure it out.

"He already knew, didn't he? He was just pumping us for information, making sure we were telling the truth."

"I told you," Song said. "He's good."

Ivelitsch picked up the front page, which was covered with a series of red and black X's and O's.

"What's this?"

Song peered at it. "I'm not sure, but I think it's an old cipher system dating from the forties. It's hugely complicated. You take your message and the particular page of newsprint you're using and create an algorithm that encodes the former onto the latter. There are only a handful of agents who can break it without a computer."

"Huh." Ivelitsch was about to say something else, but, twenty feet away, Melchior had turned to look back at him.

"Did you double him?"

A little smirk played over Ivelitsch's lips. "I'll tell you in fifty years, if we're both still alive."

Melchior nodded, turned back around. "Song keeps petting you like that," he muttered, "I'm pretty sure you'll be dead long before then."

The men flanked him, the smaller one ahead, the bigger one behind, as they descended the staircase and made their way toward the front door. They spoke to each other in Russian, more or less confirming BC's earlier suspicion. This was a bad sign. It was one thing for Melchior to go rogue. It was quite another for him to cross to the other side. Or had word of Orpheus simply crossed international channels? Still, for some reason he wasn't afraid. He was already bucking the FBI and CIA, after all. What was one more acronymed agency?

When they reached the bottom of the stairs, the first man turned back to him. "We know you are traveling with Orpheus. You will take us to him, or Nazanin Haverman will die."

"Of course," BC said. "If you'll go get me a pen and, uh"—a glance over his shoulder—"your partner tracks down some paper, I'd be glad to write down the address."

The lead agent smiled at BC's attempt at a joke. "We are strangers in the city. We would be very appreciative if you took us to him yourself."

BC shrugged. "Whatever floats your boat."

The second man pressed so close as they made their way through the thronged front hall that BC could feel the man's belly pressed against the small of his back. He couldn't resist.

"Is that a gun in your pocket, or are you just glad to see me?"

"Why can't it be both?" the man said.

The crowd seemed to have thickened. The parlors oozed smoke and music and body heat, and people eddied back and forth between them, making the hall a swirling mass. The three men inched their way forward, the lead Russian unwilling to shove through. Probably didn't want to attract attention, BC thought. The agent's hesitation bought him a few seconds, but to do what?

A fresh surge of people pushed the three men against a sleek modern console. An expressionist portrait hung over it—a woman looking like she'd been dismembered and reassembled by a blind surgeon. More helpfully, there was a medium-sized brass vase on the console beneath the painting.

Another press from the crowd. BC slipped his left hand into the vase as though it were a big brass glove. A puff of ash floated into the air as his hand sank into the metal canister. Great, he thought, I've stuck my hand in an ashtray. He hugged it quickly to his stomach, thankful he wasn't wearing one of his new suits.

"So, uh . . ." He squinted at the signature on the painting. The man's handwriting was the most recognizable thing on the canvas. "What's your opinion of de Kooning?"

Even as the front man was turning around, BC whirled, leading with his metal-capped hand. The big Russian behind him was fast, he had to give him that. His gun was already out and leveling off. The vase struck it with a loud clang. The gun bounced off the console and went flying across the room.

"Whoa, bad trip!" someone yelled as BC whirled back to the front. He wasn't so lucky this time. He heard the sound of a shot as he turned, saw the smoking barrel of the gun in the lead Russian's hand even as a ripple traveled up and down his skeleton, shaking his bones one from the other. He wobbled on his feet, only his skin holding him together.

The Russian smiled. He seemed about to say something, then stopped. His brow furrowed, his smile leveled out. Blood leaked from his mouth and a second stain was flowering on his chest.

"*Blyat,*" he said, and fell backward.

BC held up the vase and saw the dent on the base. He'd gotten lucky after all.

Not that he had time to enjoy it. Something hard struck him in the small of the back and he was thrown forward. He landed on the fallen Russian and grabbed for his gun, trying to shake the bullet-dented vase off his left hand the whole time, but all he got was a cloud of ash. Still, he had the gun in his right hand, and he rolled onto his back and waved it at the second Russian.

"Back off," he said, inching backward across the marble floor, the brass vase clanking with every step.

"This shit is the *best!*" someone said. "You would not believe what I'm seeing right now!"

Other partygoers were less sanguine, or less stoned.

"Call the cops!"

"Take it outta here, man. You're bringing down the vibe!"

Just then Peggy Hitchcock came into the hall.

"Oh my God," she yelled, looking not at the gun in BC's right hand but the vase on his left. "Grandma!"

"Call Billy," BC told her. "Tell him you've got a dead KGB agent in your foyer. He'll know what to do."

To her credit, Hitchcock just nodded and ran from the room.

The Russian seized the moment, diving behind the console beneath the painting. From his position on the ground, BC tried to aim underneath it, but before he knew it the console had flipped up in the air and was coming down top-first on his body, looking for all the world like a coffin falling from the sky. His right hand slammed into the marble floor and his fingers lost their grip on the gun.

Before he could move a second weight crashed into him. The console exploded in pieces, and he found himself staring at a pair of quivering jowls.

"If you think de Kooning is bad," the grinning Russian said, "wait till you see what I do with your face." He grabbed BC's throat with both hands and banged his head against the marble floor.

BC slammed the urn into the side of the Russian's head. It wasn't a strong blow, and all the Russian did was blink as a cloud of Peggy Hitchcock's grandmother's ashes burst into the air, but at least he stopped banging BC's head against the floor. BC hit him again, angling for the man's bulbous nose this time, which showered his own face with blood. A third blow. A fourth. It was the Russian's face that resembled the de Kooning painting, but still he refused to let go of BC's throat. Spots dancing in front of BC's eyes obscured the Russian even more.

He was about to go for one last blow when the Russian's head fell on his chest and his hands finally slackened their grip. BC looked up to see Peggy Hitchcock standing over him with an African-looking totem in her hands. She was holding it by a penis the size of its abdomen.

"Just go," she said before BC could speak.

BC lifted his left hand, still stuck in the dented urn. Peggy Hitchcock waved it away.

"Grandma's seen worse."

BC retrieved the unconscious agent's gun and stumbled into the hall, pressed the button for the elevator. He'd just managed to extricate his hand from the urn when the doors opened. A shower of ash shot into the air like a desiccated thundercloud. The elevator operator pretended not to notice the ash or the blood or the skewed wig.

"Find what you were looking for, sir?"

BC straightened his vest and walked onto the elevator. "More like it found me."

The operator was nice enough to hail a cab for BC when they reached the street level, and he raced back to the Village. The cab got stuck in a traffic jam at the end of Fifth, and BC had to run the last five blocks to the hotel. Sweat mixed with the ash and blood on his face to form an acrid gruel that kept dripping into his mouth, but as soon as he pushed the door to the hotel room open, he realized he needn't have bothered.

Chandler was gone.

Sam Giancana's guards didn't just frisk Melchior: they un-tucked his shirt and lifted it up to check for a wire, took off his shoes, felt inside the band of his hat, leafed through his wallet. They even opened his pen and scribbled on a piece of paper to make sure it was real—then kept it for themselves. Satisfied he was neither armed nor miked, they ushered him into Giancana's private office.

"I'm gonna want that pen back before I go," Melchior said to the guards as they left, then turned around to face the kingpin of the Chicago mob.

Giancana didn't get up as Melchior, still disheveled from his frisking, approached his desk. He was a lean, nattily dressed man, with a sharp dimpled chin and a softly rounded head, largely devoid of hair. Melchior'd only seen him in photographs, usually wearing a pair of Hollywood shades and a spiffy hat to hide his baldness, but now he wore thick horn-rimmed glasses and looked more like a businessman than the lady-killer who, in addition to a long-term relationship with Phyllis McGuire of the McGuire Sisters, had dated Judith Campbell at the same time she was seeing Jack Kennedy (this was after Miss Campbell was done with Frank Sinatra). The then-candidate was looking for a little help with the Chicago ballot, and rumor had it that his mistress had helped to broker a deal between him and the man sitting on the other side of the desk, whose well-tailored suit did nothing to mask the street-kid accent that filled the room like squealing brakes as soon as Giancana opened his mouth.

"So. Who is this mook who's been calling every two-bit con artist, numbers man, street hustler, and pimp in Chicago saying he wants to meet Momo Giancana?"

There was a chair in front of Giancana's desk just as there was in front of Drew Everton's, but Melchior remained standing. He knew the theatrics that had so annoyed Everton wouldn't fly here.

"My name is Melchior," he said, biting back the urge to add, "sir."

Giancana swatted the answer away like a fly. "I didn't ask your 'name.' I know your 'name.' I asked who the hell you *are.*"

"I work for CIA. I was in Cuba for most of '62 and '63—"

Giancana's nostrils flared as he let out a frustrated sigh. "You're wasting my time, Mr. Mook Melchior of the Central Fucking Intelligence Agency, or whoever you work for. Now. Who in the hell *are* you, and why the fuck did you wanna see *me?*"

Melchior found himself fiddling with his lapel, feeling for the familiar, comforting bullet hole. But although he was still wearing a dead man's suit, this one had come from a man he'd killed himself, and he'd taken care not to leave any marks. He knew he had to tread every bit as delicately here.

"Here's the situation, Mr. Giancana. I know you helped Jack Kennedy carry Chicago in 1960, and I know you've been helping the Company try to knock off Fidel Castro for the past couple of years. And I also know that you feel double-crossed because, despite the money and manpower you've expended in good faith, Bobby Kennedy is still trying to throw your ass in jail."

Giancana's expression didn't change, but for the first time he paused.

"Look, you wanna go tit for tat," he said, "I can talk shit too. I got letters on CIA stationery thanking Lucky Luciano for his help fighting the Commies in Italy and France right after the war. I got photographs showing Company agents shipping Southeast Asian heroin to San Francisco in order to outfit a private army to fight the Viet Cong. And I got a unique collection of souvenirs—cigars packed with C4, pens filled with cyanide, and a couple-a fungusy-looking things that I don't wanna get too close to—all made in Langley labs and destined for our good friend on the other side of the Florida Straits."

Melchior took a moment to absorb this. On the surface, the words were as hostile as everything else Giancana'd said, but the tone was different. The boss was curious. Was sending out feelers to see just how much Melchior was willing to say.

He took a deep breath. It was going to be all or nothing.

"I was in Italy in '47. I was seventeen years old. Lucky liked me so much he wanted to set me up with his daughter. And I spent nine months in Laos raising funds for the private army you mentioned, and another two years in Cuba, where I went with the task of delivering one of those exploding cigars to El Jefe. I'm not here to accuse you of anything, Mr. Giancana. I'm here to offer you my help."

Melchior wouldn't want to get in a poker game with this guy. Giancana's face didn't twitch when Melchior rattled off his list. He just sat back, the rich leather of his chair creaking beneath him, and let an amused smile spread across his face. It was a dangerous, disarming smile, like a cobra's hypnotic swaying just before it strikes.

"Siciliano?"

"My mother was born in the shadow of Mount Aetna," Melchior said in perfect Sicilian.

A sound, half-laugh, half-bark, burst from Giancana's mouth. "All right, then. Tell me what it is that *you* can do for *me*."

Melchior nodded. "Just over three weeks ago, I shot Louie Garza."

Giancana flicked a bit of lint off his cuff. "That name don't mean nothing to me."

"I shot him in Cuba, while he was trying to steal a nuclear bomb."

Another pause. Melchior couldn't tell if Giancana was considering what he'd just said, or considering how to get rid of his body after he had his guards shoot him in the back. Finally:

"Louie never mentioned no nuke to me."

"That's because he was planning to sell it and keep the money for himself."

"You kill the bastard?"

"Yes."

"Good. Saves me the trouble." Then, almost as an afterthought: "So what happened to the nuke?"

"It's still in Cuba."

Giancana leaned forward, reaching for a cigar on his desk. "Oh well, *que sera, sera,* as Doris—"

"The way I see it, Mr. Giancana, that bomb belongs to you."

For the first time Melchior got a reaction. An eyebrow twitch, but he'd take it. Giancana took the time to light his cigar before speaking again. Melchior glanced at the band. Cuban, of course. Montecristo. Also of course.

"I done a little-a this and a little-a that in my day. Girls. Booze.

Even a few guns here and there. But a nuke? Why don't I just tape a bull's-eye on my forehead and hand the gun to Bobby Kennedy?"

"The way I see it, Mr. Giancana, the bull's-eye's on you already. Bobby Kennedy's made the mafia public enemy number two—after Jimmy Hoffa. One way or another he's going to nail your ass to the wall in the next year to make sure Jack wins the election, and he's gonna ride that wave all the way to the White House in '68. It's gonna be sixteen years of the Kennedys unless someone does something about it."

The number two was a good gambit. As the Montecristo suggested, Giancana liked to be tops in everything. Even the most-wanted list. "What do you want me to do, shoot Bobby Kennedy?"

Melchior shook his head. "Shoot him and you make him a martyr. Breaking the mafia will go from being his crusade to being the nation's. The only way to stop him is to get him out of office, and the only way to get Bobby Kennedy out of office is to get Jack Kennedy out of office."

Giancana puffed out thick gray wreaths of smoke until a bright red nubbin the size of a thimble glowed at the end of his Montecristo. He turned the cigar toward his face, brought the end so close to his eye that Melchior thought he was going to burn himself, but all he did was watch the glowing tip slowly fade like a dying star. Only when it had dimmed to the palest orange did he look back at Melchior.

"Say it straight," he said. "Tell me exactly what you want, or I'm gonna use this cigar to write my name on your forehead."

Melchior came closer to gulping than he ever had in his life.

"What I'm saying, Mr. Giancana, is that if you take this bomb off my hands, I'll take care of your Kennedy problem. For good."

Two hours later, he called Song from Midway. Ivelitsch answered, and before Melchior could say anything, the Russian relayed what had happened at Peggy Hitchcock's apartment in New York. The story seemed fuzzy to Melchior, like a TV station on a rainy day, but he was too wired to pay it any real attention. He was so jumpy after his interview with Giancana he was practically twitching.

"Yeah, whatever, Pavel, great men you've got working for you. I don't give a shit right now. Put Song on."

There was a disgruntled pause, the sound of muffled voices, then Song came on the phone.

"Is this line secure?" Melchior asked.

"We change it every month."

"It's the nineteenth. The Company's had nearly three weeks to tap it, if they're watching you. Is this line fucking *secure?*"

"Calm down, Melchior. Why would CIA be watching me?"

"Because they're watching me. Jesus Christ, get with the program."

"Melchior—"

"Look, just shut up and listen. Things are gonna happen fast now, or they're not gonna happen at all. Our friend in the Windy City tells me you know Jack Ruby."

There was a pause. Song's frustration came through the line like radiation.

"*Song!*" Melchior could barely keep from shouting. "Do you know *Jack Ruby?* The Carousel Club? Dallas fucking *Texas?*"

"I don't exactly *know* him," Song said coldly. "The Carousel gets its dancers through the Guild of Variety Artists—the Strippers Union— which is run out of Chicago, if you take my meaning. I once sent our friend in Chicago a rather beautiful blonde to dance for him at a private party. Somehow Ruby got wind of it and developed the notion that I'm in the habit of supplying girls to every whiskey-soaked dance club from here to Vegas."

"Yeah, well, his dream's about to come true. I want you to call him and tell him you're sending Nancy to Dallas. Chul-moo is your pilot, right?"

"Yes—"

"Bring her in your plane. We're gonna need it afterward. Just the three of you. There's a little strip in north Dallas called Addison. Use that one instead of Love Field."

"After what? And what's wrong with Love?"

"Jesus Christ, Song, are you out of your fucking mind! Air Force One is gonna be at Love. The place'll be crawling with Secret Service."

"Melchior? What the hell are you planning?"

"You'll know soon enough. Now, get your ass to Dallas. Just you, Chul-moo, Nancy, and the plane. Got it?"

"I can't just close up shop for a couple of days to ferry—"

Melchior banged the receiver against the side of the booth.

"Are you fucking *listening* to me, Song? If this works, you're going to be closing *permanently*. Now, call Ruby, tell him you're sending Nancy to Dallas, and get your ass *down there!*"

The phone was silent so long that Melchior wondered if he'd broken it when he smashed the receiver. Then:

"Jesus Christ, Melchior." Song's voice was hushed. Not frightened, but awed. "They'll send an army after you. You'll be running for the rest of your life."

"I already am running. But once this is over, they won't know who they're chasing."

A crackly voice in the background called Melchior's flight to Dallas.

"Listen to me, Song. Don't lose faith in me. This was your idea, remember? This whole damn thing was your idea. Believe in it. Believe in me. Now, put Pavel on the phone."

"I've been on the whole time."

"Of course you have, you eavesdropping fuck. I need you to send a couple of telegrams. One to Cuba. The other to Dallas."

"Ah." There was a pause. "To whom should I address the second one?"

Ivelitsch's voice was flat. Incurious. Unimpassioned. Melchior remembered what he'd said in Union Station yesterday afternoon, just before he'd shot one of his own men and forced Melchior to kill two Company agents. *Everyone who knows you has to die.* It was all in a day's work to him.

"Send it to Alik. Alik Hidell."

"And what do I tell—"

"Tell him it's time. Time to do what you trained him to do in Russia."

In the house on Newport Place, Song and Ivelitsch sat in her
office, their conversation punctuated by an occasional whip crack from
the second floor, where Chul-moo was helping one of the girls with a
prominent lobbyist for the tobacco industry. The lobbyist had just seen
a draft of the Surgeon General's impending report on smoking and
health and felt he needed to atone for the sins of his profession.

"The idea of the sleeper took hold in American intelligence right
after Stalin detonated his first bomb," Song told Ivelitsch. "Suddenly it
was undeniably clear that the Soviets were way ahead in the spy game.
The Americans lacked experience. What they did have was dollars, and
a willingness to try just about anything. Joe Scheider, who was then
little more than a hyper-patriotic postdoctoral student with degrees in
psychiatry and chemistry, floated the idea of trolling orphanages in
search of bright kids who could essentially be raised by the Company as
intelligence agents, placed in situ as children, and activated when and if
they were needed. There were any number of problems with this plan,
but chief among them was the fact that Caspar, Scheider's star recruit,
turned out not to be an orphan. His mother left him at the orphanage
Monday through Friday, but took him home weekends. Most weekends anyway. Scheider refused to give up, however. He directed Frank
Wisdom to act as a paternal surrogate—Caspar's own father had died
before he was born—and, although Caspar was raised by his mother
and a couple of stepfathers, the Wiz and other Company men had frequent contact with him through various extracurricular activities. They
helped him develop a dual identity. Publicly he was an outspoken socialist, carting around copies of *The Communist Manifesto* and *Das Kap-
ital,* but privately he was training to become a double agent inside the
KGB, joining the Civil Air Patrol in his early teens, then dropping out
of high school to enlist in the Marines when he turned seventeen. But,
as you saw in Russia, juggling both identities proved too much for him.
Caspar wasn't sure if he hated America or loved it, if he was working for

the triumph of the proletariat or trying to expose the duplicities of the Communist paradise. The only thing that never wavered was his loyalty. Not to the Company or the Wiz or Scheider. To Melchior. I can't believe he'd ever shoot him."

Pavel Semyonovitch Ivelitsch listened to Song's lecture respectfully, smiling when the tobacco lobbyist moaned particularly loudly. He didn't understand masochism. The world was full of people trying to lord it over you—why pay someone to add to that? He'd much rather be the one holding the whip. Now he looked at Song pointedly.

"Would it be such a bad thing if he did?"

Song's eyes narrowed. "You think we can go it alone?"

"I think Melchior's ambivalence could be our undoing. His loyalty to the Company is essentially mercenary, but his loyalty to the Wiz is, like Caspar's loyalty to him, personal, and considerable."

"But with the Wiz gone, Melchior knows there's no place left for him in the Company. They already sent Rip Robertson to kill him, and now they're trying to get Caspar to do it. He's got no one else to turn to *except* us."

"For our sake, I hope you're right."

"Maybe you don't understand what just happened on the phone."

"What do you mean?"

"Dallas? Jack Ruby? The Carousel Club? Melchior could've sent us a coded telegram, but he mentioned those names out loud. On purpose. He's trying to find out if anyone in the Company besides Everton is spying on him."

"Because?"

"Don't play dumb, Pavel. He's not just going rogue. He's going away. He's going to kill everyone who can identify him. When this is over, only you and I will know that he ever existed, let alone that he still does."

A smile flickered over Ivelitsch's mouth. "I'm almost impressed. But can he pull it off?"

"You mean logistically? Or temperamentally? Logistically I think it's doable. For twenty years he's been in the field. He's virtually unknown by Company brass, let alone other agents. Everton's the only person in Langley besides the Wiz who's seen his face in the past decade."

"What about the other Wiz Kids?"

Song shrugged. "As near as I can tell, that's a story Melchior made up himself."

"And Caspar? Can he kill him?"

"I don't know. Something's changed in him since he came back from Cuba, and it's not just getting hold of this bomb, or even Orpheus. He's become more calculating. Maybe he's just realized that with the Wiz out of the picture, he has to plan a different future for himself, but he's a much more ruthless man than the one I met a decade ago."

Ivelitsch shook his head. "I meant, will Caspar try to kill Melchior?"

Song looked at Ivelitsch sharply. "You know why Caspar was sent to Russia, don't you?"

"Presumably to infiltrate—"

"Caspar couldn't have infiltrated his mother's house. He carries a sign over his head that says 'SPY' in neon letters."

"Then why send him to the Soviet Union?"

"Because even if he *was* a spy, he was still a self-proclaimed defector. A former Marine. A man who could confirm the existence of the U2 program, which evidence could have been used to execute Francis Gary Powers had the Politburo chosen to go down that route. He could have been sent on a whistle-stop tour of the hinterlands to lecture on the evils of capitalism while simultaneously keeping him away from state secrets. TASS and *Pravda* could have had a field day with him. All he needed was a single photo op with Premier Khrushchev."

"To—kill him?" Ivelitsch's eyebrows went up, though it was impossible to tell if he was amazed or merely amused. "This sounds more like Mother than the Wiz. It also sounds like a suicide mission."

"Be that as it may, it didn't work. And now Caspar's back in the States, still looking for a leader to kill."

Ivelitsch shook his head. "What a curious profession we have. So. I take it this is your way of saying Caspar will do it."

"I think he'll try. Whether he'll pull it off is another thing. Among other things, he's not a particularly good shot."

"And if he misses? Melchior will kill him?"

"Like I said, something's happened to alienate him from the Company. I don't know what he's capable of now."

"You think he wants revenge?"

"It's more than that. He wants to prove them wrong. He has to make himself believe that he's not just the Wiz's pickaninny after all."

"I don't like it. An intelligence agent's actions should be convoluted, but his motivations should always be crystal clear and simple. Zeal or greed I understand, even glory, but this is oedipal—messy—and it has a damn good chance of blowing up in our faces."

"Well, for now we have to trust him. He's brilliant in the field, and every king needs a general." She looked at Ivelitsch pointedly. "I can manage him."

"Every king needs a queen as well," Ivelitsch said, giving Song a tight-lipped smile. "Just make sure you're not trying to manage all of us."

Suddenly there was a crash in the hallway, and Ivelitsch jerked upright.

"What the hell—"

Song felt a familiar dull thud in her head. Immediately she understood.

"Orpheus!"

Ivelitsch looked at her sharply. "How do you know?"

"No time to explain. We have to get out of here."

"Nix that," Ivelitsch said, pulling his gun from his jacket. "I'm going to take care of this Orpheus problem once and for all."

"Pavel, no—"

But it was too late. Ivelitsch pulled open the door and strode into the hall.

Chandler paced the floor of the SRO for all of five minutes after BC headed to Peggy Hitchcock's apartment in his ridiculous getup, then grabbed one of the ex–FBI agent's new blazers and headed out into the bright fall afternoon. An idea had come to him when BC showed him his beatnik costume. It was a long shot, but if it worked he'd be on his way to Naz before BC even got to Hitchcock's home. And if it didn't, he'd be back in the hotel before BC returned, none the wiser.

It was only a few blocks to Washington Square Park. The Village was another country to the one that existed north of Fourteenth Street, another world to Beacon Hill. Chandler had laughed uproariously at BC's thrift store finds, yet they were tame compared to the outfits he saw here: men in vests that appeared to be made of bear fur, flared black leather pants that rode below what would have been the waistband of the underwear, had the people in question been wearing any. The only ties he saw were wrapped around foreheads, the only dresses were dashikis and sarongs, and just as likely to be on men as on women. At one point he saw a slim man in pressed chinos and starched white shirt and severely parted hair, but when he got closer he realized it was actually a woman, her breasts flattened by some kind of binding, her upper lip darkened with pencil. There were several interracial couples as well—black girls and white men, but also black men and white girls. Sweet-smelling home-rolled cigarettes were passed freely from hand to hand around the park's central fountain. It was one big party, and Chandler was there to get in on the fun. Not marijuana, though. He needed something stronger.

He walked through the park searching for the right person. Finally he saw a young man sitting with a tall drum between his dungarees, the only thing that covered his skinny body in the nippy evening besides a length of light brown hair. The man's eyes darted from place to place, as if he were watching butterflies or hummingbirds flit through the air. The sky was empty, though. The man was clearly hallucinating.

Chandler took off his tie and opened the top couple of buttons on his shirt, then ambled up to the man and sat down on the bench a few feet from him.

"Nice day, huh?"

The man's head continued to dart this way and that.

"I said, nice day, isn't it?"

The man looked over at him. "Oh, sorry, man. I didn't realize you were real."

You don't know the half of it, Chandler thought. Aloud he said again, "It's a nice day, isn't it?"

"You think that changes things?"

"Beg pardon?"

"If you call the day nice? Do you think the sun hears you and decides to shine brighter? The wind decides to ease up just enough to rustle the leaves? The day don't need any compliments from *you*, man. The day just *is*. All you got to be is *in* it."

"Oh, uh, right." Chandler paused. "Do you think maybe you could help me with that?"

"I don't think you're ready for my trip, man." The man flicked the shiny lapel of BC's jacket. "I think it'd blow the mind of a square like you."

"You'd be surprised."

It took Chandler a half hour more to convince Wally to give him a taste. There was just enough LSD in the grubby little square Wally pulled from his pocket to set Chandler's mind a-tingle, but it was enough. He was able to push Wally to give him the rest of his stash—four more light hits—and then he wandered around the park, reaching into people's minds to see if anyone was carrying. By the time he left he had six hits of LSD, as well as three hundred dollars in cash. He hailed a cab on the corner of Fifth Avenue and Washington Square North.

"Where to?" said the old Italian man behind the wheel.

"Washington, DC."

"You mean Penn Station?"

"No," Chandler said. "I want you to drive me to Washington, DC. Now."

o   o   o

Chandler had never seen the gray-eyed man who stepped into the hallway of Song's establishment, but he recognized him from the snippets he'd pulled from BC's mind. This was the man who'd taken Naz.

The man jerked his pistol at Chandler. Chandler concentrated. The acid he'd scored in Washington Square Park was substantially weaker than the stuff Keller had been giving him, and he'd used a lot of it getting the cabbie to drive him out of New York City before ditching him at a rest stop on the New Jersey Turnpike. He'd downed everything he had left ten minutes before he knocked on the front door of the Newport Place house. It would have to be enough. He forced his way into Ivelitsch's mind and grabbed.

As Ivelitsch leveled his gun at Chandler, the weapon suddenly turned on its holder, hissing like a cobra. He screamed and threw it from his hands.

Chandler picked up the gun while Ivelitsch blinked in confusion—not just at what had happened with the gun, but how quickly Chandler retrieved it. He'd never seen a man move so fast.

As Chandler was aiming the gun at Ivelitsch he saw a flicker of movement to his right. Song, leaping for him with a knife in her hand. He reached, pulled, thrust.

Melchior had briefed Song on what to expect. She knew the pit that opened in the floor beneath her feet was just an illusion. But even so, the vision was too real to resist. She screamed as she fell into the void.

As Song fell to the carpet, Chandler pounced. He'd never struck a woman before, but he kicked her viciously in the head. Her skull smashed into the wainscoting and she lay inert.

Ivelitsch had recovered enough to charge. Chandler used the gun this time. He'd never shot anyone either, but he squeezed the trigger and a globe of blood burst from Ivelitsch's shoulder. Ivelitsch slammed against the flowered wallpaper and slumped to the floor.

Chandler advanced with the gun extended. Ivelitsch's eyes flickered up the hall, where Chul-moo's bare legs protruded from the security booth. He saw no sign of Garrison or Junior, but it wasn't difficult to imagine that they'd been similarly dispatched.

"Where is she?"

A trained professional, Ivelitsch didn't react. He pulled his handkerchief from his pocket and pressed it to his shoulder to stanch the flow of blood.

"Who?"

Chandler's eyes narrowed, and he pushed as hard as he could. A wave of fire washed over Ivelitsch's body and he screamed hysterically until Chandler relaxed. Even so, he continued rolling on the ground in an effort to douse the flames for several seconds, until Chandler kicked him onto his back and put the gun in his face.

"Where?"

Ivelitsch stared up into the face of Orpheus. It was implacable and otherworldly. The face of a man possessed by love and hatred. His flesh still scalded and he couldn't believe he was alive.

"Wh-what *are* you?"

But Chandler didn't respond. The answer to his question had floated to the top of Ivelitsch's brain like a drowned corpse rising from the bottom of a lake.

A nightclub, a portly balding man. He pushed at Ivelitsch's brain until he had a name, a location.

Jack Ruby.

The Carousel Club.

Dallas.

He brought the butt of the pistol down as hard as he could on Ivelitsch's skull and, like an unplugged TV, the picture snapped to black.

PART 4

THE TRUMAN DOCTRINE

The integrity and vitality of our system is in
greater jeopardy than ever before in our history.
Even if there were no Soviet Union we would face the
great problem of the free society, accentuated many
fold in this industrial age, of reconciling order,
security, the need for participation, with the
requirement of freedom. We would face the fact that
in a shrinking world the absence of order among
nations is becoming less and less tolerable. The
Kremlin design seeks to impose order among nations
by means which would destroy our free and democratic
system. The Kremlin's possession of atomic weapons
puts new power behind its design, and increases
the jeopardy to our system. It adds new strains to
the uneasy equilibrium-without-order which exists
in the world and raises new doubts in men's minds

whether the world will long tolerate this tension
without moving toward some kind of order, on
somebody's terms.

The risks we face are of a new order of magnitude, commensurate with the total struggle in which
we are engaged. For a free society there is never
total victory, since freedom and democracy are never
wholly attained, are always in the process of being
attained. But defeat at the hands of the totalitarian
is total defeat. These risks crowd in on us, in a
shrinking world of polarized power, so as to give us
no choice, ultimately, between meeting them effec-
tively or being overcome by them.

   —NSC-68, issued April 14, 1950; signed by
President Truman, September 30, 1950; declassified 1975

This is a serious course upon which we embark. I
would not recommend it except that the alternative is
much more serious.

     —Harry S. Truman, March 12, 1947

"Boo."

The slim, russet-haired man gasped when Melchior stepped from behind the flaking bark of a sycamore tree. He stumbled backward several steps, barely managing to keep from falling. Melchior might've liked to think he still had that kind of effect on Caspar after all these years, but the sweet smell of whiskey carried in the warm air.

When the man had finally recovered his balance, he squinted against the shadows, his right hand already inside his jacket.

"Tommy? Is it really you?"

"Hey, Caspar," Melchior said. "It's been a while."

When BC got back to the hotel and found Chandler gone, he stared at the whorls of grime crusted beneath the radiators as though Chandler might take shape out of the shadows. But all he saw was a stack of empty suitcases—six of them, because, like a turtle, a snail even, he had to carry his clothes on his back. A rack of clothes sagged beneath the weight of the brightly colored suits and shirts and sweaters and slacks BC had purchased when he tried to reinvent himself as some kind of playboy–cum–private eye. Who in the hell did he think he was? James Bond? Sam Spade? Philip Marlowe? He wasn't even Paul Drake, the nebbishy gumshoe Perry Mason used to do his legwork. He was just the ugly duckling who'd tried to convince himself he was a swan—or a peacock, judging by the clothes. All that was needed was a feather boa and the wardrobe would've fit in perfectly in a showgirl's dressing room.

Somehow in less than three weeks he'd lost everything. Not just his job but his career. Not just his home but his inheritance. Not just Chandler and Naz: himself. How had he let Chandler slip away? And why had he run? Didn't he realize BC had given up everything—*everything*—to help him get Naz back, to get back at Melchior and get his world back on track?

He lifted a silk tie from the riotous lattice of color that covered the bureau. The tie was black and narrow, woven of wool rather than silk. Matte rather than shiny, like a pencil line. He should just save everyone the trouble and hang himself with it.

He continued looking at the tie until suddenly it occurred to him that it was also the same color as Naz's eyes. As her face flashed in his mind, he understood how it could captivate you. Capture you really. Take hold of your soul and never let go. He remembered the dance in her room at Madam Song's, felt her hip bones beneath his fingertips, the gentle press of her chest against his. And he remembered the feeling that had filled the room when Song came in. Hatred as palpable as an undertow, as toxic as poison gas, and every bit as indiscriminate.

He continued staring at the black tie, only now it reminded him of Millbrook's shadowed forests. And then a lightbulb went on over his head: Millbrook.

It was one of the basic tenets of investigation. When you can't go forward, go backward. He didn't know where Chandler had gone—or where the presumed KGB agent had taken Naz—but he knew where they'd started from. And Chandler'd wanted to go to Millbrook in the first place. He knew how dangerous Melchior was: surely he wouldn't go after him without all the LSD he could get his hands on? BC tried to tell himself it was the logical choice, but really, logic had left the building a long time ago.

He cinched the tie around his neck, just tightly enough that he felt each breath as it squeezed past the knot like an egg swallowed whole. It was uncomfortable, but it also reminded him he was alive. He grabbed his wallet, his jacket, his gun—at least Chandler had left him that—and headed for his car.

"Damn it, Chandler!" he muttered to himself as he raced for his car. "After everything I've *done* for you!"

Caspar's hands twitched as he uncorked the bottle Melchior'd brought with him—his whole body twitched, not like a drunk's, but like a man who feels bugs crawling over his skin. He scratched and rubbed and slapped at imaginary pests, pausing only long enough to down one shot of whiskey, then a second.

"You hear 'bout the Wiz? They say Joe Scheider fried his brain. Say he sits around in his bathrobe all day and pisses his pants like a god-damn nutcase."

"Don't you believe it," Melchior said, sipping at his own glass. For once he didn't feel like drinking. "The Wiz'll be running ops long after you and I are rotting in some unmarked grave."

Caspar's face lit up. "You remember when you shot him? With that slingshot? I wish you'd shot the doc. I never liked him. I liked the Wiz well enough, but I never liked Doc Scheider."

Melchior sipped his whiskey and let Caspar talk.

"I was just Lee then, wasn't I? No Caspar then. No Alik. No Alik Hidell or O. H. Lee. Just Lee. I liked it when I was just Lee."

"You were all alone then."

Caspar shook his head like a rag doll. "I had my mother. I had you, too." The assertion was almost violent. "And I had me," he added in a tiny, self-pitying voice. He downed another shot of whiskey. Then, smiling brightly: "I got a wife now. She had a daughter. Today."

A wife, a daughter, Melchior thought. Another man would have said their names, but all Caspar did was smile at him hopefully, as if begging Melchior to confirm the truth of what he'd said.

"I got two daughters now," Caspar said beseechingly. *"Two."*

"Who does?" Melchior said. "Caspar? Alik? Or Lee?"

Caspar looked at him with a stricken expression. *"I do."*

Melchior tipped more whiskey into Caspar's glass. Caspar looked at it as though it was one of Joe Scheider's potions, then, like a good boy, took his medicine. His shirt opened as he leaned forward, and Melchior noticed something around his neck. A string of beads. Skulls, it looked like. Hundreds of them, hanging down inside his shirt.

"They're trying to make me do things," Caspar said. "Not me, though. They want Caspar to do them."

"You are Caspar."

Caspar shook his head. "I'm Lee."

"Marina thinks you're Alik."

"I'm *Lee*."

"You can be whoever you want to be."

Caspar stared at Melchior with a stricken expression. "Alik Hidell bought the guns," he whispered. "Not me."

"Alik Hidell can do it then."

"I don't want to do it," Caspar said.

"Caspar can do it too. Or Alik. Or O. H. Lee."

Caspar got up and began pacing Melchior's motel room. He'd placed his .38 on the bureau when they first came in, and he walked to it, stood facing it with his back to Melchior. Melchior's gun was a warm lump under his arm, Ivelitsch's telegram a slip of paper in his pocket.

"What's with the skulls, Caspar?"

Caspar's left hand slipped under his collar. "I'm Lee," he whispered. He worried a bead between thumb and forefinger, and Melchior imagined bones breaking beneath the boy's fingers, cranial plates cracking, teeth snapping out like kernels of corn.

"What's with the skulls?"

Caspar whirled around to face Melchior. If he'd had his gun in his hand, he could have shot Melchior before the latter had time to react. But he didn't have his gun in his hand.

"I went to Mexico."

Melchior sat calmly, not reaching for his gun, not setting his drink down—although an agent with more wits about him than Caspar would have noticed that Melchior's jacket was unbuttoned now, that he'd moved his drink to his left hand.

"Who went to Mexico? Caspar? Alik? O. H. Lee?"

"*I* did." Caspar's fingers moved from one bead to the next like the housemaids at the orphanage saying their rosaries. "I was trying to get away. But I couldn't."

"You were trying to go to Cuba, weren't you?"

"I wanted to get away."

"You were trying to kill Castro."

"It was the Day of the Dead," Caspar said.

"You wanted to go to Russia, too. To kill Khrushchev."

"People were walking around with skulls hanging around their necks and painted on their faces. It was like they'd already died but their bodies hadn't figured it out yet."

Melchior shook his head. "Lee went to Mexico in October, Caspar. The Day of the Dead is in November. Did you think Lee was already dead?"

"*I'm* Lee," Caspar said. "*I* am."

"But you know they don't really want Alik to kill Castro, don't you? Or Khrushchev?"

"They do," Caspar said angrily, plaintively. "They want him to shoot everyone."

"Who?" Melchior didn't bother to distinguish between target and master.

"Anyone. Everyone." He was pulling so hard on the string of beads that Melchior thought he was going to break it.

"Who do they want Alik to shoot, Caspar?"

"Lee." Caspar's eyes dropped to the floor. "I'm Lee." And then, in a quiet voice: "You."

"Who do they want Alik to shoot, Caspar? You know who."

Caspar lurched across the room again, walked straight into the wall, knocked his head against it over and over.

"They want me to shoot you."

He was by his gun again. He picked it up this time, then turned and walked over to Melchior as steadily as he could, the gun resting flat on his palms like a dead kitten.

Melchior had something in his hand too. Ivelitsch's telegram.

"Who do they want Alik to shoot, Caspar?"

Caspar stared at the slip of paper in Melchior's hands. At the name written there. He looked up at Melchior, his shaking hands outstretched, the gun vibrating on his palms, until finally Melchior took it from him and set it on the table and Caspar threw his face in Melchior's lap like a humbled dog. Melchior put his hand on Caspar's head and stroked the wiry hair, resisting the urge to bring his glass down on the back of the boy's head and put him out of his misery.

"You said you'd take care of Lee, Tommy. You said you'd always take care of Lee."

Very gently, Melchior lifted the string of skulls from Caspar's neck and slipped it in his pocket.

"He will," Melchior said. He stroked the hair and tried not to think of the orphanage. "Tommy will take care of Lee. Right up until the very end."

It was nearly one in the morning when BC arrived, but the Big House was ablaze with light. When he burst into the house he found a half dozen Castalians sprawled around the common rooms on the first floor. He counted twenty-two infractions of the law, along with eleven nipples (two were marble, on a statue of Dionysus, and five more were painted on canvas or the bare plaster of the walls), plus one completely naked baby.

No one noticed him at all.

He managed to track down Leary on the second floor in a round garret with a lighted chandelier and rugs draped from the ceiling. Leary sat on a pillow in the middle of the room, his legs folded into a painful-looking knot. BC had to call his name three times before the doctor opened his eyes.

"Is he here?" he demanded, although he knew it was a pointless question. Leary would not be contemplating his navel if Orpheus was on the premises.

"Agent Querrey?" BC was still wearing his hipster getup—was still stained with blood and ash for that matter—and Leary stared at him in confusion. "I would never have recognized you."

After the circulation had come back to his knees, Leary led BC to his bedroom. A twelve-inch carpet of clothing and books and used dishes covered every square foot of floor space. In the center of this chaos rose a bed whose yellowing sheets reeked of a smell BC remembered from certain of his bunkmates' cots in the academy: not just sweat, but something else. Something funky. Something . . .

Sex, BC told himself. Just say it.

"Sex," he said out loud, and he still didn't blush, though Leary glanced at him sharply.

"In the past two weeks, Dr. Leary," BC began, "I've seen things that would surprise even you. Things that, for better or worse, have changed my life irrevocably. But this isn't about me. It's about a man named

Chandler Forrestal and a girl named Nazanin Haverman and a third person—though I hesitate to give him that much humanity—whose real name might never be known, but who needs to be brought to justice."

Fear added itself to the confusion on Leary's face. "But I thought Chandler and the girl were—"

"Dead? That's what Melchior wanted you to believe."

"Melchior? He was the dark-complected man?" Leary shuddered. "There's something *off* about him."

BC paused to kick a pair of boxer shorts off the tip of his shoe.

"If you'd asked me two months ago, I would have told you the Bureau was my life. Was all I had, all I wanted even. Now I realize that's not true. What I had was a desire to sort truth from lies—the kind of lies men like the ones who run the Central Intelligence Agency tell, but also, as it turns out, men like the ones who run the Federal Bureau of Investigation tell. Men who believe that truth is relative, or subjective, or the provenance of victor over vanquished. I do not believe that, Dr. Leary. I will never believe that. There are facts and there are falsehoods, and never the twain shall meet. Before, the Bureau served as the most natural outlet for me to express that belief. Now I just have myself. My faith, my desire. My will. What I'm saying, Doctor, is that I need you to tell me everything you know about Project Orpheus, not just for your sake, but for mine."

Leary fiddled with a statuette that BC thought was a chess queen until he saw the bare breasts—all eight of them, which the doctor was running his finger over absently, like a little boy playing with the teeth on a comb.

"I told you the last time you were here, Agent Querrey. Agent Logan kept me out of the loop."

BC stood up and stepped very close to Leary. Close enough for the doctor to see that the flesh beneath his strange new getup was every bit as real as the doctor's. The bones. The muscles. The fists.

"You need to understand, I'm a desperate man, Dr. Leary. I've given up everything to get to the bottom of this story. My career. My home. My reputation. Don't make me give up my morals as well."

A faint smile curled the side of Leary's mouth. "You said story."

"What?"

"You said 'the bottom of this story' instead of 'the bottom of this case.'"

BC wasn't sure what Leary's point was, but the doctor's tone seemed to be softening, so he just stood there. After nearly a minute of silence, Leary nodded.

"There is one thing. I don't think the CIA is aware of it. It concerns Miss Haverman. I did a little digging, and I discovered that before Logan drafted her, she'd been a subject in Project Artichoke, one of the precursors to Ultra and Orpheus."

"Artichoke was about ESP, wasn't it?"

Leary nodded. "Miss Haverman's test results were, I don't want to say extraordinary, but consistently above average. And the more emotionally fraught the context became, the better she scored. Over the course of her final experiment, she became sexually involved with one of the scientists administering it, and her apparent telepathic abilities increased dramatically as she became more intimate with her experimenter. He'd been instructed to conceal his participants' results from them—they would all either 'fail' the tests or score just high enough above a statistical mean that they could go home thinking they were special. But anyone who scored over a certain percentage was to be sent to me on some pretext or other. In Miss Haverman's case, it was the idea of LSD as a therapeutic agent for survivors of trauma. Unfortunately, I'd left Harvard by the time Naz tried to contact me, so we never connected until three and a half weeks ago."

The whole time Leary spoke, BC was remembering the feeling in Madam Song's. The hatred—the loathing—pouring from Naz like heat from the open door of a furnace. The way she'd haunted his thoughts ever since he'd laid eyes on her, so much more than Chandler.

"Are you telling me Chandler isn't the real Orpheus?" he said now. "That it's actually Naz?"

"I wish it were that simple. In chemical terms, I would call Naz a catalyst. I think it was some innate ability on her part that made it possible for LSD to change the way Chandler's brain works. To make it possible for him to project his own hallucinations onto outsiders."

"So you're saying Naz is the key? That, in the right hands, she could be used to create a legion of Chandlers? Of Orpheuses?"

Leary shook his head helplessly. "I don't know."

"And what about her? Was she changed too?"

Again Leary shook his head. "I'm sorry, Agent Querrey. I just don't know."

"Did you write your suspicions down anywhere?"

"Yes. But after—after the incident, I caught Billy trying to find my notes, and I destroyed them."

"So you're the only person who knows the role Naz might have played in Chandler's transformation?"

"Well, there's you now." Leary offered BC a weak smile. "You're not going to kill me, are you?"

"I should," BC said in a voice so cold that the doctor recoiled. "But as long as no one suspects you have secret knowledge, you should be fine." He stood up abruptly. "You'd better pray no one followed me here however."

"CIA—"

"Melchior's not CIA," BC said as he headed for the door. "Not anymore. And if he comes after you, you're going to wish I *had* killed you."

It was nearly midnight when Chandler pulled into the parking lot of the Carousel Club. He'd flown into Dallas just after noon, but it had taken him most of the day to track down a single hit of acid—if Dallas had well-marked Bohemian hotspots like New York, he couldn't find them, and, following a chain of hints, recommendations, and flat-out guesses, he eventually managed to score in, of all places, Neiman Marcus, where he also picked up several compliments on the clothing he'd taken from BC's suitcase.

The tab in his hand was of unknown provenance, like a package of batteries lacking an expiration date. It could charge him up all the way or give him only enough energy to emit a dim glow. If he took it and Naz wasn't in the club, he'd be forced to go after her—after Melchior—unaugmented. But Ivelitsch couldn't have lied about her whereabouts. Chandler had read it in his brain like a neon sign. She had to be here.

He popped the tab in his mouth. He could process the chemical and normalize the hallucinations and fine-tune his mind in minutes now. The acid, thank God, was good. Not great, but good. When he opened his eyes there was a greenish tint to his vision, but it seemed less impediment than augmentation, like some kind of night-vision lens.

He got out of the car. A tall man sat beside the front door, his lardy ass spilling over either side of the narrow stool that held his linebacker-gone-to-seed frame.

"Evenin', bub," he drawled in a voice that could've been hostile or friendly, Chandler didn't know and didn't care. "It's five tonight."

Chandler's fist caught the bouncer square in the face. The man's nose exploded in blood, and the stool splintered beneath his flailing limbs and he hit the ground like a rotten tree knocked over in a storm.

Chandler grabbed the man by the wrist and dragged him into the shadow of some crepe myrtle that didn't so much adorn the front of the club as shrink away from it. He tossed the pieces of stool after him, then pushed open the smoked-glass door. As he went in he noted a flyer pasted to the glass:

BILL DEMAR

Versatile Ventriloquist And Comic
master in the art of extra-sensory perception

PLUS: FIVE EXOTICS

kathy	little	joy
kay	lynn	dale

marilyn	felisa
moone	prell

A mephitic glow illuminated a long narrow corridor that sloped toward a black curtain. Mid-tempo jazz pushed through the curtain, and smoke, sweat, and stale alcohol saturated everything. Another bouncer sat on the far side of the curtain, and Chandler fought back the urge to use his power to reach into his mind. He had to save his energy. Pick his battles.

"Has the new girl come in?"

The bouncer didn't take his eyes from the peroxide blonde shimmying off-tempo on stage.

"We got a lotta girls, bub. They're all good."

"The new girl," Chandler insisted. "Short, dark, black eyes."

"Our girls aren't really known for their eyes, if you catch my meaning."

"Olive complexion," Chandler said, his throat tight. "Dark hair."

The bouncer must've heard the edge in Chandler's voice, because he turned to him, his mouth curled in a snarl.

"Little Lynn?" The man licked his lips lasciviously. "Jack's saving her for prime time. Why don't you grab yourself a beer and a chair and enjoy the show till then? Either that or get the hell out, makes no difference to me."

Chandler hit him then. He couldn't help it. The idea of this creature—

this crowd—mooning over Naz, waving dollar bills at her, pawing at her, was just too much. Their lust surrounded him like a locker-room funk, and bits and pieces of their disgusting fantasies flickered in his mind like pages ripped out of a blue magazine.

As soon as the bouncer went down, Chandler knew he'd made a mistake. Shouts came from the tables and chairs fell over as men stood up too rapidly, spoiling for a fight to liven up the evening. Chandler could feel their excitement, knew he had to deal with all of them now, instead of just Ruby, wherever he was, or Melchior, if he was here.

Suddenly he noticed the fallen bouncer was reaching inside his jacket, pulling out a gun. He was in Texas, after all. Chandler's foot lashed out and the gun sailed all the way across the room, smashed into the racks of bottles above the bar.

The music continued to play, but the dancer slowed to a little shake, her bare breasts swaying, her heavily painted eyes staring at the two men like a barbarian queen looking down on a pair of warriors. Chandler caught glimpses of himself and the fallen bouncer through the dancer's eyes. Apparently the bouncer'd been pressuring her to sleep with him and she was hoping he was about to get his ass kicked but good.

"This is for Felisa," he said, dropping to one knee and slamming his elbow into the side of the bouncer's face. He heard the man's jaw snap over the thumping bass.

A big man in a Stetson was bum-rushing him when he stood up. Chandler felt him before he saw him. The man had no interest in what was happening. He just wanted to hit someone.

Chandler sidestepped, sent the man flying into the wall. There was another patron, this one with a chair. Chandler barely managed to get out of the way. He bumped against a table and his fingers closed around a lowball. He hurled it at the man's temple and the man went down like a deer shot at close range.

There were four, no, six more patrons. The dancer was among them, a bottle in her hand like a club. Now that her man was down she wanted nothing but to defend him. Chandler had no choice but to push.

"Okay, folks," he said in the most authoritative voice he could muster. "That's enough excitement for tonight."

The six men and one girl paused, blinking. The dancer even rubbed her eyes, wondering how she'd failed to notice the troublemaker was a cop.

"Get on outta here," Chandler said, adding a little local color, "before I see fit to call your wives' and mommas and tell 'em where you been keeping yourselves."

He continued pushing until the last of the men, supporting the patron Chandler had clocked with the rocks glass, filed out the front door, while the dancer retreated through a curtain at the back.

Chandler sighed now, let his concentration drop. The effort of reaching into so many minds had used up a good portion of his energy, and he needed to save what little he had left.

Something was wrong, though. Where was Ruby? How come he wasn't out here trying to figure out why he'd been raided? Chandler sent out the lightest feelers he could, trying to discern who was still in the club. He counted three girls in the dressing room, all of them thinking about stuffing their tips into their purses before Ruby could take his cut. There were the two unconscious bouncers, the barman hiding behind the bar. Nothing that felt like Ruby. But . . .

He pushed toward a mirror set in the wall high over the bar. Not a mirror, he realized. A window. It must be the office. There was a . . . cloud on the other side of the glass. Not a mind, not as he'd come to understand it, but not a void either.

He looked around, saw a door off to one side of the bar. He went to it, pushed it open. A narrow staircase led up.

He mounted the stairs slowly, pushing all the while at the cloud. It had edges but no dimension. He kept trying to see around it, but there was just more cloud.

His head came up to the floor level of the office. He saw a carpet littered with cigarette butts, coffee cups, soda bottles, the kind of stains you don't want to look at too closely in a place like this. He mounted higher, reached the landing, turned around.

A voice spoke from the shadows at the opposite end of the room. "Hello, Chandler."

He squinted, and Melchior's face jumped out of the darkness. He pushed then, pushed with all his might, but all he felt was the cloud, and he stumbled forward and nearly fell.

Melchior smiled, and only then did Chandler see the gun in his hand.

Chandler heard the click when Melchior pulled the trigger, but instead of a shot he heard a hiss of compressed air followed immediately by a stabbing punch in his abdomen. He looked down to see a barb dangling from his chest, then felt himself falling to the floor.

At first glance, it seemed that Charles Jarrell had acquired several new stacks of newspaper in the eleven days since BC'd seen him last. The foyer was barred by a wall of densely packed newsprint; to get into the rest of the house you had to veer into the living room, following a trail that led almost all the way to the far wall before doubling back into the front hall. Jarrell led BC through this maze into a room that had apparently once been a library or study: several thousand books still filled the built-in shelves, but they'd been turned spine in, so that all one saw was the different colored pages aligned in faded vertical strips like one of the abstract paintings in Peggy Hitchcock's house.

Jarrell tipped his bottle of rye into the two glasses that sat on the stack of papers in front of the couch. BC was sure they were the same glasses from his last visit.

"Excuse the mess. You caught me in the middle of refiling."

"Refiling?"

"Goddamn Company broke in here night before last. They break in pretty regularly, so I need to make sure they can't find anything." Even as he spoke, Jarrell grabbed two feet off the top of one of the stacks, moved it to another.

BC looked around the room. In addition to the stacks, loose papers lined the floor and snaked up the walls. He felt like he was inside a giant papier-mâché sculpture.

"The, uh, Company breaks in?"

"Once a month, sometimes more. They try to put things back, but I can always tell when they've been here." Jarrell split a stack into a half dozen units, reshuffled them like cards, then moved the whole pile to a corner of the room. "Bureau probably comes half that often."

"That just leaves KGB," BC said, his voice light but tight.

"They've only been here once or twice." Jarrell busied himself building what looked like a castle wall complete with gun emplacements. "That I know of."

"I meant in New York. I, um, had a run-in with them."

"I know." Jarrell grunted now, continued moving paper. "In a mere eight weeks you've gone from being a COINTELPRO weasel to being a person of interest to both the Bureau *and* the Company, albeit they don't know it's you they're looking for. But I gotta admit even *I* was surprised to hear that you took out Dmitri Tarkov."

"You heard about that?"

"Heard that you caused a bit of a ruckus at Madam Song's, too." Jarrell paused to regard BC through his stacks of paper. "What *have* you stumbled into, Beau-Christian Querrey?"

"I had him," BC said then. "I had him, and I let him get away."

"Melchior?"

"*Orpheus,*" BC said. "Chandler. I had him. I had Naz, too, and I let them both get away." He looked up at the crazy man spreading paper around with the frantic energy of a rat lining the walls of its cage. "I'm sorry I came back here, but I didn't know what else to do. I've run out of leads."

Jarrell met BC's gaze, then looked away. He grabbed his glass, saw that it was empty, walked over to BC and picked up his drink, and drained it in a swallow.

"I don't know why I'm telling you this," he said then. "Must be those puppy-dog eyes."

"What?" BC demanded.

"Melchior got called into Langley day before yesterday about a little dustup at Union Station."

"The gunfight? I read about that in the, uh, paper."

"He said he'd been contacted by a Soviet agent with a cipher no one'd ever heard of, wanted to ask him some questions about Cuba, then pulled a gun on him when he wouldn't talk. Story had more holes in it than a loaf of bread after a mouse has been at it, but instead of keeping him locked up until they got to the bottom of it, Angleton and Everton sent him to Dallas instead. They want him to retrieve an agent known as Caspar."

"One of the other Wise Men?"

"He just got back from almost two years in the Soviet Union. Angleton thinks he might've been doubled by KGB, told Melchior he wants him brought in for more debriefing."

"Do you have an address for him?"

"I took the liberty of looking that up, just in case." Jarrell reached into a stack of papers. It was impossible to conceive that he could find anything amid the thousands and thousands of sheets of paper, but he had to sift through only a couple of pages before he pulled out a copy of the *Dallas Times Herald*. The front page was covered with hatch marks—no, not hatch marks, but a series of red and black X's and O's drawn around single letters. Jarrell scanned them a moment, then began copying out an address a letter at a time.

"I meant to ask you about that," BC said. "The X's and O's."

"Old cipher system from OSS days," Jarrell said, moving on to a second address. "Computers made it pretty much obsolete, but I still use it. Keeps my mind sharp." He was on to a third address, a fourth.

"Good lord," BC said.

"Guy seems to move around a lot," Jarrell said, although BC had been referring to the fact that somehow Jarrell had managed to encode four different addresses on the front page of a newspaper that had come out only that morning.

"This is the most recent address Everton had," Jarrell said, tapping the first, "but they gave him these others too. This is the wife, who lives in Irving, a suburb of Dallas. The Bureau's sent men out there a couple of times, but apparently he's only around on the weekends."

BC nodded absently. His eyes had been caught by the two-line headline that stretched almost all the way across the page.

PLEA FOR SPACE PLAN
KICKS OFF JFK TOUR

"BC?" Jarrell said.

"Melchior isn't the only one going to Dallas, is he?"

Below the headline was a map of the president's motorcade route. BC and Jarrell stared at the diagram—Main Street, Houston, Elm, and on to the Trade Mart—and then Jarrell wrote down a fifth address on the page, labeled it "Texas School Book Depository."

"What's that?" BC said.

"It's where Caspar works."

"Why are you—"

"Because it's right there," Jarrell said, circling the intersection of Houston and Elm on the motorcade map. "Right across from—"

"From Dealey Plaza," BC finished for him, and reached for Jarrell's bottle.

He was on his hands and knees. He had no idea how long he'd been—

A foot caught him in the side of the head and he went sprawling.

"I'm starting to wonder why I've invested so much energy in you," Melchior said. "I mean, if you're this easy to take out, what good are you?"

It felt like ice water was flowing through Chandler's veins. His hands and feet were numb, his head a sodden pillow, save for the sharp pain where Melchior's shoe had made contact.

Melchior kicked him again, and Chandler's shoulder slammed against the wall. He slumped there, too heavy to move, head hanging, eyes staring at the dart dangling from his chest.

"What's in the dart?" he said weakly.

"I believe the preferred term is fléchette." Melchior giggled. "Thorazine mostly. Keller figured out that it protects our minds from you, although we have to chew amphetamines like vitamins to counteract the sedative effects. Between that and the other downers flowing in your veins, you should be out cold. I've been wondering for a while if whatever Logan gave you did more than change your brain. Now it looks like the answer is yes. Fortunately, however—"

Melchior popped another dart into the gun, leveled it at Chandler.

The numbness seemed to have peaked. Chandler felt that if he could just stay conscious for a few more seconds, he could figure out how to fight it.

"Why *do* you want me?" he said, stalling for time.

"Duh. You can do things no one else can. You could walk right up to Nikita Khrushchev in front of the Politburo and kill him with no one the wiser. You could kill anyone else for that matter, from the president of the United States to some two-bit guerrilla that someone was willing to pay five or ten grand to have knocked off. No facility would be secure, no mind safe, no target out of reach."

"You have to know I'd never do those things for you."

"You'd be surprised what people can be convinced of doing. A tape recording of Miss Haverman's screams might prove to be very motivating."

Chandler would have launched himself at Melchior if he could have mustered more than a twitch. But he could feel things changing inside him, the warmth coming back into his body, the strength beginning to return to his muscles. Just a few more minutes . . .

"Of course you're right," Melchior continued. "Coercion's a poor substitute for voluntary action. At this point we're less interested in you as an operative than a research tool. We're pretty sure Logan gave you nothing but garden-variety acid, which means that whatever made you into you is inherent. In your genes, or your blood, or your brain. But wherever it is, whatever it is, Dr. Keller's gonna find it and cut it out of you, and then we're gonna make us a whole army of Orpheuses. So if you don't mind"—Melchior raised his gun—"let's just put you back to sleep and get you as far from Dallas as we can, cuz in a couple-a days no one's gonna want to be anywhere *near* this town."

Chandler gathered himself. He heard the click of the trigger, saw the dart's needle emerge from the barrel. It was too late to dodge. He would have to—

His arm swung, his hand smacked against something. He wasn't sure it was the dart until it thudded into the far wall.

The expression on Melchior's face was half-stunned, half-delighted.

"Well now, that *is* impressive."

Chandler launched himself at Melchior. The spy didn't panic. Just brought the handle of his gun down on the back of Chandler's head, slamming him to the floor. He stepped to the side and kicked Chandler toward the staircase. The spindly rails snapped and he clattered down the narrow treads.

"Yep," he heard Melchior say at the top of the stairs. "I'd say the changes are definitely more than mental. Keller's going to have a lot of fun taking you apart."

Chandler managed to roll his bruised body through the doorway just before another dart pounded into the wall. He wasn't sure how many darts Melchior had, but he wasn't shooting like a man with a limited supply of ammo.

He ran toward the bar. As he ducked under the drop-down door, a figure stood up in front of him, gun in hand. The bartender. He wasn't a threat—Chandler punched him six times before the man managed to open his mouth—but he'd had no sense of the man's mind. His juice was gone. He was on his own.

He grabbed the gun on the floor, sighted on the doorway, and waited for Melchior to come through it. But no one came. Instead a voice called through the curtain.

"Chandler?"

The curtain rustled. A figure stepped through. It was BC.

"Chandler? Are you here?"

"BC! Get down!" But it was too late. Melchior'd somehow gotten behind BC, and now he pressed a gun to his temple—a real gun, Chandler saw, not the tranq shooter.

"Hail hail, the gang's all here. Put down the gun, Chandler."

"Chandler, go," BC said firmly, calmly. "I'll deal with Melchior."

"Chandler, stay," Melchior said, "or I deal with BC." He knocked his gun against the detective's temple. "I gotta tell you, Beau, you surprised me when you showed up at Song's. I didn't think you had that kind of initiative. But then I read up on you. You're like a latter-day Melvin Purvis, ain't you? Spotless case record, bright future ahead of you, but then you made the mistake of getting your picture in the paper, at which point J. Edna pulled you out of Behavioral Profiling and made you write book reports. You ever read that novel by Mr. Dick?"

"Get out of here, Chan—"

Melchior smashed his gun into the side of BC's face.

"Put the fucking gun *down*, Chandler. Or that little speech become's Beau's eulogy."

Chandler looked back and forth between them. Finally he set his gun on the bar.

"Good boy," Melchior said. He fished in his pocket with his free hand, tossed something to Chandler. It was a small pouch containing a syringe and a vial of clear liquid.

"Fill the syringe all the way and inject yourself."

"Don't, Chandler," BC said. "I'll be fine."

Chandler filled the syringe. "I'm not just doing it for you," he said as he put the needle in his vein. "I'm doing it for Naz."

This time there was no fighting the rush of chemicals. His legs wobbled, his vision blurred. But just before he blacked out he saw BC turn suddenly, strike the gun in Melchior's hand. The gun fell behind Melchior, and before the spy could retrieve it BC had thrown himself over a booth. Shots echoed in Chandler's gauze-filled ears as BC ducked from one piece of cover to another. The last thing Chandler heard was the smash of glass as BC's body crashed through a curtained window into the parking lot.

Sergei Vladimirovich Maisky followed the directions Pavel Sem-
yonovitch had sent him via encrypted cable. In addition to the map,
there had been the explicit directive to take no one with him or tell
anyone what his business was. If word got out to the Cubans or, God
forbid, the Americans, that officers in the Red Army were stealing nuclear warheads, the fallout—all puns intended—would be catastrophic.
Reluctantly, the engineer set out alone.

God, how he hated this little country! Its dingy people with their
dark rums and noxious cigars stuffed in their mouths like amputated
darky dicks. Alcohol, like skin, should be colorless—odorless, too, for
that matter—and if you had to smoke, the only dignified way to do it
was with a pipe. But what he really hated about these dusky peasants
was their naive belief in the Communist bullshit spouted by their ridiculous leader with his ridiculous beard of an Orthodox priest, along
with his sidekicks: worshipful younger brother Raúl and swashbuckling
Argentino midget Che. Together the three of them were like some
Dostoyevskian version of the Marxist Brothers, all of them pretending
to be half saint Alyosha and half rational Ivan, when the truth was they
were all 100 percent Mitya: drunken vainglorious blowhards fighting
for a Caribbean atoll only slightly larger than Vasilevsky Island in Len-
ingrad. They could have it as far as he was concerned.

Sergei Vladimirovich was a Tolstoy man. He hated Dostoyevsky.
Hated Gogol even more.

When he finally reached the outpost Pavel Semyonovitch had sent
him to—even village was too grand a word for the dozen stuccoed huts
squatting along the edges of a pair of muddy crosshaired lanes—he had
to drive around for two hours on the rutted cart paths that passed for
roads before he found the spot on the map. The locals stared at his
truck as though it were some variety of medieval monster (or perhaps
they were just staring at his bald scalp, pink and blistered like a snake
shedding its skin), and everyone seemed to him to be sick or crippled,

though whether this was poverty or *la revolución* or radiation leeching into the water supply was anyone's guess.

The building was on the outskirts of town, shielded by a ten-foot-high cinder-block wall whose stucco had all but washed off, but whose glass-sharded heights looked recently installed. The key Pavel Semyonovitch had sent him opened the gate and he drove the truck through. Inside was the hull of yet another burned-down hacienda and a few intact outbuildings.

Sergei Vladimirovich donned his hazard suit before entering the old stables, which, though missing a roof, had their doors and windows solidly bricked up; the only working door was, like the glass shards embedded in the top of the wall, an obvious recent addition. Steel over wood. Probably stronger than the walls themselves. The same key that had opened the gate opened its lock. By the time he got the door open, he could feel the sweat coursing down his back and soaking into his underpants. The sweat was due to the heat, not nerves. Sergei Vladimirovich was made nervous by all animals larger than carpenter ants, food that hadn't been cooked to a tasteless, colorless pulp, anyone in a uniform, and women—especially women—but he thought of nuclear bombs the way a pastry chef thinks of a chocolate soufflé: a concatenation of ingredients that need only be put together in the proper way to produce the most splendid effects. Only nuclear bombs were better than soufflés, because you could take them apart after you'd made them, put them back together again better than they'd been the first time around.

But not this one. The warhead sat in a bed of straw like a giant metal egg—a cracked egg, its olive plates dented and coming apart at their seams, which oozed a powdery ocher albumen. Someone had ripped open the bomb's housing and soldered it back together as though it were a cast-iron tub. They'd really done a number on it. It looked more like they'd tried to dismantle it than steal it.

Condensation fogged the inside of Sergei Vladimirovich's visor, and his drawers were so wet it felt like he'd pissed himself, but there was nothing he could do about that now. It took more than an hour to uncover the explosive assembly, at which point he saw what was really going on.

"Son of a whore," he said, and his visor completely fogged over, and he had to wait five more minutes before it cleared. But when it did, the problem was still there, staring him in the face. Well, not his problem. Pavel Semyonovitch's. Sergei Vladimirovich had only to render what was here safe for transport. Working carefully, he stitched, soldered, and glued the whole thing together, then welded the external plate back on. When he was finished, he removed the sodden hazard suit and stowed it in a radiation-proof bag. He'd just finished when he felt a pair of eyes on him. He looked up to see a young man standing in the open doorway of the barn. He leaned heavily on a cane and carried a gun in his free hand.

"Pavel Semyonovitch wanted me to thank you for plugging our leak," he said in perfect American English. "Unfortunately, now I have to plug a leak of my own."

Two shots rang out, and the last thing Sergei Vladimirovich saw as he fell to the ground was the legend on the bag, written in Russian and English.

WARNING:
HAZARDOUS MATERIALS
DO NOT OPEN

He was disoriented when he opened his eyes. His senses were cloudy: vision blurry, hearing muffled, skin floating a fraction of an inch off his body. His limbs were so sluggish that he thought he was tied up again, and he thrashed to free himself.

"Easy there," a voice came to him. "You're okay."

He sat up quickly, his head whipping from side to side. A bed. A sour-smelling room. Grimy green walls, cigarette-scarred furniture. A strange man sitting in a straight-backed chair with a glass in his hand, his delicate-boned face full of concern—first for the man on the bed, but then, when he realized what the man was going to do, for himself.

"Chandler, no! It's BC! I'm your friend!"

The man on the bed launched himself into the air. His hands shot from his sides like striking snakes. A blow to the chin, the gut, the chin, the gut. The man in the chair toppled to the floor and his assailant ran for the door.

"Chandler, wait! I can help you find Naz."

The man paused.

Naz.

He turned.

"BC?"

BC daubed at the blood on his lip. "Chandler? Are you back?"

For a moment Chandler just stood there, wavering slightly. Then his nose wrinkled. "Since when do you drink whiskey?"

BC retrieved his glass, poured a fresh round for himself and Chandler. "I've learned that a little drink takes the edge off."

He handed a glass to Chandler, which the latter tossed back gratefully, then poured himself another.

"You sure you want to do that?" BC said, sipping at his drink. "You've been out for twenty-four hours."

"Twenty-five actually. And eleven minutes. How'd you get me away from Melchior? No, wait. How'd you find me in the first place?"

"The Company has a tap on Song's phone. A friend in Langley pulled the tapes for me. Turns out she put in a call to Jack Ruby two days ago, right after Melchior was sent here, asking if he was looking for any new dancers."

Chandler nodded. "And? After you got there?"

"One of the dancers called Dallas's finest. I flashed my badge, told them you were wanted in connection with a major drug trafficking ring."

"Melchior—"

"He got away. I'm sorry."

BC would have expected Chandler to be bothered by this news, but all he said was, "What about Naz?"

"I spoke to Ruby. He said Song never sent him a girl."

"He's lying. I saw it in Ivelitsch's mind."

"What did you see?"

Chandler wracked his brain, trying to sort through the thousands of fragments of various consciousnesses that now took up space in his own head.

"Melchior. He called them. He told them to send Naz here."

"But did you ever see them actually send Naz here?" When Chandler shook his head, BC said, "I think the whole thing was a trap. Melchior's order, Song's call to Ruby. It was all designed to get you here."

"I don't understand."

"Melchior knows it's impossible to lie to you, so he did the next best thing. He fed Ivelitsch and Song false information, figuring you'd probably end up at Song's establishment sooner or later. The call to Ruby was just insurance. In case—oh, Jesus."

BC jumped for the phone.

"What's wrong?"

BC ignored Chandler. He screwed ten digits into the phone, tapping his foot impatiently as the dial scrolled back between every number.

BC swilled his drink. "Come on, Jarrell, pick *up*."

"What is it?" Chandler insisted.

"Melchior must've suspected someone was watching him at CIA. If he finds out it was Jarrell—" He slammed the phone down, dialed another number. "May I speak with Charles—I'm sorry, with Virgil Parker?" There was a pause, and then BC's face fell. "When did this happen?" he said, and then, "No, I don't need to speak to anyone else. Thank you."

"BC?" Chandler said. "What's going on?"

"Charles Jarrell's house burned down this afternoon."

"He was killed?" Chandler said, and when BC nodded: "You think it was Melchior? But what's this Jarrell fellow got to do with me or Naz?"

"Nothing."

"Then—"

"Don't you get it? Melchior *wanted* us to know he was going to be here. He's killing everyone who's seen his face or knows something about him."

"You think he's going to kill us?"

"Me? Yes. You, I don't know. Depends on whether he still thinks he can use you." BC's hand trembled as he reached for his glass. "It's my fault. Jarrell told me I compromised him by going to his house, and then I kept going." He looked up at Chandler. "But he was my only lead to you."

"You can't blame yourself, BC. Melchior dragged you into this. Melchior had him killed." When BC didn't say anything, Chandler said, "Why's he here anyway, if he wasn't bringing Naz to Ruby's club?"

"He was sent here to bring in an operative called Caspar."

"Do you have an address for him?"

"Four, plus his work. The addresses are all in rooming houses, though, which means there are going to be other people around."

"So?"

"Chandler, please. I know how anxious you are, but you have to be reasonable. In the first place, if we cause a disturbance, someone's likely to call the police. And since you're supposed to be in federal custody, that's not going to look good—especially when they find out I'm carrying forged FBI credentials. And if Caspar's armed, someone could get hurt."

"I'm not worried—"

"Not *us,* Chandler. Other people. We can't risk their lives to save Naz."

Chandler slammed his fist into the bedside table.

"Look," BC said. "I know you're frustrated. But it's two in the a.m. Melchior's either already seen Caspar, or he'll find him tomorrow. We'll intercept them in the morning."

Chandler was so jumpy his hands were twitching. He was afraid he was going to hit something again—he was afraid he was going to hit BC—so he got up and paced the tiny room, trying to stamp the nervous energy out of his body.

As he passed the bed, he saw the newspaper lying on top of the blanket.

PRESIDENT ARRIVES IN FT. WORTH FOR CAMPAIGN TRIP

He picked it up, stared at it a moment, then tossed it away.

"I meant to ask you. That picture in the paper."

BC looked up in confusion. "The president?"

"The boy. The burning boy." Chandler walked to the bottle, poured two more drinks. "How did you know that was me?"

"Oh." BC's eyes glazed over for a moment, then he snapped back into focus. "Because it came from my mind."

"It's—you?"

BC shook his head. "It's my nightmare. You must have seen it when I came to Millbrook."

"You were at Millbrook?"

"At the end. When Melchior took you and Naz." He sipped at the drink Chandler handed him. "My father was in Korea. It was a horrible war, he said. Pointless. Millions of civilians killed on both sides, only to end up right where we were before the whole thing started. He said they used a new kind of weapon. It's called napalm. A liquid, extremely flammable. The infantry was usually far away when the bombers went in, but my father told me one time they got the timing wrong. His unit was only half a mile outside the drop zone—a city of about fifty thousand. The flames were two, three hundred feet high. Entire buildings turned into ash in seconds. Most of the inhabitants died instantly, of course, but the people on the outskirts of town weren't so lucky. My father said he could see them. Dark shadows outlined against the flames. They'd jerk around like puppets and then fall down. But one boy got a little farther. Far enough for my father to see that he wasn't dark at all. His entire body was consumed by flames. My father said he ran straight at them and they just watched him come. It was like, if he reached them, if he touched them and set them on fire, it was what they deserved." BC shook his head slightly. "But he fell down before he reached them. Of course. It was a quarter mile. No one could've covered that distance. Not on fire."

Chandler's mouth hung open a moment.

"I'd say something about what a terrible world we live in, but what's the point?"

BC shrugged. "I don't know why it made such a big impression on me. I mean, it was my father's memory, not mine. But I've dreamed of him for years. That boy. I don't think he was going to attack them. I think he was going to tell them something."

"Tell them what?"

"I don't know. Warn them maybe."

"Warn them?"

"That there are consequences. That no victory is ever clean, or total." He looked up at Chandler. "We'll find her, Chandler. I don't care how long it takes."

Chandler didn't say anything for a moment. Then: "Do you have any acid?"

BC pulled a small rectangle of blotter paper from his pocket. "Courtesy of Richard Alpert. If you'd just waited for me—"

"Okay, okay," Chandler said, laughing BC's protest away. "At least we don't have to worry about that." He reached for the bottle and poured a couple of tall drinks. Six hours later, when BC woke up, thick-headed, dry-mouthed—and completely naked—Chandler was gone.

Giancana'd provided four men with the boat, and Ivelitsch made them row the last mile to shore. The coastline was free of settlement as far as the eye could see, but Ivelitsch wasn't taking any chances that someone might hear the motor.

Garza was waiting for them on the dock, his cane in his left hand, a shuttered lantern in his right.

"Comrade. It's nice to meet you again."

"Again?" Ivelitsch squinted in the moonlight. "It was you? In Camagüey? I take it the medicine worked."

Garza smiled. "Sorry to send you on a wild-goose chase."

"Water over the bridge, as the Americans say. Well, let's do this. The sun will be up soon."

"The fishing boats will be out before that." Garza flashed his light behind him, illuminating an old pickup that seemed more rust than metal. "It's in the back."

Even with five men—Garza's hip wasn't strong enough to support that kind of weight—it was still almost an hour before the half-ton bomb was in the boat. Dawn glimmered on the horizon, and a bird had started to sing a loud, tuneless solo.

"I understand you have something for me," Garza said when they were done.

Ivelitsch went below, came out a moment later with Naz's unconscious body draped over his shoulder. He laid her on the dock, then handed Garza a brown glass bottle with an eyedropper built into the lid.

"Keep her out until you get to the safe house. Trust me, you'll have a much easier time of it."

"Uh, sure," Garza said, looking at the wisp of a girl lying on the dock. "Is that all?"

"I think I can handle this last thing myself," Ivelitsch said, pulling an automatic pistol from his jacket.

"Wha—" Garza said, but Ivelitsch was already firing. Ten seconds later, all four of Giancana's men were dead. Ivelitsch got back in the boat. Garza expected him to toss the bodies overboard, but all he did was kick away the man slumped over the wheel.

"You've joined a very select group, Mr. Garza," Ivelitsch said, starting the boat. He gunned the motor—something about having a nuclear bomb in the hold had apparently made him unconcerned about detection. "I'd advise you to remember just what the price of admission is. I'll dump the bodies in the Straits," he added. "Save you the trouble of having to bury them."

"Uh, thanks. I must've missed that entry in Miss Manners." Garza nudged the girl on the pier with his left foot. "Any other instructions?"

Ivelitsch was backing the boat from the dock. "Keep her alive. What happens to the kid is up to you."

"The kid?"

Ivelitsch didn't bother to look back. "Apparently she's knocked up."

The boat's nose pointed seaward now; Ivelitsch opened the throttle and it roared out of the lagoon. When it was gone, Garza looked down at the beautiful sleeping face of the girl on the dock. Only then did he realize the Russian hadn't told him her name. So much for Miss Manners.

He reached down for her—it was going to be awkward dragging her to the truck with his bum leg—but just as his hand touched hers, the girl's eyes fluttered open. Despite himself, Garza jumped back.

The girl looked neither right nor left, but stared straight into Garza's eyes.

"Where am I?"

The girl's eyes seemed as deep as a lagoon as well, and the longer Garza stared into them, the deeper he fell. He suddenly realized he didn't know if the girl had spoken to him in English or Spanish.

"Eres en Cuba," he said quietly, then added, "Miss Haverman." It occurred to him again that Ivelitsch had never told him the girl's name, but really, what else could it be?

Still Naz stared straight into his eyes. She didn't speak—at any rate he didn't see her lips move—but even so, Garza was sure she'd asked him a question. Requested a favor. There was only one answer possible.

"*No te preocupadas,* Miss Haverman," he said, his voice more sincere than it had ever been in his life. He dropped his cane and hoisted her into his arms; if his leg hurt him, he didn't feel it. "Don't worry. I'll take care of you."

"Stupid, stupid, stupid, stupid, *stupid!*" BC yelled at himself as he ran onto the—*splash!*—wet balcony of his motel. This was the second time Chandler had given him the slip in three days. Why the *hell* hadn't he handcuffed him to the bed?

The sky was clotted with clouds leaking gray drizzle; an oily puddle filled in the space where he'd parked last night, so Chandler'd been gone for a while. A young couple was loading suitcases into a pale bluish greenish Rambler and BC yelled down to them.

"Wait!"

"What's the holdup?" The husband smiled brightly at BC as he ran up.

"FBI." BC flashed a counterfeit badge he'd purchased for all of five dollars. "I'm commandeering this car for official business." He'd backed out of the space before he noticed the baby in the seat beside him, handed it off to its startled-looking mother through the window.

There was no map in the car, so it took him the better part of an hour to find the first address Jarrell had written down. Thank God he'd committed them to memory—Chandler'd taken the list, even though he said his own memory had become virtually eidetic. The place was all the way out in north Dallas, a withered single-story ranch with a picture window veiled by wrinkled blinds. BC drove right past the house and parked the Rambler halfway down the block, then made his way to the house using a few stunted live oaks for cover. The rain had stopped by then, but the air was thick with moisture steaming off the ground in the rising heat. The brown lawn, though wet, was otherwise unwatered and unmown. Moreover, the strands of grass that had sprung from the cracks in the driveway were a good six inches long, which is to say: no one was using this driveway.

No one lived here.

Two scenarios sprang to BC's mind. The first, unlikely, was that the house was a decoy to draw BC and Chandler away from Melchior's real target. The second, more probable, was that it was a trap.

BC immediately ducked behind a straggly hedge that separated the house from its neighbor and made his way toward the back fence. He peered through a crack, saw nothing, vaulted the fence, and crept toward the corner of the house. The first window he came to was uncurtained, the room beyond empty save for a bare mattress and box spring, an open closet with a few bent hangers on the rod. He tried the sash. It was locked. He went to the second window. This one was narrow, opened onto a small bathroom. More to the point, the lock had been forced and the wet ground below was trampled with fresh footprints. Somehow BC knew: Chandler. His first thought was Thank God! and his second was I am going to *kill* you!

He had to take his jacket off to squeeze through the narrow aperture, and even so a button snapped off his shirt as he shimmied into the house. The little noise it made as it bounced off the linoleum sounded loud as a gunshot in BC's ears, but the rest of the house remained quiet. The bathroom door stood open to the hall. Bedrooms to the left, living quarters to the right. It seemed unlikely that Melchior would be waiting in a bedroom. BC drew his gun and went right.

It was only three steps to the end of the hall—carpeted, so his feet made no sound. He peeked around the corner, and there he was. Not Chandler.

Melchior.

He sat with his back to BC in a wooden chair, facing the front door. Something lay across his lap, and in the shadows BC took it for a rifle at first, then realized it was just an umbrella. It seemed to be dry, which meant that he'd been here for a while. His breathing was slow and deep, but BC knew he wasn't sleeping. He was waiting.

He leveled his gun at Melchior's head and cocked it.

"Don't move."

Melchior didn't move. Didn't even twitch. He was so still that BC wondered if maybe he actually was sleeping, but then:

"Why, Beau-Christian Querrey. You got the drop on me. Congrats."

"Put your hands in the air where I can see them."

"Here?" Melchior extended his arms to either side like Christ on the cross. "Or here?" He pointed them straight up in the air like Superman.

"Get down on the floor. Keep your hands away from your body."

"Stand up, sit down, lie down. I feel like I'm back in mass." He stood up, and the umbrella on his lap fell to the floor. He stepped over it, his arms still raised, sank to one knee, then both, then lowered his upper body to the floor. The whole time he never looked back at BC. "From all the rigamarole, I'm betting you don't have any handcuffs on you, do you? What are you going to do, use your tie?"

In fact, BC had been wondering just that, and, angrily, he reached for the knot and pulled it sharply.

Melchior moved at exactly the same moment. BC didn't even know what he'd done, but suddenly the chair was flying toward him. It smacked the gun and a shot went off, slanting into the wall and blowing out a piece of plaster the size of his thigh, but BC managed to keep hold of his weapon. Melchior, meanwhile, had rolled to his knees and grabbed his umbrella and was holding it out like a sword.

BC couldn't help but smile.

"What is that, some kind of—"

There was a *pfft* and something that felt like a linebacker's helmet smashed into BC's gut and he staggered backward. His back hit the wall behind him and the gun fell from his hand and then he fell forward onto his face.

He was dead before he hit the floor.

BC had no fewer than five addresses for Caspar. Five, and Chandler had no idea where any of them were. Thank God there was a map in BC's rental car.

The first was way up in north Dallas. Chandler wasn't sure what sort of dosage was in the blotter paper BC had procured from Richard Alpert, so he ripped it in half and downed the first part on the drive over; he pushed at the silent single-story ranch when he finally found it, but felt nothing. He broke in anyway. Circled around to the backyard and popped a half-rotted window frame out of its housing. His eyes only confirmed what his mind had already told him: the place was empty and, judging from the layer of dust that covered everything, long deserted.

The next address was on Marsalis Street. It was just after five when Chandler got there, but an old woman was already up, washing the breakfast dishes. Her tenants, she told him, worked first shift at the string bean factory in Fort Worth, had to be in by seven. She remembered Caspar vividly, although she knew him by another name. It was only because Chandler could see the face in her mind that he knew she was talking about the person he was looking for.

"Oh, sure, Lee Oswald. Troubled boy, what with all those Cuba pamphlets and that Communist wife. Pretty girl, though, when her face wasn't so bruised you couldn't see it."

"He hit her?" Chandler couldn't help but think of Naz.

"He'd fly into these rages," she said matter-of-factly, as though describing the propensity of flies to work their way through a window screen. "I couldn't tell you what brought 'em on. News stories usually. One day it was Castro, the next day the president. Then it was Khrushchev or some mob boss that that Kennedy brother was grilling on the TV. He was one of them people who have an opinion about anything and everything, but God help the poor soul who tried to make sense of 'em all."

"Did he leave any word where he was going?"

"Well, his wife was in N'Orleans last I heard. He went after her, I guess to try to get her back." She shuddered. "He'll find her. He was a confused boy, but you could tell he was one of them who never stops till he gets what he wants."

Chandler pushed then, just a little, to make sure she was telling the truth, and all of it. There was nothing else there. Caspar seemed hardly to have made an impression on her.

Beckley Street next. It was six thirty when he got there. The landlady confirmed Caspar lived there—she knew him as Lee as well, but he'd told her it was his surname and went by his initials, O.H. She told Chandler that Mr. Lee had spent last night with his wife out to Irving.

"Irving?" Chandler held out the piece of paper with the list of addresses on it. "This one here—2515 West Fifth?"

"Why, yes, I do believe—"

But Chandler had already turned and gone.

Morning traffic was starting to pick up, and it took another hour to get out there. Chandler could feel the juice trickling from his veins and knew time was running out. He was kind of surprised he still had any left actually. He'd taken the hit almost three hours ago. Massive hits seemed to jump-start his metabolism, racing through his body before leaving him exhausted, whereas small doses metered themselves out slowly, such that he was hardly aware there was any drug in him—save for the fact that he could pull images from people's minds, of course, push other ones in their place.

The thirty-year-old woman who answered the door in Irving told him that Caspar had left to catch a ride to work with—

Chandler couldn't wait. He pushed, and grabbed the name from the woman's mind. Wesley Frazier. He lived right up the block. Chandler ran there. The door was answered by a young woman. Frazier's sister.

"Wes and Lee have already gone—"

Chandler pushed so hard that Frazier's sister stumbled backward. He saw Caspar putting a long brown-paper package into the backseat of Wesley's '59 Chevy and then get in the passenger seat.

Frazier's sister was wavering back and forth in the doorway like a blade of grass in the wake of a speeding car. Chandler pushed more, saw Wesley telling his sister he'd got a job at Texas School Books a couple of months ago, saw his sister asking him if there was maybe another job there for Marina's husband, Lee. "Although I heard her call him Alik once," he saw Wesley's sister saying. "You think maybe that's Russian for Lee?"

Chandler pushed so hard that Frazier's sister fell back on her sofa. She didn't know the exact address of the School Book Depository, but she knew it was on Dealey Plaza. Something flickered in her mind, and with the last of his juice Chandler pulled it out of her. It turned out to be the cover of the newspaper. A map. The president's motorcade route. He followed the arrows. Main. Houston. Elm.

"W-why, yes," Frazier's sister said absently, though Chandler hadn't said anything. "That *is* where it's at."

"That's handy," Chandler said, and ran for his car.

Five minutes later Frazier's sister blinked rapidly, noticed the open door.

"Durn pollen," she said, getting up slowly and shuffling to the door. "Give me a helluva headache."

o   o   o

Wesley kept up a steady patter as he drove them to work: the rain, the fact that his car battery was low, the president's visit. In the passenger's seat Caspar sat quietly, eyes forward, hands on thighs. The absurdity of it all, he thought. He's a *spy*, for God's sake. He's worked for the Central Intelligence Agency of the United States of America and the Committee for State Security of the Union of Soviet Socialist Republics. Has more aliases than the nitwit in the seat beside him has brain cells. *A Wiz Kid,* for Christ's sake, yet here he is, hitching a ride to work because he can't afford a car of his own, and doesn't have a driver's license either. Today was not the day to risk a moving violation.

"I heard the only reason he got in in '60 was because Joe paid the mob to stuff the boxes in Chicago or some such," Wesley was saying, "but I don't think Johnson can give him Texas and Georgia this time around. Not with the Civil Rights Bill hanging over—"

The Chevy went over a bump and the paper-wrapped package in the backseat reverberated with a loud metal clank.

"Curtain rods," Caspar said, even though Wesley didn't ask. Even though he'd said it when he first got in the car, had said it yesterday, too, when he'd asked Wesley for a ride to work this morning. He'd told Wesley he was going to spend the night with Marina in Irving to see his daughters and pick up some curtain rods she'd bought for him so he could have some privacy in the rooming house he stayed in on Beckley Street.

"All the same I think I'll go see him." Wesley was prattling on. "The newspaper said the motorcade's supposed to pass by work around noon, twelve thirty, so maybe I'll eat lunch in the park and wave to him and Jackie when they go by. *She's* a classy lady. Motorcade," he added. "Mo-tor-cade. Kind of a strange word when you think about it."

"I think it's a combination of motor and parade," Caspar said.

"But then it'd be motor*ade.* It's more like motor and arcade."

"Arcade?"

"You know," Wesley said. "A shooting gallery."

When they got to work Caspar got out of the car almost before it stopped and grabbed the package from the backseat and tucked it up under his arm to make it as inconspicuous as possible. As soon as he did that, however, he thought that maybe it looked like he was trying to hide it, but at the same time he was afraid that if he rearranged the package it would draw too much attention to it, so he left it where it was and started off at a fast walk to the main building. Wesley stayed in the car gunning the engine to charge the battery, but he rolled down the window and asked if Caspar needed a ride home. Caspar said he wasn't going back to Irving that night. Wesley didn't ask why.

"Damn it, damn it, damn it, damn it, *DAMN* it!"

Melchior stared at BC's facedown body, the umbrella still quivering in his hand. This wasn't the way it was supposed to have happened. *Chandler* was supposed to have come. The tranq was for *him*, not BC. Keller'd phoned him the new formula yesterday, and Melchior'd raced around town after he got out of jail, buying some ingredients here, stealing others there, but even so, he'd only been able to rig up a single shot. Keller was sure it would be enough to knock even Chandler out. Melchior'd asked how strong it was. "Don't prick your finger" was all Keller said, "unless you want a chemical lobotomy."

The fallen detective's bladder had released, and a dark stain was spreading out in the dingy flat pile of the carpet. Melchior kicked BC over, did a cursory pulse check, but it was clear he was dead. The fat needle hung from his stomach. A button was missing from his shirt and the skin underneath was stained with a few drops of blood. It was the shirt that got Melchior. Not the blood, not the corpse itself. The goddamn shirt. Mercerized white cotton, with silk piping and French cuffs held closed with knots of silver. This wasn't the same man Melchior'd met on the train three weeks ago. He'd remade himself entirely to pursue this thing. To pursue Melchior, and Chandler, and Naz. Remade himself first into a dandy, and now into a corpse.

"Aw, fuck it. Fuck you, BC Querrey. Fuck *you*."

Melchior fell to his knees, careful to avoid the puddle of urine, ripped the man's shirt open so violently that three more buttons flew across the room. He reached into his jacket pocket and pulled out a flat zippered case, opened it. There were more syringes in there, including one with a three-inch needle, and a couple of vials, one of which was filled with epinephrine (there was also a Medaille d'Or tucked into a corner of the case, which Melchior planned on smoking after he got Chandler on Song's plane). Keller had made Melchior carry the epinephrine in case the sedative cocktail proved too strong even for Chandler's souped-up constitution. Melchior prepared the shot, then slammed it into BC's chest so hard he heard a rib crack. BC's body convulsed so violently that the needle on the syringe almost broke off inside his body, which really would have been the coup de grâce, but Melchior was able to jerk it out and step out of the way before BC coughed and choked and spewed a thin spray of vomit into the air.

Before BC was fully conscious, Melchior plopped him into the chair and duct-taped his wrists and ankles to it, making sure to pull the man's sleeves and pants out of the way so the tape adhered directly to BC's skin. He did this not out of any concern for BC's expensive clothes but to make sure the detective wasn't going to get himself free in a hurry. By now some semblance of awareness was coming back to BC's eyes, but his limbs still seemed beyond his control. His head sagged on his shoulder, and he could only watch dully as Melchior tied him to the chair. He was so quiet that when he did finally speak Melchior almost jumped, because he'd almost forgotten BC was there.

"Why?"

Melchior didn't answer. He'd secured BC's thighs now, his upper arms, his chest.

"Why did you save me?"

Melchior pulled a long piece of tape from the roll.

"Spit."

"Wha—"

Melchior slapped him in the face.

"*Spit.*"

BC spat a thin stream of blood, bile, and saliva onto his thighs, and then Melchior put the piece of tape over his mouth and wrapped it all the way around his head, twice. Only then did he answer BC's question.

"I don't know really," he said, stepping back and looking at the trussed detective as though he were a mannequin being dressed for a window display. "Call it a hunch. An impulse. Everybody needs someone to keep him honest, and I guess that's what you are for me. In case I ever forget what I'm doing is illegal, immoral, and entirely selfish. In case I start to confuse it with virtue or vision. I'm just a thug, Beau, and having you on my ass reminds me that that's all I'll ever be. *Timor mortis exultat me*," he said. "The fear of death excites me."

He leaned in close now, so close that BC could feel the heat radiating off his face.

"The way I see it," he said quietly, "you didn't really get into this fairly. Started off at a disadvantage, as it were, a pawn in somebody else's fight. Hell, I thought you were completely incompetent when I first met you, but somehow you managed to survive, and learn, and look at you now: you came this close to taking me out this morning. So I'm going to give you a piece of advice: next time you see me, shoot first, ask questions later. Because that's what I'll do to you."

He paused a moment, looking into BC's eyes with equal parts contempt and curiosity. Sweat rolled out from beneath the wig he was wearing, and his exhalations were wet on BC's skin.

"They're going to say that what happened today changed things," he whispered finally. "Don't you believe them. The shift happened a long time ago, and it's a lot bigger than you or me or Chandler or even Jack Kennedy. You should read that book the director gave you—or *Fahrenheit 451*, or *1984*, or, hell, *The Manchurian Candidate*, the very novel that inspired Project Orpheus. The sci-fi guys have always known good and evil aren't mutually exclusive, let alone capitalism and communism. That two opposing forces come to look more and more like each other the longer they fight. Up till now it's been fiction. But after this it'll be truth. The thing is, though, the truth will have turned into lies, because everything will be about 'subjectivity,' everything will be about 'distrust of authority.' It'll be chaos masquerading as reason until someone or something comes along with the authority to lull people into believing that some truths really are incontrovertible: God, maybe, or country, or, who knows, maybe just selfishness as opposed to self-inspection and self-improvement. But no matter how it plays out, it translates into big profit for anyone willing to exploit people's fears." Melchior stepped back slightly. "Twenty years in intelligence and I never really got that," he said, shaking his head. "Not till I met you—someone idealistic enough to actually believe everything his government told him, even though it resulted in his own persecution. And to show you how much I appreciate your gift, I want to give *you* something too."

With grotesque intimacy, he leaned in again and put his mouth on BC's, pressed hard enough that BC could feel his lips through two layers of tape. It didn't hurt. It didn't even feel like a kiss. But BC felt his stomach churn and had to fight the urge to vomit.

After what seemed like an eternity Melchior stood up. He smiled down at BC like a proud father, then brought his hand to the tip of BC's nose to wipe away a drop of moisture. It could have been a bead of sweat or mucus or even a tear. Even BC didn't know.

"Beau-Christian Querrey," Melchior said in a voice whose solemnity was all the more oppressive for being genuine, even caring. "*You* are the burning boy. You—are—a—*faggot.*"

But he wasn't finished. He stuck his fingers in BC's pants pocket and wormed his hand over BC's thigh. BC turned his face away, his eyes squeezed closed, his breath whistling out of his nostrils with drops of snot.

Suddenly the hand was gone. It was a moment before BC could open his eyes. Melchior was holding Naz's ring up to the faint light.

"I don't think you need this anymore, do you?"

Before he left he turned on the television.

"I know daytime TV's for housewives," he said as he headed for the door. "But keep your eyes peeled. There just might be something interesting on today."

As soon as he left Wesley, Caspar went straight to the sixth floor. He wove his way through the dusty stacks of book boxes until he reached the southeast corner window, where he stood his package upright behind a stack of boxes. The tall parcel made a heavy metallic clunk as he set it on the bare concrete floor. He moved a few stacks of boxes to create a blind around the window, set three more underneath it to serve as a stand. He couldn't bring himself to look out the window, but he did notice that the clouds were breaking up and the sunlight streamed into the little nest he'd made for himself. It was going to be a beautiful day.

The park would probably be full of people at lunchtime, all waving at the president and First Lady as they drove by.

Chandler loitered in the shade of an oak on the eastern edge of Dealey Plaza, as far from the Book Depository as he could get without losing sight of the entrance. He'd waited to take the second half of the acid after he arrived, then maneuvered close enough to the six-story building that he was able to sift through the minds of the dozens of people inside. He didn't have to look far. Caspar's anxiety was like a beacon, and there, front and center in his thoughts, was Melchior. Melchior and President Kennedy and a rifle he'd hidden on the sixth floor, right by a corner window. What Chandler didn't see was Melchior himself.

When he saw the gun—saw what Caspar planned to do with it—he was brought up short. If he confronted Caspar now or, God forbid, dragged the police in, he knew he was losing any chance he had to catch Melchior and extract Naz's location from him. And he could see also that Caspar didn't want to do it, and didn't expect to. Melchior was supposed to make contact. Supposed to call it off before Caspar had to pull the trigger. Caspar seemed to think he was actually going to show up here. Chandler was inside Caspar's head, so he knew the would-be assassin wasn't lying to him—it was just a question of whether or not Melchior had lied to Caspar in the same way he'd lied to Song and Ivelitsch about sending Naz to Dallas. Chandler knew he was risking a lot—not just a man's life, but the president's and, who knows, the country's. But the alternative was losing his last, best chance of finding Naz, and so he found the most sheltered spot he could and waited.

Searching Caspar's mind from such a distance had used up a lot of his juice, however, and now there was the familiar fatigue. It wasn't nearly as bad as it'd been other times, but still, yawns were splitting his jaws, and he had to smack himself in the face to stay awake. He should've waited, he realized now, not taken the second hit until he saw Melchior.

"Excuse me," he said, stopping a middle-aged black woman pushing a white baby in a stroller. "Do you know what time the president's supposed to come by?"

"Why, you early, ain't you? Didn't the paper say he wasn't supposed to get by here till half past noon? It's only—"

"Ten forty-two," Chandler said. He made a show of looking at his wrist, but since he wasn't wearing a watch, it didn't help. The woman frowned and pushed her charge away.

The thoughts of passersby flickered in and out of his head. It was amazing how banal the minds of most people were. Something to eat, something to drink, something to screw. God, I hate my boss/my wife/my husband/my parents. A man sat down on the retaining wall beside the little reflecting pond. He was waiting for his secretary, with whom he was having an affair, and when he said to himself, Could you take some dick-tation, Miss Clarkson, he and Chandler chuckled at the same time. The man peered at Chandler nervously, and Chandler quickly turned away. He realized that at some point over the past month this state had become natural to him. That the time he spent unaugmented had come to seem not only vulnerable but incomplete and, even worse, *boring*. The thought filled him with self-loathing, and the self-loathing filled him with fantasies of revenge. He would make Melchior pay for what he'd done to him, and then, if he couldn't find a way to reverse the condition, he would take his own life to end this terrifying cycle of flight and violence. Once Naz was safe, he would bring it all to an end, one way or another.

But where was Melchior?

All morning long he had the intermittent sense that someone was peering over his shoulder. He'd whipped his head around so many times that one of his coworkers said he was acting jumpier than a man in his marriage bed with another woman. Finally, at a couple minutes before noon, he stood up from his desk.

"Guess I'll take lunch," he said. His manager waved at him without looking up.

He walked to the stairwell slowly, but as soon as the door was closed he bounded up the stairs to the sixth floor. As he was walking past the elevator it opened, and Charlie Givens stepped out and asked him if he was going downstairs to eat.

"No, sir," Caspar said. He just stared at Givens, and after a moment

Givens shrugged, picked up the pack of cigarettes he'd left on top of a stack of boxes, and got back in the elevator. Caspar waited until the doors closed before he headed to the southeast corner of the building. He passed a plate with some chicken bones on it, but saw no sign of anyone else. The faint sound of motorcycles floated through open windows.

He retrieved his package from behind a wall of boxes, ripped it open as quietly as possible. He assembled the Carcano quickly, rested it on the short stack of boxes beneath the window, and then, for the first time that day, looked outside.

"Fuck."

A line of live oaks blocked his view of this end of Houston Street, as well as the beginning of Elm. He'd seen the trees dozens of times before, of course, but never really noticed just how much they shaded the street in front of the depository—it wasn't the kind of thing you would notice unless you were planning to shoot someone from an upper-story window. He would have to wait until the motorcade turned on Elm and was directly below the building and moving away from him—and he would have to lean halfway out the window to get a clear shot to boot. Someone in Dealey Plaza would almost certainly see him and shout, warning the president's guards.

Not that he would do it. But Melchior had said he had to play it straight. Right to the end.

There were dozens of people in the park already. Caspar put his eye to the scope of his rifle and moved it from face to face.

Where the hell was Melchior?

Traffic had thickened in the past hour, and the lunchtime rush was backed up for blocks around the motorcade route. Melchior was coming in from the north, so he missed most of the tie-up, but still it slowed him down, and it was after noon when he finally reached Dealey Plaza. He abandoned BC's Rambler behind the depository and made his way around the west side of the building, figuring that if Chandler was already at the scene he'd most likely take cover in the park itself— probably in the line of trees that skirted the park's eastern edge. It had turned into a warm, humid day, and, what with the wig Song had packed for him, he was sweating buckets. It was almost like being back in Cuba. Fucking Cuba, where this had all started. It seemed like years ago, but it had only been a month. Four fucking weeks.

But four weeks, four months, four years, four centuries, it didn't matter, it could all come to an end in the next four minutes if he didn't figure out what he was going to do now. Why in the *hell* had BC shown up at the house without Chandler? And how had the detective gotten the drop on Melchior, forcing him to use the tranq meant for Orpheus—who, presumably, had followed what was otherwise a pretty obvious trail of bread crumbs leading straight to the Book Depository. All Melchior had now was a vial of acid and the Thorazine-phenmetrazine combo that protected his brain from Chandler's when the latter's was souped up. Oh, and the dart-shooting umbrella Ivelitsch's techies had cooked up for him. He had that, too. He was going to have to wing it.

As he came around the side of the depository he saw that a substantial crowd had gathered in Dealey Plaza. Spectators sat on a grassy ridge this side of Elm, and more stood along both curbs. At least a hundred people were in Dealey Plaza itself. Dozens of them had cameras out, and Melchior saw one man with an eight-millimeter movie camera aimed at the gap between the two courthouses at the top of the park. That's what he should have had Ivelitsch rig up. Not a ridiculous umbrella that managed to shoot a single dart at a time, but a bullet-shooting camera. Something that would give you a chance to fight your way out, if it came to that. Oh well. Next time.

He slipped a beret from his pocket and pulled it low on his forehead, added a pair of glasses with thick black rims, then eased himself into the crowd. He was conscious of the Book Depository on his left, row upon row of open windows looking straight down on him. For the next several minutes he was wide open. It was all up to Caspar. Either he was loyal to Melchior, and he would wait for the president to show, or someone had supplanted him in Caspar's esteem—Scheider, the Wiz, Giancana, who knows, maybe even Ivelitsch himself—in which case Melchior was dead to rights. Here's hoping Caspar's marksmanship hadn't improved in the last few years.

"All right, Chandler," he said under his breath. "Show yourself."

o o o

Chandler wasn't sure how long the void had been there before he felt it. Two minutes? Ten? It crept up on him like white noise until suddenly it was all he could hear.

Melchior.

But where was he? It was hard to pinpoint a silence, especially in the midst of so much commotion. He barely had any juice left and didn't want to waste it. He did his best to ignore his brain, searched the crowd with his eyes instead. The feeling came from the north, toward the depository, and he began to make his way in that direction as stealthily as he could.

It was hard to see people's faces because everyone was turned toward the eastern edge of the park, waiting for the first sign of the president's motorcade. (Funny word, motorcade, he thought as he walked past a young black man sitting on the grass eating a sandwich. Probably supposed to be a combination of motor and parade, but it sounded more like a combination of motor and arcade—a shooting gallery—which didn't make any sense when you thought about it.) He searched the sides of people's faces, their physical profiles, anyone big enough to be Melchior. He found himself staring at a lot of plump women with beehives—what more unexpected disguise could there be for a man as aggressively masculine as Melchior? But unless he'd found a way to alter the shape of his face, none of the women was him.

Suddenly it came to him. Cavalcade. That's where the cade in motorcade came from.

Jesus Christ, Chandler, he said to himself. That's really not important right now. *Focus.*

He made his way closer to Elm. On the far side of the street, on the edge of a grassy embankment, a large man carrying a closed umbrella caught his attention. The man was staring right at him, holding his umbrella in the middle so that it pointed out from his abdomen, and Chandler mistook it for a gun at first. He started to look away, then glanced back at the man's face. A black beret was pulled down over a dense cap of stiff, straight black hair, and the rims of the man's glasses were nearly as thick as a raccoon's mask. Chandler had been looking for an elaborate disguise, but now he saw that the simplest could be just as effective: he wasn't 100 percent positive it was Melchior until the rogue spy smiled at him.

Chandler kept his eyes on Melchior's hands as he crossed the street, but the big man merely stood there with that smile on his face. He heard motorcycles a few blocks away, a sputtering rumble punctuated by frequent backfires pulsing out of the canyon of Main Street. People strained to see the president and First Lady. Their thoughts flitted through Chandler's head like whispers from a hidden PA system. *Almost here,* he heard, and *I wonder if she's as pretty in real life,* and *He may be a Yankee and a papist, but he's still the president,* and then, louder than all these other thoughts, more desperate:

Where are you, Tommy?

The cry was so urgent that Chandler looked up at the School Book Depository. The anguish was like a beacon drawing his eyes to the sixth floor. The southeast corner. The window. He saw an outline low above the sill, as if someone was kneeling just behind it. He couldn't see the face, though, because it was concealed behind a—

He heard the *pfft* and tried to jump to the left, but it was too late. Something punched his abdomen just below the ribs, hard enough to knock the wind from him. Spots danced in front of his eyes and he braced himself for the numbing effect. Instead the spots danced faster, gained size, intensity, color, and he realized Melchior hadn't shot him with a tranq. He'd shot him with LSD—a *lot* of LSD. Chandler fought to get control of the trip, but the world got brighter and brighter and louder and louder. Jesus, he thought. Melchior must have injected him with thousands of hits. He'd never felt anything like this before.

He felt a hand on his shoulder, looked up in confusion to find Melchior beside him.

"Come on, old buddy. Let's get you out of the street."

"What did you . . ." He couldn't get the words out. The ground was churning beneath him and it was hard to stay upright. He clutched Melchior's arm for support. People's thoughts knifed through his brain, a thousand Technicolor razor blades cutting his mind to mush. Someone was thinking of the case of Ken-L Ration he needed to get on the way home, and someone else was wondering how to tell her boyfriend she was pregnant. An eleven-year-old boy was dreaming of being the first black superhero and a forty-seven-year-old woman was wondering what would happen if she put a little dill in the mashed potato salad, or a little ground glass.

But none of the minds was more potent than Caspar's. Chandler saw him in the orphanage again, looking up at Melchior adoringly, saw him as a little boy in his home in New Orleans with his mother and stepfather and brothers, nervously sitting apart from the group, knowing he was different from them. Saw him as a thirteen-year-old in New York City facing a truant officer, a seventeen-year-old enlisting in the Marines, saw him in California, Japan, Russia, England, Finland, America again, rafting through the South like a latter-day Huck Finn until he ended up in Dallas, dressed all in black with a rifle in his hand, telling Marina to hurry up and take the picture. So much travel for such a young soul! He'd seen half the world before most men had finished college. And everywhere he went, he was looking for someone to love him, and someone to kill.

And still there was more: Caspar in Mexico at the Soviet Embassy. Caspar in a Dallas hospital looking down on his newborn daughter. Caspar looking through the scope of a rifle at Melchior at this very moment and not knowing it was Melchior.

"Here you go, Chandler."

He felt something in his hand, looked down to see Melchior wrapping his fingers around the handle of a cane. No, not a cane: the umbrella. Despite the fact that it came from Melchior, he leaned on it gratefully. There were red spots on Melchior's fingers and he focused on these. If he could just make these spots go away, he told himself, he could get control of the trip. But a moment later he realized the world had in fact stopped spinning, that the voices and pictures slicing through his brain had subsided to an indistinct murmur. He *was* in control, or at least as much in control as a mahout astride a seven-ton bull elephant. But still the stains remained on Melchior's fingers.

He looked up at his enemy's face.

"What have you done?"

Melchior peered into his eyes. "Don't you know?" His eyes opened wide then, and for a moment it seemed his mind did as well. Chandler saw Melchior standing in front of a sharply dressed bald man sitting behind a highly polished desk, saw Caspar on his knees in front of Melchior, saw BC fall on the floor at Melchior's feet, saw Melchior stab him in the heart and drag the body—

"C'mon, Chandler," Melchior said. *"Push."*

Chandler pushed, harder than he'd ever done. Melchior staggered, took a step back. His eyes closed, but his mind opened wider. Chandler had seen the beginning of his incarnation as Melchior. Now he would see the end.

He beat Song to the airstrip in north Dallas, parked BC's Rambler in the hangar she'd rented, and paced the concrete for the next ninety minutes. Just after nine, Song's Gulfstream finally taxied through the wide-open doors. Melchior couldn't help but be amazed. A little more than a decade ago, Song had been a homeless runaway in Korea, caught in the middle of a proxy war fought by the newly christened superpowers, with 500 million Red Chinese thrown in for good measure. Now she ruled her own empire, not just of girls, but of intelligence services and a series of shrewd investments that had boosted her net worth to millions of dollars. Ivelitsch had told him: she was worth a lot more than a few compromising pictures or a roll in the hay. She could bankroll them for years, until their own schemes began to pay off. But now Melchior had to ask himself: was it worth the price?

Chul-moo killed the engines and the hangar went silent. The hatch opened and a staircase descended from the fuselage with a nearly silent whine of hydraulics. The fur collar on Song's jacket was more suited to DC than Dallas at this time of year, and she pulled at it as she descended into the stale air of the hangar. By way of greeting, all she said was:

"Have you heard from Pavel?"

"He docked at No Name Key about twenty minutes ago. They're in the process of moving the bomb from Giancana's boat to ours. They should be ready to head north by ten."

"And Naz is with Garza?"

Melchior nodded. "What about Everton?"

Song's smile was tired but, underneath that, mischievous. "Like I told you: second and fourth Thursday of every month." Then, more seriously: "How did your meeting with Caspar go?"

Melchior was silent a moment. "Don't worry," he said finally. "He'll play his part."

She was on the ground now. She reached up and adjusted Melchior's wig slightly, let her hands sit on his lapels while she inspected his appearance like a mother about to send her child off to his first day of school.

"The whole world's going to be looking for you."

Melchior shook his head. "I don't exist anymore. With Everton and Jarrell out of the picture, Caspar's the only person who could ID me, and he'll be gone soon enough."

"Gone?"

"Giancana's going to call in a favor."

"You think he'll do that after he finds out you double-crossed him in Cuba?"

"He has to. There are enough bread crumbs between him and Caspar that he'll face indictment as an accomplice if he doesn't shut Caspar up."

"Melchior." Song's voice softened, but only slightly. "It's *Caspar*."

He shook his head. "There's no Caspar. There never was. There was just Lee, and there's not much of him left anymore. I'll be doing him a favor."

Song took this in. Then, hardening again: "What about the Wiz?"

"Scheider took care of him for us. His brain is fried. He doesn't know himself anymore, let alone anyone else. Trust me, he's not long for this world."

Again Song paused, studying Melchior. There was something different about him. Something she couldn't put her finger on, but she didn't like it.

"I don't understand why we have to go through with it if you're not actually planning to work with Giancana. We've got Orpheus. We've got the bomb. What does killing—"

But Melchior was shaking his head.

"We're not going to kill him."

"I don't understand. You just said Caspar was in play."

"Like you said: it's *Caspar*. He couldn't make this shot with a bazooka, and I've seen his rifle. It's a goddamn mail-order antique. Plus there's a tree blocking his view of the road. He'll fire, he'll miss, he'll be taken into custody, Giancana will have him taken care of. End of story."

Song shook her head incredulously. "You're betting a lot on a bad shot. Never mind the fact that a man's life is at stake. If Giancana doesn't take Caspar out, if the Bureau finds out about his CIA connections, this could start a scandal that brings down the government. Why don't you just call the cops and get him picked up?"

"I call the cops and they know it's a conspiracy, they'll dig that much harder. Caspar's got to fuck this up on his own."

"Melchior, think this through. Caspar's Company connections are bad enough. But if his ties to KGB come to light, this could kick off World War Three, for God's sake."

"You think I don't know that?" Melchior's voice went up a notch, and Song had to work to keep her face calm. "I have no doubt Caspar's past is going to come out. It's there for anyone to see. I mean, Jesus Christ. A teenager running around spouting a Communist line about the coming revolution, but still joining the Civil Air Patrol and the Marines. A recruit whose boot camp nickname is Oswaldkovitch, who gets posted to the base of the U2, the single most valuable weapon in the U.S. espionage arsenal. A soldier who announces his intention to defect and provide military secrets to the Soviet Union, who formally renounces his citizenship yet conveniently forgets to bring his passport when he does so, who's set up in a luxury apartment in the Soviet Union and marries a girl he's known for barely a month and is allowed by the Soviet authorities to return to America, where, after a hey-how's-it-going interview with the FBI, he's left free to run around taking potshots at retired generals and skip across the border to Mexico to get a visa to knock off Fidel Castro. An idiot might try to chalk this up to a broken personality, but anyone with half a brain can see the lifelong construction of a cover—a boy with the outward appearance of a Marxist, but who's really the Company's attempt to get a sleeper inside KGB, and who might well have been doubled by them. Do you really think I'm so stupid I didn't think anyone would notice all—of—*that?*"

Melchior's voice grew louder and louder as he spoke, until Song was genuinely disturbed. Where was all this anger coming from, and at whom was it directed?

"Calm down, Melchior. I didn't mean—"

"They'll find it, Song! Every last bit of evidence revealing Caspar's ties to U.S. and Russian intelligence—real things, plus a lot of stuff that's probably totally innocent but that'll come to seem suspicious in hindsight. Someone—a G-man, a Company agent who's never heard of the Wiz Kids, a nosy reporter—somebody'll root out everything and bring it to light, and the government will either suppress it or deny it because, like you said, the scandal could bring down administrations or kick off a nuclear war. Do you understand what I'm saying, Song? *We* don't have to cover anything up, because the goddamn government of the United States of America will do it *for* us."

Melchior's hands were balled in fists and his face had gone beet red. The sweat rolling out from beneath the wig had thickened into streams that stained his collar.

"But Melchior," Song said, grabbing his left hand. "What if he makes the sh—"

She stopped. Turning Melchior's hand over, she opened his fingers, saw something that looked like a handful of seeds. He spread his fingers and the seeds fell open in a long oval, revealing themselves to be a string of beads. No, not beads.

Skulls.

Song looked up at Melchior, her confusion giving way to genuine horror. Not fear, but a sense of betrayal so profound that she couldn't find words for it.

"Then he makes the shot," Melchior said, and he slipped the necklace over Song's head while she just stood there, frozen in place.

"A gift," he said. "From Caspar."

"Melchior?" Song's right hand touched the beads on her chest. "No."

"Don't you understand, Song? History doesn't care about individuals, let alone individual actions. It only cares about symbols. It's not the shot that matters. It's not who pulls the trigger, or who it hits, or even if it hits. It's what we can make it *mean*."

Song blinked her eyes as if she was coming out of a trance. "My God. You *want* him to make it. You want him to kill the president." She started to say something else, but then her eyes saw the knife in Melchior's hand. "You—you can't be serious."

"I'm sorry, Song. Your entire career has been built around your ability to play one side off against the other. A thousand intelligence agents could identify you, and who knows how many more have bedded you."

Song tugged at the skulls around her neck, but it was as if the cord that held them together was made of piano wire. She stepped backward, but the staircase was directly behind her. She stumbled and the long string of skulls clacked against the metal treads with a sound like knucklebones shaking in a rattle, then she caught herself and stood on the bottom step.

"I don't understand. The whole thing—the partnership between you and Ivelitsch, going rogue, it was all my idea."

Melchior nodded. "It was. I can't deny it. And my career in intelligence was the Wiz's creation. But if I'm going to make this thing work, I've got to start making decisions on my own."

Song took another step up and back.

"Pavel was right about you. Your motivations are too complex. Too messy."

"Don't be naive, Song. Pavel wanted you out of the picture long before I did. Triumvirates never work, especially when two of them are alpha males and the third's a beautiful woman."

"Melchior, please," she said as she climbed backward up the staircase. "I have money. Connections. Resources. This plane. Houses in—"

"Pavel's made me aware of all your assets." Melchior shook his head. "You should have made a will, Song. As it is, all your property will pass to your brother."

"My—" Song whirled around, only to bounce off something barring the door. She stumbled backward, barely managing to catch herself from falling over the rail. She looked back at the door, at the figure standing there. Her face was pale with confusion and fear.

"Chul-moo? You're not—" She turned back to Melchior. "He's not my brother."

Melchior shrugged. "Identity, like property, or history for that matter, is just a matter of the right documents. Chul-moo is as much your brother as the boy who died in Korea."

Chul-moo pulled a gun from his jacket but Melchior put up his hand.

"I have to do this myself," he said. He reached his hand down to Song, and, as if in a spell, she took it. "I owe you that much," he said, then added, "Balthazar," and drove the point home.

But even as the blade was piercing fabric and flesh, the scene seemed to melt. First the airplane disappeared, then the hangar and the airport and Dallas, and in its place there were palms and mangroves, a white-sand beach and the roar of surf. Chandler felt the blood rushing over Melchior's fingers, but they weren't Melchior's fingers—they were his. He looked up into Song's face, but it wasn't Song.

It was Naz.

Her dark eyes bore into his, and the worst thing of all was that there was no surprise there.

"I always knew you would do this to me," she said. "You pretended you were different from the rest of them, but I always knew you were just the same."

And then she died in his arms.

A gunshot brought Chandler back.

No, not a gunshot: the backfire of a motorcycle. The motorcade's escort had arrived, was turning onto Elm Street.

Chandler staggered backward. Only the umbrella he was leaning on kept him from falling over. His senses were still screwed up, and instead of throwing himself at Melchior, he almost fell on him. The people around them took a few steps away, their hands shielding their eyes as they looked at the approaching vehicles. A thousand versions of *There he is!* flashed in Chandler's mind.

He leaned on the umbrella heavily. "Where is she?" he demanded.

Melchior's smile was a sickening parody of innocence. "What do you mean, where is she? You're Orpheus. That means she's in hell."

Another image of Naz's dying face flashed in his mind, and Chandler shook his head to clear it. That was a mistake: again Melchior had to grab him to keep him from falling over. Chandler shook him off roughly, doing his best to steady himself as the acid continued to flood his system.

"You—you added something to the LSD."

Melchior's smirk grew wider. "Several somethings in fact. Among others: psilocybin to increase the hallucinogenic power, sodium pentathol to render you open to suggestion, and a heaping spoonful of methamphetamine just to make you crazy."

"Yeah, well, crazy or not, I'm going to rip your brain apart."

"I don't think so," Melchior said. "I may play fast and loose sometimes, but I never make mistakes." He reached into his pocket and pulled out an empty pill bottle. "While you went fishing in my brain, I took another pill. You won't be getting back in for a while."

Chandler pushed—pushed hard—but it was like trying to get the water out of a sponge with a needle. It would take ten thousand pricks before he accomplished anything. Melchior's nose wrinkled. It was obvious he was feeling something, but not enough to really hurt him.

"I'll save you the effort," he said. "She's in Cuba. Trust me," he threw in, when it looked like Chandler might turn and run. "I can have her killed a dozen different ways before you could get out of the country, let alone into Cuba. Listen to me," he hissed, stepping closer to Chandler. "I know you know Caspar's in the building behind me. I know you know he's got a rifle, and I know you know he's going to shoot the president. I want you to help him."

Chandler was fighting a fresh wave of dizziness, and he barely heard what Melchior said. "Help him?"

"Caspar never was the best marksman. Help him find his target. Steady his hand. Pull the trigger for him if you have to."

"Help him?" Chandler said again, but even as he spoke Chandler's brain was reaching out. It was like Melchior's words were a map, guiding Chandler to Caspar's brain.

"But . . . but why?" he said, trying to fight the connection, feeling it grow stronger instead.

"Why? Because at any point in the past two weeks you could have gone to the police, and you refused to. Because all you could think about was getting your girlfriend back—a girl you spent less than a week with, who you slept with all of *one time*. For her you were willing to sacrifice your duty not just to your country but to your beliefs. It's time you learned that there are consequences for putting yourself ahead of everyone else. This morning *I* killed the only woman I might have ever loved—and now you and everyone else are going to learn what it means to cross me. Now, help Caspar make his shot or I swear to God I'll pull the top of Naz's skull off with my bare hands and eat her brains for dinner."

The whole time Melchior spoke, the connection to Caspar grew more and more palpable. Chandler felt the gun as if it were in his own hands, smelled the dust from thousands and thousands of boxed books. The concrete was hard under his knees, and he had to fight the urge to fidget. No, Chandler told himself. *Caspar's* knees. *Caspar* was fighting the urge to fidget, not Chandler. *Caspar* was looking desperately for Melchior, the scope of his rifle ignoring the motorcade as it moved from one face in the crowd to the next. Chandler could see the faces through the crosshairs. Male and female, black and white, their attention focused on the long line of motorcycles and limousines, their hands shading their eyes from the death pointing down at them from sixty feet above, and as he looked at one innocent face after another he had an idea. He pushed deeper into Caspar's mind, found what he was looking for, pulled it out, and put it before Caspar's eyes. The gun angled to the left.

The few seconds it took the motorcade to complete its left turn onto Elm and enter the shelter of the live oaks growing in front of the depository seemed to take all of Caspar's life.

He stopped looking through the crowd for Melchior and instead angled the rifle just past the last oak and waited. Melchior had told him he had to play it straight right up until the end.

Suddenly a thought flickered through his head and he jerked the gun a few inches to the left. The view through the scope blurred, settled, and there he was.

Melchior.

He stood on the edge of the street, casually talking to a second man who leaned on an umbrella. He never once looked up at the window.

He hates you.

The thought seemed to come out of the ether, and Caspar twitched so hard he nearly pulled the trigger.

He'll sacrifice you to his game.

Caspar took his eye from the scope, shook his head to clear it. KGB had said things like that to him, when they were trying to turn him. Had said the Wiz sent him behind enemy lines to be slaughtered, just like he'd done with all those poor boys in the Ukraine and Korea. Caspar could almost believe that about the Wiz. But Melchior? Melchior was his friend.

You're just his patsy.

Caspar leaned forward, looked through the scope again. Melchior was still right there. He could do it. Do what the Company had asked him, and maybe then he could be Lee again. Just Lee. But in order to do that he would have to kill Tommy. But—but Tommy was already dead. Melchior had said so. Just like he'd said Lee was dead. There was just Melchior now. Melchior and Caspar. If Caspar killed him, he'd be all alone.

Do it, the voice hissed in his ear. *Do it!*

A tap on the shoulder brought Chandler's attention back to the street. Melchior's smile hadn't faded, but his voice was deadly serious.

"I should tell you that if I don't check in at exactly 1 p.m., Naz will be killed anyway. Just in case you're getting any crazy ideas about having Caspar shoot me instead of the president."

Chandler glared at him. If pure hatred could have killed Melchior, he'd have burst into flames. But all he did was return Chandler's gaze with that implacable smile on his face. Chandler pushed at Melchior's brain again, but all he got was that spongy nothingness.

"Not me," Melchior said, shaking his head. "The *president*."

The president. Chandler looked up. He could see him now. His car had just made the turn off Houston onto Elm. In a minute or two he'd pass through the Triple Underpass and get on the freeway and be away, safe to lead America to a new era of peace and tolerance, to Africa and Asia and all the way to the goddamned moon. His smile was as bright as the noon sun.

In desperation Chandler cast his mind wider, looking for someone in the crowd who could help him. But who? If he tipped off one of the policemen or Secret Service agents and got Melchior arrested, he was as good as killing Naz. If he started some kind of mass panic like he had in Texas, who knew how many people might die.

He found himself thinking of the burning boy. Even though the figure was nothing more than a figment of his imagination—his mixed with BC's and all the other minds he'd come into contact with—he somehow felt that it would know what to do. A part of him willed the flaming angel to make an appearance, but it refused to come.

"It's now or never, Chandler," Melchior said. "Do it. Or Naz dies."

Not knowing what else to do, Chandler reached out to the only other mind he could think of: the president's. He felt the ache in the man's arm as he waved at the crowd, in his jaw as he flashed that famous smile. The ache that throbbed in his lower back beneath his brace despite all the painkillers and other drugs that flowed through his veins. In the past week alone he'd taken Demerol, Ritalin, Librium, thyroid hormone, testosterone, and gamma globulin, and before he consented to get in the car this morning he'd had two injections of procaine to ease the pain in his back. Good lord, Chandler thought, the president of the United States was on more drugs than he was!

As he smiled and waved at the last of the spectators, Jack Kennedy suddenly found himself thinking about Mary Meyer. How funny to think about her now! He glanced over at Jackie guiltily, then looked away again. It wasn't the fact that he'd slept with her that made him feel guilty—he and Jackie had worked out that part of their marriage a long time ago. It was the fact that she'd given him marijuana and LSD several times, and in the White House to boot. Jackie would've flipped if she'd found out about that—she had enough trouble covering up his affairs and his illnesses. Jack hadn't cared much for the hallucinatory aspects of LSD—he saw enough unbelievable things in his daily security briefing—but the euphoria was the best painkiller he'd ever experienced. For twelve blissful hours the pain in his back had been like a glob of Silly Putty he could knead and play with. God, that'd be nice right now. Here it was just after noon and his back was killing him, and instead of relief he had to face an interminable luncheon at the Trade

Mart, all for the sake of securing a half dozen votes that probably wouldn't make any difference at all next November.

As Chandler absorbed all of this he stared at the president's retreating form. So Jack Kennedy was one of the chosen few who'd been turned on to LSD. Who'd've guessed?

Then, with a start, he realized someone else was looking at Kennedy, his gaze doubly focused through the sights of his rifle and Chandler's own attention. Chandler felt Caspar's finger on the trigger, realized it was starting to squeeze, and, not knowing what else to do, he pushed at Caspar's mind, and at the same time snapped open his umbrella.

"What the—!" Standing on the edge of Dealey Plaza, James Tague jerked his head as something stung his cheek. At the same time, he heard a loud pop from off to his right.

"Oh no, no, no!" John Connally said in the seat in front of the president's. Chandler heard him clearly. He knew that the governor of Texas had recognized the sound of a gunshot, unlike the president and his wife and most of the security detail—including the limo driver, who, mistaking the sound for a blowout, stepped on the brakes instead of the gas. At least Caspar had missed. But he was getting ready to fire again, and this time it was Kennedy Chandler pushed. *Duck!* he screamed into the president's mind, and the president leaned forward. But it was too late. Chandler felt the bullet slam into the base of Kennedy's neck, nick his spine, and spit out of his throat just below his Adam's apple. Somehow, though—a miracle!—it missed hitting any vital organs, even as it ripped its way through Governor Connally's abdomen and wrist.

But the gun was still in Caspar's hands. He wasn't thinking about Melchior now, or why he was doing what he was doing. His Marine training had kicked in, and he'd shot the bolt on his rifle and re-aimed. His attention was focused squarely and solely on the president. It was as if the two were linked by a high-tension wire.

Desperate now, Chandler dove deep into Caspar's mind, trying to find someone Caspar could never shoot. But it seemed that Caspar wanted to shoot *everyone*. The president's visage gave way to Castro's first, then Khrushchev's, and then to the man with the pointed beard who'd plucked him from the orphanage with the Wiz all those years ago, and then Frank Wisdom himself, beery, bloated, and bellicose. Then Melchior. Not Melchior as he was now but Melchior as a teenager: thin, scrappy, defiant, adaptable. A survivor, unlike Caspar. Unlike Lee. And then that image faded away before another, wavering, indistinct, two-dimensional—a black-and-white photograph that Chandler was only able to flesh out with the greatest effort of will.

"Lee," Robert Edward Lee Oswald said. "Son, what are you doing?"

"Daddy?" Caspar peered through the scope.

"Put down the gun," Robert Oswald said. "Come on, Lee. That's not how your mother raised you."

Melchior stared at the retreating limousine. A dozen cops and agents had drawn their guns, and people were starting to yell and point in every direction. A Secret Service agent was jumping onto the trunk of Kennedy's limo. In another second he would throw himself over the president's body and the opportunity would be gone.

Melchior pushed Chandler's umbrella down with one hand, reached into his pocket with the other.

"She's pregnant," Melchior said. "It won't be just her who dies." And then, opening his hand, he showed him what he'd pulled from his pocket.

Chandler looked down at Melchior's hand. At first he thought Melchior was holding a ball of blood. A ball of blood connected to a silver loop of tissue. But then he realized the ball was actually a ruby—Naz's ruby—and the loop was the ring on which it was mounted, and the ring was still on—still on—

It was still on her finger.

"This is just a taste of what I'll do to her," Melchior said. "Now, *shoot* him."

Chandler stared at the finger. Sixty feet above him, Caspar saw it—

saw a finger stained with blood at any rate, and knew it to be his own. He looked down at his father in the limousine.

"Lee's dead," he whispered. "He died when you did." And then his severed finger squeezed the trigger.

Chandler felt Caspar's finger pull the trigger. The president's thoughts vanished from Chandler's brain like light disappearing from a shattered bulb. A thousand other minds rushed in to fill the vacuum. The First Lady's, and the agents in the car, and the sheriffs on their motorcycles, and the hundreds and hundreds of spectators all staring with horror at the fleeing limousine, but over it all came Melchior's voice.

"Good job, son. I knew I could count on you."

Chandler whirled on him. He was about to throw himself on him but he was overcome by a fit of dizziness and almost fell over.

"Why don't you sit down for a spell?" Melchior said as everyone began running—after the limousine, away from the shots, toward anything that would pass for cover. Everywhere Chandler looked he saw open mouths, but the roar of the gunning motorcycles drowned out all the other sounds, so it seemed that the people around him were screaming silently. On the trunk of the president's car Jackie was crawling toward something that looked like a bloody toupee.

Melchior pulled a small zippered case from his pants. He held it up to his face for a moment as though it were a walkie-talkie, but when he took it back down Chandler saw a man running past him, a camera stuck to his eye. Melchior unzipped the case, and Chandler saw that it was empty save for a single cigar, which Melchior pulled out and unwrapped casually, as though he were in a drawing room rather than at the scene of an assassination.

The familiar exhaustion was setting in now. An immense tiredness that seemed to leech the marrow from Chandler's bones, leaving him as helpless as a marionette whose strings have been cut off.

"What—what is that?"

"This?" Melchior brought the cigar to his lips, lit it with a series of lip-smacking puffs. "As Dr. Freud says, Chandler, sometimes a cigar is just a cigar."

He stood up then, glanced at the Triple Underpass through which the last of the motorcade had disappeared, then reached down and pulled Chandler to his feet.

"You—you killed him."

Melchior puffed ruminatively at his cigar. "Who can say who really killed JFK? Was it me? Was it Caspar? Was it you? Was it that guy up on that grassy knoll?"

Melchior pointed. Chandler looked. He didn't see anything, but Jean Hill and Tom Tilson and Ed Hoffman did. The figure was blurry and disappeared almost as quickly as it appeared. Who knows, maybe their own minds made it up, but they would all swear till their dying day that they'd seen a man with a gun there.

The two men started walking up the grassy slope toward the rear parking lot where Melchior had parked BC's Rambler. After only a few steps, though, Melchior stopped. He was staring at a small russet-haired man walking quickly out the front entrance of the depository. His hands were clenched in fists and his small, nearly lipless mouth was set in a hard line; it was obvious he was doing his best not to run. He looked neither left nor right but Chandler thought he saw his eyes flicker in their direction, a glance filled with a combination of fear and confusion and pride. His face, too, winked across Dealey Plaza. For most people, it merged with the image that showed up on their televisions later that night, but for some—for Deputy Sheriff Roger Craig especially—it would haunt them for years. Craig swore he saw a man matching the description of Lee Harvey Oswald get into a car on the far side of the grassy knoll, a light green Nash Rambler driven by a dark-complected man.

"Where are you taking me?" Chandler said as he slumped in the car.

"Into the future," Melchior said as he climbed behind the wheel. "Into the brave new world that you and I made together."

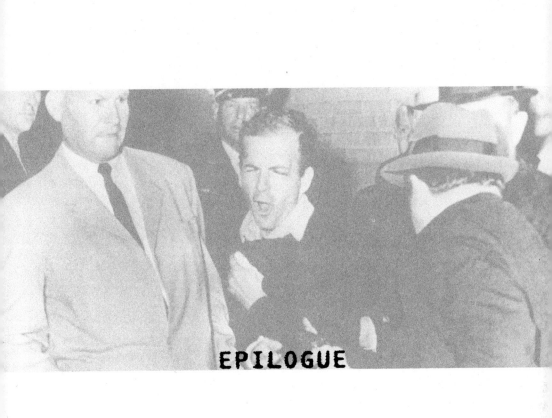

EPILOGUE

On the television, a middle-aged woman and an old man sip
from ornately patterned coffee cups. Despite the seriousness of the
situation, BC can't help but think of J. Edgar Hoover and Clyde Tolson
and their talk of gravy boats and butter dishes. He stares at the TV out
of one eye even as he continues to try to work his right arm free of the
duct tape binding it to the chair. The tape has bunched into a gooey,
fibrous strand, making it stronger than ever, but also slightly looser. BC
has yanked so hard his skin has torn, and a trickle of blood encircles his
wrist like a bracelet. He wiggles even more, using the blood as lubricant.

"I have some *very* interesting information," the woman says even as
the old man slurps his coffee like someone who's just wandered out of
a desert. "Your great-grandson and his mother are going to have
Thanksgiving dinner with us."

"I must say, I'm surprised," the old man responds, although all his
attention seems focused on his cup. Maybe his lines are written there?
He's lowering his face for another slurp when the whine of feedback
shrieks from the TV's single speaker, and the picture fades to a black
screen emblazoned with white letters.

A moment later, the articulate, assertive voice of Walter Cronkite takes shape out of the black screen like God speaking from the void. But it's not the beginning of the world Cronkite is narrating. It's the end.

"Here is a bulletin from CBS News. In Dallas, Texas, three shots were fired at President Kennedy's motorcade in downtown Dallas. The first reports say that President Kennedy has been seriously wounded by this shooting."

For a moment BC has the distinct thought that his mouth would be hanging open if it weren't taped closed. He stares at the screen, but there are just the white letters, the black background, the preternaturally calm voice of the nation's first anchorman.

"More details just arrived. These details about the same as previously. President Kennedy shot today just as his motorcade left downtown Dallas. Mrs. Kennedy jumped up and grabbed Mr. Kennedy. She called, 'Oh no!' The motorcade sped on. United Press says that the wounds for President Kennedy perhaps could be fatal. Repeating, a bulletin from CBS News: President Kennedy has been shot by a would-be assassin in Dallas, Texas. Stay tuned to CBS News for further details."

In the background another voice is heard—"Connally, too"—and then the screen cuts to a spoon swinging back and forth like a pendulum, a heart beating with the regularity of a metronome—or, rather, a metronome beating with the regularity of a heart. "It takes more than an instant to make a real cup of coffee."

A commercial for Nescafé. Behind his gag, BC finds himself giggling. Maybe that's what the old man was drinking. A promo for that evening's episode of *Route 66* follows. BC stares at the face of George Maharis, his dark hair rippling as he sits behind the wheel of the famous red Corvette, and then for some reason he remembers hearing that the car Buz and Tod drive is really light blue. Apparently it photographs better in black-and-white than an actual red car. Just one more sign, if you still needed it, that things aren't always what they seem.

Be that as it may, BC thinks as he resumes his struggle to get free, it's doubtful *Route 66* is going to be on the air tonight.[1]

---

[1] Police officer J. D. Tippit fatally shot by Lee Harvey Oswald at approximately 1:12 p.m.

The apartment's right on the Moskva. Picture-postcard views, even if the wind off the river comes colder and harder than bullets, and reeks of rotten fish besides. Four rooms, each practically as big as a swimming pool. Fourteen-foot ceilings, eighteen-karat gold detailing on the paneling, marquetry on the floor so intricate that it looks more like embroidery than oak and sandalwood and mother-of-pearl. It's the kind of place that would have belonged to a minor noble or major bureaucrat under the tsars, and now only goes to one of the Party faithful—or a prominent defector.

"Caspar's apartment in Minsk wasn't half as nice as this, I can tell you that much," Ivelitsch says when he shows it to Melchior. "And it's a hell of a lot nicer than my place."

"I'm not a defector," Melchior growls. "Neither was Caspar."

"Yeah, yeah, tell that to your neighbor, Kim Philby."

Right now, though, Melchior's less concerned with his new home than the man he's sharing it with. He's asleep right now, on a hospital bed outfitted with shackles at wrist, ankle, and waist, and enclosed inside a big steel cage to boot. He's been asleep for two solid days.

"Why isn't he waking up?"

"I don't understand," Keller says, flipping pages on his clipboard, flitting from one instrument to the next. "I've given him Preludin, epinephrine, methamphetamine. I even gave him cocaine—enough to give an elephant a heart attack. But his pulse is barely ten beats per minute. Are you sure you didn't give him too much sedative?"

"I told you, I didn't give him anything. He collapsed in the car on the way to Song's—on the way to the plane. Hasn't woken up since."

"Melchior." Ivelitsch is standing in the living room doorway. "You might want to look at this."

"I'm not letting you out of that cage until you figure out what's wrong, Doctor," Melchior says, striding into the other room. "Either you wake that man up or you die in there with him."

The living room is empty save for a huge console television and a massive broken chandelier hanging over it like a glacier punching a hole in the sky. Beneath it, the TV looks more like Pandora's box than a modern technological conveyance. It even sounds creepy, voices from six thousand miles away booming out of the shot speaker like ghosts looking for a way out of hell. The tiny screen shows a shallow brick alcove crammed with people. Flashing lights, garbled voices, an air of eager, almost greedy expectation so palpable you can almost see it, although it's probably just static.

An announcer is speaking, but Melchior concentrates on the noises coming from the alcove itself. Suddenly the pitch heightens several notches, the camera flashes grow even more frenetic; a moment later Caspar melts out of the shadows. His hands are cuffed in front of him, his hair is mussed, and there are bruises on his forehead and lip. He walks slowly, as though dazed or drugged. His right elbow is held by a man dressed all in white, his left by a man dressed all in black, the two men towering over him like a pair of angels bickering over the soul of a little boy.

"It's a police station," Ivelitsch says. "What the hell can—"

"There," Melchior says, pointing to a flicker of movement from the right side of the screen even as a voice rises above the din of the crowd:

"Do you have anything to say in your defense?"

A gunshot rings out. The crowd yells, but Caspar's groans are louder. The men holding him try to support him, but he falls to the floor.

"He's been shot!" the announcer says. "He's been shot!"

"I told you," Melchior says, heading back to the other room. "We don't have to worry about Caspar."[2]

---

[2] Lee Harvey Oswald killed by Jack Ruby at 11:21 a.m. as he is being transferred from Dallas Police Headquarters to the Dallas County Jail.

It's been a long pregnancy. Eleven months, maybe more, yet the mother has borne it stoically. Indeed, she doesn't seem to have suffered at all, and, despite the worries of the women in the village, who dote on her like one of their own daughters, she insists her baby will be fine. She refuses their gifts of spicy food, warm rum, doses of castor oil. He will come when he's ready, she tells them, not a moment before.

He is ready now.

Louie Garza stands at the back of the room, leaning on his cane more out of habit than necessity. Tropical Storm Isbell is gathering strength off the western coast of the island, pushing cold damp winds ahead of it that aggravate the old injury to his hip. A stiff breeze whips the curtains, the bed skirts, Naz's hair, but she has insisted the windows be left open.

Louie's angled himself so he can't see what's happening beneath the sheet that covers Naz's legs but can still see her face. It's unreal. Her face, that is. Serenely calm and beautiful, like that of a woman waking up after a peaceful night's sleep rather than engaged in the agony of childbirth. One of the women who styles herself Naz's *abuela* has embroidered her a brightly colored pillowcase, so that it seems her face rests on a kaleidoscopic rainbow.

"Empuja," the midwife says, but quietly. Furtively. *"El viene ahora."*

Naz smiles wider. If she is pushing, it doesn't show on her face. "I know he's coming. Just like the storm."

"Empuja," the midwife says again, and crosses herself behind the sheet.

A gust of wind shakes the whole house and a ceramic pitcher smashes on the floor. A thread of water snakes across the floor toward Louie's feet, but he doesn't notice. His eyes are glued to Naz's face. For a single moment her brows knit together, more in concentration than pain, as if she is willing her child into existence. The next minute the midwife is calling,

"¡Es aquí! ¡Es aquí!"

Despite his yearlong gestation, the baby is normal-sized, even a bit small. But his limbs are strangely articulate and fine—not thin but lean, as if he has already started to tone his muscles and burn off his baby fat. He is as calm as his mother. His eyes are open, and he doesn't cry as the midwife wipes him clean, wraps him in a blanket, and carries him across the room. He looks not at his mother or the woman holding him but directly at Louie, and when the midwife offers him the baby, Naz's guard hesitates, looks at the mother.

"Do you want to hold him first?"

Naz shakes her head. The wind whips her hair around, a dark halo at the center of the riot of color on the pillowcase. Her dark eyes stare at nothing—nothing in the room anyway—and her smile grows even wider.

"Take the boy to him. I've already told him everything he needs to know."

"To—the father?" Louie still hasn't accepted the baby from the midwife, who seems eager to have it out of her arms.

"To Melchior," Naz says, smiling radiantly. "I want him to see the face of the man who will kill him one day."[3]

---

[3] Mary Meyer murdered on a towpath along the Chesapeake and Ohio Canal in Georgetown. Henry Wiggins, the only witness, reported seeing "a black man in a light jacket, dark slacks, and a dark cap" standing over Meyer's body. Meyer's diary, in which she is alleged to have recorded the details of her affair with the murdered president, was first given to CIA associate deputy director of operations for counter-intelligence James Jesus Angleton, and later destroyed by her sister.

Arlington National Cemetery
November 22, 1965

Beneath its hollow cross the tombstone reads only:

FRANK
WISDOM
JUNE 23, 1909
OCTOBER 29, 1965

The grave is almost a month old, but for some reason the sods haven't taken yet. Though the rest of the cemetery is uniformly, immaculately green, the grass over the Wiz's grave is brown and friable—so dry that the man carrying a bouquet of forget-me-nots imagines it would crunch beneath his shoes if he dared to step on it. "Happens sometimes," a passing groundskeeper tells him. "Don't worry, sir, it's already scheduled for resodding."

The man with the flowers nods. He doesn't bother to point out that the brown strands extend well beyond the rectangle of cut sods laid atop the grave itself—that its tentacles spiral out a good six inches in every direction like a negating kaleidoscope sucking the color from everything it touches. As soon as the groundskeeper is gone, the man pulls a bullet-shaped lead from his pocket. The lead is attached to a long coil of wire and the man drops it in the center of the brown patch, then glances at what looks like a watch on his wrist to confirm what the grass has already told him. He reels the lead up, drops it in his pocket, and turns away; almost as an afterthought, he tosses the flowers behind him.

Something about the gesture stops him in his tracks. A memory shakes him like a muscle spasm. A hot spring day in New Orleans in 1942, a marble toss he made without looking. The day it all started. He knew it even then, even if the Wiz didn't, or Caspar.

He turns, and when he steps on the grave to lean the flowers against the headstone, the grass does indeed break beneath his shoes. There's

not enough radiation to worry about—not for a few seconds anyway—
but even so, he takes care not to touch the ground or the stone or the
rotten flowers that already adorn the site, and then he turns and makes
his way to the pay phones outside the chapel.

Only someone watching would notice that he doesn't put any money
in the machine or place a collect call, just punches several long strings
of numbers. It takes nearly two minutes for the connection to be made.
Finally a click, a hollow *"Da?"*

"It's leaking," Melchior says, and hangs up.[4]

[4] Frank Wisdom found dead in his home October 29,
1965, of an apparent self-inflicted gunshot to
the face. The shotgun in question belonged to his
son.

"Credentials?"

The police officer guarding the hospital door is soft but solid and has a no-nonsense air about him. He peers at the badge the man in the white coat shows him, then scrutinizes the face that goes with it.

"I ain't seen you before."

In answer the man pulls his coat open, revealing a Star of David hanging from a chain around his neck.

"Oh. Go on in, Mister, uh"—the man glances at the badge—"Rabbi Gaminsky."

BC slips past the guard. Once in the room he pulls a plastic-bottomed steel wedge from his pocket and slides it beneath the door, just in case the room's occupant makes a fuss. But the person on the bed doesn't wake up, so BC pulls out a needle and, ignoring the IV line, slides it directly into an arm. Epinephrine, aka adrenaline. The same stuff Melchior had used to save his life just over three years ago.

Jack Ruby's eyelids flutter apart, barely, his lips part the tiniest sliver as though a knife has sliced them open.

"Who . . ." His voice breaks. He swallows and tries again. "Who are you?"

"You haven't got much time left, Mr. Ruby. I've come to give you the chance to make things right."

Ruby stares at him a moment and then, as if it takes all his strength, turns away. His body is so desiccated that when he turns, strands of hair break from his head and fall to the pillow. The thin lines wavering on the white background remind BC of staff paper for some reason, the blank pages of an unfinished symphony that he has been desperately trying to complete for the past three years.

"Mr. Ruby, you told Dallas Deputy Sheriff Al Maddox last month that someone gave you an injection for a cold but that it really contained cancer cells. It wasn't cancer cells, Mr. Ruby. It was a radioactive poison taken from a Soviet nuclear bomb stolen from Cuba. You said:

'The people who had an ulterior motive for putting me in the position I'm in will never let the true facts come aboveboard.' Who are these people, Mr. Ruby? Tell me their names so I can bring them to justice for President Kennedy's murder—and yours."

It is a long time before Ruby answers. Then: "No one," he says.

"You know that's not true, Mr. Ruby. You gave Sheriff Maddox a note in which you said that President Kennedy was killed as part of a conspiracy. Who was involved in that conspiracy? What were their names?"

Ruby's head shakes again. More strands of hair fall to the pillow. "There was no one."

"Mr. Ruby, please. You told a psychiatrist named Werner Teuter that you were framed to kill Caspar—to kill Lee Harvey Oswald, just as he said he was a patsy for someone else. Who, Mr. Ruby? Who framed you?"

At the name Caspar, Ruby's eyes sharpen, but then his lids fall closed and a long, wet breath bubbles from his nostrils.

"Does the name Caspar mean anything to you, Mr. Ruby? What about Orpheus? Melchior? Do these names mean anything to you, Mr. Ruby? *Please,* Mr. Ruby. This is your last chance to make it right."

Ruby's voice, when it comes, seems to leak from him like his breath, as if he is not speaking but expiring.

"There is nothing to hide," he whispers. "There was no one else."[5]

[5] Jack Ruby dies of cancer in Parkland Memorial Hospital, the same hospital where John F. Kennedy had been pronounced dead just over three years earlier.

Camagüey Province, Cuba
June 19, 1975

Over the course of the past twelve years her garden has grown remarkably. Her corn is the sweetest in the province, her tomatoes the largest, her beans more numerous. It helps that the local children come over after school to work with her, that women give her fish heads to sow and men give her a share of the manure the state has allocated them for their own plantings. No doubt the time and energy expended on this half acre of land are a profligate waste of resources in a managed economy. But they produce some gorgeous fruits and vegetables, a small portion of which she trades for rice, the rest of which she gives away.

Her garden has matured, but she hasn't. For twelve years he's been watching her, and Louie Garza would swear she hasn't aged a day. Only sometimes, when he's standing across a field, say, or on the second floor of the house he shares with her, watching her toil away in her garden, he seems to see cracks in her facade—gray hairs among the black, wrinkles at the sides of her eyes and mouth, the beginning of a sag in her breasts. It makes no sense, of course. Even if these signs *were* real, he wouldn't be able to see them from so far away. And when he approaches her, they always disappear, and she becomes ageless again, perfect. It is as if, in waiting for the day when Orpheus comes for her, she has decided to keep herself exactly as she was the last time he saw her.

But all that is changing now. The icy Russian stands on the porch of the house Naz and Louie have lived in for more than a decade, looking out at her as she weeds a patch of amaranth.

"Do you have to take her?" Louie does a poor job of keeping the pleading note out of his voice.

"Melchior's convinced she's the only thing that can wake Chandler up."

Louie has no idea who Chandler is. Which is to say, he knows that Chandler is the same person as the Orpheus Naz sometimes speaks of, and knows that for the past twelve years Melchior and the Russian have been trying to wake him from a coma, but what they expect him to say or do when he wakes up has never been specified. It seems a little unreal to him. As unbelievable as Naz's unchanging beauty must sound to anyone who doesn't live with her. But who is he to doubt? It isn't Chandler he cares for. It's only Naz.

As the Russian heads out into the garden, Louie hooks the tall man's arm with his cane.

"I've protected her for twelve years. I won't let you hurt her."

The Russian looks first at Louie's cane, then at Louie. His eyes are as cold as the land he comes from and wants to take Naz to.

"I don't think I could hurt her even if I wanted to. But just to put your mind at ease: I'm under strict orders to bring her back unharmed. Melchior's convinced himself that she's somehow the key to everything."

Louie nods, and releases the Russian. As Ivelitsch turns and heads into the garden, he glances at the syringe he's palming in his right hand.

"He didn't say I couldn't have a little fun, though," he says, and, baring his teeth in a smile that practically causes the plants to wilt, he strides toward Naz.[6]

---

[6] Sam Giancana executed in the basement of his home in Chicago, shot once in the back of the head, then six more times in the face. At the time of his death he was scheduled to testify before a Senate Committee investigating the possibility of collusion between CIA and the Mafia in the Kennedy assassination.

It takes BC a moment to find the light switch in his basement office—it's hiding under a piece of paper he must have taped up the last time he was down, and the room's two tiny windows, similarly covered, let in no light at all. He finds it finally, clicks it, and, one by one, the fluorescent rectangles flicker into life. The steady, measured brilliance of American industry illuminates the seven-hundred-square-foot space, every inch of which is covered with newspaper clippings and photographs and Xeroxes and other bits of evidence and clues. Even the door, when it falls closed, is revealed to be covered with flowcharts and diagrams scribbled in marker, pen, pencil, something that looks like lipstick or blood. Red, blue, and green threads connect various faces and places with one another in a system not even he fully understands anymore. He is like a spider who has woven a web around his own body, trapping himself. At least there's Scotch.

He pulls a bottle and crystal tumbler from a cabinet, pours himself a finger of rich amber liquid, knocks it back, pours himself another. It's his birthday, after all. His forty-third. There's no mirror in the room but he knows what he looks like well enough. Knows that he looks good for his age—damn good—but that, even so, he's not the twenty-five-year-old kid who got sucked into this wild-goose chase eighteen years ago. There's gray at his temples, even more in his beard when he doesn't shave, lines at the corners of his eyes and mouth that don't go away even when he's not squinting or frowning.

As he sips his second drink he remarks, not for the first time, the similarity between his office and Charles Jarrell's home, and thinks he will have to let Duncan down here to vacuum and dust and put things in piles. But he knows that sooner or later—a few days, a few weeks, the difference means little measured against eighteen years—a new inspiration will strike, a connection he missed before, a lead he failed to follow, and he will come down and tape things to the wall again, draw lines between them as, for the thousandth time, the ten thousandth, he tries to figure out where Melchior disappeared—and Chandler, and Naz, and Ivelitsch. Song, well. Song he found a long time ago. Her body had been dropped outside of Brownsville, Texas, just north of the Rio Grande. She was dressed in a peasant blouse bordered with a floral Mayan collar, a chain of Day of the Dead skulls draped around her neck. Her hair had been hacked into a crude bob, her face bludgeoned to conceal the more Asiatic of her features, but one look at her unlined hands should have told anyone that she wasn't another illegal immigrant hoping to toil her way out of Mexican fields and into the service of some middle-class white American woman looking for a maid— even if, for some reason, Melchior had cut off a finger and taken it as a trophy. BC hadn't bothered to point any of this out to the local PD, however. It wasn't Song he was looking for.

He sips at his Scotch and tries to tell himself that his fervor is as strong as ever, but the fact is, it's been so long since the last time he was down here that everything is covered under a layer of dust. In his head, Naz's face shines as brightly as it ever did, and Chandler's, and even Melchior's, but the truth is nearly two decades have gone by. God only knows what they look like now. More than likely at least one of them is dead, and it's a fair bet they all are. For, of them all, the only one he's gotten any leads on at all is Pavel Semyonovitch Ivelitsch, who, as far as BC can tell, still works for KGB. The most likely scenario is that he duped Melchior into turning Chandler over to him, probably as a way of recovering the bomb that had been stolen in Cuba, and then, when he got it back—Jack Ruby's death is proof that he got it back—he killed them all. Gunned them down like the Bolsheviks gunned down the Romanovs. The only thing that gives him any hope at all is the trips that Ivelitsch continued to take to Cuba, but the last one happened in 1975, and though BC has visited the island three times, he's never figured out what Ivelitsch was doing there. It's a beautiful country, after all. Not even Communism can sully the Caribbean or dim the tropical sunshine. Maybe he was just going on vacation.

He goes to take another drink and discovers that his glass is empty. He shrugs and pours himself another. It's his birthday after all. Forty-three. He never thought he could be a forty-three-year-old.

Sometimes on nights like this, after two or three Scotches, or four, or five, he asks himself what would have happened if the president hadn't died. If Chandler had managed to stop Melchior, if Caspar had missed? Or if Jack Ruby hadn't been able to walk up to Caspar in a crowded police station and shoot him dead and the president's killer had talked and told the bizarre story of his life that people have been piecing together ever since? Would things have turned out differently? The good things—Civil Rights and the War on Poverty and the sexual revolution—and the bad: the Vietnam War and Watergate and the sexual revolution. Would the country have turned out the same? The world? Would he?

The question makes him think of the book he was reading on the train the day it all started. *The Man in the High Castle.* A novel that asks what would have happened if the U.S. lost World War II. He's kept the book with him all these years, but he's never tried to read it because, frankly, he doesn't think it ends well, and he doesn't want it to prejudice his investigation. A lot of things about him have changed over the years—or, more accurately, he now acknowledges things about himself he never would've admitted before all of this started, and one of them is that he's not the rationalist he thought he was. The believer in causality and consequence. The truth is, he's a bit superstitious. More than a bit even, and a part of him believes it wasn't an accident that this of all books should have fallen into his hands when it did. A book that asks if the facts of history have any meaning at all, or if we're all on a one-way train to apocalypse.

But still. He hasn't read it and won't. Not till he's found Chandler and Naz. Not till Melchior is brought to justice.

Which brings him back to the original question: would things have turned out differently if Chandler had stopped Oswald? He can't help but think that Melchior was telling the truth in his parting words: that the shift started a long time ago before Oswald pulled the trigger, that the change would have happened regardless of what played out in Dealey Plaza. Maybe so. But that still doesn't change the fact that an innocent man was killed, and a lot of innocent people were dragged into a crime that had nothing to do with them as the nation tried to find scapegoats for their own feelings of vulnerability, and culpability, and failure.

The whine of feedback from the small TV behind him cuts into his thoughts. Eighteen years disappear, and he's back in the chair in Dallas, watching the screen fade to black and hearing Walter Cronkite's voice flood out of the darkness. Somehow he knows even before he turns around.

"This is a CBS News Special Bulletin. In Washington, DC, shots have just been fired by an unknown gunman at President Reagan as he left the Washington Hilton Hotel. It is unclear whether the president was hit or not. However, we do know that James Brady, the White House press secretary, was injured, as well as a Secret Service agent. The gunman fired at the president from approximately ten feet away and was immediately subdued by the Secret Service. Any details about his name or motivation have yet to be released. Stay tuned to CBS News for further details."

BC stares at the screen for a moment. He's not sure what he's waiting for until a commercial comes on. The inescapable theme song to Pac-Man. After eighteen years, history is still told courtesy of its commercial sponsors.

BC presses a button on the intercom. Duncan answers almost before the buzzing stops.

"Yes, BC?"

"Get me on the first plane to DC."

A pause. "Under your name, or—"

"An alias," BC says, then releases the intercom. He looks at the half inch of Scotch in his glass, then sets it undrunk on the desk. "It's starting again," he says to no one but himself. "It's finally starting."[7]

---

[7] John Warnock Hinckley Jr. attempts to assassinate Ronald Reagan as the president leaves the Washington Hilton Hotel. Hinkley claimed to have shot the president in order to make himself as famous as Jodie Foster, with whom he was obsessed. At his trial, he was found not guilty by reason of insanity.

About the Authors

TIM KRING is one of the creative community's original transmedia story-tellers using film, TV, broadband, computers, mobile devices, and the printed page to engage audiences around the world in narrative and immersive story arcs. Internationally, 76 million fans know Tim's work as the creator and executive producer of *Heroes*, NBC's Emmy-nominated epic saga that chronicles the lives of ordinary people who discover they possess extraordinary abilities.

Kring has written numerous feature films, series pilots, and television movies. Before creating *Heroes*, he was a producer for television shows including *Chicago Hope* and *Providence*. He also created the procedural drama *Crossing Jordan*.

Kring studied film at Allan Hancock Junior College and then the University of Southern California's renowned film school. After graduation he worked his way up in production as a grip, a gaffer, and on camera crews.

Kring resides in Los Angeles with his wife Lisa, a social worker, and their two children. In his spare time, he enjoys photography and collecting acoustic guitars.

DALE PECK is the author of nine books, including, most recently, *Body Surfing* and *Sprout*, both novels. His fiction, essays, and criticism have appeared in numerous publications, including *Atlantic Monthly*, the *London Review of Books*, and the *New York Times*. Since 1999, he has taught in the New School's Graduate Writing Program. A co-founder of the Mischief and Mayhem writing collective, he lives in New York City.